# The Snake Charmer's Tale

by

VINCENT GILVARRY

*A story about snake charmers, holy men,
a hidden treasure and a time-travelling spirit*

*This novel was selected as a finalist
in
The 2019 Book Excellence Awards.*

Published by the author
All rights reserved.
Copyright
2024
©

## Table of Contents

FOREWORD ........................................................................ 7
CHAPTER 1 .......................................................................... 9
CHAPTER 2 ........................................................................ 12
CHAPTER 3 ........................................................................ 16
CHAPTER 4 ........................................................................ 20
CHAPTER 5 ........................................................................ 23
CHAPTER 6 ........................................................................ 24
CHAPTER 7 ........................................................................ 27
CHAPTER 8 ........................................................................ 30
CHAPTER 9 ........................................................................ 34
CHAPTER 10 ...................................................................... 36
CHAPTER 11 ...................................................................... 38
CHAPTER 12 ...................................................................... 41
CHAPTER 13 ...................................................................... 45
CHAPTER 14 ...................................................................... 48
CHAPTER 15 ...................................................................... 51
CHAPTER 16 ...................................................................... 55
CHAPTER 17 ...................................................................... 58
CHAPTER 18 ...................................................................... 59
CHAPTER 19 ...................................................................... 61
CHAPTER 20 ...................................................................... 64
CHAPTER 21 ...................................................................... 67
CHAPTER 22 ...................................................................... 69
CHAPTER 23 ...................................................................... 71
CHAPTER 24 ...................................................................... 73
CHAPTER 25 ...................................................................... 75
CHAPTER 26 ...................................................................... 79
CHAPTER 27 ...................................................................... 82
CHAPTER 28 ...................................................................... 85
CHAPTER 29 ...................................................................... 87

CHAPTER 30 .................................................................................. 92
CHAPTER 31 .................................................................................. 99
CHAPTER 32 ................................................................................ 104
CHAPTER 33 ................................................................................ 106
CHAPTER 34 ................................................................................ 109
CHAPTER 35 ................................................................................ 111
CHAPTER 36 ................................................................................ 115
CHAPTER 37 ................................................................................ 118
CHAPTER 38 ................................................................................ 120
CHAPTER 39 ................................................................................ 122
CHAPTER 40 ................................................................................ 123
CHAPTER 41 ................................................................................ 125
CHAPTER 42 ................................................................................ 127
CHAPTER 43 ................................................................................ 128
CHAPTER 44 ................................................................................ 131
CHAPTER 45 ................................................................................ 133
CHAPTER 46 ................................................................................ 136
CHAPTER 47 ................................................................................ 139
CHAPTER 48 ................................................................................ 141
CHAPTER 49 ................................................................................ 144
CHAPTER 50 ................................................................................ 147
CHAPTER 51 ................................................................................ 151
CHAPTER 52 ................................................................................ 155
CHAPTER 53 ................................................................................ 158
CHAPTER 54 ................................................................................ 160
CHAPTER 55 ................................................................................ 162
CHAPTER 56 ................................................................................ 164
CHAPTER 57 ................................................................................ 166
CHAPTER 58 ................................................................................ 168
CHAPTER 59 ................................................................................ 170
CHAPTER 60 ................................................................................ 172

| | |
|---|---|
| CHAPTER 61 | 177 |
| CHAPTER 62 | 180 |
| CHAPTER 63 | 187 |
| CHAPTER 64 | 190 |
| CHAPTER 65 | 193 |
| CHAPTER 66 | 196 |
| CHAPTER 67 | 198 |
| CHAPTER 68 | 202 |
| CHAPTER 69 | 206 |
| CHAPTER 70 | 210 |
| CHAPTER 71 | 213 |
| CHAPTER 72 | 217 |
| CHAPTER 73 | 222 |
| CHAPTER 74 | 225 |
| CHAPTER 75 | 228 |
| CHAPTER 76 | 233 |
| CHAPTER 77 | 239 |
| CHAPTER 78 | 241 |
| CHAPTER 79 | 244 |
| CHAPTER 80 | 246 |
| CHAPTER 81 | 250 |
| CHAPTER 82 | 252 |
| CHAPTER 83 | 258 |
| CHAPTER 84 | 261 |
| CHAPTER 85 | 264 |
| CHAPTER 86 | 268 |
| CHAPTER 87 | 271 |
| CHAPTER 88 | 273 |
| CHAPTER 89 | 278 |
| CHAPTER 90 | 282 |
| CHAPTER 91 | 286 |

CHAPTER 92 .................................................................... 289

CHAPTER 93 .................................................................... 292

CHAPTER 94 .................................................................... 296

CHAPTER 95 .................................................................... 301

CHAPTER 96 .................................................................... 304

CHAPTER 97 .................................................................... 308

CHAPTER 98 .................................................................... 312

CHAPTER 99 .................................................................... 315

CHAPTER 100 .................................................................. 318

CHAPTER 101 .................................................................. 324

CHAPTER 102 .................................................................. 329

CHAPTER 103 .................................................................. 333

CHAPTER 104 .................................................................. 336

CHAPTER 105 .................................................................. 343

CHAPTER 106 .................................................................. 347

CHAPTER 107 .................................................................. 351

CHAPTER 108 .................................................................. 354

CHAPTER 109 .................................................................. 358

CHAPTER 110 .................................................................. 361

CHAPTER 111 .................................................................. 364

CHAPTER 112 .................................................................. 370

CHAPTER 113 .................................................................. 372

CHAPTER 114 .................................................................. 375

CHAPTER 115 .................................................................. 377

CHAPTER 116 .................................................................. 381

CHAPTER 117 .................................................................. 384

## FOREWORD

The Snake Charmer's Tale is a story that weaves its way across two centuries and two continents. It's a story about love, loss and the pursuit of a legacy, but it is also a story about two generations of snake charmers whose destinies are shaped by a mysterious and all-knowing holy man.

And if it had not been for a unique experience that I had in the Golden Temple of Dambulla in Sri Lanka, this story would not exist at all.

Dambulla is one of the most sacred places in Sri Lanka, a temple that's over two thousand years old. And as soon as you step inside, you are surrounded by images from Buddhist mythology and numerous statues of Lord Buddha.

In the Cave of the Divine King is a 14-meter statue of Buddha that has been carved out of solid rock, but I ventured further afield into The Cave of the Great Kings.

I was in a sacred space infused with centuries of divine spiritual energy but I was immediately attracted to a large seated Buddha. And as I was gazing upon the radiant face of this enlightened being I beheld the impossible.

The Buddha's face came alive as if it was imbued by celestial magic, and I realised that he was not only nodding his head, but his eyes and lips were moving as well.

A silent message whispered to your soul is an extraordinary experience and one that you would never forget, but it was responsible for this enchanting tale. I hope you enjoy it.

# PART ONE
# THE SNAKE CHARMER'S TALE

# CHAPTER 1

Govinda is an orphan, a rudderless boat in a sea of uncertainty. He sleeps in the stables behind a mudbrick shed on a floor of dirt and straw, and it is not just the mosquitoes that he has to contend with. Sometimes it's the monsoons, those balmy winds that blow in from the south for one half of the year, and then from the north for the other half.

On the day that his life changed, he wakes from a dream, yawns loudly, dusts himself off and ties up his faded sarong. A gecko in the rafters chirps loudly to cheer him on his way.

He gives it a quick smile and then has a wash in a water trough. The face that he sees has dreamy soft brown eyes which suggest deep wells of quiet thought.

'Hello,' he says. 'And who are you?'

Govinda has said that a hundred times before but he had never expected to hear a reply.

'I am the voice of the whispering wind.'

The ear is just one of many gateways to the soul, but before the day is over, Govinda will encounter yet another. And for a fleeting moment, he will experience a quickening, his heart will race, his mind will follow along behind, and he will arrive at the shores of a different world.

Govinda lives in a village on the banks of a quietly flowing river, one that flows down from the mountains, winds its way through the jungle, and merges with the sapphire blue water of the Indian Ocean.

The creatures of the forest watch closely as he makes his way to the village square, but another pair of eyes also has him in their sights. Govinda is about to cross the path of Chohan the holy man and his faithful dog Kosala.

A holy man is never seen unless he wants to be seen. He can hide behind the drooping leaves of a banana tree, or the upturned feather mop that is the ever-present coconut tree.

Every morning without fail Govinda heads for the river to visit his grandmother, but he is distracted by a busy little messenger bird dancing around his head.

It follows him to the marketplace, where Pamu, an old man who has been tending the same stall ever since he was a boy offers Govinda a fresh banana.

'And what are you going to do with your day Govinda?'

'That I do not know yet,' he says.

'I have heard that there will be a snake charmer at the dagoba this afternoon.'

'Oh, I must go and see that.'

The bell-shaped temple is believed to be over 600 years old. It sits on a base of three concentric circles, and on the very top is a golden spire that reflects the light from the early morning Sun. In days of old it was covered in copper plates, but now it's a faded and shabby shade of grey.

According to legend, the temple contained a treasure which a holy man had acquired in the kingdom of heaven.

The story came to the attention of a meddlesome Prince who desired it as a gift for his wife, but to his dismay, he discovered that the temple was protected by some sort of spell.

The prince was not to be deterred, so one dark night, he returned with an army of faithful retainers. And as soon as they started to hack away at the door, a woman in golden armour appeared on a beautiful black stallion.

The prince marvelled at her beauty, but this was no ordinary woman, and in an effort to win her over, he raced her to the top of the fabled mountain known as Adam's Peak.

They rode off into the night and up the narrow, death-defying path that led to the temple at the top, but the prince was never seen again.

No one really knows what happened to him, but on some mornings, it is possible to see a mournful black stallion wandering through the ghostly blue mist.

Adam's Peak has been an attraction to countless people over the centuries, but it is a precipitous climb and is not for the feint hearted.

Pilgrims have been making the journey to the summit for over two thousand years, and one of those was Sinbad, an adventurous sailor from Baghdad.

The main attraction is not just the windswept temple but a sacred relic, an indentation in a boulder that resembles an oversized footprint, and one which has been there since the beginning of time.

The Buddhists call it Sri Pada and claim that it belongs to the Buddha. To the Hindus, it is the footprint of Siva, the divine hero Rama, who rescued his wife from a demon king. And according to Muslims, this is where a remorseful Adam ended up after he had been banished from paradise.

To those of many faiths, Adam's Peak is a sacred mountain, but it is also the home of a holy man called Chohan.

Dressed in a long white robe, his hair hanging loosely over his shoulders, Chohan sits in a state of mystical union. He has been following Govinda closely as he has a task for this young man, and today is the day that it starts.

## CHAPTER 2

Ballangoddi is an isolated village in an unexplored region of the mountains, a three-day trek along a jungle path, and one that would test even the sturdiest bullock wagon.

There is precious little to buy in the marketplace, other than a woven mat, a tortoiseshell comb, or cheap silver jewellery. And on the odd occasion, you can even find the intricate lace that originates from the coastal city of Galle.

Other than a gaggle of noisy children and numerous stray dogs there isn't much to see, and on a fine day, the elders hold a meeting under the shade of an old banyan tree.

A silversmith fashions a bangle dripping with silver beads, while lean and scrawny men carry buckets of fish from one house to another.

The menfolk sit on their haunches contemplating the progress of their crops, while the women sit on a mat making curry seasoned with dried fish and fiery hot chilies.

And when they are not boiling rice over an open fire or scraping the skin off a coconut, they spend the day weaving mats from the leaves of a plantain tree.

Their homes are windowless mud huts thatched with dry straw, but most people spend the day on the streets where everyone knows everyone else's business, and during the monsoon season they have no choice but to take refuge inside.

It is early morning; the heat is oppressive and thunderclouds have gathered overhead. The wind grows in strength, and a storm, followed by a deluge of heavy rain drenches the landscape, and in a matter of minutes, the river is a rushing torrent.

Govinda takes shelter under a tree, but he is worried about his grandmother. Achchie is not his real grandmother, but she has looked after him ever since his mother died.

Achchie lives in a houseboat on the river and makes a living by washing clothes. Govinda appears like clockwork every morning, and his staple breakfast is a bowl of rice and a cup of tea, but before he leaves, she always gives him a freshly laundered sarong.

'Thank you achchie.'

'Who will look after you when I have gone?'

'Somebody will. I had a dream about snakes last night.'

'Good snakes or bad snakes?' she said.

'Good ones mostly, and there was a man as well.'

'A good man or a bad man?'

'A good man achchie.'

'I hope so my boy.'

'So, what are you going to do today.'

'I am going to see a snake charmer at the temple.'

'Well, don't get too close.'

'No, achchie, I won't.'

The sky is often a blaze of colour before sunset, but on that afternoon, a great shaft of light streams up from the horizon.

A few moments later, a snake charmer dressed in his finest clothes appears on the steps of the temple. And before the show even starts, Chohan entertains the children with a few simple magic tricks.

Snake charming has a long and interesting history, and to some it is a mystical cult. Snakes have been worshipped in almost every ancient civilisation.

To the Dravidians of India, the snake is regarded with both admiration and respect, and one of the most venomous of all serpents, the Cobra de Capello has been the focus of veneration.

Whereas some snake charmers squat on the ground and whisper a mystic incantation, others go into a trance, but that is not Chohan's style.

He moves around playing a richly decorated flute and does his best to coax a rather lethargic old snake out of its basket. And once the performance has finished, he bows to the children and introduces himself and his assistant.

'Boys and girls, I am the great Irrawaddy, snake charmer extraordinaire. Some snake charmers work alone, but I work with my faithful companion, Kosala the wonder dog.'

Kosala stands on his legs and barks loudly. The children have never seen such a thing before, and they cheer and clap loudly.

Chohan wanders around playing an intoxicating melody on his flute, and to the delight of the children, two golden cobras rise out of the basket. They sway sinuously back and forth, their eyes trained on the those of their master.

The children have seen countless snake charmers over the years, but they have never seen one like Chohan before, and for his efforts, he receives another round of applause.

'Thank you, my friends, but you must be very wary of cobras. Does anyone know why that is?'

'I do,' Govinda says.

'In that case, come up here my boy and I will show you something that every snake charmer knows.'

Govinda does so but hesitantly. He has no idea what he is letting himself in for, but he is about to find out.

'Now, hold out your hand.'

'But why?' he says.

'You can die from a cobra bite, but you don't have to, if you know the secret.'

'And what is that?' Govinda says.

To Govinda's horror, a cobra leaps out of a basket and bites him on the hand.

'I don't want to die,' he cries.

'You won't,' Chohan says. 'Give me your hand.'

He removes a highly polished stone from his pocket, applies it to the deathly blue mark on the back of Govinda's hand and holds it firmly.

'This will absorb the poison. You will see.'

Govinda is terrified, so Chohan taps him on the head and a sensation such as he had never felt before ripples through his body. A few minutes later, he removes the stone and inspects the wound.

'There now, look at that. Your hand has healed. What do you think of that?'

'Are you sure I am not going to die.'

'If you were, you would be dead by now.'

'Did you know that once you have been bitten by a cobra, you spend the rest of your life as a snake charmer.'

'No, I did not know that.'

'Would you like to be a snake charmer, my little friend.'

'I think I would.'

He whispers something in his ear so that none of the other children can hear.

'Then come to my camp before sunset and we will talk.'

# CHAPTER 3

Sinhala is a land of legends but it is also the home of those mystical gems called star sapphires. And if you know where to look you can find them in cerulean and midnight blue.

Hold one up to the light, twirl it this way and that and you will see a curious silky sheen, but if you place it in the hands of a jeweller, he will transform it into a perfect six-sided star.

I will tell you a story of a holy man who found a simple rough-hewn stone, which in some places are as thick as hailstones after a summer storm.

He deduced from sheer perspicacity that if you polish a dull brown stone, a metamorphosis will ensue, but if you release it from its earthly prison, it will shine with more than enough light to create a new and lasting future.

And on that overcast afternoon, Govinda, a simple uncut stone makes his way down a winding forest path to Chohan's camp site.

His little heart is beating faster than it has ever done before, the quickening he felt at the temple is still pulsing away, but he has no idea what it means. He is a little apprehensive and a little excited because nothing like this has ever happened to him before.

Chohan is sitting by a campfire but gets to his feet when he hears the sound of twigs being trampled underfoot.

'Boy, come closer so that I can see your face.'

Govinda creeps out of the shadows, wary of the barking dog.

'Kosala will not harm you, my friend. Please take a seat.'

'So, what is your name?'

'I was called Govinda by my mother.'

'And where is she.'

'She died in her sleep, a long time ago.'
'So, who looks after you now?'
'I look after myself, mostly.'
'Would you like to make a lot of money?'
'Oh yes, I would, but how will I do that?'
'I will teach you to be a snake charmer.'
'I would like that.'
'Then, as of today I will be your master. You can accompany me on my travels, and you will never go hungry again. What do you say to that?'

Govinda suddenly remembers his dream of the night before and smiles.

'That sounds good, but what is your name?'
'I have many names, one of which is Chohan.'
'But I must tell achchie first, or she will be worried.'
'Yes, you should.'

Govinda races back to the riverboat, unaware that he has just made a decision which will change the course of his life.

'Achchie, achchie,' he cries. 'I have good news.'
'What is it my boy.'
'I am going to be a snake charmer.'
'It's not that gypsy who was here last month, is it?'
'No achchie. Chohan is a good man. I can see it in his eyes.'
'Then I want to meet this man for myself.'

With Govinda at her side, she hobbles along a path that she has travelled a hundred times before, but Chohan is not the sort of snake charmer that achchie had expected to see.

He is a very impressive looking man with piercing brown eyes, and his distinctive bearing may have something to do with the fact that he was born into a high caste family.

On his head, he wears a turban decorated with a silver buckle, and around his neck he wears an amulet of golden amber.

On his wrist he has a heavy gold bangle, but on the index finger of his left hand is the symbol of eternity, a golden ouroborous, a ring that depicts a serpent swallowing its own tail.

Chohan holds his hands together and bows his head respectfully. 'I am honoured to meet you achchie and I can assure you that your grandson will be in good hands.'

'He is not my grandson, but someone has to look after him.'

'Then allow me to thank you on his behalf.'

'It seems that you were right,' she says to Govinda. 'Chohan looks like a good man.'

'He is achchie.'

But she is not about to leave Govinda in the hands of a total stranger, not without an interrogation.

'Tell me why I should hand him over to you.'

'I can assure you that Govinda will have a long and happy life and he will never go without.'

'What does that mean?'

'I will teach him everything he needs to know, and one day, he will have opportunities such as he never thought possible.'

Achchie cannot imagine such a thing. She has struggled all her life. Her husband drowned in a flood many years before, but she is old and ailing and her time is almost up. And if she doesn't agree to this plan, Govinda will end up like any other orphan.

'In that case, I will let him go with my blessings.'

'If this is to be your destiny Govinda, it is a road you must follow,' she says.

She removes a little box from her pocket and places it in his hands. 'But you must take this.'

'What is it achchie?'

'They were your mother's earrings. I was going to give them to you on your wedding day, but I think you should wear them when you become a snake charmer.'

'Oh, thank you achchie.'

'It is the very least I can do, my boy.

Govinda takes one last look at the only person who has ever cared for him, and tears stream down his face as she disappears into the darkness, never to be seen again.

# CHAPTER 4

Govinda spends his formative years travelling with a man possessed of excellent sensibilities. Chohan is a delightful companion with a sense of humour, but he can also conjure up food from an invisible oven, and at mealtimes, there is always something different to eat.

Those splendid fruits, the mango, and jak fruit are to be found everywhere in Sinhala. The banana, which is also known as the fig of paradise, is a handsome yellow fruit that is usually eaten raw, but it can be a gourmet meal in the hands of a master.

Over the next five years, they wander from one village to another; Govinda gets more exercise than he has ever had before, and in time, he grows into a handsome young man.

They travel through great tracts of forest where people fight an on-going battle with nature and even the occasional wild animal.

As a rule, elephants are harmless creatures, but one day, they encounter a rogue male blocking their path, and to anyone else, that would mean certain death.

'Get behind me,' Chohan cries.

Govinda is glued to the spot and is white with fear, and just as the bull is about to charge, a white elephant appears out of nowhere. The bull bows respectfully and disappears into the forest, but if it had not been for that, Govinda's life may have ended there and then.

A few hours later, they set up camp not far from a bleak and forbidding temple covered in the grime of ages. Govinda plucks up the courage and ventures over to take a closer look, but he has no idea that this is a long-forgotten Hindu temple.

In times gone by, it was revered as the abode of the gods, and while some images are obviously deities, others are creatures with apish faces and a multitude of breasts, arms, and legs. He has never seen such a thing before and races back to the safety of the camp.

'That temple is the doorway to a cave,' Chohan says, 'and some say that it is haunted, but I know for a fact that it's not.'

'I once knew a man called Mathika who could cure people just by looking at them.'

'And how did he do that? Govinda says.

'He had to pass through that doorway to find what fate had in store, and if you wish to fulfil your destiny Govinda, that is where you have to go.'

'But what's in there, Master?'

'That is for you to find out.'

Concealed by a tangle of thorns and creepers, the temple peers ominously through the foliage, its splendid facade worn away by centuries of dust, wind, and the rain.

As soon as he steps inside, Govinda looks around warily, only to see even more grotesque creatures lining the walls and ceiling. Images swirl through his mind, of stories told by the village storyteller, of children who were taken by tigers and others by demons of the night.

He moves along tentatively, only to find himself surrounded by hundreds of little fireflies swirling around in a hazy circling dance, but way up ahead he sees a door that glows with a shimmering blue light.

'What will I do?' he says.

He turns on hearing Chohan's familiar voice. 'Step through and see for yourself.'

'Master, I can hear you, but I cannot see you.'

'Keep going Govinda.'

He does so, only to see a white elephant wandering lazily along a silky white beach. And way up above, a magnificent temple floats on a fluffy white cloud, but a storm is brewing.

In the distance, a ship, being tossed about by a raging sea appears as quickly as it disappears and moments later, it collides with an outcrop of rock.

Not long after, a man and a girl start searching through the debris, only to stumble on the body of a boy who has washed up onto the beach.

When Govinda finally emerges from the cave, he looks as if he has seen a ghost. Chohan sits him by the fire and places a cup of tea in his hands.

'So, what did you see?'

'You may not believe it, but I saw a beautiful temple floating in the sky and a white elephant on a beach.'

'Very interesting. Anything else?'

'Yes Master. I saw a ship that was wrecked in a storm, and the only survivor was a young boy but he was saved by a man and a little girl.'

'What does that mean Master?'

'You had a glimpse of your future.'

'I did, but who were those other people?

'The man on the beach was you.'

'And the girl?

'She is or will be your daughter.'

'My daughter, so who was that boy?'

'You will find that out for yourself, but the temple means one thing and the white elephant means something else altogether.'

'What do they mean Master?'

'The temple does not exist yet, but you will have a part to play.'

'Do I have to build a temple all by myself?'

'No, Govinda, you will have to help someone else do that.'

'That's good because I don't know anything about building temples, but what of the elephant?

'It means that your spirit guide is a white elephant, and in times of danger, it will appear out of the blue and save you from certain death.'

'That is good, isn't it Master?'

## CHAPTER 5

They usually head off after breakfast along paths that wander through fields both rich and green, on roads barely wide enough for an ox cart. And wherever they go, they see people with smiling faces, and picturesque huts that are the perfection of village life.

On one such day, they stop to watch a couple of children chasing butterflies and a man in a loin cloth who is harvesting sweet potatoes in his garden.

He greets them with natural politeness, selects a freshly harvested coconut, removes the fibrous outer layer, pours the juice into a wooden bowl, and offers them a cool and refreshing drink.

In any given village, it is not uncommon to see an indolent man stretched out on a wooden bench, happy in his idleness. Little black pigs are everywhere, as are ducks and fowls, but most places are swarming with dogs.

Sinhala was once a stage for sordid little tragedies, but today, it is the embodiment of contentment, people with open faces, an open-hearted friendliness, and a detached interest in the metamorphosis of life.

Men usually wear a comboy, a lose piece of fabric wrapped around the waist, their hair twisted in a knot above their heads, whereas the women tie theirs back with a tortoise shell comb and a silver pin.

The scenery changes from hour to hour, and after a long day on the road, they usually find somewhere to set up camp. And on one occasion, it was under an ancient fig tree, one so large that it was held in place by a maze of roots that had anchored themselves deep into the ground.

## CHAPTER 6

No one else can do what Chohan can do, but he never made a show of it, not in front of others at any rate. As to who taught him how to cook, Govinda has no idea, but every meal is different, and on some nights it is a veritable feast.

After a long day on the road, Govinda wanders down to bathe in the river, and when he gets back, it is only to find a that Chohan has prepared a feast fit for the king. His eyes almost pop out of his head when he sees what they will be eating that night.

'Just help yourself,' Chohan says.

Govinda rises early the next morning, only to find his Master contemplating the majesty of nature. A solitude reigns over the landscape, and the first quivering rays of light are stirring the world into life.

Birds are singing in the trees. A palm squirrel races up a tree. A lazy green lizard stretches its neck, and in the trees far away, a troop of monkeys bicker over a bunch of ripe bananas.

'Good morning,' Chohan says. 'Did you sleep well.'

'I did Master, but what are you doing.'

Chohan has been watching a flock of crows, hopping about with heads awry and beady eyes askance. Crows can be found almost everywhere, but they are not only interested in food scraps; they love anything that glitters.

Chohan removes a small bag from his pocket and offers it to Govinda.

'They're little seed pearls. Scatter them around and see what happens.'

Govinda does so, only to find himself laughing out loud. A prize is on offer, and the crows come from everywhere.

'Crows are a lot smarter than they look.'

'But Master, what do they want with pearls?'

'They usually carry them to the top of a building and watch as they roll down the roof, but if you look closely, you will see something very useful.'

'A hungry serpent has them in its sights.'

It slithers through the grass, propels itself into the air and strikes out, but the crows are ever watchful. A flurry of squawking follows, and all that remains of the cobra's early morning meal are a few feathers floating in the air.

'That is one way to find a cobra but it's not the only way,' Chohan says. 'If you are to be a snake charmer Govinda, you must learn how to catch a snake first.'

At any hour of the day, the jungle is alive with the sound of birds and birdsong. After breakfast, they investigate an enormous white anthill in the middle of a field, and then watch closely as a flock of noisy parakeets fly overhead.

Very few people know the song of a thrush from a blackbird or a croaking frog from a toad. Chohan points out things of interest, a colony of beaver birds building a nest, the song of a golden oriole, an orange woodpecker, a turquoise kingfisher, and a golden sunbird hovering above a flower.

'A snake charmer must have a knowledge of the creatures of the forest, and not just those that creep, crawl or burrow,' Chohan says.

'Listen closely, and you will hear something in the undergrowth.'

'What is it, Master?'

'It's a palm cat but it is actually up there in the crest of that coconut tree.'

'Kings of times past used cobras to protect their treasure houses and they are often found in pairs.'

With a forked stick in hand, he removes a sleepy cobra from its nest, holds it up to his face, looks it in the eye and kisses it on the nose.

'It is not just the fangs of which you must be wary, it is the death giving gland in the mouth.'

'When the flesh is pierced, the poison enters the bloodstream. For a small animal, death is instantaneous, but for a man, it can take a little longer.'

'You can remove the gland, but the cobra will not live for much longer after that.'

## CHAPTER 7

The fabled land of Sinhala was once the home of over one hundred and sixty-five kings and queens. And on one occasion, they spend the night in the remains of an ancient city called Anuradhapura, a faded reminder of the might and glory of the old empire.

In times long gone, this was a vast and mighty metropolis, but now it is buried beneath centuries of jungle growth and fifteen feet of soil.

Mighty monoliths inscribed with the deeds of ancient kings have long since been consumed by a tangle of roots and vines, and even the great stone temples, palaces, monasteries, shrines, and bathing pools have all but disappeared.

And it is here that you will find the most venerated tree in all of Sinhala, an ancient fig known as the Bodhi Tree. This is the very same tree under which Buddha found enlightenment and it is believed to be over two thousand years old.

'Are there ghosts around here?'

'Yes Govinda, this was once a thriving and a most exceptional city in every way.'

Chohan describes its splendours and Anuradhapura comes magically to life.

'Behold the mighty gate and the city that once rose like a flower in a desert. The walls of the palace were surrounded by stately palms and gardens.'

'But the most impressive building of all was the great Dagoba, a temple that rose over 260 feet into the air.'

At any time of the year, the paddy fields are a hotbed of mosquitoes, so the next morning they take a shortcut through the jungle instead.

An hour later, Chohan stops in his tracks when he hears the sound of hysterical elephants and the smell of burning flesh.

They leave the barrow behind and creep along like hunters on the prowl, and wherever they look it's apparent that the undergrowth has been trampled underfoot.

'An elephant kraal,' Chohan says. 'It's just as I suspected.'

'This could be dangerous Govinda. Stay close.'

Elephant hunting is a repulsive past-time, but elephant baiting is even worse. The poor creatures are subdued by any means at all and locked away in huge enclosures called kraals.

Elephants have roamed the length and breadth of Sinhala for centuries, but elephant hunting has become a very lucrative business over the last few years.

Hidden deep in the forest, they come upon a stockade, and just inside the gates is a mound of burning flesh. The stench is overpowering and it is driving the other elephants mad.

'Barbarians,' Chohan cries. 'Another vile sport is about to begin.'

An overweight man with a German accent barks out an order, while a group of wild-eyed coolies herd the terrified animals into the stockade.

'What are they going to do?' Govinda says.

'Kill them, but not if I have anything to do with it.'

'Stay here and do not move. I will be back in a few minutes.'

A dozen grizzly-looking outlaws have been taunting an old cow until every muscle in her body starts to convulse. Unable to take any more, she drops to the ground with an enormous thump.

They are stopped in their tracks by a flash of blinding light. The gates are torn from their hinges and when the smoke finally clears, a man in a black turban and long black robe steps forward.

'There is no place in this world for such heartless cruelty,' he roars. 'Now taste the fruits of your labours.'

Chohan raises his hand and dozens of cobras appear from everywhere. The men are surrounded on all sides but they are no match for a creature that can kill on sight.

The cobras strike out in rapid succession, and a few seconds later, they are rolling around and gasping for breath.

Their faces turn red and then purple, and with one final spasmodic jerk, their horrible lives fritter uselessly away.

These are men who have raped, pillaged, and ravaged their way across darkest Africa and then trained their sights on Asia.

Chohan releases the elephants, burns the krall to the ground, storms off into the forest and doesn't even bother to look back.

'I have seen their kind a thousand times before,' he says. 'This world will be a better place without them.'

## CHAPTER 8

Govinda never imagined that his life would be any different to that of any other boy in the village. He used to watch the potter at his wheel, but he never expected to end up as a snake charmer, and he never realised that the jungle could be such a dangerous place.

Chohan is obviously distressed by the experience of the day before, and spends hours in a state of contemplation. Govinda has never seen his Master like this before, and when he does eventually speak, it is not until late afternoon.

'If you ever do anything like that Govinda, it tears away a piece of your soul.'

'You saw what happened, didn't you?'

'I did Master.'

He saw something that he will never forget. He saw what his master really could do, but he also saw a cobra in action. He saw them strike and then strike again, but he will never forget the look of horror on the faces of those men.

'However, word will soon spread. I think we should get as far away from here as possible.'

'Where are we going Master?'

'Up into the mountains.'

They head off with all haste, with their two-wheeled barrow in hand, and Kosala following along behind. The woods are alive with the hum of bird life and the almost deafening sound of cicadas.

They leave the forest far behind and venture up a long winding path on the edge of a precipitous ravine, and several hours later, they reach the high mountain plains.

Visible in the distance is a vista of undulating hills, and beyond that is a natural pyramid which towers over the landscape, the almighty mountain known as Adam's Peak.

They head for the foothills and follow a descending path that leads to the door of a cave. And as soon as Govinda steps through, it is only to find himself in an enormous underground cavern.

'I call this The Cave of the Ancients,' Chohan says, 'and you will soon see why.'

He lights a series of torches attached to the walls, and a few moments later, Govinda sees a sight such as he has never seen before.

Decorating the cave from one end to the other are faded murals that have long since lost their lustre and stories written in a long-forgotten language.

'What is this place?' he says.

'It's a temple of sorts, a sacred space.'

'You see, at some point in the distant past, the Earth was inhabited by a different race of people.'

'What happened to them Master?'

'A great cataclysm devoured every continent and they disappeared into the ocean, but others rose to take their place. Many people lost their lives but some survived and ended up in other lands.'

'Were you one of them Master?'

'I was, but my people are long gone now, and I am the only one left.'

'This beautiful land of ours has a long and ancient history, but it has also been an attraction to rogues, thieves and invaders from other lands.'

'Do you know anything of its history Govinda?'

'No Master, I do not?'

'Well, we have had a very long day, but before we eat, I think you should bathe in that pool over there, and then I will tell you a story.'

Govinda's little world is changing but his education is in the hands of a master. He would love to click his fingers and start a fire, but that is not the sort of education he agreed to.

It was a long and strenuous climb up the mountain path, and after he has bathed, Govinda is far too tired to even think about food. He curls up beside Kosala, and before long, they are both fast asleep.

Govinda is not the first orphan whose life has been changed by Chohan and he will not be the last. In a few years, he will travel the roads of Sinhala by himself, but after breakfast the following day, his education begins in earnest.

'There are several ways to protect yourself from a cobra bite,' Chohan says as he removes a black stone from his pocket.

'Do you remember this?'

'I do Master, but it doesn't look like it could save a life.'

'It saved yours but you must learn how to use it first.'

'Now, hold it between your thumb and forefinger so that the cobra can see it clearly, and then move it around in a circular motion.'

Govinda watches closely as the cobra concentrates on the stone, and before long, it is fast sleep.

'That is a very good trick Master, but what did I just do?'

'You made it drowsy, and it fell asleep.'

'Where did you learn that?'

'Now, that is a very good question. After the floodwaters receded, there were snakes all over the place, dangerous ones mostly.'

'One day, I encountered a leopard that had been cornered by a cobra and I had to distract it so that it wouldn't turn on me.'

'So, what did you do Master?'

'I used an old trick that I learnt in the temple. The high priest often went into a trance but he never did so alone. Another priest held a highly polished diamond in front of his face and moved it around ever so slowly.'

'So, I searched around and found a stone to divert the cobra's attention.'

'And did it work?'

'Not at first, but it did eventually.'

'Can you do that to people, Master?'

'Yes, you can, but only if they are susceptible to the power of persuasion. Otherwise, it is a waste of time.'

'Would it work on me?'

'I have no doubt about that at all Govinda.'

'Now, another way to hypnotise a snake is to play a very slow, soporific melody on the flute.'

'I will try that, Master.'

Govinda removes the lid from a basket and plays a barely audible monotonous tune, and then watches with interest as the cobra succumbs to the intoxicating power of music.

'It works Master.'

'You will make an excellent snake charmer, Govinda, once you have had a bit more practice.'

# CHAPTER 9

Govinda spends the next few days rehearsing for his first ever public performance, but at night he is happy to sit back and listen to one of Chohan's stories.

'That was a very good story too Master, but please tell me another one.'

'Okay, I will tell you about an elephant called Kandula.'

'Now, on the day that a certain queen gave birth to twin boys, a miracle happened.'

'What's a miracle master?'

'A miracle is when something amazing happens. You have already experienced a miracle, Govinda.'

'I have. When was that?'

'Remember the white elephant that saved your life. That was a miracle.'

'Ah, yes.'

'Miracles are like magic, you could say.'

'So, what was the miracle, Master?'

'A ship from a faraway land docked at the harbour with a present for the queen.'

'What sort of present was it, Master?'

'You may not believe it Govinda, but it was an elephant clad in golden armour and beautiful gems.'

'Was it a spirit elephant, Master?'

'No, it was a real elephant. The king passed away many years later, so his first-born son claimed the right to rule. However, his twin brother did not like that idea at all.'

'He wanted the throne for himself, so he kidnapped Kandula and took refuge in a palace on the top of a mountain.'

'Gamani was not about to submit to his brother's demands, so they met on the field of battle.'

'But when Gamani saw Tissa riding his favourite elephant, he leapt from his horse, knocked his brother to the ground, and took his place on Kandula's back.'

'Did his brother die Master?'

'No, but Kandula didn't like Gamani at all, so he threw him to the ground, raced back to Tissa and they made a triumphal return to the palace.'

'And is that the end of the story, Master?'

'No, it's not. Many years later, a war broke out with a wicked king called Damilas who ordered his army to destroy the temples and plunder the sacred relics.'

'Tissa sent warriors to destroy Damilas but that was no easy task. You see, Damilas lived in a stronghold surrounded by lofty walls and deep trenches.'

'Dressed in his war armour, Kandula charged the stronghold and destroyed the iron gate. Unfortunately, his armour could not protect him from buckets of red-hot iron.'

'Did Kandula die Master?'

'No, he did not, but for his bravery, Tissa made him a Lord of the Realm.'

'Is that the end of the story Master?'

'Not quite.'

'Kandula fought by Tissa's side in thirty other battles, and when the land was finally at peace, he retired to the good life. Kandula had over one hundred slaves at his beck and call and spent the remainder of his days wandering through the city.'

'And when he did eventually die, he was given a most extraordinary and very memorable funeral.'

'That was a good story too, Master.'

# CHAPTER 10

'If you are to become a celebrated snake charmer Govinda, you must learn how to control seven cobras at once.'

'Is that possible Master?'

'That is the thing for which you will become famous, but I know a secret that no one else knows.'

'And what is that Master?

'Let's just say that it's a gift, one that will give you the power to talk to a cobra.'

'Oh, that could be useful.'

'Cobras are not just snakes, Govinda. They are gods that must be treated with respect. And even though they cannot hear, they do understand.'

'Now, take a cobra from a basket, hold it up to your face, gaze deeply into its eyes and then kiss it on the nose.'

Govinda does so but somewhat hesitantly. 'But how do I speak to it?'

'Like this,' Chohan says, as he taps him lightly on the head.

A tingling sensation ripples up his spine, and for the first time in his life, Govinda sees the world through very different eyes.

'Come forth my friend and stand before me as you really are,' Chohan says.

'You have a task to complete, but you do not have to do it alone. I will be there whenever you need me. Do you understand?'

'I do Master, but tell me. Why are we surrounded by a golden light.'

'That is the light of the Kundalini. It's a serpent of a different kind, you could say.'

'The Kundalini is an energy that resides at the base of your spine, but once activated, it travels up your spine.'

'It is truly a miracle Master. I feel like I am in heaven?'

'In a sense, you are. You have one foot in this world and one in the next.'

'But why have you shown me this?'

'You can now talk to a cobra, but if you look into its eyes and kiss it on the nose, it will be yours to command.'

'However, Govinda, you cannot keep a cobra for too long. The fangs grow back after they have been removed and that makes them dangerous.'

'That's a very good secret too Master.'

'It is, but you must know this as well. A cobra does not react to the flute but to the vibration of sound. It reacts because it wants to strike out at the snake charmer.'

'What is a vibration, Master?

'It's an energy that exists inside of everything, like the rocks and trees and water. You cannot see vibrations, but sometimes you can feel them.'

'You see, hidden inside your body is a very powerful organ called a heart, and your heart sees all and knows all, and it will tell you immediately if something is good or if it's bad.'

'Like the feelings that you had for achchie, for example. That is a very special vibration called love.'

'Think of it like this. If you encounter a dog wagging its tail, your heart tells you that it's a good vibration, and it means that the dog is friendly.'

'But if the dog is barking angrily, your heart tells you that it's not friendly and it's time to get out of there.'

It's the same with people. If someone has good vibrations, your heart knows about it immediately, and it definitely knows if they are mean or cruel or evil.'

'Like those men who killed the elephants.'

'Yes, Govinda. That is exactly what I mean.'

## CHAPTER 11

Govinda is about to make some money, and his first performance will be in the seaside village of Negombo. It's a balmy night, the sun has set, the lights of Negombo are visible in the distance and the aroma of cinnamon wafts through the air.

After dinner, they sit on the beach and watch as a phosphorescent light cavorts across the waves like a pair of ghostly hands.

Govinda is now a young man of fifteen, but he is no longer a beggar boy, nor does he wear a faded sarong. He is well fed and healthy and spends his time in the company of a man who has gone out of his way to give him a purpose in life.

Snake charmers wander from one place to another, and it is not always easy to make ends meet. That could have been Govinda's fate if it had not been for Chohan.

On this occasion, he will have a talented accomplice by his side. Kosala is no stranger to the stage. Whereas he will be wearing a jeweled collar around his neck, Govinda will be dressed like a prince of the realm.

The bazaar is a hive of activity and the aroma of spices wafts through the air. The marketplace has exotic fruits and fabrics, a myriad of precious gems and hand-carved boxes but there are just as many soothsayers.

A rather large fortune-teller dripping with bracelets steps forward and offers to read Govinda's palm.

'Your future is not a mystery to me,' she says.

Govinda just bows his head and smiles, but her companion, a beautiful young gypsy girl with copper coloured skin and vibrant brown eyes is immediately attracted to Govinda.

'This is no ordinary love potion,' she says as she dangles a little bottle in front of his face. 'It has

38

the power to make a woman swoon at the sight of a handsome man.'

'I won't need that, but thank you all the same.'

'It wouldn't hurt,' she says.

The moment of truth is almost at hand, so Kosala steps forward and barks loudly to get everyone's attention. Chohan places an oversized basket on a colourful rug, and with a small gong in hand, he makes an announcement.

'Ladies and gentlemen, boys, and girls, gather round and prepare to be amazed. Govinda the Magnificent is a snake charmer like no other.'

'He has travelled across stormy seas with his companion, Kosala the wonder dog, and not one, but three little messenger birds.'

He throws a handful of powder onto the fire which erupts into a puff of black smoke. Govinda steps forward and he looks resplendent in a red and gold turban, a red vest, loose-fitting pants, and his mother's golden earrings.

He bows politely, makes himself comfortable, places the flute to his lips and plays a slow and haunting melody. A sinuous blue and gold cobra rises out of the basket, peers around carefully, and then strikes out this way and that.

And to the delight of the audience, Kosala races around, barking loudly, and manages to avoid one fatal bite after another.

Moments before the cobra turns its gaze on Govinda, three busy little messenger birds come to his rescue. They are brave-hearted creatures renowned for their speed and daring.

Messenger birds fear nothing at all, and to the delight of the bystanders, they dart around trying to tempt the cobra with a bite-sized delicacy.

The tempo of the music changes, and as soon as the cobra starts to sway languidly from side-to-side, Govinda returns it to the basket.

And for his efforts, he receives a hearty round of applause, but to everyone's surprise, Kosala walks around with a begging bowl in his paws.

'It worked Master. I got it right this time.'

'You did indeed. Well done, my boy.'

It was a captivating performance, especially for the young gypsy girl. She could not take her eyes off Govinda, and accompanied by a couple of talented musicians, she starts to sing and her voice travels through the air like a solitary wind whispering through the night.

## CHAPTER 12

Over the next three years, Govinda performs in the markets of every town and village in the land but just before he turns eighteen Chohan takes him to Colombo.

It's a three-day walk through the outskirts of the city, along dusty roads, an endless sea of poverty and a sea of mud brown huts plastered with mortar.

Chohan's house is an isolated bungalow several miles from the fashionable Cinnamon Gardens, a pleasure ground that is popular with Europeans, all of whom live in elegant houses nestled amongst exotic gardens.

'The charm of my house lies in the fact that it has an excellent view of the ocean,' Chohan says. 'The owner died of complications, and I acquired it for a song, shall we say.'

'Is that all you had to pay for it.'

'Not entirely, but more of that later.'

'The house was believed to be haunted. People said they heard sounds in the night and saw demons perched on the roof.'

'Apparently, the owner was jilted by a beautiful woman, so he embezzled her father's gold and hid it in the house.'

'He took his life not long after, but his neighbours believed that he was haunting the house as a ghost.'

'And was he?'

'I decided to spend a night there just to see what was going on, and I discovered that there was a zoological reason for the rumours.'

'And what does that mean?'

'It means that they were mostly bipeds and quadrupeds, creatures with two legs or four.'

'The ghost was nothing but a tomcat. The demons were bandicoots and the pest on the roof was a flying fox.'

'The gardens were as wild as a mad woman's hat and that suited me fine. It meant that no one would come anywhere near the place.'

'But you will like what you see, and you can stay here whenever you like.'

Situated on the edge of the bay where the river meets the sea, the house is of ample proportions with a verandah on all four sides. It was not as bad as it sounded, not until twilight, a time of day that engenders thoughts of another nature.

After they have eaten, they take a seat on the verandah, and watch closely as a purple light dances across the ocean.

'Govinda, I have something to tell you.'

'And what is that Master?'

'My work is done, and I will be leaving soon.'

'But why Master? Where are you going?

'I have things to do, but you are a man now and there is a wonderful life waiting for you out there.'

Govinda realises that this will be their last evening together, but when the brooding wings of night sweep over the landscape he is engulfed by an almighty sense of despair.

'You have been like a father to me,' he sniffles.

'And you have been like a son to me,' Chohan says. 'But one day soon, you will meet the love of your life, and you will be the father of a beautiful little girl.'

'Now, that is something to look forward to, isn't it?'

'Yes, it is,' Govinda says.

'Let's go down to river as I have something to show you.'

Govinda gets down on his knees and peers into the depths of the water, and a few minutes later, he sees a face looking back at him.

'Now, what do you see,' Chohan says.

'It's that gypsy girl from Negombo.'

'Well, that's the woman you will marry, which means that one day you must return to Negombo.'

'In that case, I will. She is very beautiful, isn't she?'

'She certainly is.'

'But Master, I can see a little girl as well. Is that my daughter?'

'Yes Govinda, but she will not be your only child.'

'Oh Master, I cannot believe that I am going to have a family of my own.'

'There's a boy as well, but I will tell you about him another day.'

That night, Govinda has dreams upon dreams, and when he wakes up the following day, he feels a lot better.

He is about to see the sights of the city, but to his dismay, Colombo has a distinct lack of spirit. It is hot and oppressive with a very disagreeable odour. The roads are lined with bullock carts loaded down by huge bags of coal.

Half-starved coolies stumble along with heavy loads on their backs, and sluggish, stern-faced traders skulk about like tomcats in the night.

A shop with a display window is something that Govinda has never seen before, and he has no idea what to think about a tailor's dummy dressed in a hoopskirt with enormous sleeves.

The emporium sells everything from a needle to a crowbar, but when he realises that it also sells guns, Govinda just turns around and walks away.

The next day, they leave Colombo far behind and head south to the town of Galkissa. As they wander along a quiet dusty road, Govinda is doing his best to hold back the tears.

Chohan is all too aware of how he feels, but before he goes, he hands the barrow over to Govinda.

'This is yours now, but when we reach the fork in the road, I will go one way and you will go the other.'

'Will I ever see you again Master?'

'Of course, you will, but you have something important to do. Somewhere out there is a little girl who needs a father.'

'Make sure that you teach her everything you know, for she has something important to do.

'I don't want you to go Master.'

'I will be looking after you at all times my boy, and whenever you call, I will answer.'

He takes him in his arms and brushes the tears from his eyes. 'The roads are not always safe, and danger lurks around every corner.'

'But cobras are your constant companions, and you can call upon their assistance whenever you need to.'

'Believe me, my boy, you really do have a very special life ahead, but now, it's time for me to go.'

Chohan bows from the waist, turns around and wanders up the road but Kosala decides to follow along behind.

'You stay with Govinda,' he says. 'He is your master now.'

## CHAPTER 13

For the next few days, Govinda travels from one village to another but it's not the same without Chohan. Life on the road can be very lonely, so he turns the barrow around and heads for Negombo.

'Kosala, we are going to look for that girl. I wonder if I will even recognise her.'

Kosala barks happily and when they reach the outskirts of Negombo, the road is swarming with people heading for the markets.

It's a tropical evening and the bazaar is alive with people, cinnamon vendors and spice stalls, hawkers of spurious love potions, soothsayers, palm readers, and jugglers.

The smell of smoking resin fills the air, and a crowd has gathered around a makeshift stage to watch a ritualistic ceremony. And to the beat of pounding drums, a shaman wearing a loin cloth and a grotesque mask struts around a smoking fire.

He works himself into a frenzy, accompanied by devil dancers dressed in equally gruesome masks with big bulging eyes, but a few minutes later, the crowd steps aside.

Four men enter the arena carrying a comatose woman strapped to a bamboo chair and deposits her in the middle of the stage. Word soon passes around that she has been possessed by the demons of the graveyard.

The shaman waves his trident in the air and babbles away in a language that only he understands. After which, he lops the head off a chicken and makes a sacrifice to an invisible god.

A long bout of chanting follow as he tries to retrieve her soul from the cold hands of death. The crowd is on tenterhooks waiting for something to happen, and then, the woman starts to shiver and shake and finally releases a gut wrenching cry, and to everyone's surprise, she comes back to life.

Once the onlookers have dispersed, Govinda gathers up his things and is about to head off when he encounters the very same girl whose face he saw reflected in a watery pool. This is the woman that Chohan said he would marry.

Suleka wears a vibrant red dress with golden earrings in her ears, bells on her wrists, a wicker basket perched on her hip, but she recognises Govinda immediately.

'You're that young snake charmer, aren't you?' she says.

'Yes, I am, but what have you got in your basket?'

'A python.'

'So, do you dance?'

'Yes, we do sometimes, if he's in the mood, but I don't think he is today.'

'Are you going to perform at the festival?' she says.

'Yes, I am, if I can find a space.'

'I might be able to help. Follow me.'

Her brother Raja and two handsome young men dressed in gypsy regalia are performing in a corner of the square.

'As soon as they have finished, I will join in,' Suleka says.

A few minutes later, she leaps onto the stage, crouches like a tiger, whips her hair from side to side and releases a high-pitched trilling sound.

To the sound of a gypsy guitar and a beating drum, she stomps around the stage and engages in a sensuous and exotic routine that titillates every man in the audience.

And when it's over, she gets a healthy round of applause, but to her dismay, she barely gets any money at all.

'It was hardly worth the effort, but every little bit helps,' she says to Govinda. 'So, now it's your turn. Do you need any help?'

'Yes, I do,' he says.

She introduces Govinda to her brother Raja, and another young man called Drago, and a few minutes later Govinda appears in his red and gold outfit.

He takes his place in front of a woven basket and starts to play, but everyone steps back when seven cobras rise out of the basket.

They strike out one way and another, but they are no match for Kosala or three busy little messenger birds. And as soon as the music changes to a slow melodic refrain, the cobras settle back and drift off into a long deep sleep.

Govinda bows to one and all but Kosala wanders around with a bowl in his paws and collects more money than Suleka has ever seen in her life.

'I wish we made that much.'

'Please take it,' Govinda says. 'I have more than I need.'

'Really. In that case, the least I can do is invite you back to our camp for dinner.'

'I would welcome the company as I spend most of my time talking to Kosala.'

'Well, things can change, can't they?' she says curiously.

## CHAPTER 14

They venture down a jungle path to a gypsy camp that is alive with the sound of music, voices raised in song and people dancing around an open fire.

If Govinda had turned up alone, it may not have been the same but he is closely guarded by Suleka who sits him around an open fire.

They talk until just after midnight, and after everyone else has gone to bed, Suleka takes him by the hand and leads him up the steps to the door of her caravan.

It is just after sunrise when they are roused from their sleep by the sound of someone knocking on the door.

'Suleka, it's time to get up. We are about to leave.'

'We'll be there soon Raja.'

Govinda has a speedy lesson in how to harness a horse to a wagon, and they follow along behind as the caravan makes its way deep into a jungle that is alive with the sound of birds and monkeys.

A few hours later, they stop to hunt for food. Honey is an essential part of their diet and if you know where to look it can be found in abundance. A young boy shimmies up the side of a cliff, while others lay in wait to trap a few of the native cocks.

They travel until sunset and then set up camp in the ruins of an abandoned city, but the most unsettling thing of all is not just the silence but the looming gaze of a huge time-blackened idol.

The jungle conceals many secrets, including savage dogs and a multitude of bodies buried in the undergrowth. It's all very eerie, surrounded as it is by a great pile of stones and numerous shallow graves covered in thorns.

'What is this place? Govinda says.

'No one knows. Some say that it's inhabited by evil spirits,' Raja says. 'I have even seen the skeletons of newborn babies.'

'I don't understand. Why?'

'They were probably left here to die.'

An evening of merriment follows, and while the women cook food over an open fire, the men swill palm wine from a leather pouch, but Govinda is deep in thought.

He has been pecking away at a bowl of seasoned rice but puts it aside and gets to his feet when he hears the sound of something racing through the forest.

'What's wrong?' Suleka says.

'Did you hear that?'

'Hear what?'

'I thought I heard dogs barking and a baby crying.'

He listens closely. 'There it is again.'

He races down the road, followed closely by Suleka and Kosala, and arrives on the scene only seconds before two hungry dogs are about to attack a helpless little baby.

Wild dogs can be skittish at the best of times, but they are no match for an angry man with a big lump of wood and an equally ferocious dog.

'It's all right. You're safe now,' Govinda says as he takes the child in his arms.

He removes the swaddling cloth, only to see a beautiful little face looking back at him.

'It's a little girl. Why would a mother abandon a baby in the forest?'

'Maybe an astrologer told her to do it.'

'But she's so helpless.' Govinda says. 'Well, I found her and she's mine now.'

'My Master said that I would find a little girl, but he also said that I would find a wife.'

'He knew that too.'

'Yes, he did. She's beautiful, isn't she? I am going to call her Kashmira, the mystery girl.'

'That's a beautiful name, but a baby needs a mother as well,' Suleka says curiously.

'Perhaps we could talk about that later. Let's get her back to the camp as I think she is hungry.'

If fate had not intervened, Kashmira's life could have ended in that moment, and it may have done so, if not for Govinda.

He would never have known what to do if he had found a baby on the side of a road, but he is surrounded by women with a wealth of experience.

After a long and interesting night, everyone gathers at the river bank the following morning to watch a herd of elephants bathing in the river.

The mothers stay close to the bank with their little ones, but dark clouds are gathering overhead and a storm is brewing.

A few minutes later, a gale force wind roars through the trees. The bull elephant sounds an alarm and the babies race into the forest. The males huddle together and stand their ground as a huge wall of water roars down the river.

The storm lasts for five long minutes and when it finally subsides, Raja races around to see that everyone is okay, but he stops in his tracks when he sees the ghostly form of a white elephant disappearing into the forest.

'Did you see that. It was a white elephant?'

'Yes, I did,' Govinda says. 'It came to my rescue once before.'

'And why would that be?'

'Because he is lucky, that is why,' Suleka says.

# CHAPTER 15

Their courtship is a display of stolen glances, a smile here, a gentle caress there, and silent messages sent from one youthful heart to another.

It does not go unnoticed that Govinda and Suleka only have eyes for each other, so after dinner one evening, they wander down to the river and lay side-by-side in the grass.

Govinda gazes up at the Moon and listens to the sound of a heron wailing in the night, but Chohan's words are always at the forefront of his mind, so takes a long deep breath and decides to broach the subject of marriage.

'Suleka, would you like to be my wife?' he says hopefully.

'I would love that,' she says. 'But you will have to talk to my brother first.'

A gypsy wedding is an extravagant affair and an age-old tradition with numerous rituals, but the first thing he has to do is talk to Raja.

'You usually have to pass a few tests first,' he says.

'Like what?' Govinda says.

'Firstly, you have to kidnap the bride and keep her hostage for three days. If no one comes to her rescue, then she is yours.'

'But you and Suleka have been living together for two weeks now, so you won't have to do that.'

'Is that all?' Govinda says.

'No, you have to pay for the wedding as well.'

'I can do that as I have lots of money.'

'In that case Govinda, you have my permission, but you will need the approval of the Queen of the Gypsies as well.'

'Have you met Ravanna the fortune teller yet?'

'No, I haven't.'

'Well, she's in that caravan over there. Come with me and I will introduce you.'

Ravenna is an impressive sight to behold, a rather large woman dressed in exotic silken veils, huge golden earrings, and hundreds of glistening bracelets.

'Ravenna, I would like you to meet Govinda. He has asked for Suleka's hand in marriage, and I have given my permission.'

'Come inside young man and we will talk,' she says.

The caravan is dark and mysterious, and the only light comes from a single candle. Ravenna makes herself comfortable and removes the cloth that covers her crystal ball.

'Now, let's see what the spirits have to say about this.'

She waves her hands across the ball and waits for the smoke to clear.

'I see a man gazing back at me, a man with deep brown eyes and a turban on his head.'

'Do you know who this is?'

'Yes, that's my master,' Govinda says.

'Very interesting. Now I see a white temple floating in the air, and a young couple standing at the very top but there's more. I can also see two white doves flying above their heads.'

'Does that mean something too?' Govinda says.

'It's a good sign, I know that much. Love birds if I am not mistaken. I think it means that you and Suleka are made for each other.'

'But before you go, please tell me about your master.'

Raja has been waiting patiently to hear the verdict, and the moment that Ravenna steps out of the caravan, he races up to hear what she has to say.

'So, is the news good?' he says.

'It seems that Govinda is a lucky young man, and I will be happy to give my blessings,' Ravenna says. 'But where will we have the wedding?'

'I know of a place,' Govinda says. 'It's the great rock of Sigiriya and it's not far from here.'

'That is an excellent choice, a temple in the clouds, just like the one I saw in my crystal ball.'

Sigiriya is a megalithic stone mountain that rises seven hundred feet into the air. And from a distance, it resembles a crouching lion, but on the very summit are the remains of an elaborate palace.

According to some people, it was a pleasure garden in the sky, conceived in a time long gone by a heavenly being, or even the great god Rama.

Here on the very doorstep of heaven, he created a vision of paradise, surrounded by terraced gardens, and a bevy of scantily dressed women in transparent veils and jeweled headdresses.

Very little remains of the palace or of its splendid gardens, but with a lot of effort, the ruins are transformed by glittering candles and flaming lamps.

It is just after sundown, and under the gaze of an indigo sky, the scene is set for a resplendent gypsy wedding. The aroma of food roasting over an open fire permeates the air. Garlands hang precariously from the ancient walls. Leaves and petals float across the surface of the murky old pools, and flower petals have been scattered across the ground.

The moment has all but arrived and the guests wait patiently for the bride and groom to appear.

Accompanied by an entourage of children dressed in colourful clothes, Suleka and Govinda pass through the remains of the fabled Lion Gate, after which they make the long trek to the top on an old wooden staircase.

To the sound of a single horn and a reverberating drumroll, followed by exultations of joy, the bride and groom finally make an appearance.

Dressed in lavish costumes and jewellery borrowed from everyone they know, they take their place on the edge of a pavilion.

In the background is a panoramic view of the landscape and the ever-present holy mountain. Raja raises his hand to quieten the congregation, and a few moments later, the Queen of the Gypsies makes an appearance.

Dressed in a flourish of glittering veils, Ravenna bows respectfully, looks from one face to another, and says, 'Is there anyone who does not find favour with this union?'

As no one replies, she continues. 'In that case, it is in my power to grant your heart's desire.'

She places a golden ornament around the necks of the bride and groom, pricks their fingers with a knife, recites a gypsy prayer and binds their hands together with a silken cord.

According to tradition, the groom must skip over a bed of warm coals, and to prove that she will follow her husband anywhere, the bride must do the same.

A night of grand celebration follows, but it was not until later in the evening that Govinda had a chance to talk to his special guest. No one had any idea who Chohan was, and they were too drunk to care.

'So, Master, what did you think?'

'That was a very beautiful ceremony my boy, and I would not have missed it for anything.'

## CHAPTER 16

It takes five long days for the caravan to reach the hilltop city of Kandy, a picturesque location 7600 feet above sea level and the home of the king of Ceylon.

Thousands of people have come from all over the island for the most important festival of the year, The Festival of Buddha's Tooth. And the highlight of the day will be a grand procession with over one hundred elephants adorned in lavish garments.

The ancestral home of the tooth is The Dalada Maligawa, and on this occasion it will be carried through the streets in a golden casket on the back of a majestic white elephant.

The King will make his way to the Mahaveli Ganga to celebrate the water ceremony, followed by a procession of public figures dressed in their finery.

Moments before the festivities begin, the sound of flutes and drums can be heard throughout the city. Dancers, musicians, and jugglers in elaborate costumes fill the streets but the firewalkers are the attraction of the day.

A young priest, his face painted with a pattern of red and yellow powder is the first contestant of the day. He waits patiently for an elderly priest to raise his arm, and as soon as he does so, he leaps into the fire pit.

To the dismay of the crowd, he stumbles and falls but carries on regardless, and for his efforts, he receives a garland of flowers to wear around his neck.

A spectator, a man in a white sarong decides to have a go as well, so he takes off his shoes, races across the pit and survives without a scratch, and for his efforts, he receives a resounding hurrah.

'Suleka, I am going to do that,' Govinda says.

'But you can't. You'll burn your feet.

'Not if I kiss one of my snakes first. Besides, it will be good for business. Now, watch this.'

Govinda steps into the pit and wanders along from one end to the other, then turns around and does it again. To prove that he is worthy, he throws a handful of burning ash into the air and then shows everyone the bottom of his feet.

'My friends, I am Govinda, a master snake charmer and this is my beautiful wife, Suleka. We will be performing in the marketplace tonight. Please come and see our wonderful show.'

Word soon spreads about the snake charmer who can charm seven snakes at a time and hundreds of people flock to see this unusual show.

Govinda looks resplendent in his red and gold outfit, but Suleka looks ravishing in an emerald-green dress and a headdress of beaten gold.

People are watching nervously and expectantly, waiting for the moment that she leaps into the flames with seven dangerous serpents.

This is something that no one has ever seen before, but by some magic they do not understand, several baby cobras appear on her head and disappear just as quickly. It's a triumphant success and cries of awe and wonder follow a thunderous round of applause.

Accompanied by Raja and Gonzaga, Kosala steps forward with a begging bowl and happily collects several bowls full of money.

Not long after, an old man dressed in a white comboy races up to Govinda.

'I am Ramus, and this is my wife, Rani. Master, we beg your indulgence. May we speak with you please?'

'Yes, of course you can.'

'We have been looking everywhere for you.'

'And why is that?'

'All the blessed signs have brought you here on this day. We need your help Master, to remove a curse from the landscape.'

'And how can I do that?'

'You are a Master, blessed by the gods themselves, but when I saw your golden aura, I knew that our prayers had been answered.'

'So, what do you want me to do?'

'Our home is many leagues from here, but it is plagued by men with guns. They are British elephant hunters Master, very bad Englishmen.'

'They are but a curse on the landscape as I said, men who show no mercy to those beautiful animals.'

'We do not know what to do about this, but I had a dream in which you used your magic power to scare them away.'

'But I do not have magic powers.'

'Oh, but you do master, I saw it in my dream. Will you at least come and see what they are doing?'

'Once you do, you will be so enraged that you will want to kill them with your own hands.'

Raja has been listening closely to this conversation. 'Ramus, where do you live?' he says.

'Do you know the ancient city of Polonnaruwa?'

'Yes, we have passed through there many times.'

'Then, we will come with you, but we must keep this a secret,' Govinda says. 'If word gets out that we killed an Englishman, our lives will be in danger.'

'Oh, thank you Master. We will not exclaim one single thing about this. You have my very word.'

## CHAPTER 17

The pear-shaped island known to some as Sinhala and to others as Ceylon has attracted gold diggers of every shape and form.

The history of colonization was a litany of horrors but the first to make landfall were Portuguese merchants, only to be followed by missionaries, pirates and finally the administrators.

In the name of one Imperial Majesty or another, the Europeans went out of their way to rape and pillage in the name of that insatiable god called money. And if the word of the Lord did not work its magic, the sword always found its mark.

Vasco da Gama made landfall in 1505, but the country he encountered had a weak and ineffective king. Ceylon was not under his control, but that of petty chiefs, the Moors, the Tamils, the Malabars and numerous vassal kings.

The Portuguese had a diplomatic battle on their hands from day one. The Ceylonese were a lot more astute than the Portuguese realised, but they made their presence known with guns and cannons.

In the year 1517, the Portuguese set up a trading station on the western coast of Sinhala, a place that the Arabs called Kalambu, and a city that would eventually be known as Colombo.

A steamship docks at Colombo harbour and one of the passengers is an Englishman in a safari suit.

Moss Burton is a game hunter with a face like a desert hawk, and on this occasion, he is accompanied by three men of the same persuasion.

'Colombo hasn't changed,' Burton said. 'It is still a rampant cesspit of a place.'

'Let's get out of here. We have a long journey ahead.'

## CHAPTER 18

A few days later, Govinda is sitting around a campfire with a group of men trying to work out what they can do.

'Ramus, tell me everything that you know about elephants,' Govinda says.

'Oh Master, they are the lords of the jungle, but they are also the wisest of animals. Why, they even work out how to do things for themselves.'

'Elephants walk in single file, but the Mamma elephant is very wise and she always tells her baby to walk in front. That is very sensible for a tiger sometimes wants to pounce on the baby and take it away.'

'The mother elephants are protected by the papa elephants. You see, the mammas and the babies are always in the middle, safe from all harm.'

'Now, did you know that if two elephants start to quarrel like naughty boys, the papa elephant will punish them?'

'No, I did not know that.'

'Do you know how an elephant drinks?'

'Through his trunk,' Govinda says.

'No, he does not. An elephant has to dip his trunk into the stream so that he can squirt the water into his mouth. Of course, he has to do that many times to get enough water.'

'But you may say, why doesn't he go into the stream?'

'And why is that?'

'The answer is that he does not want to stir up the mud and therefore dirty the water. Now you see what a wise animal the elephant is.'

'As to how his nose became so long, that I do not know. But Master, did you know that an elephant can walk under water?'

'I do know that. I have even seen it for myself.'

'But an elephant also likes to play tricks.'

Everyone is intrigued by what Ramus has to say, but Gonzaga has had enough of this never-ending story.

'Govinda. Aren't we supposed to be planning something?'

'We are but I am the one who has to come up with an idea.'

Early the next morning, Ramus races into the camp, puffing from his exertions.

'Master, I have very bad news indeed. Those British Englishmen are going to kill those beautiful elephants. If you wish to see such a horrible thing and with your own eyes, then follow me,' he says.

The elephants wander freely through the jungle, but the one place they do feel safe is the remains of Polonnaruwa, the ancient capital of old Ceylon.

Not long after, a hunter on horseback appears, accompanied by four scantily dressed men with drums.

His hunter's heart is beating as he sneaks up on a lone elephant and presses the trigger. The remainder of the herd race into the forest but this one suffers a slow and agonising death.

The ivory trade is big business and an elephant's tusk is worth a small fortune. The hunter places his rifle to the elephant's head and delivers the fatal blow.

'I should make a pretty penny from this one,' he says.

# CHAPTER 19

It was a horrible thing to have to see, but it got a lot worse after that, much worse and what followed was nothing less than unmitigated carnage.

The hunter hacked off the tusks, his retainers chopped away at the carcass with bloody axes, loaded the meat onto a cart, and left the remains to rot in the sun.

That was as much as Govinda and his men could stomach, so they head back to camp but the evening that follows is a muted and sombre affair.

They are gypsies, resilient men who have spent their lives foraging in the forest in an effort to survive. And even if they were tempted, they would never take the life of a beautiful creature such as an elephant.

But that was not foraging, that was an act of vicious and bloody violence, and an experience that leaves everyone in a state of mind-numbing shock.

Ramus is almost heartbroken and he begs Govinda to do something about it.

'See what I be meaning Master. That was a very bad man indeed,' Ramus says. 'What will you be doing?'

'We have to find a cobra's nest, Ramus.'

'Yes Master, there are very many in the old city. What is your plan?'

'We will let the cobras do what they do best. They can take care of those murderers.'

'Ooh Master, that is a very clever plan indeed and I think that idea will work.'

Armed with his flute and a digging stick, Govinda sets off for the ruined city in the company of twenty other men.

He coaxes a cobra out of a hole, seizes it by the tail and stretches it out until he has a stranglehold on the head, after which, he places it in a basket.

'Cobras cannot resist the sound of a flute.'

'Music must make them very joyful Master.'

'No, Ramus. Snakes do not have ears like we do.'

As soon as he has a dozen cobras, Govinda ventures into the undergrowth and finds just as many in the trees.

'That's a good one. Here Raja, put it in the basket.'

'Ah ha,' he cries. 'It's a monster.'

'This place is crawling with snakes, especially if you know where to look.'

After dinner that evening, they sit around the campfire and listen closely to what Govinda has in mind.

'We will position ourselves around the city, and each of you will be in charge of a cobra.'

'Are you going to kiss every one of them?' Raja says.

'Yes, otherwise they will run away, and we will have wasted our time.'

Early the next morning, Ramus races into the camp with news of another hunting party.

'We have to hurry Master. Those Englishmen are going to kill more elephants.'

Govinda and his men arrive just in time to see a hunting party closing in on its prey. Accompanied by beaters banging away on drums, Moss Burton and three other riders are preparing to take down as many as they can.

There is no time to waste, so Govinda races along from one basket to another and kisses each of the cobras in turn.

'When you hear me whistle like this,' he says as he imitates a birdcall, 'that's the signal to let them go.'

'Now spread out and make sure that no one sees you.'

62

Burton fires the first shot and brings an elephant to its knees. Govinda's men respond immediately and thirty cobras slither along the ground, their eyes set firmly on their prey.

The beaters make a speedy retreat. The horses whinny and rear and Burton and his men are thrown to the ground.

A scene of mayhem and carnage ensues as the cobras emit a bone-chilling death rattle of a sound. The hunters are immobilised after the first bite. Shock sets in. They gasp for breath and jerk spasmodically back and forth. Their faces turn blue, and a few minutes later, the cold hand of death takes its toll.

'Another bunch of murderers have gone to hell,' Gonzaga says, 'but they won't be the last.'

'Quickly, let's get out of here.'

## CHAPTER 20

Dark clouds are gathering overhead, the air is hot and balmy, and the monsoon season is about to start, but Govinda is still troubled by that experience.

'I never thought I would do such a thing.'

'You did what you had to,' Suleka says.

'But that was murder.'

'They deserved what they got,' Raja says.

At that moment, Ramus hobbles into the camp

'Master, it is not safe to be around here anymore.'

'Why, did someone see us?'

'That I do not know, but the British soldiers have found the bodies.'

'If they work out that we are behind this, we are done for,' Govinda says. 'I think we should get out of here.

'Maybe we should split up and go our different ways,' Raja says.

'No, we should stay together for a long as possible.'

They pack the wagons and make their way along paths known only to gypsies, but it rains every day and night for the next week.

'We can't go on like this.' Suleka says. 'Kashmira is teething and she won't stop crying.'

'Then we will find somewhere to stay until she settles down.'

'Raja, we are going to hide out in Ratnapura, but we will leave the wagon with you.'

'Okay, but if we decide to move on, we will let you know.'

Govinda and Suleka assume the attire of a middle-class couple from Colombo. Govinda shaves off his moustache and changes into a loose-fitting shirt and a pair of white trousers, whereas Suleka is dressed in a neat white jacket, her hair fastened with silver pins and a tortoise shell comb.

Pilgrims from many lands use Ratnapura as a stopover on the way to Adam's Peak but today it is almost deserted.

The City of Gems is the centre of the gem mining industry, and it is here that a prospective buyer can purchase rubies, sapphires, emeralds, and other precious stones.

Suleka waits with Kosala on the verandah of a local tea house while Govinda searches for somewhere to stay.

The Ratnapura markets are normally a hive of activity, but this is the wet season, the pilgrims have not yet arrived, and today is a quiet day.

Dressed in long white caftans, the Moors are a common sight at the markets. An old moneychanger sits at a desk counting a multitude of copper coins, while most of the traders just while away the time polishing their goods.

An old peddler with a tray of charms approaches Govinda, hoping to sell a few trinkets.

'Not today,' he says. 'I am looking for somewhere to stay.'

'Then you should speak to Sudhra, that man over there,' he says. 'He is a cloth trader from Colombo and he has a place.'

Govinda approaches Sudhra, a short round man with an agreeable face and explains that he is looking for a place to rent until the rain has settled down.

'Then you are in luck my friend. I have a guest house that I am willing to rent for a small fee. You will not find a finer view in all of Ratnapura. '

'Follow me,' he says.

They head to the outskirts of the city and follow a path through the jungle and Govinda is impressed by what he sees.

The house is small but clean and well-furnished and sits on the edge of a tea plantation, and in the distance, shrouded by mist, is the sacred mountain known as Adam's Peak. This will be the perfect place to hide out for a while.

He thanks Sudhra, pays him what he is due, and races back to the teahouse.

'Suleka, I have found a nice little guest house and it's just perfect.'

Now that they have time on their hands, they take pleasure in each other's company. Kashmira's baby teeth have finally come through and she is no longer crying, so Govinda removes her from the cradle and places her on the bed beside Suleka.

'Look at those new teeth Tada.'

'You are so beautiful, aren't you?' Govinda says as he kisses her on the forehead.

'I could get used to living in a house,' Suleka says.

'Then I will buy you one.'

'Something on a hill with a view of the ocean would be good.'

'Yes, I like that idea. I am tired of wandering around from one place to another.'

'So am I and it would be the perfect place to raise a family.'

'Did you hear that Kashmira? You are going to have a baby brother one day. '

# CHAPTER 21

A week later, the streets of Ratnapura are alive with pilgrims, all of whom are eager to make the trek to the top of Adam's Peak. The markets are a bustle of activity, but everyone races outside when a group of soldiers march down the street.

'Suleka,' says a worried Govinda. 'They're British and they are probably looking for me.'

'They don't know who you are or what you look like.'

'I hope you are right.'

After dinner that evening, Govinda sits on the verandah and gazes out across the plantation. He is barely aware of the sounds of the forest, the chirping cicadas or a bird singing a strange lullaby. When Kosala starts barking, he looks up, only to see an unusually bright light on the hill.

'Suleka,' he cries. 'Come and look at this.'

'Oh, that is so beautiful, but what is it?'

'Fireflies, perhaps.'

'I don't think so.'

'Maybe we should take a closer look.'

'I don't want to leave the baby by herself.'

'We won't be long. Let's go and check this out. Kosala, keep a close eye on Kashmira while we are away.'

They are only halfway to the top when Suleka looks up, only to see a man dressed in the outfit of an Indian prince.

'Look Govinda. Look up there. Who is that?'

'It's my Master, Suleka.'

He takes her hand, and they race to the top of the hill.

'Master, what are you doing here?' he says.

'I said that I would keep an eye on you, that is why.'

'Greetings, Suleka, I am Chohan, Govinda's master. There is no need to be afraid, not of me, at any rate.'

'But you must pack your things and head for the coast at daybreak. You are not in any danger yet, but the British are rounding up every snake charmer in the district.'

'They are already here. We saw them this afternoon.'

'They have vowed to scour every inch of the island until they get their man. You should head for the town of Dehiwala and then go south to Galkissa.'

'But what will we do Master? '

'Go to Aditya and find a man called Tihali. Give him this ring. He is an old friend of mine. Take this as well. It's a bag of gemstones. That should tide you over for quite a while.'

'But whatever you do, never mention your profession to anyone for several years at the very least.'

'But why are you doing this?' Suleka says.

Your daughter Kashmira is the reason. She has a destiny, and one that she must fulfil, but she will not do so, not in your lifetime.'

'Master, can you tell us what it is?'

'She will be doing the world a favour, but that will not be for a very long time. Your task is to see that she gets that opportunity.'

## CHAPTER 22

It takes three days to reach a beachside settlement not far from Galkissa, a busy place bustling with half-naked children and dozens of fishermen, some of whom cast their nets into the sea while others fly through the water in fast moving canoes.

It's a hot and humid night so they decide to sleep outside on a woven mat. The next morning, Suleka joins a group of women bathing in the ocean, and after they have washed their hair, they rub it with coconut oil and pin it back with a tortoise shell comb.

A woman called Radhini invites them to share a bowl of rice for breakfast. Her husband, Kapila, is a wiry man with leathery skin and a mouth tinged red from chewing betel nut.

'Do you know of a man called Tihali?' Govinda says.

'Is he a friend of yours?'

'He was a friend of my father.'

'I have heard of a physician called Tihali. You will find him in the temple at Aditya. If he is not the Tihali you seek, then the priests may know of another.'

They rent a little bungalow in Galkissa, a two-roomed house with a row of columns at the front. A shade tree in the garden and a bougainvillea vine across the front offers all the privacy they need.

The next day, they take a bullock cart to the temple and travel along a bumpy road that winds its way through an avenue of coconut trees, past labourers working in the fields, and men carrying buckets of fish.

When they arrive at the temple, an over-excited young priest called Tharanga rushes up to a group of monks in yellow robes and begs their indulgence.

'I have a most remarkable tale to tell,' he says. 'I have been most fortunate on this day.'

'And why is that?' says one of the elderly priests.

'I found a Bodhi tree in the jungle. That's the very same tree under which the Buddha reached enlightenment.'

'But how can you be sure that it was.'

'I was travelling down the river when I heard the sound of drums.'

'Why I do not know, but I got out of the boat. And to my surprise, there were no drums to be found, but there in front of me stood a Bodhi tree.'

'It must have come from the old city of Anuradhapura,' the old priest says. 'This is most portentous indeed.'

'Then I will make it my mission to build a new temple on that very site,' Tharanga says.

'But the swamp is full of snakes.'

'In that case, I will need a snake charmer to dispose of them.'

Govinda steps forward and uses this as an opportunity to introduce himself.

'Most reverent brother, I am a snake catcher, and I will be happy to be of service.'

'Praise be to Buddha,' Tharanga cries. 'Then we must work together my friend, as the snakes outnumber the trees by two to one. But what brought you here?'

'I am looking for a man called Tihali. I believe there is a man of that name, here in the temple.'

'There is indeed. This is a fortunate day for both of us. And you have come to the right place. Allow me to take you to him.'

## CHAPTER 23

Tharanga chatters away as he leads them down a long winding path that weaves its way through well-kept gardens to a small building at the rear of the temple.

'Are you a relative of Tihali?' he says.

'He is a friend of a friend, you could say.'

'Then you will find him to be a most interesting old man.'

'Is he a priest? Govinda says.

'No, he is a healer who attends to our needs. This is the place you seek. I will leave you now, but we must talk later as we have much to do.'

'In that case, we will catch up before I go,' Govinda says.

An old man in a long white robe opens the door and inquires of their business.

'My name is Govinda, and this is my wife, Suleka. I believe you are Tihali the healer.'

'Yes, that's true. How can I be of help? Are you ailing in some way?'

'No, I am not. I have been sent here by a friend.'

'And who might that be.'

'My Master, Chohan. Do you remember him?'

'I have not heard that name since I was a boy. You may not believe this, but he was my master as well.'

'Please come in as I think we have many things to talk about.'

They step inside only to find that this really is the domain of a healer. The infirmary is spotlessly clean with sunlight streaming in through every window.

Numerous cupboards line the walls, each of which is bulging with bottles of exotic herbs, elixirs, remedies, salves, and ointments.

Govinda and Suleka listen with interest to Tihali's story, of the day he nearly died, of how he tumbled down the side of a mountain, and of the man who came to his rescue.

'Chohan taught me everything about herbs and potions and set me on the path of a healing man. But that was over sixty years ago. Is it possible that he still lives?'

'If it is the same man, then you will remember this,' Govinda says, as he places a blue sapphire ring in his hand.

'I do indeed remember this ring. Then it is truly a miracle.'

'I believe Chohan might be a holy man.'

'I can assure you that he is Govinda, but what brings you here?'

Tihali listens closely to what he has to say about the elephant hunters and of their need to keep a low profile.

'My Master told us that we would be safe here.'

'As long as no one finds out who you are, you will be, but what will you do now?'

'A young priest called Tharanga has just found a Bodhi tree in the jungle, and says that he is going to build a temple to the Buddha.'

'Tharanga is a determined young man and I have no doubt that he will succeed.'

'I am going to dispose of the snakes,' Govinda says. 'Apparently, the swamp is riddled with them.'

'It is indeed. I spend most of my time curing people of snake bites.'

## CHAPTER 24

Some people believe that if you kill a snake, its mate will seek revenge. Other people place them in a basket and send them down the river, but everyone knows about the dreaded Mapilla.

It usually resides in the roof of a house, and as a few unfortunate people have found out, a mapilla will bite without provocation. But their favourite routine is to hang from the rafters and descend on its victim as it sleeps.

The news that Tharanga is going to erect a temple in the jungle spreads like wildfire and it's not long before everyone in Galkissa is talking about it.

One morning, he and Govinda wander through the markets looking for men to eradicate the snakes, but no one is interested, and everyone has a different excuse.

'There are too many crocodiles, the first man says. 'Oh, but what about the wild pigs.

'There are very many great big spiders in that jungle.'

'Have you not seen the size of those leeches?'

'I do not like rats, and I do not like mosquitoes.

'Why, only last year, I was bitten by one of those monkeys and I almost died.'

'Have you not seen that dreaded devil bird?'

By the end of the day, Tharanga is crestfallen. 'I am thinking that we will have to think of something else.'

'Perhaps we should talk to Tihali,' Govinda says.

Tihali is not surprised but he does have a suggestion.

'Do you know that old saying, if you want to build high, then you have to dig deep. Well, in this case, you will have to climb high.'

'I don't understand,' Govinda says.

'Several days walk from here is a temple dedicated to the snake goddess. It is there that you will find a tribe of Veddhas. Have you heard of them?'

'Yes, I have encountered them once before. A fearsome bunch of people.'

'Not all of them. I know of one tribe that would be willing to help.'

'On one occasion, I saved the life of a young Veddha boy and Pomorola promised to repay the favour.'

'The journey will not be an easy one, not unless you have some experience of the wilderness.'

'I have seen more than my fair share of this country,' Govinda says.

Pomorola gave me this,' Tihali says, as he removes a rather large piece of bone from a box. 'Give it to him and he will remember me immediately.'

'What is it?' Tharanga says.

'It's the jawbone of a cobra.'

'That was a big snake.'

'That's a relatively small one, compared to some.'

'I'd hate to see a big one.'

'You probably will.'

'I am having second thoughts about this,' he says. 'Perhaps we should forget about it for now.'

'Unfortunately, you cannot. You found a Bodhi tree, which means that you have a temple to build.'

'That could take a lifetime,' Tharanga groans. 'Oh, why I ever went there, I will never know.'

## CHAPTER 25

Govinda would rather stay home than venture into the wild lands but he has no other choice. He spends his last few minutes bouncing Kashmira on his knee.

'Tada loves his little girl, but Tada is going away for a while, and you will have to look after Mama while I am gone.'

'How long will you be away?' Suleka says.

'About five or six days.'

'I have heard that there is a group of gypsies to the south of here, and I have a feeling that it's probably Raja.'

'Just be careful,' Govinda says.

'You're the one who should be careful.'

'I won't be doing any snake charming for quite a while, maybe for years.'

'Good. Make sure it stays that way.'

After he has packed a few things in the barrow, he meets Tharanga on the outskirts of the town, and with Kosala following along behind, they travel high up into the mountains.

Their destination is one of the most remote parts of the island, and in his usual style, Tharanga chatters all the way.

'I have heard that the Veddhas are the wild men of the jungle. I have also heard that they live in trees and dry their meat in the trunk of a tree, and they never bathe or wash their hair.'

'I have heard that they have a God peculiar to themselves,' Govinda says. 'And they dance around a fire to appease that God, but there are no finer hunters than the Veddhas.'

'I hope they do not have a taste for human flesh.'

'Tihali has assured us that these people are different.'

'I hope so. I do not want to be roasted over an open fire.'

As they make their way up the mountain, the heat is intense, and the humidity is rising. The jungle is a mass of dense foliage and Tharanga has had enough.

He has been assaulted by one vicious plant after another and is about to scream. For all he knows, he could be surrounded by snakes and scorpions and other unmentionable creatures.

It is late afternoon when they chance upon a well-hidden gorge, and he is astonished to see the bones of hundreds of elephants scattered from one end to the other.

'This is most un-natural, is it not? I have heard of such a place, but I never expected to see it for myself.'

'I have seen stranger things than this in the jungle,' Govinda says.

'Truly, like what?'

'I once saw an abandoned city with babies that had been eaten by wild dogs.'

'Ooh, I do not like the sound of that at all. I will not be going there very soon.'

'Just be careful where you walk Tharanga. This place could be booby trapped.'

'And why would that be?'

'The wild men of the jungle have many ways of catching their prey.'

'But we are not prey, are we?'

'It depends on who we meet first.'

Oh, my goodness me. Look up there,' he cries. 'The cliffs are riddled with snakes.'

'Then the temple can't be far from here,' Govinda says.

'I am hoping you are correct.'

To Tharanga's dismay, the ground is littered with skeletons propped up on sticks.

'I am thinking that there are a lot of dead people here. Someone must have lived here once, and they obviously died here as well.'

Kosala takes off to investigate but stands his ground when he realises that they have company. A moment later, a group of scantily clad men armed with bows and arrows emerge from the undergrowth and Tharanga almost wets himself.

'Oh no, Govinda. It's the wild men. We are doomed.'

'Just wait and see Tharanga.'

A half-naked man with knotted hair and penetrating eyes steps forward and says, 'What is your business?'

'We are here to see Pomorola,' Govinda says.

'Then follow us.'

Surrounded by a dozen men with flaming torches, they head deep into the forest, pass through a long dark tunnel, and then cross a rickety bridge suspended over a deep ravine.

'We are not going to walk on that thing, are we?' says a very worried Tharanga.

'Keep going,' the leader says.

This is not what Tharanga had in mind when he agreed to this trip. He just wants to go home, but there is nowhere to go but forward.

They pass through another dark tunnel, but the last thing that Tharanga expected to see is a well-concealed city that overlooks the valley below.

'Oh no,' he cries. 'Where are we now?'

'Where we are supposed to be,' Govinda says.

A solid young man dressed in a loin cloth, steps forward and looks them up and down.

'I am Pomorola, chief of the Uniga tribe,' he says. 'Who are you and why are you here?'

'I am Govinda, and this is Tharanga. We are not here by accident. We have come with the blessings of someone you know.'

'Do you remember a man called Tihali? '

'Yes, I would not be here if it was not for him. Has he passed on?'

'No, he hasn't. He sends his greetings, but he asked me to give you this,' Govinda says as he hands over the jawbone.

'I have not seen this since I was a boy, but why did you bring it back.'

'You promised Tihali that you would return the favour.'

'Yes, I always keep my word.'

'We need your help to get rid of a few snakes, lots of them in fact.'

'Then you have come to the right place. The Uniga have no fear of snakes.'

'What about crocodiles, pigs, and leeches?'

'We eat them.'

'Good, I was hoping you'd say that.'

A shaman dressed in animal skins suddenly steps out of the shadows.

'This one has the power to talk to snakes, he says as he points his staff at Govinda.

'Is that not so?'

'How do you know that?'

'Saya Kyanga does not know but the Goddess does. She is calling and you must obey.'

'Why? Did I do something wrong?'

'It is not my place to say, but the Goddess has spoken. You must climb that peak and cross the bridge of snakes. And if you survive, we will do as you ask.'

'Survive,' Tharanga gasps.

## CHAPTER 26

'What is this all about Govinda?'

'I have no idea, but we are about to find out. I hope you are not afraid of snakes.'

'I am afraid of everything, which is why I became a priest. I don't like the look of this Govinda.'

'Would you rather face the wrath of that old witchdoctor?'

'No, no, no, definitely not.'

'Then follow me.'

After a thirty-minute climb they reach the summit of the mountain and it is here that they have a breath-taking view of endless miles of airborne peaks.

To reach the temple, they pass through a serpentine gateway and then have to cross another rickety old bridge.

'Govinda, what did he mean that you can talk to snakes?'

'It's a skill that I have had for years, and it comes in useful as a snake catcher.'

Thunderclouds are getting closer with every passing minute, but a flash of lightning followed by a crack of thunder is the last straw for Tharanga. He screams at the top of his voice and dives for cover.

'Oh no. It's time to get out of here.'

'Just stay calm,' Govinda says.

'That's easy for you to say.'

'There it is, just up ahead.'

Kosala decides to check out the temple but doesn't venture any further than the doorway.

'See, even the dog won't go in.'

'The Goddess awaits,' Govinda says.

'I think I'll stay here.'

'Whatever you wish, Tharanga.'

The temple is a vast open space with a domed roof adorned by serpents of every shape and form, and seated on a throne at the far end is the goddess herself.

Govinda takes one hesitant step at a time, but Kosala races down to take a closer look. The goddess reaches out and pats him on the back and Kosala barks excitedly.

'Boy, come closer so that I may see your face,' she says.

'Master, is it really you?'

'This is just one of my many faces, Govinda.'

'But why have you called me here?'

'Were you expecting the worst?'

'I wasn't sure what to expect, but what do you want?'

'You were given a gift for a reason, and so far, you have used it wisely.'

'But the elephant hunters Master, and the British soldiers. I live in fear for my friends and family.'

'They will eventually tire of searching Govinda, but be warned, you will have one close call. Be on your guard nevertheless.'

'I don't want anything to happen to Suleka and Kashmira. They are the only family I have.'

'You will have other children, but one of those will not be your own.'

'On the day of Kashmira's tenth birthday, a ship will be wrecked on a beach just south of Galkissa.'

'You must save a young boy's life, raise him as your own and teach him to be a snake charmer.'

'If that is what you wish Master. I will do as you say.'

'He will be an important part of Kashmira's life, and it is vital that they meet.'

'However, before you go, give this staff to the old witchdoctor. It won't stay gold for long, but he definitely needs a new one.'

'Thank you, Master, but will I ever see you again.'

'Of course, you will, my boy, but probably in some other form.'

When Govinda finally emerges from the temple, Tharanga heaves a sigh of relief.

'Thank the almighty one that you are safe Govinda. Did the Goddess give you that?'

'Yes, but it's not for me. It's for the witchdoctor?'

'Oh, I wouldn't mind one of those. So, tell me everything. What did the goddess say?'

'She said that I was going to have more children.'

'We came all the way up here just to hear that. The local soothsayer could have told you that.'

'Are you sure that is all?'

'I promise Tharanga. That's all she said.'

'Well, I suppose it's important, isn't it?'

'It is Tharanga.'

# CHAPTER 27

Tharanga had the inspired idea to boat the Uniga tribesmen in under the cover of darkness, but then decides against it. The boatman will probably tell everyone he knows, so the only option is to creep through the jungle in the early hours of the morning.

Before they can do anything at all, an astrologer selects a suitable day and a suitable hour at which to conduct the ceremony.

Two days later, a procession of priests wander around chanting and waving bells this way and that. And an hour later, they declare that the site is free of malevolent demons and unfavourable spirits.

But before they get down to business, Govinda has a job for Tharanga.

'Oh no,' he says. 'What is it this time?'

'The swamp is full of leeches. Ask Tihali if he has a potion as we will need to get rid of them.'

Tharanga sighs with relief. 'I thought you had something else in mind.'

'I do, but I will save that for later.'

Before Govinda can get rid of the snakes, he has a problem with just as many monkeys.

'That isn't going to be easy,' Pomorola says.

Fifty Uniga tribesmen venture into the swamp, and the monkeys know immediately that something is up. Word passes around and the battle to protect their homeland starts with an onslaught of nuts and berries.

'They've gone mad,' Govinda cries.

'I know how to fix this,' Pomorola says. 'We will be having monkey brain soup tonight, that's for sure.'

'What are you going to do?'

'Scare them away.'

'But where will they go?'

'Across the river. There's plenty of forest over there.'

Pomorola's plan involves a lot of loud noise and high-pitched squealing, and the monkeys are prepared for the worst, but his men are not fazed in the least.

After a very chaotic battle, the Uniga are the victors, and the monkeys finally get the message. The jungle is normally a very noisy place, but two hours later, peace finally reigns supreme.

'Well, that's one less problem to worry about,' Pomorola says. 'Now, for the snakes.'

'I know how to tame a snake,' Govinda says.

'And how is that?'

'Have you ever kissed a cobra before?'

'No, I haven't but it sounds dangerous.'

'Watch and see for yourself,' Govinda says.

Pomorola doesn't have much faith in this idea and just shakes his head when the cobra heads for the river.

'It was supposed to go into the swamp,' Govinda says.

'And do what?'

'Do what I told it to do, of course.'

'Where did you get that idea?'

'A master snake catcher. Who else?'

'And did it work for him?'

'Yes, and it usually works for me.'

'Well, it didn't this time. There are probably thousands of snakes in there. You can't kiss every one of them. It would take weeks at that rate.'

'Then I will try something else,' Govinda says.

'So, what do you have in mind this time?'

'A lullaby.'

Govinda ventures into the swamp and plays a low monotonous melody on his flute. As to whether it's working on the snakes it is impossible to say, but a few of the tribesmen start to nod off immediately.

'Well, it works on your men,' Govinda says. 'Let's see if it had the same effect on the snakes.'

'You can only hope,' Pomorola says.

To his surprise, most of the snakes are as timid as the day they were born, but not long after, the men race out covered in leeches.

Govinda grabs a smouldering stick from the fire and hands it to Pomorola. 'Here, burn them off with this,' he says.

'No, we peel them off and throw them onto the fire.'

Tharanga comes racing up the road with a bag of salt, lemons, pig fat and vinegar and Govinda mixes them into a paste.

Pomorola's men head back into the swamp covered in a greasy solution of aromatic pig fat, and by the end of the day, they have a mountain load of leeches and hundreds of catatonic snakes.

'So, what do we do with them now?' Pomorola says.

'We load them onto a bullock cart and take them to another swamp,' Govinda says.

After a very tiring but successful day, it's time to reap the rewards of their efforts. Tharanga watches in horror as Pomorola throws the leeches into a smouldering firepit.

'We won't starve tonight, that's for certain,' he says.

'You're going to eat those things?'

'Yes, Tharanga. They're delicious.'

He stabs a barbequed leech with a pointed stick and offers him one.

'Try it.'

'I have taken an oath never to eat the flesh of a living creature.'

'That's your loss, Tharanga, not mine.'

# CHAPTER 28

After an experience of that nature, Govinda is hot and sweaty, and when he finally gets back home, he just collapses on the floor.

'Thank God you're back,' Suleka says. 'Was your mission successful.'

'Yes, it was. We cleared the swamp of just about every wild animal in the area, but I do have some good news.'

'And what is that?'

'We are going to have children of our own.'

'Oh, and who told you that?'

'I was summoned to the Temple of the Snake Goddess, and she told me.'

'It was actually my master in disguise, but he also said that we have to be on the beach on the day that Kashmira turns ten.'

'And why is that?

'A ship will be wrecked in a storm and the only survivor will be a boy. We will have to raise him as our own.'

'Really?'

'Yes, it's important.'

'That must have something to do with what he said in Ratnapura.'

'It does.'

'Well, that is interesting, but we have plenty of time to think about it.'

'So, did you find Raja?' he says.

'Yes, they set up camp not far from the beach, but they keep a close eye on the passing traffic just in case any British soldiers pass by.'

'Sounds like a good plan, but the Goddess did say that the soldiers will eventually give up searching. However, I will have one close call.'

'When?'

'She didn't say. I just have to be careful. But where is our little angel.'

Govinda adores his little girl, and she obviously loves her daddy as well, but this is an auspicious day. This is the day that she utters her very first words.

'Ta-da. Ta-da.'

'Has she ever said that before?'

'Not that I am aware of.'

'You will be bossing us around soon, won't you? But you really are going to have brothers and sisters. Won't that be good?'

'Govinda, I have wonderful news,' Suleka says.

'Don't tell me that you are pregnant. Are you going to have a child?'

'Yes, but I think it will be a girl.'

'That's wonderful, I don't care what it is. It will be ours.'

'I never thought I would ever have anything, but now I have a family of my own.'

'Of our own,' Suleka says as she takes him in her arms. 'I fell in love with you the first time I ever saw you, Govinda.'

'In that case, we must celebrate.'

'Not until you have had a bath. You stink Govinda. Get down to the ocean and go for a swim. And after you come back, we will spend a few days with Raja.'

'Whatever you say, my darling.'

## CHAPTER 29

Ever since his experience with the elephant hunters, Govinda has kept a low profile. He is all too aware of Chohan's warning and prays that he will never get caught.

Every now and then he sneaks out to buy a few supplies at the local marketplace. The staples of everyday life are displayed on huge plantain leaves. Yams, jackfruit, breadfruit, and coconuts can last for weeks, but that is not the case for the noble mango. By the end of the day, they lose their tantalising appeal, but they pale into significance compared to the aroma of the formidable durian.

Govinda has learnt to steer clear of the king of fruits as it's sometimes known. The durian is a big spiky beast with an unforgettable aroma, and according to some people, the taste is not unlike rancid onions or rotting meat. But to those with a discriminating palate, it is not unsimilar to a finely aged cheese with a hint of caramelized garlic.

There is no hustle and bustle in the marketplace, and people rarely squabble over anything at all.

A stallholder usually spends the day chatting with his neighbour or chewing away on a pepper flavoured betel nut.

Up until that moment, Govinda's life moved along at a quiet pace, but a gut-wrenching sound brings everyone to a standstill.

A distraught mother races out of a nearby house screaming hysterically. 'Help me please. A snake bit my son.'

'I might be able to help,' Govinda says. 'Where is he?'

Everyone watches closely as he sucks the poison from the boy's leg, then pounds some charcoal between a couple of rocks, mixes it into a paste and applies it to the wound.

'My son is going to die,' the hysterical woman cries.

'No, he will not,' Govinda says. 'We must get him to the temple immediately. He will survive, Tihali the healer will see to that.'

It has been several months since the death of the elephant hunters, but word passes around about the snake catcher who can charm a serpent with a flute.

And it's not long before Govinda comes to the attention of a British Army Colonel. A week later, he is dragged out of his home and detained in the army barracks.

Over the next few days, he is questioned by Sir William Walleran, an overweight Englishman with a well-trained handlebar moustache.

Govinda knew that this day would come, and he had his story all worked out, but Colonel Walleran is not easily convinced.

He has been on this case for six months, he is determined to pin the blame on someone, and he has his eyes set on Govinda.

In desperation, Govinda reaches out to Chohan from his jail cell.

'Master, if you can hear me, I need you now.'

Chohan appears at his side a few seconds later.

'Just relax Govinda, I will get you out of here.'

'Oh, thank you Master, thank you, but what are you going to do?'

'I know for a fact that the Colonel has a fear of snakes. This is a job for the snake goddess. Leave it to me.'

'I hope it works.'

'I can assure you it will.'

It's a very humid night and the Colonel is sweating profusely. Sleep is almost impossible, but he wakes with a start, only to see an enormous snake easing its way down the bed post.

He reaches for his gun, only to find another on the bedside table. He leaps out of bed and races down the corridor, and in desperation, he ends up in Govinda's cell.

'You, snake catcher. I will let you go if you rid me of these accursed demons.'

'What are you talking about,' Govinda says.

'The barracks is infested with snakes.'

'I can't see any.'

'There are hundreds of them out there. Get rid of them now, for God's sake.'

Govinda creeps down the corridor and whispers quietly.

'Master, what will I do?'

'They're harmless Govinda. Just collect them by the handful and put them in those barrels.'

Govinda does as he is told and ten minutes later, he heads back to the cell, only to find the Colonel hiding under a blanket.

'The coast is clear, Colonel Walleran. You can come out now.'

'What did you do with them?'

'What any snake catcher does. I caught them, of course.'

'So, where are they?'

'Follow me and I will show you.'

The Colonel does so, but hesitantly. Govinda removes the lid off one of the many wooden barrels that line the walls of the central corridor.

'They're in here,' he says.

'In that case, they will probably be dead by now.'

'And why is that?'

'They're for gunpowder. We were going to get rid of them, but we haven't got around to it yet.'

'I owe you an apology Govinda. You saved my life.'

'See, I am what I said I am. I am just a snake catcher.'

'And a jolly good one at that, my lad. I am sorry for the inconvenience.'

'I don't think I will ever find the blighter who killed those elephant hunters, and if the truth be known, I couldn't care less. They deserved what they got. Damn fine animals those creatures are.'

'Once again, please accept my apologies,' he says as he offers his hand in friendship. 'But I'll know where to go if I see any more of those dashed things.'

'It's the mating season,' Govinda says. 'That probably has something to do with it.'

'I hope not. They give me the willies. So, my lad, off you go. I believe you have a lovely wife at home, and she will be missing you.'

'She is about to have a baby.'

Suleka's time is almost at hand, so they pack up their things and head for Raja's camp. A gypsy woman never gives birth alone and Suleka is about to do so surrounded by women who have been delivering babies for years.

Everyone is sitting around the caravan and waiting for the moment that they hear a familiar sound.

'Any moment now Govinda, and you will be a real father,' Raja says.

'I am a real father. I have a beautiful little girl.'

'I think you are about to have another one.'

Raja gets to his feet and quietens everyone down. A few moments later, a woman pokes her head through the door and makes an announcement.

'It's a girl,' she says.

Raja slaps him on the back.

'See, I told you so. Now, go and have a look.'

This is the first newborn that Govinda has ever seen, so he takes it in his arms and holds it to his chest.

'She's so beautiful, isn't she, but what will we call her?'

'Well, I was thinking about Rania,' Suleka says. 'That was my mother's name.'

'That's a beautiful name.'

Kashmira is overjoyed to have a little sister, but Rania is a reason to celebrate, and a night of festivities follows.

# CHAPTER 30

## ROSHAN'S STORY

It was an overcast day in the summer of 1844 when a cargo ship set sail from Barcelona harbour. Apart from my father and the crew, I was the only other passenger.

I knew from an early age that I would eventually take over the family business, and I often accompanied my father from one seaport to another.

As I stood on the outer deck watching as the city disappeared into the distance, I had no idea that I was leaving my homeland behind, or that it would be many years before I saw the face of my mother again.

She was never at ease when my father took long sea voyages, but even before we left for Japan, she knew that something was going to happen.

She accompanied us to the harbour and held my hand until it was time to board the boat. And as we disappeared over the horizon, she prayed for our safe return, but in her heart, she just wanted us to come back.

It was just before sunrise of the third day when the ship encountered a storm at sea. Dark storm clouds loomed ominously overhead. The wind was howling, and the ship was rolling from side to side.

I leapt from my bed and raced up onto the deck, and then watched in horror as twenty-foot waves battered the ship from all sides.

The prow rose up into the air and the bridge house was ripped from its moorings, but the most gut-wrenching sound of all was the screams of the ill-fated crew as they disappeared into the depths of the ocean.

The formidable hand of nature reached down and swept me over the side, and when the storm finally subsided, there was nothing left, other than a tangle of broken boards.

By morning light, the beach was scattered with debris from one end to the other. I was the only survivor of that ill-fated voyage, but if it had not been for a snake charmer called Govinda, I may never have survived at all.

## A GYPSY CAMP

On the night of the storm, dark clouds are gathering in a dull grey sky. The winds are howling, and monstrous breakers are rolling onto the shore. Govinda closes the shutters and takes refuge in the house along with his family.

If it had not been for the generosity of his Master, he would never have been able to afford a tract of land to the south of Galkissa. He had chosen a dramatic site on a headland overlooking a rocky beach, and it was here that he built a home for his family.

It is the day of Kashmira's tenth birthday, and a day that he has been dreading. Govinda is up earlier than usual, and with his wife and daughter by his side, they head down to the beach.

Normally it would be to check on a few crab pots, but on this morning, the beach is littered with debris from one end to the other.

'What happened Tada?' Kashmira says.

'A ship went down in the storm. Perhaps we should look for survivors.'

At the far end of the beach, they find a boy with a gash on the side of his head. Govinda and Suleka always knew that they would have to raise someone else's child, a boy who would play a significant role in their daughter's life.

He is bedridden for several days, and when the boy finally recovers, he is in a state of shock. Kashmira is entranced by this golden-haired boy, but she is all too conscious of the look on his face, so she makes it her mission to look after the handsome young boy with glistening green eyes.

'That's the boy my Master spoke of,' Govinda says. 'But what will we do with him?'

'My brother Raja might know,' Suleka says. 'Perhaps we should talk to him.'

They pack up their wagon and head north to a remote beach settlement, one that is only frequented by gypsies.

Raja is sitting around a fire with several other men but gets to his feet when he hears the sound of barking dogs. He races off to investigate but he had not expected to see his sister and her husband.

Raja is a handsome young man with a pale brown complexion and deep brown eyes. He wears a pair of loose-fitting pants, a leather vest, and a chain of gold around his neck.

'It's wonderful to see you again,' he says as he welcomes them with open arms. 'But who is that boy?'

'We found him on the beach after a shipwreck,' Govinda says. 'And we are going to raise him as our son.'

'Then it would be a good idea to teach him our ways.'

'Kashmira is doing a good job of that. He follows her around everywhere and she has even named him Roshan.'

'And does he answer to that?'

'He does, strangely enough.'

The sound of laughter, dancing, and music fills the air that night. Suleka has not performed in front of an audience for many years, but this is a night of celebration and Raja wants to see her dance.

'In that case, you are in for a treat,' she says, 'because this is a family affair now.'

Govinda makes himself comfortable in front of a smoking fire, and with his flute in hand, he summons a mighty cobra with a soulful melancholy tune.

He throws a handful of sulphur onto the fire, and a few moments later, Suleka appears, dressed in the clothes of an exotic belly dancer. She crouches like a tiger, whips her hair from side to side and releases a high-pitched trilling sound.

This is her routine, and it never fails to impress, and as soon as she has finished, she bows to one and all, the music fades away and Govinda returns the cobra to the basket.

Their fame has not spread far and wide but they are famous amongst their relatives, and for their efforts, they get a resounding round of applause.

ಚಿಲ್ಲ ✱ ಲ್ಲಚಿ

Kashmira rises early the next morning, only to find a very lost and lonely Roshan sitting quietly under a tree. She wanders over to the fire and scoops a spoonful of honey rice into two wooden bowls.

'Would you like some?' she says.

Roshan mumbles something under his breath, pecks away at the rice and then puts it to the side.

Kashmira is all too aware of his pain, so she picks up two wooden balls and starts to juggle. And to her surprise, for the first time in a week, she sees a spark of life in his dull and lifeless eyes.

'Come over here and I will teach you how to do this,' she says.

'Now, you hold a ball in each hand with your palms facing up. Then you toss them from one to the other and throw them around and around.'

'It's easy with two balls, but I am going to show you how to do it with three.'

Roshan watches closely as the balls fly through the air in perfect formation. The dappled sunlight streaming through the trees adds a touch of magic to what he sees.

To a boy whose mind is a blank canvas, this is a wondrous thing to behold. And at that moment he takes a long deep breath and comes back to life.

'Now you try,' Kashmira says.

He starts with one ball and then another and it's not long before he is juggling three balls at once. And everyone including Raja and Govinda take notice.

'He's a fast learner,' Raja says. 'That knock on the head didn't do too much damage. I wonder where he comes from?'

'I have no idea,' Govinda says, 'but I agree. He definitely has talent.'

'Maybe Ravenna the fortune teller can shed some light on this situation. Why don't we go and see what she has to say?'

'Come with me Roshan,' Govinda says.

'I am going to introduce you to the local soothsayer,'

A woman of immense proportions steps out of a caravan and Roshan is immediately worried.

'Fear not young man,' Raja says. 'Ravenna doesn't eat children for breakfast.'

'So, what do you know about him,' she says.

'Nothing at all,' Govinda says. 'He was shipwrecked on our beach, and we don't even know his name, but Kashmira calls him Roshan.'

'Leave him with me, I might be able to find out something useful.'

Govinda and Raja watch closely as she takes Roshan by the hand and escorts him into her caravan.

'That boy is going to marry Kashmira one day,' Govinda says.

'How do you know that?'

'My master told me.'

'And who is he?'

Govinda relates the story of a most unusual man who appeared in his life many years before, of the strange and wonderful things he could do, and of how he trained him to be a snake charmer.

'I have often wondered about you,' Raja says. 'Does Suleka know any of this?'

'Yes, she does, and she has even met my master.'

'But there's more isn't there?'

'My master told me that they have something important to do, but he didn't say what it was.'

'I am glad you told me this Govinda.'

'Why is that?'

'You never know, I might be able to help. But it looks as if your boy is having trouble. Come on, we had better check this out.'

'It's okay Roshan,' Govinda says as he takes him by the hand. 'Everything will be alright.'

'He has been through something that no one would ever want to experience,' Ravenna says. 'The boy is in shock. You don't have to be a fortune-teller to see that. But I had a glimpse of his future and I saw a love that nothing could surpass.'

'With Kashmira?' Govinda says.

'Yes, they have something special to do.'

'In that case, young man, welcome to your new family.'

Kashmira has been watching closely and races over to see what's going on.

'Tada, what did you do to him?'

'Nothing, my darling, but I want you to teach him everything you know.'

'What do you mean Tada?'

'Roshan has a new family now, and we have to look after him. Can you do that?'

'Yes, I can Tada.'

She takes him by the hand and says, 'come with me Roshan and I will take care of you.'

'I would like to meet this master of yours,' Raja says.

'And why is that?'

'He obviously knows something. He places the lives of two orphans into the hands of another orphan.'

'In that case Raja, I will need all the help I can get.'

# CHAPTER 31

Even from the start, it was apparent that Kashmira was attracted to me and I was entranced by her, but my life could have been a lot worse.

I had a new family and two beautiful sisters, a loving father, and an equally devoted mother, but if it had not been for them, my fate might have been very different.

I often cried myself to sleep at night, but Kashmira usually sat by my side and held my hand. For a long while after, I just sat around and gazed out to sea, but Kashmira had a new brother and a playmate as well. It was she who eventually brought me out of my shell and it was she was who taught me to speak the Sinhalese language.

About a year later, Govinda came home with a brand-new caravan and a handsome horse. This was to be the beginning of a whole new chapter in our lives.

The caravan was very sturdy, plain, and unadorned on the outside, but it was very different on the inside. And we were amazed to see that you could fit so much in a small space.

It smelled of freshly hewn wood, and as well as bunk beds along the side, there were numerous cupboards to store just about anything at all.

'Tada,' Kashmira said. 'Why did you buy a caravan?'

'Because we are going on an adventure.'

'Oh, Tada. Where are we going?'

'Everywhere, my darling.'

The idea that we were about to set off on a big adventure really did take us by surprise. Govinda had travelled almost every road and byway in Sinhala, and he had stories such as we could never have imagined.

'Just ask Kosala, he knows what I am talking about, don't you?'

'Do you really,' Kashmira said.

If Kosala the wonder dog could speak, he would have told such tales that Govinda's would have paled into insignificance.

'Oh Tada, when do we leave?'

'Not for a while. We have a lot of things to do first.'

As we sat around the table that night there was a distinct sense of excitement in the air. Govinda had spent most of his life on the road, but Kashmira was surprised to hear that her father was an orphan.

'One day I will take you to Ballangoddi and you can see where I was born,' he said.

'But Tada, how did you become a snake charmer.'

'Now that is a very interesting story. My master is a man called Chohan and I suspect that he is a holy man, but I do not know that for certain.'

'What's a holy man Tada?'

'A magic man.'

'Oh, really Tada.'

'Yes, and he has been around for a very long time.'

'We often sat around the campfire at night and he told stories that I still find hard to believe.'

'Like what Tada?'

'My master travelled to distant lands where he saw snake charmers for the very first time. But these were not normal snake charmers, they were magic men. And one of those wore a crown of live cobras on his head.'

'Now, if you ever become a snake charmer, you need to know that some snakes are harmless, but those like the cobra can pierce the flesh with its fangs.'

'Its teeth are as sharp as a needle, but if you remove the gland, the cobra will die soon after.'

'My Master passed his knowledge onto me, and I am passing it onto you. You never know, one day it could save your life.'

'But he showed me how to play a special tune on a flute, and believe it or not, a snake will very quickly fall asleep.'

'It sounds like this,' he says, as he plays a slow monotonous tune. 'If I was to play it for long enough, you would fall asleep too.'

'But that's not all. You can paralyse a cobra with a special stone, but it can also be used to cure a cobra bite.'

'My master cured me of a snake bite using such a stone. You just place it on the wound and the poison disappears. I do not know how it works, but charcoal works just as well.'

'Can you use any stone Tada?'

'No, this is a special stone. They are only found in the mouth of king cobras. I do not have one, but my Master does.'

We were entranced by the idea that there was a sort of magic associated with snake charming, but Govinda had planted another seed in our minds. Somewhere out there was a magic man called Chohan and that was even more intriguing.

'Tada, will we ever meet your master?'

'That I do not know, but he can take the form of anyone at all. And for all I know, Kosala might even be my master in disguise.'

༺ ✺ ༻

I may have had a very different fate if it had not been for Govinda and his family, but I did not find out until many years later that I was the son of a wealthy shipping magnate from Barcelona.

I had lost my memory and had no idea that I had once lived a life of luxury in a mansion that overlooked that glorious if somewhat imperfect city.

As I think back on my life, I can see everything in that magical world which we call memory, but I will never forget the day we set off on our first adventure up into the high mountain plains.

We travelled along a path that wound its way through the forest, and wherever we looked we were surrounded by a rich and vibrant jungle of exotic plants and ferns.

This was a tropical wonderland, a world of living creatures of every shape and form, birds, reptiles, and insects that sparkled in the light, and as I lay awake at night, I could hear an elephant bellowing in the distance.

I was not prepared for the heat, especially when the monsoons swept across the landscape. It rained every day, and every living thing went into hiding. And when it finally passed, it was cool again, the world came back to life, and it was a splendour to behold.

This was a time when the Europeans were staking their claim to this fair country. They spent years laying waste to the jungles and building houses in the hill country.

In some places we could hear the sound of a taskmaster's whip, and we often saw half-starved men digging holes, cutting down trees, pulling up roots or burning them on a bonfire.

Many years later, we passed through Nuwara Eliya once again, and we were amazed to see how much it had changed. The countryside was no longer a forsaken wilderness. It was now a thriving tea plantation.

On one occasion, on a precipitous mountain road, Govinda had to steer the caravan into the bush to avoid a drunken Englishman. He was holding on for dear life as an out-of-control elephant raced over the side of a ravine.

We found out sometime later that it kept going for another seven miles and finally dropped to its knees and died of exhaustion.

Elephants are such gentle creatures with eyes that reflect the beauty of their souls. Most of them roam freely through the forests and some are used as workhorses, but I was impressed by one elephant in particular.

She was working away in a river lining up one log after another, and she obviously knew that they had to be in line, but sometimes the currents swirled this way and that and she had to start all over again.

I will never forget the night that we climbed to the top of Adam's Peak. It was pitch black and if we wanted to reach the top unscathed, we had no choice but to carry a flaming torch soaked in resinous tar.

We followed a jagged path and were at the mercy of the elements, and for a family of adventurous pilgrims, there was no refuge from a passing storm.

It was a long and arduous trip that took over five hours, but it was worth it in every way. No matter where we looked, we had an unobstructed view of rolling hills, and rivers that circled this way and that, and in the distance was the magnificent Indian Ocean. In my mind, the fabled land of Sinhala really was paradise on Earth.

I stood at Kashmira's side on the highest point in the land and we were entranced by the vista. A narrow slice of the Moon was still visible, the stars had all but disappeared, and then, as if by magic, the almighty hand of God reached down, and a moment later, the first rays of light spread across a darkened world.

It was a powerful experience but at that moment, Kashmira took my hand and I knew without a doubt that I had found the love of my life.

# CHAPTER 32

During the cooler months we performed in one town after another, but my career as a snake charmer did not start immediately.

Govinda had been apprenticed to Chohan for eight years before he set out on his own, but I started out as a juggler of coloured balls.

I had mastered quite a few routines in a short space of time and could throw the balls around at dazzling speed. Most people would not stop to watch a juggler, but they did stop to watch a white boy in a cotton dhoti.

Govinda was the star of the show, and he amazed everyone with his command of seven venomous snakes, but Suleka, accompanied by her two daughters always put on an eye-catching display.

The thing that worried my family was the fact that I would black out from time to time, and the last time it happened, we were visiting the Golden Temple in Dambulla.

It was a long climb to the top, but before we were even halfway there, I fainted and rolled down the stairs. They were all alone, in the middle of nowhere and had no idea what to do.

No one even noticed when Kosala started to howl like a wolf, but to their relief, a holy man appeared at their side a few minutes later.

'We must take him into the temple,' he said. 'It is there that I shall attend to him.'

The temple is one of the most sacred places in Sinhala, situated on a hill between two enormous boulders. But they were so distraught that they didn't even notice the endless line of Buddhas, the highly coloured murals or the graceful dagoba which occupies the centre of the hall.

'If you do not mind, ladies, I would like you to wait outside,' the holy man said. 'But I will need this man's assistance.'

'Now, Govinda, let's take a look at this boy.'

'Master, is it you? But how?'

'Kosala has strict instructions to keep an eye on you Govinda. You can thank him for his vigilance.'

'Master, I was so worried. All those things you told me about their future. I had no idea what to think.'

'Worry not Govinda, but I cannot do this here. We must take him to my place.'

'But how will we get there, Master.'

'The easy way, Govinda. Just close your eyes, as you are about to travel through space and time.'

## CHAPTER 33

Almost three days had passed before I regained consciousness, and I did not find out until many years later that I had met Govinda's master, but there would be many more opportunities to come.

What I do remember is that Chohan's place of residence looked like a hall in a king's palace. Ornate statues lined every wall, the floors were polished marble, and at one end was a life-sized statue of the beloved Asian goddess, Lady Kuan Yin, the Goddess of Mercy and Compassion.

And way up above was the eternal sky, it was not the sky that we see every day, but it was a sky, nonetheless.

There was no one else around, apart from Chohan and it was as quiet as a tomb, but I will never forget the view through the window. It was as if we had been transported into the depths of outer space.

The memory of that place would haunt me for the next fifty years, but it would resurface in a different fashion many years later.

It would eventually become a reality, inspired by my first experience of the Taj Mahal and a conch shell that I had found on the beach.

ಚ್ಛಲ �֍ ಲಾಲ

One day, after we had been travelling for hours, we decided to bathe our weary bones in a cool and shady swimming hole. We had spent many happy hours in the surf at Galkissa and we were all good swimmers.

On the opposite side of the pool was a waterfall that tumbled over the cliff face, and it was there that I had another unusual experience. I swam over to take a closer look and as I was splashing around, I noticed the entranceway to a cave, so I decided to investigate.

It was a dangerous thing to do as I had to climb over slippery rocks, but beyond that was an even bigger cave with pools of water that dripped down from above.

I ventured along a passageway that led to a chamber illuminated by pinholes of light. And against the back wall was an elaborate old shrine that had turned green with mold, but the last thing I expected to see was a man sitting on his haunches.

He had a live cobra coiled around his neck. His skin was blue and he was covered in lichen. His ratty hair reached to his waist, and his fingernails had grown into long twisted vines.

He looked as if he was communicating with an unknown God, but I nearly jumped out of my skin when I saw someone out of the corner of my eye.

'Stay where you are Roshan.'

'Who are you, and how do you know my name?'

That man was striking in appearance and dressed in a long white robe with a white turban on his head.

'We have met before.'

'We have,' I said.

'Yes, two years ago, in the Temple of Dambulla.'

'Ah, so you must be Govinda's master.'

'That is correct. I was the one who saved your life.'

'But what do you want, and why are you here?'

'You agreed to complete a task, but to do that you will have to become a snake charmer. And not just any old snake charmer, but the best snake charmer in all of Sinhala.'

'Why?'

'You will work that out for yourself, but you will need an accomplice.'

'And who would that be?'

'Kashmira. Your destiny is intertwined and it always has been.'

I was in the presence of a superior being and had no idea what to think, so I just bowed my head in agreement.

'But I have one question. Who is this man and what is he doing?'

'That was me, once upon a time. It is a well-known fact that you can achieve a state of Godhead through an intensive period of meditation.'

'And I did, eventually.'

'I no longer require the services of that body as I now have a different one.'

## CHAPTER 34

I never mentioned that experience to anyone, but I had been watching Govinda closely, and decided to teach myself to be a snake charmer. He had traps all over the place for bush rats and field mice, but the snakes were kept in a shed at the back of the house.

I made a flute out of a bamboo reed and decided to practice on the beach. It was some distance from the house, but when I got to the other end, I could hear someone arguing in an unfamiliar language.

As far as I knew there was no one else around, but obviously, that was not the case. I crept along stealthily, only to discover a boat in the water and footprints on the beach.

As to who it could be, I had no idea, but I was curious and had to find out. Five minutes passed and there was still no sign of anyone, so I decided to take a closer look. And that's when I heard someone with a gravelly voice barking out orders.

A few minutes later, four grisly Asian pirates rolled a boulder across the door of a barely visible cave, got back in the boat and headed out to sea. I got out of there as fast as I could and raced back to the house to tell Govinda.

'What were you doing down there,' he said.

'I was going to practice the flute.'

'Why?'

'So that I can be a snake charmer, of course.'

Govinda was a busy man who spent most of the day catching food for the snakes or tending his vegetable garden.

'In that case, we will start tomorrow, but we should go and check this out before it gets dark.'

'No,' Suleka said. 'It's far too dangerous. And if they are pirates, they may come back.'

We never did get around to checking out that cave but we should have. As I would discover to my everlasting horror thirty years later, Asian pirates had been using that cave to store goods for the black market. But they also had an interest in the slave trade, and a handsome white boy would have made a healthy profit.

So, the next day, my career as a snake charmer began in earnest. And over the weeks that followed I learnt the secrets of snake charming from a master, and it wasn't long before Govinda decided to test me out.

We packed up the caravan, and a few days later, we headed off on another tour of this beautiful country.

For Kashmira and I, this would be the beginning of a love affair that would last a lifetime. We were young adults now, and it was obvious to our parents that we had already made up our minds.

## CHAPTER 35

Kashmira had blossomed into a hauntingly beautiful woman, and unlike Suleka who had a copper-coloured complexion, hers was a soft and gentle brown, but she had the most alluring almond shaped eyes I had ever seen.

She was a refreshing breeze in our lives, and I always looked forward to seeing her smiling face at the breakfast table. She never missed an opportunity to spend time with the people she loved, and she knew every little thing that was going on.

We often took long walks on the beach and even stole the odd kiss every now and then. We had spoken about marriage several times and we knew it would happen eventually.

One day, after a performance at a local marketplace, we were approached by a man with an offer we could not refuse.

'I would like to introduce myself. I am Saminda Ranasinghe, a gem merchant from Colombo,' he said.

'That was a very impressive performance. I have never seen such artistry before, and I was wondering if you would be interested in performing at my daughter's wedding.'

'That depends on where you live,' I said.

'Colombo, but I have many empty rooms in my house, so accommodation will not be a problem. And, of course, I will pay you handsomely for your efforts.'

'However, you will never look back after that. You will have more work than you have ever had before.'

If there was ever a time to ask for Kashmira's hand that was it. At the age of twenty, in the year 1854, we were married in a traditional gypsy ceremony, surrounded by friends, and loved ones. Govinda and Suleka always knew that we would go our own way but they never thought it would be so soon.

For one glorious week we had the company of over thirty gypsy relatives who spent most of the time singing and dancing around the campfire until late into the night.

Just before the wedding, Govinda received a visit from his master. Late one afternoon, he and Suleka were sitting on the front verandah when they saw an old peddler making his way up the hill.

'I wonder who that is,' Govinda said.

A moment later, his old dog Kosala races up the hill wagging his tail excitedly.

'That's Kosala, but he disappeared years ago. Which means that our visitor is none other than my Master.'

They race down the hill and meet Chohan halfway.

'Master, it is you...isn't it?' he said.

'How did you know Govinda?'

'Kosala, of course. He is your dog after all.'

'The dog that never dies. He has been a wonderful companion.'

'But why are you here Master?'

I believe that there is to be a wedding soon, and I thought I would pay my respects to the newlyweds.'

'And...what else?'

'I just want to spend a little time with you and your family. I hope you don't mind.'

'You are welcome here at any time,' Suleka said.

'But I would not say no to a cup of tea.'

'In that case, please step this way.'

As far as everyone else was concerned, this was Govinda's uncle, Ravi Naveen. Suleka had numerous relatives but we had never met any of Govinda's family before.

Over the years, we had heard many stories about his master and the remarkable things he could do. And the fact that he was accompanied by a dog that we had not seen for years was an obvious clue.

'Uncle Ravi,' Rania said. 'Can you tell us a story.'

'Now that is a wonderful idea.'

We knew this was going to be special, but we could never have imagined how special it would be.

'Now, this is a story about a little orphan called Akila. He slept in a stable and every morning without fail he would appear at his grandmother's door.'

'Achchie was not his real grandmother, but Akila was well-fed and clean, and she loved him like a son.'

'One day, Akila met a very interesting man. He was actually a holy man in disguise, but he taught Akila everything he knew.'

'And on one occasion, he told him that he would marry a beautiful woman and have a family of his own.'

'But Akila didn't know that his children had a very special destiny.'

As to whether it happened, I will never know for certain, but I am sure that Chohan had something to do with it.

For a few glorious moments, it was as if we had been transported to another time and place. And on that day, Govinda had an opportunity to see what life had in store for his adopted children.

I waddled off to bed, none the wiser that anything had happened at all. It could have been a dream, but it stayed with me for a long time after.

Before he left, Uncle Ravi asked if he could speak to Kashmira and I in private.

'Every story has to start somewhere, and yours starts here. You two have a long and glorious future ahead, and one day, you will do something that everyone will remember for a long time to come.'

We wanted to ask more but we didn't have to. We had a fleeting glimpse of what our future held. And if I wasn't wrong, it really was going to be full of surprises.

'But it's time for me to go,' he says.

'Aren't you staying for the wedding?' Kashmira says.

'I would not miss that for anything, which means that you will see me again. In the meantime, I wish you all the best.'

He said goodbye to Rania, placed his battered old hat on his head, and accompanied by Govinda and Suleka, they headed for the road.

'Master, I had a dream last night,' Govinda said.

'I promised that you would see the reason for this with your own eyes, but your work is done now Govinda, and it is time for your children to spread their sort of magic around.'

'Perhaps I will see you in another life. You never know, but I will be back for the wedding.'

He dipped his hat and disappeared around the corner, and other than a strange man at the wedding that no one seemed to know, Govinda didn't see his Master for another twenty years.

## CHAPTER 36

As I stood beside Kashmira on our wedding day, I had a feeling that something was missing from my life. That was the day I started to remember snippets from another life, and Kashmira was the only one in whom I could confide.

'Ravenna once told me that you are Espanola, that you came from another country. I do not know of other lands, so I cannot say any more than that.'

'You do remember that we found you on the beach after a shipwreck, don't you?'

'Yes, but it never meant anything to me. This is the only life I have known.'

'That can't be right Roshan. You had another life before this one.'

From that moment on, I could think of nothing else, but whether we liked it or not, we had to pack up our things and move to Colombo. We had no idea how long we would be away, but this was an opportunity of a lifetime.

The day that we left was one of heartache and pain and it was even worse for Govinda and Suleka. Their children were leaving home, but they would not have to endure the heartache alone. They had a wonderful group of friends, and they were not going anywhere, not until they had to.

We had to buy suitable clothes for such a venture, but we would need even more when we got to Colombo, but we also had to travel with numerous cobras. As to where we would keep them, I could not imagine. What do you do with snakes in a fancy house?

With our possessions on the back of a bullock cart we headed for Galkissa where we were met by a relative of Mr. Ranasinghe.

It was only a short trip to Colombo, but that was the first time I had been on a boat since the shipwreck, and even more memories came flooding back.

Kashmira always knew when someone was having problems, and even though there was nothing she could do, she assured me that it would all work out in the end.

Several years earlier we had spent a few days at Chohan's place in Colombo, but we were not prepared for the lifestyle, or a beautiful house surrounded by equally beautiful gardens.

Mr. Ranasinghe and his family met us at the harbour, but they didn't leave us to our own devices. Apparently, he had not stopped talking about us and everyone in Colombo wanted to meet the mysteriously beautiful Kashmira.

The idea of a European snake charmer was equally intriguing, and we did nothing but talk about ourselves for weeks on end. Word spread amongst the European community, and we were soon performing in front of a very different audience.

One Sunday afternoon, as we were admiring the ships in Colombo harbour, I was approached by a sea captain.

He introduced himself as Captain Alvarez and said that he was an employee of the Barcelona Steamship Company. He spoke to me in Spanish at first, but I had no idea what he was saying.

'Excuse me sir, do you mind if I ask you a question?'

It had been ten long years since I had heard my native tongue and it took me by surprise, and in that moment a flood of memories came surging back and I almost collapsed.

'Roshan, what's the matter,' Kashmira cried. 'You look as if you've seen a ghost.'

'Quickly, help me please. He is going to faint.'

As I sat there, gazing at the captain in his blue uniform and gold epaulettes, I knew that I had seen something like that once before.

And then as if by some magic I did not understand, I answered in Spanish.

'What would you like to know,' I said.

'You remind me of someone.'

'And who is that?'

'My master, Juan Sebastian Delgado, the proprietor of the Barcelona Steamship Company.'

The captain related the story of a young boy called Juan Philippe Delgado who disappeared when a ship was wrecked on this very coastline ten years ago.

'Does that mean anything to you?'

'I think I might have been that boy. I was rescued by my family when I was ten years old. They said that I was the only survivor of a shipwreck.'

'Then there is every possibility that you are Juan Phillipe Delgado, Senor. You are your father's son in every respect, and he will be overjoyed to know that you are still alive.'

Kashmira had no idea what we were talking about, but she was a woman of refined instincts and knew that this was important.

'Your father was rescued by a fishing boat, Senor. He returned to Barcelona but he never gave up hope that you had survived.'

'Those in his employ have strict instructions to watch out for you every time we visit Ceylon. He will be overjoyed to know that his one and only son is still alive.'

# CHAPTER 37

I took to my bed and in my tortured dreams I relived the storm that took the life of fifty men and destroyed one of my father's ships. I tossed and turned for days on end, but Kashmira sat by my side and mopped my brow.

She would have stayed there all night if it had not been for Mrs. Ranasinghe. She called upon the services of three different doctors, but there was nothing they could do.

Waiting for the fever to subside had been three of the worst days of her life, but it had also been very illuminating.

Captain Alvarez was a close friend of my parents and he told her everything. Apparently, my father was a changed man after he returned to Barcelona. He was grief stricken at the loss of his only son and had never fully recovered.

'It would be a good idea to return to Barcelona as soon as possible as their time is running out,' he said.

I was hesitant to sail the high seas and I needed time to recuperate but I had to get out of Colombo and clear my head before doing that.

We went back to Galkissa and spent a few days with our family. It was a beautiful part of the world and the place where we would eventually settle down, but before that happened, I had to face the inevitable.

I had the distinct feeling that our lives were about to change in a way that I could never have imagined but it had to be done. Once again, we packed our bags and said goodbye to our loved ones.

The journey to Barcelona was as difficult for me as it was for Kashmira. I had a knot in my stomach from the moment that I set foot on the ship.

Kashmira was leaving the only world that she had ever known, but she had great inner strength and rarely succumbed to her fears. I knew what to expect but she did not.

We sailed on a 300-foot steamship, one of the finest vessels in my father's fleet. It was a commercial vessel that transported anything from wool to livestock, but it also provided accommodation for paying passengers.

We had a furnished cabin with a porthole, and when we were tired of sitting around, we passed the time in a comfortable lounge room with leather chairs.

It was not as luxurious as a cruise ship, but the food was good and we were treated like royalty. And when we had to stretch our legs, we passed our time on the upper deck.

The ship was a long and narrow three masted vessel of 2000 tons, powered by a mighty 1200 horsepower engine.

The upper deck was a busy place, and the crew had a variety of tasks, but we were a curiosity, nevertheless. I was the long-lost son, but my wife was a brown skinned Ceylonese beauty, and that did not go un-noticed by the crew at all.

I soon realised that men from every rank of society have an eye for a beautiful woman.

## CHAPTER 38

On the day that our ship berthed at Barcelona harbour, a warm wind was blowing, and dark clouds threw ominous shadows across the rooftops of that noble city. This was the scene I remembered as I sailed away, never knowing what fate had in store, but today was different.

Today, I was about to do the most difficult thing I ever had to do. I was about to see my parents again, but I had no idea how much they had changed.

My father had sent a carriage to meet us at the harbour. It was another sign that this was going to be a heartbreaking experience.

I could not imagine them in any other way than as they were. Their health had deteriorated, my father had retired much earlier than expected, and the company was now managed by an old friend called Manuel da Silva.

Kashmira knew what I was going through, and I knew exactly what she was thinking. She was anxious for all the obvious reasons.

She was not Spanish. She was not from a wealthy family. She could not speak our language, and she was not Caucasian.

I assured her that she was the most important person in my life and that would never change. Whether my parents approved or not, I did not care, I had married the woman I loved.

My family home is just one of many stately mansions in the exclusive domain known as the Avenida del Tibidabo, and beyond that is the mountain of the same name.

The house is set amongst beautiful gardens, exotic fountains, and elegant pools, and as we approached the gates, Kashmira was awestruck. She was about to enter a world of affluence on a scale she had never known.

I held her hand as if my life depended on it, and when the carriage finally stopped at the front door, I froze.

'Everything will be fine Roshan. We will get through this.'

'We will,' I said. 'Somehow or another, we will.'

I could see my parents through the window and my heart almost melted. My mother's beautiful black hair was now a silvery grey, but in a glistening white gown, she looked like a matriarch of the Spanish royal family.

My father still had a goatee beard and a thick head of hair, and for this occasion, he was dressed in the blue and gold uniform of the Barcelona Steamship Company.

I am not sure what they had expected, but they could not believe their eyes when I stepped out of the carriage. I was now a fully-grown man, and in many respects, I was the spitting image of my father.

## CHAPTER 39

Up until a few weeks ago, my parents had given up hope of ever seeing me again, but for them, this was the beginning of an emotional odyssey.

The moment I saw the two people who had brought me into the world, I could not hold back the tears. I had expected my mother to cry but not my father.

They had endured ten long years of not knowing whether I had lived or died, ten long years of heartache and pain, and ten long years lost in the depths of despair.

As I would learn for myself, that is what happens when a force beyond your control suddenly rips the most precious things out of your life, and when you eventually come up for air, you are stranded in no-man's land.

But I would never have made it without Kashmira. I had been raised by a loving family. I had met the love of my life and I was now a happily married man, but it could have been different if Kashmira had been dressed as a Ceylonese peasant.

In his wisdom, Captain Alvarez insisted that we purchase a suitable wardrobe for this venture, and he even allocated company funds to ensure that we looked our best and would be acceptable in any situation.

And the moment that Kashmira stepped out of the carriage, my parents could not believe their eyes. She looked like the Queen of Egypt in a blue silk gown with narrow sloping shoulders.

And then they did something I will never forget. They opened their arms and welcomed my beloved wife into their lives. They were simply overjoyed to have me back and they were too ill and too frail to care anymore.

## CHAPTER 40

If things had been different, I would have had the best education that money could buy. I would be in control of the family business, and I would, no doubt, have beautiful women lining up at my door, but that was not to be.

Kashmira had never had an education, but she was warm and loving and intelligent. And she had an innate ability that was uncommon amongst the genteel folk of an aristocratic society.

She was hauntingly beautiful, and she had presence, and if anyone had any reservations about who they were dealing with, they only had to look into her eyes. It was not long before my wife had charmed everyone in the house.

We had all changed, but I felt like a stranger in a strange world. We spent most of our time wandering around the garden, but I wanted Kashmira to see this city. I wanted her to see the tree-lined boulevards known as the Ramblas and the magnificent Gothic buildings.

As soon as we stepped through the doors of the Catedral de Barcelona, Kashmira was mesmerised by its power and majesty. She had no idea what the Catholic faith was about and I did my best to explain, but she was intrigued by the idea that a man called Jesus rose from the dead.

'That would be an interesting thing to do,' she said.

I had no idea what she meant at the time, and I don't think that she did either, but it had somehow struck a chord. I know for a fact that she thought about it every time we passed a Catholic church.

But it wasn't until many years later that she described a moment when she had a unique experience. Apparently, Jesus drifted down from the cross, dressed in a gleaming white robe and whispered a message in her ear.

My parents went to mass every day of the week, but once a week was more than enough for me. And while they prayed to God and gave thanks that their son was home, we went sightseeing.

It was impossible to ignore the fact that most of the population of Barcelona lived on the breadline and in the most despicable conditions. The spirit of rebellion had always been there, but it would eventually rise to the surface as it had done so many times before.

I have no idea if my parents knew that their time was almost up. Perhaps they did but they wanted nothing else, other than to spend their last days as happily as possible.

My homecoming had affected my father more than I realised, and three weeks later, he passed away in his sleep. It was a difficult time for my mother and she was grief stricken.

She locked herself away and retreated into a world of her own. A week later, I woke up early one morning only to be advised by a member of the household staff that her body had been found at the base of the cliff on the outskirts of our property.

As of that day, I inherited an empire, and I had sole possession of the family company. I was not a businessman, and I had no interest in being one.

The Barcelona Steamship Company was in capable hands, and it would continue to thrive, but not with me at the helm. A few weeks later, we packed our bags and said goodbye to Barcelona forever.

## CHAPTER 41

We were wealthy now and had more money than we would ever need, but we did not go home empty handed. We spent a fortune on presents for everyone.

For the women, it was beautiful clothes and fabrics but we did not forget about the men. They got beautiful leather boots, new leather vests, and quite a few barrels of fine Spanish wine.

'When Govinda fished you out of the sea,' Raja said. 'He had no idea that you had a treasure chest in your pocket.'

'You can thank my father for that. He worked hard every day of his life, and for that I will be eternally grateful.'

'So, what are you going to do now?'

'We are going to build a new house to start with.'

'And then what?'

'Kashmira and I are going to travel the world and do what we do best.'

'Well, in that case, you will need someone to take care of the business side of things. Have you thought about that yet?'

'No, I haven't.'

'Then I will gladly offer my services."

'What do you know about that sort of thing.'

'Nothing yet, but I am very trustworthy.'

'Okay,' I said. 'You've got the job.'

'So, how much does it pay?'

'One rupiah a day.'

'Forget it. I will not consider anything less than one hundred rupiah a day.'

'Then it's a deal,' I said.

Raja was over the moon, and on that night, he got drunk on more than his fair share of Spanish wine, but he was worth his weight in gold.

He brought fancy new clothes and then spent the next three months in Colombo learning to speak English and a few other foreign languages.

Kashmira had seen quite a few beautiful houses in Barcelona but she liked the idea of a Spanish bungalow, something with light and airy rooms, a central courtyard, and a view of the ocean.

The house might have taken a lot longer if Gonzaga had not taken charge. It was a huge undertaking that involved over fifty men. He was the overseer of the operation, and on the day that it was finally finished, Raja made a triumphant return.

To our surprise, he had not wasted his time in Colombo. He was not yet fluent in English or Spanish, but he had learnt enough to get by. And at night, he had everyone in hysterics with stories about life in a big city and the things he had done.

'But Roshan, you will be pleased to hear that I also made some very shrewd business contacts while I was there?'

'What sort of contacts?' I said a little apprehensively.

'I met an Englishman from London, a booking agent for a big theatre company, and I have signed you up for a three-month tour.'

'In what sort of places?'

'The best theatres in Europe, of course. Where else?

'Really, so, when do we go?'

'As soon as you give the word.'

# CHAPTER 42

A show called *The Snake Charmer's Tale* took the world by storm and we booked out one theatre after another wherever we went, but it was not just a snake charming act anymore.

Gypsies love to dance, and they love to sing, and we put on a show of world class standards. A cast of thirty people were dressed in glittering outfits, and the stage looked like a gypsy camp on a moonlit night.

It was an intriguing tale about a gypsy woman who fell in love with a young snake charmer, but when she realised that he was under the spell of a cobra king, she came up with a devious plan.

With the help of a few friends, she steals his magic flute, transforms herself into a sorceress, and releases the snake charmer from the cobra king's spell.

Kashmira played the part of the heroine, and her talents were there for all to see, but when the cobra king discovered that his flute was missing, he was furious.

Accompanied by the snake charmer and a band of courageous friends, Kashmira lures him into a trap. The cobra king is determined to retrieve the flute, but the last thing he expected is to be challenged to a duel by a sorceress with flaming red eyes.

And as soon as the snake charmer starts to play, Kashmira leaps into the flames and transforms herself into a cobra queen, after which she turns her gaze on the cobra king, and when the smoke finally clears, he is nowhere to be seen.

The final scene is a wedding with a stirring love song, a story that the gypsies know to be true, that when your love wears golden earrings, he belongs to you.

# CHAPTER 43

Our lives had changed in a way we could never have imagined. We toured non-stop for the next five years, but one day Kashmira had the news that I had long been waiting to hear.

'Roshan, we will have to forget about travelling for a while.'

'You're pregnant, aren't you.'

'Yes, I am, and it's all your fault.'

'I will happily take the blame for that.'

The Italian sculptor Donatello was responsible for some of the most beautiful statues of the Renaissance era, and the moment that Kashmira heard that name she fell in love with it immediately.

Donatello, as we eventually found out means a gift from God, and eight months later, we became the proud parents of a beautiful little boy.

Out little Donatello lived up to his name from the very moment he came into the world. He had the most beautiful smile, deep green eyes, a complexion the colour of burnished gold and a little dimple on his chin. And if there was ever an angel in disguise, it was our little boy.

His exploits always kept us enthralled, and even the birds and butterflies would follow him around as he played in the garden.

We always had a dog around the house, but I had never seen one as protective as Sashi. She never let him out of her sight, but one day a little kitten appeared out of nowhere and she decided to stay.

Donatello had been using Sashi as a pillow for his afternoon nap ever since he was a baby, but Mow-Mow was not about to be left out, and she usually found a spot in between.

On some days, we would wander along the beach but Donatello spent his time drawing pictures in the sand. One day, however, he built a little house surrounded by a garden of shells and little driftwood figures.

'Look,' he said. 'Tada and Mama.'

As to where this talent came from, I have no idea as he had never read a book or even seen a picture before. That was to be the first of many little houses that he created, but one day he built a temple with a dome on the top.

'That is so beautiful,' Kashmira said. 'You are such a clever boy, but what is it?'

'House,' he said.

'Whose house darling?'

'Tada's house.'

Donatello had created a replica of the Taj Mahal but where did he get such an idea? It was a mystery that I did not understand.

One day, as I was gazing out to sea, I happened to notice a cloud that looked like the Taj Mahal and I had an inspired idea.

'Kashmira, I think we should go to India to see the Taj Mahal, and we should take Donatello along as well.'

'Why?'

'It has something to do with those sandcastles that he has been making and something that Chohan once told me.'

'And what is that?'

'That we have a task to fulfil. I think we should go and see it for ourselves.'

That idea consumed our thoughts from that moment on, and we could not stop thinking about it. And in the second week of May of the year 1870, we set sail on a ship from Colombo to Bombay.

In the distant past, long before the Europeans had even heard of India, merchants from many lands wrote of the splendours of the great Mughal Empire. They had alluring tales of harems and fakirs, of mosques with pointed domes, of amber and ambergris, and of that most idolatrous custom of all, the burning of the dead.

Our first experience of India was not what we had expected. Bombay was just a few scattered islands that was central to the British cotton trade, but it was the most direct route to the city of Agra.

It took several weeks to get there, a journey of almost a thousand miles, but there was no point in rushing as life moves along at a very different pace in India.

Agra was the capital of the Mughal Empire and was once the most important city in India. In its time, it was a centre of artistic and commercial importance, but its golden age had long since passed.

The power of the Mughal empire is evident in the walled city which is now known as The Great Red Fort. And up until the time that Shah Jahan moved the capital to Delhi in 1638, it was the primary residence of the Mughal emperors.

The big day had finally arrived, and our first view of The Taj Mahal was from a distance. It was like something out of a dream and we were awestruck by its magnificence.

It was a gracious expression of love and purity, framed by a sinuous arch and surmounted by a pointed dome, but it was equally enchanting to see its reflection mirrored in an elongated pool.

We had told Donatello that we were going to see his sandcastle, but he had no idea what we meant, not until we got there.

'Look Donatello, that's your sandcastle,' I said.

He replied as he had done so many times before, 'Tada's house.'

## CHAPTER 44

One evening as we were sitting on the verandah and gazing out across the ocean, I noticed the last rays of sunlight filtering through the trees, and for a fleeting second, I thought I saw the outline of the Taj Mahal.

'Kashmira, I am going to build a replica of the Taj Mahal on that hill over there.'

'I don't think that's what Chohan meant,' she said.

'It's somewhere to start, but I am none the wiser about the task that we have to fulfil.'

'Answers to questions do not always appear at once, as I have discovered.'

I knew exactly what she meant. Kashmira had saved the life of a boy who had no idea who he was. After a series of coincidences, he ends up on the doorstep of a home in another land. And not long after, he inherited a fortune. After that, one door opened and then another, and on and on it went.

I could afford to spend money on a good quality house, so I approached an architect in Colombo and left the idea in his capable hands. And over a period of months, our version of the Taj Mahal gradually rose from its foundations.

Word soon got around amongst the European community in Colombo, and it was not long before we made the front page of The Government Gazette.'

'So, this is what you get up to while I am away,' Raja said. 'Where did this idea come from?'

'From Donatello.'

'You're joking, aren't you?'

'No, I'm not. Just ask Kashmira.'

'Donatello's just a baby. How could he have told you that?'

I explained the origins of this strange and wonderful situation, and Raja was almost speechless.

'So, what are you going to do next?'

'Govinda's master told us that we have a task to complete. I don't think this is it, but it's the only thing we have come up with so far.'

'So, it's like a riddle then.'

'And a very interesting one it is too, but I am sure we will work it out eventually.'

'Once upon a time I would have said that you were light in the head Roshan. And you were when I first met you, but now that I know you, I am absolutely certain of it.'

'Well, I might be odd sometimes, but I made you a rich man.'

'And for that I am very grateful, my friend.'

Raja was still a good-looking man, but his life had changed, and he was no longer a wayward gypsy.

He was not usually one for reminiscing, but he recalled the day that Suleka first set eyes on the man she wanted to marry.

'Govinda was responsible for all of this. Who would have thought that an orphan could change our lives?'

'Are you complaining Raja?'

'Not at all. I have nothing but respect for Govinda, and his offspring, but I believe that Rania is going to get married soon?'

'Yes, she is.'

'In that case, we will need a lot more Spanish wine as I have grown quite fond of that stuff.'

'I know,' I said. 'And the good life as well.'

## CHAPTER 45

God must have been looking kindly on me on the day that I was born, but I am just so grateful that he saw fit to raise me in Ceylon and not Barcelona.

These people took me into their life. They gave me all the love they could share, and they never asked for anything in return. What more could a person ask?

'So, when do we get back onto the road?' Raja said.

'I have no idea. We just want to be with our little boy. Besides, there's no rush and we certainly don't need the money.'

'That's true. I believe you make a small fortune every day of the week and you don't even lift a finger.'

'I am trying to work out what our task is first. And when I have done that, we will get back to work.'

'Why, do you need money?'

'No, not at all, I just need something to do. I like being a businessman and I love travelling.'

'Well, why not start your own business.'

'Doing what?'

'You know everything about booking theatres and bossing people around. There's a place for you in Colombo.'

'But we don't have a decent theatre.'

'Then I will build one.'

'Really, you are feeling generous today, aren't you?'

'In that case, I accept. When do I start?'

'Go and talk to my architect and tell him what you want. We saw some very impressive theatres on our travels. Base your ideas on one of those.'

'Yes, but that will probably mean another trip to Italy.'

'Well, I know for a fact that the Italian women were quite fond of you, so you will have plenty to do to pass the time.'

'Hush your mouth, young man. Don't spread that around.'

'It's too late for that Raja. Everyone knows that you're a womaniser.'

'How did we end up with someone like you?'

'Just lucky, I guess.'

'We certainly are.'

All we had to do was sit back and watch as our beautiful new home took shape and form, but it was just as interesting for Donatello. He would sit on the verandah and watch, and every now and then he would say, 'House, Tada.'

'Yes, my boy, and it's all because of you.'

'No, Tada, nudda house.'

'Another house, you want me to build another house.'

'Yes Tada, like dis,' he said as he showed me a little shell.

That really took us by surprise, and we wondered what he meant. There was no point in asking, as he only spoke a few words at a time, but one day Kashmira said something interesting.

'I was watching him play yesterday, and he was talking to someone.'

'What do you mean? Who was he talking to?'

'Well, I couldn't see anyone, but he obviously could.'

'Like a ghost, you mean.'

'No, I don't think it was a ghost.'

'Then what was it?'

'I don't know. Maybe we should ask Ravenna.'

Ravenna was an old woman now and lived with several other women in Govinda's old house, but her skills had never diminished.

Donatello spent as much time with them as he did with us, but one day I went over to get him, and he was playing with Ravenna's crystal ball.

'Ball, Tada, ball.'

'Did you see something in Ravenna's ball?'

'I do, Tada.'

'I think he did see something,' Ravenna said, 'but I am not sure what it was.'

## CHAPTER 46

That was very unusual for one so young, and later that afternoon, Ravenna came over to see us.

'I had a glimpse of what Donatello saw in my ball, and this morning, I realised what it was.'

'And what was it?' Kashmira said.

'It was a big shell, something like this one.'

We had collected many beautiful shells over the years, most of which were mollusks of one sort or another.

'Does that mean anything to you?' she said.

I explained what Chohan had said, that we had a task to complete, and we thought it had something to do with the Taj Mahal.

As is the way of a soothsayer, Ravenna closed her eyes and looked deep within.

'You must build a temple,' she said. 'Not here, but in another land.'

'And is that all.'

'I see a beautiful white temple, not like the one you have just built, but it must be made of marble.'

'One day in the future, you will find the answer to your questions, but it will be the last thing that you ever do.'

That was another element of the puzzle, but I was none the wiser. I was only thirty years old, and if that was the last thing I ever did, I had plenty of time to work it out.

'All you can do is wait,' Kashmira said. 'If it's meant to be, it will come to you.'

Ravenna's crystal ball had left a tangible impression on Donatello's mind and according to Ravenna, he would head straight for her room just to see it.

'Ball, Venna, ball,' he would say.

Ravenna had another ball that she hadn't used for years, and at first Donatello was happy to play with that, but he couldn't see anything, so he carried it around from one old lady to another.

They would ooh and ahh and pretend to see a bird, a face, or a cloud, but he obviously couldn't see anything and just shook his head.

'Ball no good, Venna.'

Ravenna was intrigued but she had other ways to keep him occupied. She showed him the patterns left by the leaves in a teacup, but he wasn't interested in that. Donatello only wanted to see her crystal ball.

Gypsy women are renowned for their ability to read your fortune, but one day, an old lady called Esmeralda decided to read his palm. It was just a bit of fun, and as soon as she took his hands, she gasped in horror.

She wasn't about to tell Donatello what she had seen, so she came straight over to our place, and from the look in her usually placid eyes, it was apparent that she was distraught.

'Donatello must not go near water,' she said. 'Bad men near water.'

We were somewhat shocked but Esmeralda was deadly serious. We asked what she meant but she couldn't tell us anymore than that. I suddenly remembered Pirate's Cove and the day I had a very close call.

'I haven't been back there for years,' I said. 'I wonder if they're still around.'

'Well, if that's what Esmeralda meant,' Kashmira said, 'I think you should check it out.'

When Raja found out, he related a tale that no one had ever mentioned before. After one of his performances, Govinda was approached by an old man called Ramus who had begged him to save the elephants from a group of English hunters. He was not about to endanger his friends and family, so he let the cobras do the dirty work.

'And it worked beautifully, but we had murdered six men,' Raja said. 'The British had no idea who did it, but every snake charmer in the country was a suspect.'

I approached Govinda and explained what Esmeralda had told us.

'You must be careful as I was jailed by the British for doing that,' he said. 'And if it had not been for my Master, I may have lost my life.'

'Then what are we to do,' I said.

'Go and see if the pirates are still using that cove. And if they are, then you must come up with a plan to get rid of them.'

Asian pirates are murderers, but what we were about to do was dangerous. One night, Raja organised a group of men to meet at my place, and we spent hours working out a plan of action.

'I have already checked out Pirate's Cove,' he said. 'Luckily, they weren't around, but I found their cave.'

Apparently, there's an old woodcutter's hut on the hill just above the cove, and Raja's idea was to stake the place out and see if the pirates worked to a schedule.

'I have never noticed that hut before.'

'I have, but I won't tell you why.'

'Ah, you lecherous old rascal. You take your women there, don't you?'

'No, I don't, but that's a good idea Roshan.'

# CHAPTER 47

How were we going to keep this a secret? If word got around that we were planning to murder a bunch of pirates, we would be in big trouble.

'Ah ha,' Raja said. 'Why don't we build a lighthouse on the hill above the cove.'

'What for?'

'Well, for one thing, we will have an excuse to be there. And for another, these boys will stop drinking my fine Spanish wine.'

'But who owns that land?' said a young man called Bartos.

'Govinda owns it all.'

When Kashmira heard what we were going to do, she had a better idea. 'Why not throw a few cobras into the cave and let them do the dirty work.'

'That could work,' I said. 'And we wouldn't get the blame.'

'You are a clever girl.'

'I was raised by a snake charmer, Roshan.'

And so it was that I went in search of Raja with a big smile on my face.

'You may not believe it, but Kashmira has come up with a brilliant idea.'

'This better be good. So, spit it out. What is it?'

'Do you remember how Govinda got rid of the elephant hunters?'

'Of course, I do. I was there.'

He listened closely and just shook his head.

'Women,' he said. 'You never know what they will come up with next.'

'I wouldn't say that too loudly Raja, not around here at any rate.'

'Yeah, I know what you mean. You could get a knife in your back in the middle of the night.'

Gypsies have a reputation as tramps and thieves, but these were good people who also had a safe place to live.

Govinda had purchased a large tract of land that went all the way up to the base of a mountain range. And when they were not on the road, the gypsies set up camp beside a freshly flowing stream.

We set off for Pirate's Cove and shimmied down the cliff face as we didn't want to leave any footprints in the sand.

We rolled back the stone, only to find that the cave was stashed with a veritable treasure trove of stolen goods. Not long after, we saw a ship on the horizon, so we bunkered down to wait it out.

The ship finally dropped anchor and loaded their contraband onto a rowing boat. Four very nasty-looking Asian pirates stepped ashore, unloaded the boat, and rolled back the stone, but they never came out.

An hour later, another boat was dispatched to see what was going on. Three men entered the cave, and a few minutes later, they raced back to the boat and took off.

'They'll be back,' Raja said. 'They're pirates and they kill for a living.'

'A few old snakes won't keep them at bay forever.'

'If they do come back, they'll get another surprise,' I said.

'And why is that?'

'Because I selected an even number of males and an even number of females, and five of those are pregnant.'

'You clever boy.'

We saw no sign of the pirates after that, but for all we know they may have returned. After all, they had a substantial investment in that cave.

# CHAPTER 48

Rania was a beautiful girl and she looked dazzling on her wedding day. For Govinda and Suleka, this was a bittersweet experience. Their little girl was about to marry the man that she loved.

Rania had accompanied us on all of our tours of Europe and had fallen in love with a man from Barcelona of all places.

She met her husband-to-be only minutes before we were about to go on stage. She had tripped and fallen while carrying a box up the back stairs of the theatre, and a young man called Miguel Cervantes came to her rescue, and according to Rania, it was love at first sight.

He was the son of the theatre manager who was delivering a letter to his father. Neither of them understood a word that the other was saying, but love as they say, is a universal language.

As I was the only one who could speak Spanish, Miguel asked if he could speak to me in private. We were about to go on stage, so I told him to come back later. But Miguel was a determined young man and he was waiting at the door when the performance had finished.

'Permesso, Senor. Please allow me to speak with you.'

'Give me a few minutes Miguel. I have to change first and then we will talk.'

'Roshan, what does that young man want?' Kashmira said.

'I don't know but we are about to find out.'

When we finally made an appearance, Miguel was beside himself with anxiety.

'Ah Senor, Senorita. Gracias. You have no idea how your story has affected the people of this city.'

We had received a true Barcelona welcome on the day that we arrived in this great city. Hundreds of people were waiting on the dockside, waving flags and ribbons in the air. And to my surprise, the mayor even presented us with the keys to the city.

'So, what's bothering you, Miguel?'

'Senor, I would be forever in your debt if you would give me permission to marry your daughter.'

'But I don't have a daughter Miguel.'

'You do not, but I thought that Rania was your daughter.'

'No, she's my sister.'

'Senor, but that cannot be. If the church found out, you would be excommunicated.'

'I don't care what the church thinks Miguel.'

'You do not,' he gasped.

'No, I don't. Spain is where I was born, but Ceylon is my home, as my wife will attest to.'

'Roshan, what is this all about?' Kashmira said.

'Miguel wants to marry Rania.'

'Really, that is so romantic.'

Miguel was a typical Spaniard in the bloom of youth, and he was not an unattractive young man.

'Miguel, when did all this start.'

'Oh, about two hours ago,' he said.

Kashmira could not help but laugh.

'Well, there's nothing wrong with that. I knew that I was going to marry you the first time I ever saw you.'

'What is your wife saying Senor. You take me for a Don Juan, do you not?'

'No Miguel, we do not. My wife said she knew that she was going to marry me when we were children.'

'Ah, Senorita,' he sighed. 'You have just saved my life.'

Miguel accompanied us on the final leg of our tour, but unbeknownst to anyone else, he and Rania were married in a private ceremony in Sicily.

He was insistent and I eventually agreed on the condition that they were to exchange their vows in front of Rania's parents and her family.

'But where will that be?' he said.

'In Ceylon, of course.'

'But Senor, is that safe?'

'Miguel, I think you should come and see for yourself. I have lived there for twenty years, and I can assure you that Ceylon is the most beautiful place on the face of this Earth.'

Miguel was a dreamer, a sensitive young fellow with a heart of gold, but Rania had never been any different. I was not surprised that they fell in love in a fleeting moment of time.

'Oh, Senor, you must tell me more of this fabled land.'

'I don't think that's possible Miguel. Ceylon has an ancient history, but as I said, it is beautiful.'

He had one question after another and I was exhausted by the time I got back to the hotel, but Kashmira wanted to know the verdict.'

'It seems that Govinda and Suleka have a knack of attracting handsome young Spaniards into the fold.'

'I could have told you that years ago. So, what happens now?'

'I gave them permission to get married this afternoon. After all, they have spent the last two months together and I would not be surprised if Rania is pregnant.'

# CHAPTER 49

Rania was not with child on her wedding day, but Miguel had to return to Barcelona not long after as his father passed away, which meant that he was an orphan now.

In my mind that was not such a bad thing. I had no idea what life had in store for that young man, other than an education of a kind he would never have got anywhere else.

He had trouble with the language and people laughed hysterically, but they were kind enough not to do so in front of his face.

Miguel was a lovely boy, and he had a loving wife who was as patient as the day is long. He would rush over to our place at any time of the day and ask me to explain one thing or another.

On the day of Donatello's third birthday, Rania gave birth to a baby boy called Diego. Everyone was excited and a night of great rejoicing followed.

Govinda and Suleka now had two grandchildren, but I wanted something grander than an impromptu party to celebrate their lives, but Chohan had to be there as well. So, one day, I took Govinda aside and asked where I could find him.

'Ah, that's easy,' he said. 'Come with me Roshan and I will tell you a story.'

We took a seat on a hill overlooking the ocean, and over the next few hours, Govinda told me the story of his life.

I knew a little about him, but not everything, and it was because of what I learnt that afternoon that I had the confidence to tell this story.

Four hours had passed in the blink of an eye, and I had forgotten why I went to see him in the first place, but Govinda had not.

'I have not seen my Master for many years,' he said. 'But something tells me you are asking this question for a different reason.'

'I am organising a celebration for you and Suleka, and I want Chohan to be there.'

'Then, leave it to me, my boy, and I will make sure that he is there.'

When Raja found out, he had a few complaints.

'But that means I will have to forgo at least three barrels of my favourite wine,' he groaned.

'You have at least twenty stashed away in our storeroom.'

'But's that's for an emergency.'

'Like what,' Kashmira said. 'So that you can get rolling drunk.'

'I have never been rolling drunk in my life, I will have you know.'

'So where are we going to have this big celebration, here or over there?'

'In Rania's courtyard.'

'Well, at least you have made one good decision. So, what do you want me to do?'

'Firstly, I want you to spread the word.'

'That won't be too difficult, then what?'

'We will need entertainment.'

'Ah yes, I know just the thing.'

'It's a family affair Raja, not a bacchanal.'

'Okay, so, is that it?'

'No, I have invited a special guest?'

'Me?'

'No, Govinda's master.'

'I will finally get to meet him.'

'I think you already have.'

'When was that?'

'He was at Govinda's wedding, our wedding and Rania's wedding.'

'He was. How come no one told me about that.'

'Chohan is a master of disguise, that is probably why.'

Just before the big day, an old peddler and his dog appeared at our door, and I knew exactly who it was.

'Greetings kind sir, I believe that you require the services of a master magician,' he said.

'Chohan, please come in. I was hoping you would get the message.'

The next few hours were the most fascinating that we have ever had, and Chohan was impressed by our version of the Taj Mahal. But Donatello was attracted to Chohan immediately and the first thing he did was place a shell in his hands.

'Thank you, young man. Is this a present?'

'No, Tada's house.'

'He has been saying that for years, but we have no idea what he means.'

'Well, I won't spoil the surprise, but he is trying to tell you something.'

'About our task, you mean?'

'Yes, Tada will work it out one day, won't he Donatello.'

'Now about this special night, I believe that I am to be the special guest.'

'That's the general idea, if you approve.'

'I have nurtured many people in my long life, but no one has ever offered me an opportunity like this before.'

'Well, we can, but that's because we can afford to.'

'So true, but I have one stipulation, that you do not introduce me as Chohan the Holy Man, but as Govinda's uncle, Ravi Naveen.'

'I wasn't planning to blow your cover; I just want you to be there.'

## CHAPTER 50

I was hoping that Chohan would entertain us. How, I didn't know but he accepted the invitation, and I was happy with that. Unfortunately, I had to inform Raja of the bad news.

'Chohan will not be able to attend.'

'How do you know that. Have you been talking to him?'

'Yes, we had a visit from him a few days ago.'

'A man gets one chance to meet someone special and no one bothers to tell him.'

'But Govinda's uncle will be there.'

'I thought Govinda was an orphan?'

'He is, but he has one remaining relative.'

'And who would that be?'

'His name is Navi Raveen.'

'And what does he do?'

'He's a peddler.'

'That should be exciting.'

'He's a lovely old man,' Kashmira said. 'As you will find out for yourself.'

On the big day, the courtyard looked resplendent with paper lanterns swaying in the breeze, jugglers and jesters, costumed merrymakers, singers of songs, brightly painted caravans, lots of noisy children and numerous barking dogs.

One barrel of Raja's wine disappeared before the party even started, but he was in fine form, nevertheless.

It was an occasion to dress in our finest clothes, but to our surprise, Uncle Ravi did not look like a peddler at all.

He was dressed in a frock coat, knee length boots and a jeweled waistcoat. And with a gilded dagger at his side, he looked like an Italian prince of the Renaissance era.

The table of honour was surrounded by a floral archway. The aroma of incense floated through the air. Gentle music was playing in the background and flower petals had been scattered over the floor.

A hush settled over the courtyard, the music stopped and everyone waited for Govinda and Suleka to make an appearance.

And when they did, they received a resounding round of applause, but it would not be a celebration without a speech or two. I had a few things to say, and I was not about to be left out.

'First and foremost, I would like to express my gratitude to the family who welcomed me into their life. '

'But I also want to thank all of you, the people who welcomed me into their world and treated me with love and affection.'

Raja had everyone in hysterics as I knew he would, but his idea of entertainment was to tell one bawdy story after another.

Old Uncle Ravi was not about to be left out either. He was the guest of honour and word soon passed around that he was not a peddler of goods at all, that he was in fact someone else altogether.

'Senor and senorita,' he says as he bows graciously to his hosts. 'Ladies and gentlemen, boys and girls.'

'What a wonderful night this has been, but your lives could have been very different if it had not been for a little orphan called Govinda.'

'Now, I know that you are all very curious as to out who I am, and normally, I do not reveal myself to anyone but a chosen few.'

'Govinda and Suleka know what I really look like, but this is not it, I can assure you of that.'

'I was the one who took Govinda by the hand and offered him a life that he would never have had. And I was the one who set him on the path of a snake charmer.'

'Why would I do such a thing you might be wondering?'

'Well, you could say that I am a conjurer of dreams, because that is what I do. That is my purpose in life, and I have been doing it for a very long time.'

That was not what anyone expected to hear, but you could have heard a pin drop, and not even the dogs barked.

Chohan's voice had a very ethereal quality, and we were spellbound by everything he said. I wasn't the only one who was hoping that he would do something memorable, and he did not let us down.

'Now, I have numerous skills and talents, which I have perfected over the years, but I was lucky enough to be born with special powers.'

'I could very easily use them for destructive purposes but I have never done so. I am very respectful of those gifts and only use them to better the lives of those around me.'

'As a consequence, I am going to do something that I have only done once before. I am going to take you on a journey.'

'You will not remember it for some time to come, and when you do, you will shake your head and think to yourself, that was nothing but a dream.'

'The only thing you will remember is that old Uncle Ravi said some very nice things about Govinda and his family. It will last but a moment or two and you will be none the wiser that anything happened at all.'

I know for a fact that I did not remember what Chohan said for many years to come. As to whether anyone else did, I never found out. For all I know, it could have been a dream, but it wasn't like any dream that I have ever had before.

I stepped out of my body and rose into the heavens where I was surrounded, not by people, but by beings of light with a miraculous glistening aura.

Barely visible structures floated around like jewels in a spectral mist, and then a man appeared, clothed in an armour of golden light.

'Behold, and look around,' he said. 'This is the grandeur of creation. This is existence in perpetuity.'

'This is what you really are, and this is where you come from.'

'But that world down there is the reason for everything we do. That is our future and that is why we exist at all.'

# CHAPTER 51

A few years later, I decided to build a cemetery, so I chose a site not far from the foothills of the mountains, and over time, I surrounded it with a low set stone wall.

Govinda and Suleka's resting place would be a white marble mausoleum, while ours would be a replica of the Parthenon in Athens.

That idea was inspired by the cemetery on the slopes of Montjuic in Barcelona, a city of the dead with more gravestones and mausoleums than it is possible to imagine. But this one would be different, set as it was against the background of a beautiful forest and surrounded by an orchard of fruit trees.

I had no idea that it would get so much use in the years to come. Ravenna and her lady friends were the next to go, but I never imagined that I would have to bury the people who gave me a reason to live. What we didn't know until it was far too late was that the pirates had returned to Pirate's Cove.

Donatello had grown into a handsome young boy and was the love of our life. He and the gypsy boys often went on hiking trips up into the mountains or swam in freshwater streams, but he had been given strict instructions never to go to the beach by himself or to go near Pirate's Cove.

It was late one afternoon when one of his friends raced into our house and Pauli was hysterical.

'Kashmira,' he cried. 'Donatello has disappeared.'

'What do you mean?' she said.

'We were playing around in the water and when we looked around, Donatello was gone.'

'Pauli, run up to the camp and get as many men as you can. Tell them that this is urgent. And if you see Raja, tell him to get down here immediately.'

That evening was the most horrifying we have ever experienced. We had search parties combing the beach until late into the night. Raja's men ransacked the pirate cave but it had been abandoned long ago.

The following day, there was still no sign of Donatello, but Bartos had found his golden locket. 'I also saw signs of a struggle and footprints on the beach.'

'Roshan, what are we going to do,' said a very hysterical Kashmira.

'We are going to track those pirates down, that's what we are going to do.'

Accompanied by Raja and a dozen strong-armed men, we set off for Colombo. I owned a fleet of ships, and I was going to use them for as long as I had to.

I stormed into the Colombo office and advised the manager of my intentions. He leapt into action immediately, and before the day was over, we set sail on the high seas.

That was the beginning of three solid weeks of searching. We docked at every town and city along the Asian coastline, handing out money for any information at all.

We had almost given up in despair, but not Raja. He sussed out every lowlife bar in every seedy place we went, and one day, he found what he was looking for.

'I've got a lead,' he said. 'I overheard a couple of cutthroats talking about their latest acquisition.'

'White boy from Ceylon. Him no make good money anymore. He no good at all now.'

'You followed him, didn't you,' Kashmira said.

'I did more than that, I even got the bastard.'

'Where is he?'

'Roped and bound and suffering like hell in the brig of the Isabella, that's where he is. Follow me.'

The man was a mean-looking piece of work who had been flogged to within an inch of his life.

'This is your last chance,' Raja said. 'Tell me where the boy is, or I am going to chop off one finger at a time.'

'Me not know what boy you mean,' he cried.

'You know exactly who I am talking about.'

Raja whipped out his knife and began to slice away at one of his fingers.

'Stop, stop, stop,' the man howled. 'I tell you where boy is.'

'You will do better than that mate. You are going to take us there.'

We had no idea that there was so much barbarity and wickedness so close to our beautiful island home. The slave trade was big business, but on that night, we discovered how vile and disgusting it really was.

We had been praying that our beautiful boy had survived and we did not want to think about what they might have done to him.

We crept through the backstreets to the most squalid docks I had ever seen, and a few minutes later, we heard Donatello crying out for help.

'It's coming from that old junk over there,' Kashmira cried. 'He is alive. Our baby is alive.'

'You stay here, while we take care of this,' Raja said.

It was almost midnight and there was no one else around. Raja and his men were armed with every possible weapon that money could buy, but he was not interested in taking prisoners. They crept onto the boat, only to find one guard on duty.

Kashmira and I were rooted to the spot and saying every prayer we could think of when Raja appears on the deck.

'We found him,' he said. 'It's not a pretty sight and he's in a pretty bad state.'

'I don't care, I just want to see him,' Kashmira cries.

We could not believe our eyes. The room reeked of faeces. The window had been nailed into place, and Donatello was as close to death as anyone I had ever seen.

He had been locked away like a caged animal. His body was covered with ugly green sores, and he had been used by God knows how many sick and ugly people for their own perverted pleasure.

## CHAPTER 52

Nothing could have prepared us for an experience like that and nothing did. We were the lucky ones. We lived a life of affluence, surrounded by astounding beauty.

Over the years I had seen more than my fair share of poverty in this land, and I vowed and declared that I was going to do whatever I could to help those who needed it.

But there was little I could do to help my son. He was too far gone, the sickness had eaten away at his body, and eventually it ate away at my soul.

I could afford the best physicians in the land, but there was nothing they could do. In desperation, I raced to the top of the highest hill and screamed like I had never done before.

'Please someone, if you can hear me, please help my little boy.'

I must have passed out, and when I woke up the following morning, Chohan was by my side.

'Chohan,' I said.

'Yes, Roshan, I heard your plaintiff cry.'

'Can you do anything for Donatello? Please tell me you can.'

'I cannot save his life, but I can be of assistance in another way.'

'I don't understand.'

'Donatello is one of those people who pass our way for a short period of time Roshan, but he has not completed the work that he came here to do.'

'And what work is that?'

'He has been telling you for years to build something.'

'I know Chohan, but I haven't worked out what it is yet.'

'He has already given you a clue Roshan.'

'The shell, you mean.'

'It is not just one shell that will inspire you Roshan but several. You will work it out soon enough.'

'I don't know whether you remember, but I saved your life many years ago.'

'I do remember Chohan, and I have never forgotten that.'

'I asked whether you wanted to go or whether you wanted to stay, and you chose to stay. But you could only make that decision because you were not at death's door.'

'When you pass over, you leave your physical body behind, but you do not disappear. You still exist, but in another form.'

'As a ghost, you mean.'

'As a spirit, Roshan. That is what we are, spiritual beings in physical form.'

'Donatello will always be by your side because he has as much invested in this as you do.'

'He does.'

'Yes, and he is going to do everything in his power to see that you complete your task.'

It took a while to get my head around that idea, but Kashmira understood immediately. She wasn't happy about the fact that she had lost her beloved son, but she was a sensitive and intuitive woman. Her pain was insurmountable, but her belief in the impossible had never faltered.

Donatello's funeral was a heartbreaking experience for everyone. We celebrated his life in every way that we could think of, but the very last thing we did was place his ashes in a marble casket along with a family portrait.

It was a powerful emotional experience for Kashmira, and tears were running down her face. But when she looked up, she saw Donatello's golden spirit standing beside his casket.

'He is here Roshan. Donatello is here. I can see him.'

One afternoon as we were gazing out across the ocean, Kashmira told me what had happened.

'Those pirates did awful things to him and treated him very badly. He got a terrible rash and they wouldn't have anything to do with him. They just left him there to die.'

'But Mama,' he said. 'Come with me. I want to show you something.'

'Where are we going?'

'Down to the beach. Tada has to see this too, Mama. It will give him a wonderful idea.'

'He showed me where to find the shells, but he also told me that you have to build a temple just like that.'

'Then we should check it out now,' I said. 'Come on, let's go, before it gets dark.'

We raced down to the beach, and I eventually found the spikes of four huge conch shells buried in the sand. These were not the tiny little shells that Donatello had shown me so often but fully grown shells.

The light was fading, so Kashmira put them on a table and placed a candle in the middle. And it was then that we saw the ghostly form of the idea for which we had been searching for so long.

'How beautiful is that,' she said.

It was all too much for me. It was the tail end of an agonising journey. I had lost my beloved son and I just sat down and wept tears of blood.

## CHAPTER 53

My drawing skills were not as good as they used to be, but I persevered until I had something that looked like a temple. It was the sinuous flowing lines of the shells that spoke to me, the graceful way in which they rose from the base and met at the top.

'That's as good as I can get it,' I said.

'It's beautiful Roshan, but what are you going to do with it?'

'I am going to ask one of the local woodcarvers to create a model before we do anything at all.'

I didn't have to worry. As usual, Raja came to the rescue.

'I know just the man and he is one of ours.'

A young fellow called Molti had been carving birds and animals ever since he was a boy. He had bright eyes, a cheery disposition, and the solid arms of a woodcutter.

'I make a little money every now and then,' he said. 'But I have never been offered a small fortune for my work.'

Molti set up a workshop in the courtyard of Rania and Miguel's house. I had never seen an artist at work before and had no idea what they did.

We were excited that something was finally happening, and I would pop in every day to check on his progress. Our little masterpiece was taking shape and form as every day passed, and the day finally came when it was finished.

'That is magnificent Molti.'

'Thank you, but it was a challenge,' he said. 'There were so many finnicky little details.'

Now, we could see exactly what it was. Four spiral staircases wound their way around the outside to a platform at the top, but on the inside, it looked like a heavenly chapel.

'We could perform in a place like that,' Kashmira says.

'We could, but it would have to be a lot bigger than that.'

'So, what are you going to do with it?' Molti said.

'I think it would look magnificent if it was made of marble.'

'Oh, it would,' Kashmira says.

'Do you think you are up to a task like that Molti?'

'I have never worked in marble before.'

'So, how would you like to go to Italy and learn from the masters.'

'Senor, that is the dream of a lifetime, but where in Italy?'

'To Carrara, of course.'

'Really. When?'

'As soon as you have packed your bags.'

This was a reason to celebrate and even Raja was impressed. He inspected our little temple closely and gave Molti a good solid pat on the back.

'Well done young man. That is very fine work indeed.'

'Thank you.'

'And you two, what would you do without me?'

'You know exactly how we feel about you,' Kashmira said.

'So, what happens next?'

'Molti is going to Italy.'

'Why?'

'To be a marble carver, of course.'

'In that case, my boy, you will need a chaperone, and I am the best man for the job.'

'I knew that was coming,' I said.

## CHAPTER 54

Donatello insisted that we go away for a while, that we should take a holiday. Kashmira had fallen in love with Sicily and often spoke of Naples with great affection.

So, we packed our bags and spent two beautiful months on the Amalfi coast in a little villa that had once belonged to an aristocratic Count.

It was the perfect place to rejuvenate our spirits, but Donatello was always close by and for that we were very grateful. I had always wanted to see his beautiful face again, but he was Kashmira's constant companion and he rarely left her side.

The house had a huge terrace that overlooked the Adriatic Sea and when I found out that it was for sale, I decided to buy it.

It was the first of many houses I would buy in one place or another, places we fell in love with, simply because they were beautiful.

Molti would be away for at least a year, and we had time to spare, so we decided to explore Egypt and the Holy Lands.

We could not abide the thought of going anywhere near the Far East after what had happened to Donatello, but the Middle East was very different in every way.

It was almost a year later when we got back to Ceylon, and to our surprise, Rania had given birth to her second child. Her little boy Diego was now two years old, but her second child was a girl that she decided to call Suleka.

Miguel had become quite proficient in the Sinhalese language and had decided to start a school. There were dozens of uneducated children in the gypsy camp, and with a little help from Drago, he managed to get their attention for a few hours a day.

'Why I ever decided to do that I will never know,' he groaned.

'What's the problem?' Kashmira said.

'They're little terrors, that's what. I need an armed guard in the room just to keep them quiet.'

'Well, don't give up. You can see what we have achieved. These people had nothing before Roshan came along, but now look at them.'

'Maybe you could teach the girls,' he said.

'I have never had an education, Miguel.'

'Well, it's about time you did.'

That was the beginning of another era in the lives of these people, and it may never have happened at all, if it had not been for Kashmira.

She sat in class along with everyone else, and if anyone dared to step out of line, it was the last thing they ever did.

We had no idea when Molti would be back, but one day a fancy two-wheeled carriage rolled up to our door, and to our surprise, Raja poked his head through the window.

'What do you think?' he said.

'It's very impressive. Is it for us?'

'No, it's not. Carriages are quite the thing these days. So, I am going to start a new business.'

'That idea should work, but where's Molti?'

'He's at the dockside in Colombo waiting for a block of marble to be loaded onto a bullock wagon.'

'You paid for it of course, otherwise it would never have happened at all.'

'Have you got any other surprises up your sleeve Raja.'

'As a matter of fact, I have, but I would kill for a few glasses of my favourite Spanish wine.'

'Sorry,' Kashmira said. 'There's none left.'

'You're joking, aren't you?'

'Yes Raja, of course I am.'

## CHAPTER 55

The block of marble wasn't as big as I thought it would be, but over time, it would evolve into another version of our temple. It took two solid months of work, and when it was finally finished, it really did look like a heavenly chapel.

While Kashmira spent the day learning to read and write, I was having an education of a different kind.

Marble is such a beautiful material, and I would often sit by Molto's side and carve away at the scraps. If you held a piece up to the light and turned it this way and that, it glistened like crystal, but Molti had so much to say about his experience in Carrara.

'An apprentice usually has to start at the bottom, and work with a team of men who cut the marble into all sorts of shapes, but I didn't have to do that.'

'Raja paid a man called Pietro to teach me everything he knew, otherwise I would have been there for the next seven years.'

'It helps if you have a bit of money to throw around,' Raja said. 'And you do Roshan.'

'I won't have much left when you are finished, that's for certain.'

'So, you now have your idea in solid stone, but what are you going to do with it?'

'I am going to ask my architect to create the plans for a three-storey version of our temple.'

'A three-story version,' Raja gasps. 'But that will cost a fortune.'

'I thought I would borrow the money from you.'

'Ha, ha, that's a funny one. And then what?'

'All I know is that it will eventually be erected in some other land. As to where that will be, I have no idea.'

'Another land,' Raja cries. 'A masterpiece like that belongs here in Sinhala.'

'That's what Ravenna told me many years ago.'

'Umm. Those darned soothsayers. They think they know everything.'

It took another two months before the plans were finished, and as luck would have it, Raja came up with the perfect solution.

'I was reading that crappy old English newspaper the other day and I came across an interesting advertisement.'

'And what was it about,' I said.

'Apparently, there is to be a big exhibition in Australia soon. It's called The Melbourne International Exhibition and people from all over the world will be coming to see it.'

'That sounds perfect,' Kashmira said.

'It certainly does.'

'Raja, do you know that you are worth your weight in gold?'

'Fool's gold mostly,' Kashmira chuckled.

'Now, watch it lady. Have some respect for your elders.'

'Oh, I do Raja, most of the time.'

Finally, after years of not knowing anything at all, we knew what we had to do. I spent a fortune on blocks of marble from Carrara in northern Italy, after which they were transported to Melbourne on one of my ships.

## CHAPTER 56

Raja was almost fifty but he was not ready to head off to the promised land. Kashmira and I had just turned forty and we were about to do the most important thing we would ever have to do.

We would be the first to perform in our beautiful new temple, but we would not be going alone. We had to train a new generation of performers and we had plenty of takers.

We spent three months rehearsing, and our backup team was excited at the thought of what they were going to do. And when the big day finally arrived, thirty people dressed in their finest clothes set sail for a place they knew nothing about.

Melbourne was a long way from everywhere, but it was obviously good enough to host an International Exhibition.

We booked out an entire hotel for six whole weeks, but we had not been prepared for the weather, and had to rush around and buy warm clothes.

The suburb of Fitzroy is not the sort of place you would want to raise children, but it was close to the city, and it was within walking distance of The Carlton Gardens, the site of the upcoming exhibition.

There were quite a few houses for sale and one of those was being offered at a very reasonable price, so we decided to add it to our collection.

The salesman described it as a Federation Style Cottage, a four-bedroom house with a pretty little rose garden at the front.

The packing crates were still at the dockside and our temple had not yet been erected, but a marble model took pride of place in our parlour. It had no purpose other than to allow the public to enjoy a unique performance in an outdoor setting.

Every evening, Kashmira placed a little candle inside, but one day, she had the inspired idea to call it the Chapel of Love.

What I didn't know until sometime later was that Donatello had been warning her to be careful. He never said any more than that, but one day she decided to tell me.

'Please God, no,' I cried.

'If it's meant to be, Roshan, there is nothing we can do about it.'

I couldn't concentrate and I couldn't sleep, and the last thing I wanted was to lose the woman I loved. I felt like a man possessed, but the night before it happened, we had had a few too many wines with Raja.

The following day, we decided to practice the most critical part of our routine where Kashmira steps into the fire. What we didn't know was that a drama of a very different kind was taking place on the street outside.

It happened as a horse and carriage was passing by, and it was then that a dog decided to chase a cat across the street. The horse bolted and the cat took the shortest path to freedom, and unfortunately, that was through the front door of our house.

The cat was followed by the half-crazed dog. They ran around the room, knocked over a bottle of kerosene, upended a bowl of burning coals and scattered them all over the floor, and within minutes, the house was a raging firestorm.

Kashmira, the love of my life, the woman I adored with all my heart was trapped in the middle of a blazing inferno, and there was nothing I could do about it.

The house was reduced to cinders within minutes, and there was nothing left of my beautiful wife at all, nothing but ash and bone.

## CHAPTER 57

We abandoned our plans and took the first ship back to Colombo, but the day that I placed Kashmira's ashes in our mausoleum was one that I could barely even remember. The very thought that she had died in such a horrible way cut me to the core.

I was never the same again for many long and heartbreaking years, and even Raja had trouble trying to make me laugh.

My task was not yet complete, and I had no idea what to do, but late one night, Chohan appeared at the door.

'Roshan, what are you going to do?'

'I have no idea.'

'You will have to go back to Melbourne and finish your work. This has to be done Roshan. You have created something beautiful and the whole world should know about it.'

It took five years before I could face up to that challenge, and I eventually returned to Melbourne in the year 1890, accompanied by Miguel and his son Diego.

The blocks of marble had been stored in a warehouse not far from the docks. I dreaded the very thought of going there, but one day I plucked up the courage and just did it.

I had no idea as to the staggering scale of our masterpiece. There were literally hundreds of wooden crates from the floor to the ceiling.

'Oh, Miguel,' I cried. 'Can you believe that?'

'I can see it with my own eyes Roshan, and I still can't believe it.'

The thought of such an undertaking was far too overwhelming, so we sailed back home to think about it. Many years later I embarked on part one of an elaborate plan.

I returned to Melbourne and hired a local company to erect a three-storey building in Fitzroy which would eventually become the storage place for our masterpiece.

It took over a year to complete and I decided to call it The Phoenix, named after the fabled bird that rises from its own ashes. The marble blocks were stored away on the first and second floor, but I had a different plan for the basement.

Accompanied by Miguel and Diego, I travelled to Italy to oversee the creation of two statues, one of myself and one of Kashmira. And I even employed a professional photographer to take photos of the paintings in our house.

There was one of Govinda dressed in his glittering red outfit, and one of Suleka doing her famous dance. There was one of us performing in a local marketplace, and a portrait of Donatello gazing out across the mighty Indian Ocean. But my favourite was that of Kashmira dressed in a colourful Indian sari, and in her hands, she held a pair of pure white doves.

A year later, Miguel and I travelled to Venice as I wanted someone to make solid glass paintings in the style of 17th century Indian murals. My idea was not readily accepted by the glassmakers of Venice but I eventually found a young man who jumped at the opportunity.

Franco Libertelli had his own workshop, and over a period of months he came up with a solution. The finished products were masterpieces, and along with the statues, they would be stored away in the basement of The Phoenix.

## CHAPTER 58

Part two of my plan was not as time consuming but it had to be done. I bequeathed a small share of my fortune to my family of friends, and I placed control of my empire in the hands of the Bank of Colombo. After which, I stored our valuables in a bank vault along with Kashmira's pride and joy, the marble replica of the Chapel of Love.

I had no idea who would complete this task, but I went to a lot of effort to ensure that someone did. I spent ages writing a diary, and according to my instructions, The Phoenix was not to be sold until the year 2014.

I placed a letter in the hands of the Bank of Colombo with strict instructions that it should be passed on to the new owner. The contents of the vault would be the reward for the person who could do what I could not. As a consequence, I spent a long time composing my thoughts in a diary which would also become their property.

*"I know that one day in the future, someone will discover this treasure and realise what it is. Hopefully, you will also find this diary and understand its importance. I sincerely hope that whoever does so honours it in the way that it is meant to be honoured.*

*The Chapel of Love was something I wanted to share with the world. I can only hope and pray that the universe intervenes, and that this shrine to the memory of my beloved finds its place in history.*

*If you are the person reading this diary, you are also the owner of The Phoenix. It was named for the fabled creature that rises from its own ashes and lives once again.*

*If you have successfully erected the tribute to the love of my life, it is now one hundred years later, and it is the year 2014.*

*If you have completed the task that I could not, and the Chapel is now a reality, I say to you my beloved friend, thank you from the bottom of my heart, and may God bless you for all eternity.*

*Before I take to my bed for the last time, I have one more thing to say. Hidden away in the back of this diary is a key to a vault in the Bank of Colombo. If you have done as I could not, I have left a token of my thanks for your efforts.*

*Blessings be upon you, for you are a good and honest soul. What you find in my adopted land will be a reward for your efforts.*

*I will not be for this life much longer, but I will be watching, hoping, and praying that one day, I can look down from heaven and see Kashmira's Chapel in that beautiful garden in Melbourne, Australia.*

*I will sign off now, but I will be calling to you from afar, of that you can be assured.*

*Juan Philippe Delgado, also known as Roshan the Snake Charmer, husband of the beautiful Kashmira, the love of my life and the Snake Charmer's Wife."*

## CHAPTER 59

Chohan saw the wisdom of my plan and assured me that he would go out of his way to see that our dream became a reality. And not long after that, I took to my bed and closed my eyes for the very last time.

Kashmira and Donatello were waiting for me when I stepped out of my body. They had been waiting for a very a long time, but now the waiting was over. I took my beautiful boy in my arms and I took Kashmira by the hand, and together we wandered off to greener pastures.

I had no interest in the next life and I didn't want to know anything about it. I was with the people I loved and that was how it was going to stay, but as I would soon find out, Kashmira had other ideas.

Donatello was proof that there was more to our existence than we knew. The fact that he could come and go at will was an idea that Kashmira took to heart, and in time, she would find a way to do exactly the same thing.

Our plan to erect our beautiful dream had not yet been fulfilled, but if it was to happen at all, we had to offer someone a helping hand. Kashmira would see to that.

THE END OF PART ONE

PART TWO

# A TALE
# OF
# A MODERN-DAY HOLY MAN

## PREFACE

It is said that holy men can breathe underwater, that some can walk on water, and others can travel through space and time. One young man found that out for himself, not long after he turned eighteen.

A snake charmer and his wife had been reaching out from beyond the grave, looking for someone to do what they could not.

They had failed to lure three other men into their net and came up with another plan. They had someone different in mind this time, not some egotistical, self-important, know-it-all, but someone a little more sensitive.

In the year 2000, Kashmira befriends a young boy called Jasper Powell. She has been appearing in his dreams ever since he was five years old, but Jasper never imagined that she would make an appearance in his life. He has acquired a special gift from his Lady Friend, and he is about to find out exactly what it is.

## CHAPTER 60
## 2013
## Melbourne, Australia

The year 1995 is one that not many will remember. That was the year in which the World Wide Web made itself known to the world at large. It was the year in which terrorism reared its head in the guise of the Oklahoma bombing, and the year in which the Russian space station docked with the shuttle Atlantis.

It was also the year in which the Dalai Lama proclaimed that a six-year-old boy would be the 11th Panchen Lama. However, something equally important happened in the city of Melbourne in faraway Australia. 1995 was the year that Jasper Powell made his appearance on the world stage.

His father had suffered from a medical problem, and his mother had had enough of married life, and when Jasper was five years old, she filed for a divorce.

Geraldine had her reasons. You don't walk out of a marriage of forty years if everything is sailing along smoothly. Love wasn't the problem and never had been.

On the advice of a friend, they placed Jasper's welfare in the hands of a respected childcare agency. Jasper would live with his father and could see his mother as often as he liked. From an educational point of view, it was the best thing they could have done.

Henry was a retired businessman who chose to subdue his demons with alcohol rather than prescribed medication.

Geraldine relinquished her career as a practicing gynecologist, packed her bags, moved out of their Toorak home, and opened a tapas bar in Fitzroy, a suburb of Melbourne with a long and interesting history.

At the time that this story starts, Jasper has had fourteen different carers, most of whom were university students. The last of those was a young man called Mark Jacobsen, and it was his job was to provide opportunities for Jasper's social and emotional development.

A few months before he graduates from high school, Mark decides to take him on a camping trip up into the mountains. Mark is a Physical Education student at Monash University, and he loves nothing better than to slip on his hiking boots and explore the rugged Australian bushland.

'I have it all planned out Jasper. Our destination will be a freshwater creek that flows down from the Dandenong Range.'

'We will set up our tents, check the place out and maybe do a spot of fishing.'

'It won't be dangerous, will it?' Jasper says.

'We will probably see a couple of birds, a few ground rats, maybe a kangaroo and even the occasional snake.'

'Snakes,' Jasper says.

He has every reason to be wary, he has seen quite a few in his dreams and that's where he would like them to stay.

'Besides, we will be accompanied by my friends Declan Smith, and Fabian Stella-Marcus. And if anything goes wrong, Fabian will come to your rescue.'

'Any self-respecting snake would think twice about grappling with dear old Fabian. He is, how shall I say, smarter than the average snake.'

One fine but chilly Saturday morning they set off in Mark's newly refurbished, bright orange campervan.

Jasper is dressed in a long-sleeve shirt, good solid hiking boots and a pair of cargo shorts with big roomy pockets. And as they zoom along the highway, he is bopping away to the feel-good tunes of the 1950s.

Two hours later, they arrive at their first port of call. Sassafras is a quaint little town where day trippers can soak up the atmosphere or sit back and enjoy a hot scone and jam in one of its famous Devonshire tea houses.

But these boys have something different in mind and they head straight for the local bakery. The humble meat pie is an old Australian favourite that has inched its way up the gourmet ladder. And on a chilly day in the mountains, there is nothing more appealing than a piping hot pie topped with a light and crispy golden flaky pastry.

'Ooh, they look so good,' Jasper says.

He's an old-fashioned boy with old-fashioned tastes, but he cannot resist a pie with mushy green peas and a dollop of gravy on top.

After some consideration, Declan decides to try a Saucy Mexican Salsa and Mark settles for three sausage rolls. But when Fabian finally steps out of the door ten minutes later, he has a tray piled high with a selection of mouth-watering cream cakes as well.

'Just in case we get peckish. That lovely girl gave me three pies for the price of two.'

'Probably because she wanted to get rid of you,' Mark says.

'More than likely.'

'Okay, boys, let's hit the road. We still have a few miles to go.'

After a healthy dose of flaky pastry, they pile into the campervan and head for the Dandenongs. With Mark at the helm, they venture along country roads, down narrow country lanes, past weekend retreats and even the occasional country mansion.

It is almost two o'clock when they arrive at a car park in the middle of nowhere, but this is not just a hiking expedition, this is a data collection exercise as well.

Orienteering is an accredited subject, and the boys must document their trip in detail. A map of Victorian hiking tracks and an old-fashioned compass are essential, but so is the vital data that streams to mobile phones from a satellite navigation system.

They strap on their backpacks and make their way through an old growth forest. And when they finally reach their destination, the light is fading, darkness is closing in and rain clouds are gathering overhead.

This is as far from civilisation as Jasper has ever been, but it was worth the effort just to see a little freshwater creek winding its way through the undergrowth.

'Well, we made it,' Fabian says. 'It's just like something out of Deliverance, isn't it?'

'I hope not,' Mark says.

An encounter with a couple of mean-spirited rednecks is the last thing he wants, but you never know. This is the great outdoors, and anything could happen on a bleak and miserable night in the middle of nowhere.

Jasper has never been camping in his life and he had no idea what sort of tent to buy. He paid a small fortune for a green and brown polyurethane dome, which according to the instructions, was a cinch to erect.

The boys have theirs up within minutes, so he removes each piece from the packet and places them side-by-side.

'Now what goes where?'

He lays out the ground sheet, unwraps the tent and then sits down to assemble the poles. Everything is colour coded, which is good, but that doesn't help him at all, and after a few frustrating few minutes, he finally gives up in despair.

'Oh, this is supposed to be easy,' he cries. 'What do I do with all of this stuff?'

Fabian has been watching closely and comes to the rescue.

'So, you are obviously not the outdoors type.'

'No, I don't know anything about it.'

'In that case, I will give you a hand.'

With a few deft moves, Fabian slips the poles into the sockets, pulls the tent into place, and stakes it to the ground, and two minutes later, it's all done and Jasper is impressed.

His new home is a lot bigger than he expected, a very stylish and roomy space age igloo with a zip up door. He was tempted by a solar powered tent with a heated floor and Wi-Fi but decided that would be going a bit too far.

'Very nice,' he says.

'There now, that should keep the greeblies out,' Fabian says. 'I am an expert at just about everything.'

'That's good to know. Thanks, Fabian.'

'My mother always told me to be kind to strangers. Now, let's get this show on the road.'

They scout around and collect a stockpile of twigs and branches. Fabian lights the first match of the day, and they watch closely as the flames gather in momentum. Thirty minutes later a healthy fire is blazing away, and the only chore after that is to cook up an old-fashioned Aussie BBQ.

## CHAPTER 61

It's a well-known fact that men of a certain age group are partial to a drink or two, especially when they plan to have a good time. Jasper watches with interest as Fabian removes a black leather pouch from his backpack.

'Well, we made it,' he says. 'And that deserves to be celebrated.'

'How old are you, Jasper?'

'Eighteen, but I will be nineteen in a few weeks.'

'Well, that makes you legal. Perhaps you'd like something to lubricate your mind,' he says with a wicked glint in his eye.

'It won't hurt. In fact, from what Mark has told me it might even do you good. You are a writer after all, aren't you?'

'Amongst other things,' Jasper says.

'Consider this a present. It will open your eyes in ways you could never imagine.'

Every Friday afternoon, Jasper's mates would have a quick puff before they caught the train home, but he had never been interested.

One day, he decided to give it a try and nearly passed out on the spot. He ended up at Melbourne Central Station and wandered around in a daze for the next two hours.

And on that day his life took a detour he wasn't expecting. That was the day he noticed an attractive young woman gazing at him from the opposite side of the platform.

There was just enough space on the bench for one more person, so she plucked up the courage and asked the old lady at his side if she could squeeze in.

'I have been working non-stop for the last twelve hours,' she said.

She made herself comfortable, ruffled around in her red velvet bag until she found what she was looking for.

'You don't mind if I smoke, do you?'

The old lady pointed to a sign that is visible on almost every street corner in Australia…This is a Smoke Free Zone.

'I don't care. Besides, I have had a hell of a day. Whatever you do, never take a job in the hospitality industry. People can be so tiresome when you work in a fancy restaurant.'

The old lady had obviously had a harrowing day and all she wanted was to get home, kick off her shoes and rest her weary legs, but a message over the loudspeaker was the last straw.

"The six o'clock train to Cranbourne will be delayed for another thirty minutes."

She sighed volubly, retrieved a book from her bag, and settled back with a well-thumbed copy of an old Mills and Boon love story.

The vivacious Sally Velasko was now free to devote her attention to Jasper.

'Very interesting,' she said in a voice that was just short of a sigh.

There was something about Jasper that she couldn't resist. He had a certain indefinable quality, and it wasn't just his glistening green eyes, the dimples around his mouth or his boyish good looks.

Most women in Melbourne wear black as a statement of their position in society but Sally wasn't one of those. She was dressed like a modern-day gypsy in a pair of blue spangled tights and a red velvet coat.

Her glossy black hair was hidden away under a black velvet beret. Ruby red was the lipstick of choice, and her sparkling blue eyes were accentuated by a subtle hint of eye shadow.

Jasper is a typical teenage boy but he was no match for a seductress in disguise. And within minutes, Sally had him laughing away about one thing and another, and before long, she had his phone number and he had hers.

Passengers were bored and tired and the sound of the train soaring through the tunnel was music to their ears.

'It has been nice meeting you,' Jasper said, 'but I have to go now.'

Sally was not to be deterred so she followed him onto the carriage and took a seat by his side.

'So, Jasper, what are you doing tonight?'

Sally couldn't get any closer if she tried, and as he gazed into those seductive blue eyes and ruby red lips, he knew exactly what she had in mind. He was about to venture into uncharted waters without a map or compass.

'I was just going to have a pizza and maybe watch a movie.'

'With Mum, Dad and the kids, perhaps.'

'No, I sort of live alone. If Dad is at home, he is probably in an alcoholic stupor.'

'In that case, I would love to join you, if you don't mind. I am an apprentice chef, and I could whip up a few delectable nibbles…and maybe something else as well.'

They disembarked at Toorak station and wandered down the hill and around the corner. Jasper's home is a red brick Georgian mansion and Sally was impressed.

He never did get an opportunity to watch a movie that Friday evening. Sally had other things on her mind, and as Jasper would eventually find out, Sally always gets her way.

## CHAPTER 62

Jasper's father was diagnosed with liver failure and passed away three months later. It was a difficult time as it coincided with his high school graduation and his eighteenth birthday.

But it could have been a lot worse if it hadn't been for Sally. She took a week off from work, escorted him to the ball and even made a cake for his birthday.

The funeral was a quiet affair, a simple graveside ceremony with a few close friends. Saying goodbye to a loved one is never easy, but Sally stood at Jasper's side and offered what little comfort she could.

As the only remaining member of his family, his mother also made an appearance, in body if not in spirit.

Jasper was the sole beneficiary of his father's estate, and numerous documents had to be signed and countersigned. As a result, he gets to see more of his mother in the solicitor's office than he has in ages.

'Well, Mum, that's the last one,' he says. 'Feel like a coffee before you go back to work.'

'That would be lovely Jaz.'

They spend the next hour wandering through Toorak Village, an exclusive shopping precinct for the well-heeled and the well-to-do.

'Jasper, you are a very wealthy boy now,' Geraldine says. 'What are you going to do with your life?'

'I think I'll sell the house and find somewhere else to live.'

'In that case, I know just the place. It's an interesting building in Fitzroy. Why don't you come over and check it out? It's a bargain compared to anything else in the area.'

'I might just do that,' he says.

Geraldine is the owner of a tapas bar called Donna Isabella's, an inconspicuous little shop in the time capsule that is Brunswick Street, Fitzroy. Whereas Toorak reeks of style, class and money, Fitzroy oozes old world charm and character.

Fitzroy is one of the oldest suburbs in Melbourne and a popular haunt for artists and musicians. Thousands of cottages were built in the early 20th century to cater for the influx of European immigrants and quite a few still exist in their original form.

Fitzroy has always had a colourful mix of people, including the poor, the sad, the lost and the lonely. The seedy boarding houses and brothels of days gone by have been given a new lease of life. And in the 1980s, the young urban professionals moved in and transformed Fitzroy into what it is today.

Jasper is excited at the thought of having his own place. So, he makes an appointment with a real estate agent for the following Saturday morning and meets his mother at 9.30 on the dot so that they can check it out in advance.

The building in question is a narrow red brick structure with decorative features around the top. The windows on the ground floor have been replaced by brickwork. The first and second floors do not appear to be occupied but the top floor apartment has a fancy little balcony at the front.

'Look Mum, it even has a name,' he says. 'The Phoenix, 1914, is etched into the lintel above the door. I wonder if it means anything.'

'I have no idea Jaz, but it appears to be a very solid-looking building.'

'Look up there. It even has a bell tower. I have a feeling this is going to be good.'

'Have you met the agent yet, Jasper?'

'No Mum, I have only spoken to her on the phone. I think she comes from the upper end of town.'

A few minutes later, a jet-black sports car stops at the kerb. And with the skill of a seasoned professional, the driver backs into an empty parking space. A stylish young woman with bright red hair pokes her head through the window and immediately zooms in on Jasper.

'You must be Jasper Powell,' she says.

'Yes, I am.'

'I am Jennifer Bradley. I thought I'd get here first, but you beat me to it.'

Jennifer is an attractive young woman in her late twenties. And even though it may not be her usual attire, she is dressed in a perfectly appointed, two-piece ensemble with matching shoes.

And after a few minutes of general chit-chat, they wander down a side street to the back gate of the Phoenix.

'This is the only access but it's very secure. It's that sort of neighbourhood if you know what I mean.'

Some of the houses in the street are of Victorian vintage, while others were obviously built in the 1940s. Other than that, it appears to be a perfectly respectable street.

The back fence is a bluestone wall with a series of spikes along the top. Jennifer unlocks the gate, and they step back in time to a typical 19th century courtyard.

'This was probably a stable once upon a time, but today it could accommodate three cars or a lap pool, and it even has a wine cellar in the basement.'

Being the business-minded person that she is, Jennifer launches into her sales pitch immediately. Jasper is a prospective client and there is money to be made.

'The Phoenix has had a series of occupants over time, and has been vacant for the last few years, but it is always spotlessly clean.'

'I believe that a local family looks after it, but I have no idea who they are.'

The Phoenix is built on a solid bluestone base, but the lobby is a real surprise and could easily be the entrance to a boutique hotel.

An ornately carved staircase winds its way to the top floor. Filtered light streams in through a beautiful stained-glass window, and an ornamental lamp suspended from the ceiling adds a touch of quiet sophistication.

'This is really beautiful, isn't it Mum?'

'It certainly is Jaz.'

'The design of the Phoenix is based on the Art Nouveau style, which is usually leaves and tendrils and that sort of thing,' Jennifer says.

'But if you look closely, you will see that it's actually a hotbed of snakes, vipers and serpents.'

'Oh, really,' Jasper says.

'Is that a problem.'

'Well, we'll see. Perhaps we should take a look first.'

'In that case, follow me.'

They make their way up three flights of stairs, and the moment that Jasper steps through the door he is impressed.

The top floor apartment is a vast open space with polished wooden floors and a view of Fitzroy through every window. A beautifully carved cornice eases its way around the ceiling, and at the very apex is what appears to be a bell tower.

'That's not a real bell tower, is it?'

'No, it's not Jasper. If you look closely, you will see that it is a woman with a crown of serpents on her head.'

'Snakes again,' he groans.

The very mention of the word is enough to send him into a spin, and for a very good reason, he has been dreaming about them for years.

'This is the work of a very accomplished craftsman' Geraldine says. 'Do you know anything about the builder?'

'Not much, other than the fact that his wife was the inspiration for the décor. Apparently, she was a great beauty from somewhere like India.'

'He was a snake charmer and she was commonly known as the snake charmer's wife.'

'Really,' Jasper says.

He inspects the statue closely and realises that it has the same face as that of his Lady Friend. This is the very same woman who has been appearing in his dreams ever since he was a boy.

As he gazes into her eyes, a tingling sensation slithers up his spine like a snake slithering up a pole. It stops for a few seconds and then surges up his backbone.

And at that moment, an unusual display of lights appear at the far end of the room. Unbeknownst to Jasper, this is the energetic activity that precedes the appearance of a spirit from the spirit world.

The ghostly form of a woman in silken veils steps through an invisible portal, drifts around the room, opens her arms and nods her head as if to say, this is an excellent idea, Jasper.

'Jasper, are you alright? Geraldine says. 'You're as white as a sheet.'

'Yes Mum. I'm just a little light-headed, but I'll be okay in a few minutes.'

Geraldine knows all about his Lady Friend and even took him to see a psychologist when he was ten years old but it was to no avail.

Jasper's Lady Friend continued to appear like clockwork. As to who she is, he has no idea, but her usual routine is to gaze into his eyes as if she is aching to take him into her arms.

'So, Jaz, what do you think?' Geraldine says.

'It really is beautiful Mum.'

'It would be a shame to let someone else get hold of it.'

'I know Mum. It would, wouldn't it?'

'So, what will you do, my boy?'

Jasper is in a quandary and his instincts are to walk away and forget he ever saw the place, but his Lady Friend obviously has a different idea.

From the look on her face, it's apparent that she is beseeching him to throw caution to the wind and just do it.

'I think I will take it, Mum.'

'Congratulations,' Jennifer says. 'You have made an excellent choice.'

This is the biggest decision that Jasper has ever made in his life, and whether he likes it or not, the die has been cast. A few days later, he becomes the proud owner of a prime piece of Victorian real estate.

And as he will soon find out, he is also the custodian of a major piece of its forgotten history. The Phoenix has its secrets, and it has been waiting for someone to work out exactly what it is.

Jasper never mentioned that experience to anyone. To see a ghost in the clear light of day was weird enough, but that tingling sensation and that golden light. What was that all about?

That is the least of his problems at the moment. In just over three weeks, his father's house will go to auction, and he has a million things to do.

He spent days wading through seventy years of memorabilia, but the most difficult room of all was his father's library. It was filled to the rafters with photographs that had not seen the light of day since the 1950s.

Over the next three weeks, people come and go to do one thing or another, but it could have been a lot worse if not for a very efficient young woman from a local cleaning company.

Rosanna Forenza supervised a team of busy people who prepared the house for its big day, and even Geraldine is impressed.

'I have never seen it looking so good,' she says. 'You have done an amazing job Jasper.'

'It wasn't me, Mum. It was Rosanna.'

Just about everyone at the auction is a lawyer, a doctor, or a merchant banker. And while some are doing their best to look as unobtrusive as possible, a few are obviously from the shady side of town.

To purchase a house in Toorak is an opportunity to stake their claim to a slice of hallowed ground. And for one nameless face in the crowd, it's a bargain at 4.5 million Australian dollars.

'So, Jasper, what are you going to do with the furniture?' Geraldine says.

His father was an avid collector of 19th century furniture of one style or another. And an antique dealer with an eye for a bargain would happily take everything off his hands.

Jasper wasn't about to dispose of his heritage altogether and decided to save a few things for himself, especially his father's wine cellar.

Before he wanders out the gate and up the hill, he takes one last look at his family home. That old Georgian mansion has served its purpose, but now it's time to move on. It has far too many memories and Jasper wants to leave them exactly where they are.

## CHAPTER 63

Rattling around in an empty apartment felt very strange for the first few weeks, but Jasper was never alone. His Lady Friend made an impromptu visit at least once a day.

The tell-tale sign was that all-too-familiar tingling sensation, and after that he would drift around in a daze and his feet barely even touched the ground.

Kashmira made an appearance on the night that Sally stayed over, and that was all it took. A few days later, she moved in, accompanied by a black cat called Merlin.

As soon as he saw something out of the corner of his eye, he made a beeline for the front balcony, and that's where he stayed for the next three months.

A rusty old stove was the only appliance in the kitchen, so Jasper ripped it out, activated his brand new bank card and then did a bit of serious shopping.

He spent a small fortune on a new state-of-the-art kitchen, a huge black and white couch, and several wingback chairs. But Sally wasn't about to let the dining room table or the French armoires gather dust in the basement.

They spend the next few weeks trawling through some of Fitzroy's best antique shops where she spied an exotic hand-crafted canopy bed.

Sally spent ages decorating it with exotic Indian saris, and when it was finished, Jasper christened it the boudoir of the Queen of Sheba.

A plaque at the bottom of the stairs stated that The Phoenix was completed on the 28th of March 1914, and that gave him an inspired idea.

'Why don't we have a house-warming party and invite a few people over?'

Their biggest problem was how to trim down an extensive list of friends, and the only solution was to pick a name out of a hat. It's a task for which they have to pluck up a bit of old-fashioned Dutch courage but there was plenty to choose from.

Over five thousand bottles from the Toorak wine cellar have been stored away in the basement, and it only takes two bottles of a finely aged red before they are ready to roll.

'Okay, I'll go first,' Jasper says as he selects the first name from a hat. 'Ah ha, the Queen of the Witches is a certainty.'

There are not many people who can say that the Queen of the Witches is one of their best friends, but Jasper can, thanks to his mother, of course.

Mortisha is the very essence of modern day witchiness who wears a long black dress from nine to five, and other than that, she has nothing in common with the unflappable Morticia of Addams Family fame.

As everyone knows, she is a fictitious creation, but Mortisha Montserrat has two principal interests, one of which is handsome men and the other is a passion for high-class fashion.

'Your turn,' he says to Sally.

She is just about to select a name from the hat when a gust of wind scatters little bits of paper all over the floor.

'Now that was seriously creepy,' she says. 'Is this place haunted?'

Jasper hasn't had the heart to tell her that strange things have been happening ever since he moved in.

'I think it might be,' he says.

'What do you mean by that Jasper?'

'Well, ever since I was a boy, a woman has been appearing in my dreams, but for some reason she has decided to make an appearance in my life as well.'

'So, who is she, Jasper, and what does she want?'

'I don't know, but whenever she appears, I get all sort of tingly.'

'Like goose bumps you mean?'

'No, it's like every cell in my system starts to vibrate at light speed, and I feel as if I'm out there somewhere and here at the same time.'

'I have no idea what that means,' Sally says. 'Perhaps she fancies you, Jasper.'

'A desire to seduce me is not it at all Sally. My Lady Friend has never done anything like that, not once, but she is obviously hanging around for a reason.'

'Like what Jasper?'

'It has something to do with this place.'

'So, what does she want?'

'I think she is trying to tell me something.'

'And what would that be?'

'I don't know. Maybe she was murdered in this very apartment and wants someone to find out.'

'The spirits of the departed do not rest easily, especially if they have been maligned,' Sally says in an overly theatrical manner. 'They usually hang about until their issues have been resolved.'

'That's the sort of thing Mortisha would say. Perhaps she can solve this problem.

'I have had enough of this situation. It's getting all too creepy and it's not normal either.'

# CHAPTER 64

Sally has to face a twelve-hour day slaving away in a high-class restaurant in upper Collins Street. She is usually out of the house by five thirty in the morning but Jasper doesn't drag himself out until nine, after which he sits on the balcony and savours the first coffee of the day.

His one and only dream has been to write a best-selling novel, and he would love to peck away at one of his manuscripts, but that's not going to happen, not at the moment.

When all else fails, he heads off to the Melbourne Baths to do a few laps in the pool. The City Baths are a twenty-minute walk through the beautiful Carlton Gardens, and after a hundred or so laps, he usually wanders over the road to soak up the atmosphere of the fabled Queen Victoria Markets.

The Old Vic Markets are as popular with the locals as they are with the tourists, but only the most resolute have the power to resist the aroma of freshly cooked food wafting through the air.

But today, Jasper has other things on his mind, so he decides to go and see his mother instead.

At this time of the day, Geraldine is usually preparing the delicacies for the midday rush, and she sometimes needs an extra pair of hands.

'Jasper, it's so lovely to see you,' she says. 'I'm running a little late. Mind giving me a hand?'

'Definitely Mum. What do you want me to do?'

'Peel the prawns, prepare the whitebait, and cut up the squid, to start with.'

'You mean this sloppy mess on the bench.'

'Yes Jaz.'

Desecrating a few lifeless menu items is good therapy. At least it gives him something to think about, and as far as Jasper is concerned, he has done enough thinking for one day.

'The smelly jobs for the hired help,' he says. 'No problemo, Mama.'

Geraldine loves all things Spanish and today she is dressed in a deep green skirt, a bright red scarf, big chunky earrings, a healthy application of eye shadow and a string of glitzy beads.

She doesn't regret giving up a lucrative career as a gynecologist, and she certainly doesn't miss the stress of being a medical professional. Geraldine is doing something that she loves.

'Thirty minutes to countdown,' she says. 'Just enough time for a glass of wine and a quick cigarette.'

When they step out the back door, she offers Jasper his first ever cigarette. He has never been tempted before but today he jumps at the opportunity.

'You look a little worried Jaz. Is everything okay with you and Sally?'

'Yes Mum, it's all good, but it's that apartment. I think it's haunted.'

'Really, that must explain why it was such a bargain.'

'But there's more, I am still having those dreams about my Lady Friend but she's there as well.'

'What do you mean, Jaz?'

'Well, she just pops in sometimes, not to scare me or anything, but I always know when she's around.'

'Why, what does she do?'

'Well, it's nothing awful, but I get all weird and tingly, like I am about to take flight or something.'

'Really Jasper, that does sound interesting.'

'I wish I knew why Mum, but the last time it happened all I could think about was Dad.'

'Your father experienced something like that after his mother died. He was always saying that he could see her in the house.'

'It took its toll on both of us after a while, which is another reason I moved out.'

'I have a feeling that there is something going on,' he says. 'And she wants me to do something about it.'

'This sounds like a case for Mortisha, High Queen of the Witches,' Geraldine says. 'You've got her number, haven't you?'

'Yes Mum, I have.'

'Jaz, my boy. Things happen for a reason, and I would not be surprised if you have been chosen to solve a long-standing problem.'

'That sexy she-devil might have you in her sights but don't ignore her. I think she likes you, my boy.'

'I think she does Mum, but I wish I knew why, because I can't take much more of this.'

## CHAPTER 65

Jasper often pops in to have a quiet chat with Mortisha but it's not a good idea to rock up unannounced. The last time he did that, she was entertaining a coterie of like-minded souls.

An eerily cat-like woman swathed in long silken veils took a fancy to him immediately. Lucrezia Lavarre was a vaporous spirit on two legs whose primary means of expression was through long breathy pauses.

In an effort to cleanse his aura of a few unwanted visitors she spent ages showering him with invigorating little molecules. Or that's what she said at any rate.

Jasper knocks politely and just hopes for the best. To his relief, Mortisha opens the door and not Mademoiselle Lavarre.

'Is this a good time,' he says.

'Yes Jasper. My lady friends have taken flight.'

After a compulsory kiss on both cheeks, she stands back and scrutinises him in the way that only a witch can do.

'I have a feeling that something big is about to pop up.'

'I hope not, Mortisha.'

'There is definitely something going on with you, young man. Now come on in and tell me everything.'

Mortisha has long black hair and deep black eyes, and today, she is dressed in her work clothes, a close-fitting black dress with a tail that usually attracts little bits of lint, fluff, and dust.

As to her age, Jasper has no idea. She could be a hundred or she could be forty. She is a witch after all and probably knows the secret of immortality.

Her house looks like every other house on the street, until you get inside that is. The focal point of the lounge is an enormous crystal ball, and above that is a ceiling which resembles an elegant if not creepy spider's web.

Jasper has never had the courage to ask about the strange green glow emanating from a door at the far end of the room.

For all he knows it could be a portal to the world beyond. But he is relieved to see that there is not another soul in sight, other than her shaggy old cat, Methuselah.

'Would you like a cup of tea?' she says.

'Anything Mortisha, as long as you don't spike it with something.'

'You are in a bad way, my boy. I think you are in need of sedation.'

While she attends to a simple domestic task, Jasper just goes for it and tells her everything.

'So, when your Lady Friend appears, you experience a heightened sense of arousal, shall we say?'

'Not that sort of arousal, Mortisha.'

'Okay, tell me more.'

'It starts at the base of my spine, like a tingling sensation at first, and then every cell in my body goes into overdrive.'

'So, you feel energised, you could say.'

'Yes Mortisha, big time, like a power plant on two legs.'

'Jasper, have you ever heard of the Kundalini?'

'No Mortisha, I haven't. What is it?'

'It's a reservoir of power at the base of the spine, and once activated, it flows up to the brain and opens the way for experiences of a non-physical nature.'

'It's not life-threatening, is it Mortisha?'

'For first timers, it can be temporarily debilitating, but for the experienced, it is unadulterated bliss.'

'If the Kundalini ever makes an appearance, magic can happen. Your energy system operates on full power for a few glorious hours, and you feel as light as the proverbial feather, so to speak.'

'Then that must be it, Mortisha. What else could it be?'

'What you have described is what the Holy Men of India experience Jasper. It happens for a reason in their case.'

'However, once this situation has been resolved, you will never experience it again, but you never know.'

'But why is it happening to me, Mortisha.'

'Your Lady Friend obviously activates that energy when she makes an appearance. It seems that she is determined to communicate something to you and to you alone.'

'You obviously have a connection with this woman. Perhaps you were lovers in a previous life.'

'I don't think so, Mortisha. I think she has something to reveal, and she has chosen me to do it. Why I cannot imagine, but she has.'

'In which case, I will look into this in my own way, and I will let you know what I find out.'

'You never know what else might pop up, Jasper.'

'In the meantime, did you enjoy the tea?'

'You didn't put hemlock in it, after all, did you?'

'No Jasper, that would have been fatal. Not that I would have. You were doing perfectly well without any help from me.'

## CHAPTER 66

To Jasper's mind, that idea does make sense, but it leaves him with a lot to think about. Not knowing what else to do, he wanders along Brunswick Street, and on an impulse, he decides to investigate a spiritual bookshop.

Entering *The Lighthouse* is like stepping into a highly charged sanctuary. The air is infused with incense, and hundreds of crystals suspended from the ceiling allude to a very otherworldly feeling.

*The Lighthouse* has an interesting selection of books on all sorts of New Age topics, including channelling, spirit guides and other out-of-the-world things.

Jasper works his way through one shelf after another until he finds a book called *Meditations on the Kundalini* by a man called Swami Jagatpati.

'That's just the thing,' he says.

He races up to the counter, hands over the money and then heads for the peace and quiet of the Fitzroy Public Library.

According to the cover, Swami Jagatpati is a holy man who claims to have reached a state of Godhead through intensive meditation, and he is also a self-professed expert who has spent most of his life in a state of Kundalini-inspired bliss.

This is new territory and Jasper is intrigued. The Kundalini has a long and ancient history but the thing that really takes him by surprise is the fact that it has always been depicted as a serpent.

'Ah ha, that explains all that weirdness. Now it's starting to make sense. My never-ending snake dreams have nothing to do with snakes at all.'

But it's what the Swami has to say about the effect of the Kundalini on lovers both young and old that really wins Jasper over.

'Ooh, Sally will love to hear about that.'

Now that he knows that he is not possessed by evil spirits he starts to relax, but before he goes, he decides to inspect an exhibit on the local area.

Brunswick Street has had several incarnations over time and many of the grander buildings date from the 1850s. Melbourne went through a building boom following the discovery of gold but everything changed after the 1850s.

Entire blocks were razed to the ground. Living conditions were abysmal. Houses were in a pitiful state, and immorality and drunkenness were rife.

'And the lives of the inhabitants were nothing if not deplorable,' he says. 'Things must have been absolutely horrible in those days.'

He is just about to give this idea up as a lost cause when it moves into even stranger territory. Jasper has never been one to hear voices in his head, but he has the distinct feeling that someone just whispered in his ear.

'Jasper, search and you will find.'

'I am doing my best,' he says.

He suddenly remembers a conversation he had with Jennifer Bradley.

'So, what's in the other two apartments?' he had said.

'No one knows, Jasper. We don't have the keys.'

'What about the pub on the ground floor?'

'I can't say as no one has ever seen it. The real estate company only have the keys to the top floor apartment.'

'But the contract clearly states that they will be transferred to the new owner after they take possession. Apparently, the owners of the building can only be contacted through a private mailbox in Colombo.'

# CHAPTER 67

All the clues are probably staring him in the face, but the last thing that Jasper wants is to pack his bags and head off to Sri Lanka.

He delays his return for as long as possible and decides to have a coffee to pass the time, but when he gets back home it's only to find the back gate unlocked.

'Oh no, this isn't good,' he says. 'What will I do?'

He doesn't have a macho muscle in his body, and no martial arts skills at all. Sally won't be home for another hour so it couldn't be her, and the last thing he wants is to wrestle an intruder to the ground.

'There is no way that they could get in, not unless they are some sort of modern-day cat burglar.'

He had the locks changed to an electronic system, and only he and Sally know the password. That can only mean that the intruders are in one of the other two apartments.

He has been up and down the stairs at least five hundred times in the last two months and has often wondered what lies behind the other doors.

He has a feeling that he is about to find out, so, he creeps up to the door, and to his relief it is locked.

'So, they're in the other one,' he says.

He moves along quietly, his heart pounding away in his chest, but to his dismay, the door on the second floor is ajar. Not much, but it is.

Oddly enough, he just happens to notice an old-fashioned fragrance wafting through the air.

'Cashmere Bouquet. That's what my grandmother used to wear.'

Jasper is not about to rush in unannounced, so he braces himself and takes a long deep breath.

'Come out whoever you are. This is private property, and you are trespassing.'

The worst thing about living in the modern age is the fear factor. Television has been brainwashing people for decades, making them believe that everything is dangerous, that their food is carcinogenic, that their neighbours are the enemy, and at any given moment, they will strike you down and that will be that.

But the last person he expected to see is a lovely white-haired old lady peering cautiously around the door.

'Don't hurt us sonny,' she says. 'Please don't hurt us. We don't mean any harm.'

'Are you Jasper Powell by any chance?'

'Yes, I am, but who are you?'

'My name is Bella, Arabella José and this is my husband Paz, Pasquale. We are your neighbours, Jasper.'

Jasper is not about to be mugged by two of the loveliest old people you could ever wish to see. And they really are his neighbours. He has often seen Paz pottering around in the back garden.

'But what are you doing here?'

'Jasper, we are here to give you the keys,' Bella says. 'But before we do, perhaps you could oblige us with a cup of tea.'

'I could,' he says. 'I definitely could.'

'Please take my arm as I am an old lady now and it takes ages to get up these stairs.'

There are exactly thirty-three steps between each floor, and it's slow going with Bella on one arm and Paz on the other, but they eventually make it to the top.

'Jasper, your apartment is beautiful,' Bella says. 'But where is your girlfriend?'

'She'll be here soon.'

'Jasper, you boil the kettle, and we will sit down and wait. We have a few things to tell you.'

Jasper sends a quick text message to Sally, alerting her to the fact that they have company. And while he's at it he sends one to Mortisha and his mother as well.

He races back and forth with cups and saucers, milk, sugar, and biscuits, and is just about to pour the tea when all three appear at the door at once.

'I know you,' Geraldine says as she races over to Bella. 'I've seen you before.'

'Yes, we pass your shop, but only on a Thursday,' Bella says. 'We have never stopped in for a chat but I have often thought we should.'

'You're Donna Isabella, aren't you?'

'Yes, I am, but my real name is Geraldine Powell.'

As to how he was going to get hold of the keys, Jasper had no idea, but this is the last thing he expected.

Bella and Paz have a story to tell, and everyone is waiting on tenterhooks to find out the secrets of The Phoenix.

'Our parents arrived as immigrants just after the Spanish Civil War of 1937,' Bella said.

'The Franco regime targeted anyone who was still loyal to the king, and my family barely escaped with their lives.'

'Paz and I were born in Melbourne, and we have been married for over fifty years. This building has been here for at least a hundred years and my father was the third caretaker.'

'We lived here for many years but after my parents passed on, we brought the house next door.'

'We had to move out, Jasper. There are too many stairs to climb for one thing but that's not the only reason.'

'It's haunted, isn't it?' he says.

Paz knows exactly what he's talking about.

'Yes, it is,' Bella says. 'This is not a good place for a man to live as you have probably found out, but it does have its secrets.'

'Tell us everything you know,' Jasper says.

'Well, I don't know as much as I would like, but maybe you can find out more.'

According to Bella, The Phoenix has a resident ghost who targets any able-bodied male.

'But that isn't all. On the two floors below, there are hundreds of wooden boxes.'

'Really,' Jasper says.

'Yes, we have no idea what they are. I don't think its treasure but it's big, whatever it is.'

'This building was constructed several years after the Melbourne International Exhibition of 1880. My mother told me that and I am sure it's important but I don't know why.'

'There were other caretakers before my father, and if they knew anything about this place, they took the secret to their graves.'

'Do you have any idea who built it Bella?'

'No Jasper, I don't.'

'I believe it has something to do with the woman who has been appearing in my dreams,'

'The ghost you mean?' Bella says.

'Yes, she has been doing it for the last ten years, and I suspect that she has something to do with this place.'

'She even whispered a message in my ear when I was in the library this afternoon.'

'She did,' says an astonished Mortisha. 'What did she say?

'Search and you will find were her exact words.'

# CHAPTER 68

Jasper's Lady Friend appears in his dreams again that night but not as a puff of smoke. This time she is waiting at the edge of a cliff adorned in long silken veils.

It's a wild and stormy night, the winds are howling and monstrous breakers are rolling onto the shore, but this is no sightseeing tour, it has another purpose altogether.

Jasper is about to witness the destruction of a ship trapped in a raging storm. The sails are in tatters, and it's heading for an outcrop of rock, and in a tempest such as this it doesn't have a hope.

The storm eventually subsides, and by morning light, there is nothing left but debris scattered along the beach. The fate of the only survivor may have been different if a little girl and her father had not come to his rescue.

'That boy may have died,' his Lady Friend said. 'If it had not been for us.'

Another part of the puzzle is falling into place, and if Jasper is correct, that was the coastline of Sri Lanka.

As to who the boy was, he has no idea, but if he wants to find out, he has no choice but to check out the other two apartments.

He ventures downstairs with a flashlight in one hand and a cast iron key in the other, and to his relief, the lock opens with ease.

He pokes his head around the door, expecting to see rats, mice, and cobwebs all over the place but it's spotlessly clean.

To his amazement, this really is a storage place for hundreds of wooden crates, all of which are stacked from the floor to the ceiling.

'Holee, this is massive,' he says. 'How did they get them in here? And how would you get them out?'

The only way would be to remove the front wall, but that would cause chaos for three days at the very least. Brunswick Street is a busy road with trams and cars coming and going every other minute.

He wanders along, only to discover that every crate is numbered. As to what they contain, he could not even imagine, but someone obviously went to great lengths to protect this treasure.

'But who were they and why?'

He is just about to lock up when he hears someone coming up the stairs.

'Jasper. Are you there?' says a familiar voice.

'Yes Mortisha, I am. Come on in and feast your eyes on this.'

'Oh, my goodness. What is this?'

'An undiscovered treasure, I presume. It's pretty impressive, isn't it?'

'Oh Jaz, you're right. This is truly extraordinary, and it's been here for how long?'

'One hundred years at the very least.'

'I would love to take a quick look. Wouldn't you?'

'Yes of course Mortisha, but I don't think now is the time. My Lady Friend might not approve.'

'Do you have any idea who she is?'

'No, but she appeared in my dreams again last night. Only this time she was waiting on the edge of a cliff.'

'Any reason why.'

'A ship was wrecked in a storm and the only survivor was a young boy.'

'Let's go upstairs and have a cup of tea Jasper, so that we can discuss this in the clear light of day.'

While Jasper potters around in the kitchen, Mortisha wanders back and forth, conscious of the fact that this really is the discovery of the century.

'I had a feeling about you when we first met.'

'Like what, that I'm a deviant or something.'

'No, Jasper, that wasn't it at all. However, I know a lot of people who are.'

'You said that you were going to do a bit of investigating, Mortisha. Did you come up with anything?'

'Oddly enough, I did.'

'What special powers did you use?'

'Nothing at all, other than a bottle of red wine, but I didn't get anything, not until three o'clock this morning.'

'That's power shower time for anyone of an unearthly nature.'

'I drifted off into the distant past, a marketplace in an exotic Indian city with people buying and selling just about everything you can imagine.'

'A bazaar,' Jasper says.

'Yes, incense, caged birds and monkeys, the whole shebang, but the star attraction was a snake charmer.'

'A snake charmer, that is interesting.'

'Exactly, but get this Jaz, everyone else was Indian, but he wasn't. He was Spanish or Portuguese or something like that.'

'He might have been the survivor of the shipwreck,' Jasper says.

'You mean the boy on the beach.'

'Yes, and when I woke up this morning, I knew that it was Sri Lanka.'

Mortisha sits bolt upright and casts a witchy eye around the room. 'Ooh, I think your Lady Friend might be listening in on our conversation.'

'Well, that's good,' Jasper says. 'Now would be a good time to let us know if we are on the right track.'

They are half expecting their teacups to become airborne at any given moment but nothing happens.

'She is obviously not the vindictive type.'

'No, she never has been, So, tell me more about this snake charmer.'

'He was a handsome young man with the most magnificent physique you have ever seen.'

'He had a gift with the flute and it was enough to stop people in their stride, but he wasn't working alone.'

'An old man in the background was stoking the fumes of a slowly burning fire, and his companion was a woman in silken veils.'

'But this was no ordinary woman, Jasper. She was hauntingly beautiful.'

'And what did she do?'

'She had everyone in her spell as she danced around the flames and enticed seven cobras out of a basket.'

'Seven,' Jasper says.

'Yes, and when the smoke cleared, the cobras had vanished, and she was wearing a crown of serpents on her head.'

'Like that,' Jasper says as he points to the statue in the bell tower.

'That's exactly what she looked like.'

# CHAPTER 69

Sally usually gets home around six thirty in the evening but it's almost seven and Jasper is beside himself with excitement. And when she finally appears at the door he just has to tell her everything.

'Sal, you have to see what we've got.'

She follows him down to the second floor, but Sally doesn't know what to think when she sees hundreds of packing crates lined up in perfect formation.

'Oh my God, there's so much of it, Jasper. It's probably a monument of some sort.'

'I wouldn't be surprised if it is Sal.'

'And you have no idea where it came from?'

'Possibly Sri Lanka. Maybe we should have a closer look at the legal documents. They might tell us something.'

They dash back upstairs and read one letter after another.

'Here it is,' Sally says, 'I have found it.'

'It says that The Phoenix has been held in trust since 1914 by the Bank of Colombo. A primary clause states that it is not to be offered for sale until the year 2014.'

'They obviously have no idea that it's packed to the rafters with something valuable,' Jasper says.

'But someone must have established a trust or something like that Jasper. It's a legal transaction, for one thing.'

'Things were different back then Sal.'

'Jennifer Bradley did say that the Bank of Colombo would send me all of their correspondence.'

'Have you checked the mailbox lately, Jasper?'

'Not for a while.'

'Then pop downstairs and take a look.'

The mailbox was empty the last time he looked, so Jasper opens it tentatively and the contents spew out onto the floor.

'Holee, what is this?'

He gathers it up, races up the stairs and dumps it all over the dining room table.

'You were right Sal. Look at this, and it's all from the Bank of Colombo.'

'You pour the wine while I track down my trusty old letter opener.'

The envelopes are the old-fashioned brown paper variety with stamps from every decade of the 20th century.

'Sal, they might be worth something,' he says.

'Who cares about that Jasper?'

She places bank statements at one end of the table and legal documents at the other, but the most interesting thing of all is a parcel wrapped in some sort of animal hide.

'It's a book, possibly a diary, and it may hold the answer to this mystery. I think we should leave it to last.'

'You go first,' she says. 'Pick a letter, any letter.'

Jasper removes a faded piece of paper from an old brown envelope, a letter that looks like a page from a long-forgotten history book.

'It's from the Barcelona Steamship Company in Spain and it's addressed to someone called Juan Philippe Delgado.'

'Read it,' Sally says. 'I can't stand the suspense.'

*Senor Delgado*

*This is to inform you that we have dispatched your goods to Melbourne, Australia. They should arrive three months prior to the Melbourne International Exhibition. They will be stored in the warehouse of the Adelaide Steamship Company at the dockside in Melbourne.*

*We have been advised that it will be collected by a Mr. William Sergeant, a local businessman who will see that your goods are safely delivered to the Exhibition site. An engineer called Mr. Robert Peterson has been engaged to erect the structure according to your instructions.*

*Your Trusted Servant*

*Manuel da Silva, Managing Director, Barcelona Steamship Company.*

'I believe that part one of this mystery has just been solved,' Sally says. 'And we really do have a treasure on our hands.'

Jasper places the letter on the table, slumps into one of his new wingback chairs and just sighs.

'I don't want to read any more Sally. I need a breath of fresh air. Why don't we go for a walk?'

Jasper is a million miles away, totally oblivious of the passing traffic, or that he is surrounded by the time capsule that is Brunswick Street by night.

'I have a feeling that there's an interesting story behind this, one that features a snake charmer and the snake charmer's wife.'

'I am beginning to agree with you Jasper, but she must have been something special if he wanted to create a memorial in her honour.'

'Well, she is hauntingly beautiful, and I should know because I have seen her every night for the last ten years.'

'And they must have had a wonderful love life as well.'

'Sally Velasko, there are names for people like you.'

'Overly amorous, perhaps.'

'I suppose that's one way of describing it, but lust and love are two different things, as you no doubt know.'

**208**

'That I do know, Jasper, at least I do now. But it does help if that person is someone special.'

'That's true,' he says.

Jasper had no idea what love was, not until Sally came along. She appeared out of the blue when he needed someone to replace fourteen carers, one deceased father and a mother he rarely ever saw. Sally just kept coming back and he wasn't about to complain.

The thing that really brought them together was the passing of his father. To lose someone you love is a powerful experience, but Sally was there from the start. She held his hand by the graveside. They cried their hearts out for the next few days and they have never looked back.

'I love you Sally, you know that don't you?'

'Of course, I do Jasper.'

'Ooh,' she squeals in a particularly playful voice. 'I have just had a wonderful idea.'

Jasper is immediately worried. He has heard that titter of excitement before but only in the bedroom.

'No, we can't do it here, Sally, not in the middle of the street.'

'Not that, Jasper. I think we should celebrate. I just happen to know this lovely little tapas bar called Donna Isabella's and it's just up the road from here.'

'Sounds good to me, but don't be surprised if you end up waiting on tables and ladling out the soup.'

'Easy as,' she says. 'I do that all day long.'

## CHAPTER 70

Every table at Donna Isabella's is packed to capacity and Geraldine is about to lose the plot, but she thanks her lucky stars when Jasper and Sally appear at the door.

'The casual staff called in sick. Care to help me out for a while.'

'Sure thing,' Jasper says.

He spends the next four hours washing dishes and ladling out the soup, but Sally is a godsend, and she really does know her way around the kitchen.

They work non-stop until just after midnight but there's nothing much to clean up, Sally has it all under control. And when the last of the customers finally stumble out the door, they sit down for a well-earned glass of wine.

'Thank you,' Geraldine says. 'I had no idea what I was going to do but you saved the day.'

'What can I ever do to repay you?'

'Nothing Mum. It's all good,' Jasper says. 'But you will never believe what we have got.'

Geraldine listens closely as he tells her about the horde of mail they received from the Bank of Colombo.

'We will probably start reading the diary tomorrow. And somehow or another, I think it's going to be a lot more interesting than one old letter.'

'You've gotta be there Mum.'

'I wouldn't miss out on that for anything, Jasper, but Sunday would be better as I have the day off.'

'In that case, food and drinks are on us.'

'Why don't you invite Bella and Paz along as well. They would love to find out the truth.'

'But I will have to invite Mortisha along as well, otherwise she will curse me until the end of time, especially if she misses out on the find of the century.'

'She would never do that Jaz. She is a white witch after all.'

It's almost two o'clock when they finally get home, and the moment his head hits the pillow, Jasper is out like a light. He isn't used to working in the fast-paced world of a modern-day restaurant or anywhere else for that matter.

They sleep in until ten and then take a seat on the balcony, along with the first coffee of the day.

'I am absolutely starving,' Jasper says.

'Why don't we have breakfast at the Old Vic Markets,' Sally says. 'And after that we can do a spot of grocery shopping.'

'I'll vote for that,' he says.

The Queen Victoria Markets was once the site of a graveyard, but that's ancient history now. People travel from far and wide to spend a day at the Old Vic Markets. And they have a lot more to offer than just the ambience, they also have the best food in town.

'Jasper, I have the menu all planned out,' Sally says.

'So, what have you got in mind?'

'A slow cooked leg of lamb basted in freshly squeezed orange juice, which I will serve up with baked vegetables, of course.'

'You will love it, Jasper. It will literally melt in your mouth. And after that, we will have an Asian-style dessert followed by a delicious homemade cake with coffee.'

'How does that sound?'

'Positively scrumptious, but we have to get a few nibbles for me too Sal. I get absolutely ravenous after my Lady Friend comes a-calling.'

'That's good to know Master. You can have anything that your heart desires.'

Saturday morning is the busiest time at the Markets, but you don't have to battle your way through the crowds every step of the way, and if you do, that's half the fun.

The Old Vic Markets sell everything from home-made treats and delicacies to freshly caught seafood. But if you are an epicurean, a pleasure-seeking hedonist or just a lover of fine food, the Vic Markets have it all.

They also have the best delicatessens in town, and if you are so inclined, you can even do a gourmet tour and sample a few things on the way.

Sally wanders around and selects the finest local produce, while Jasper munches away on anything that takes his fancy.

But he is powerless to resist a Bratwurst roll with grilled onions and mustard. He scoffs down a whole punnet of fresh strawberries, and to finish it off, he has a triple scoop of peppermint ice-cream.

Three hours later, their shopping trolley is full to overflowing.

'Sally, I think we brought way too much of everything.'

'That's not a problem Jasper. We have a brand-new refrigerator, and we also have the biggest pantry in the known world.'

'We could rent it out as a refuge for the homeless.'

'Oh, you wouldn't do that, would you Sal? What if they were a little light in the head or something?'

'I have no doubt that your Lady Friend would come to your rescue.'

'She doesn't have a body, Sal. She's just a spirit-like thing.'

'In that case, she could scare them to death.'

## CHAPTER 71

Sally spends the next few hours preparing a few delicacies for their Sunday lunch, but Jasper sits at his desk exploring the world of modern-day transport vehicles.

He has decided that he wants a car and is currently inspecting the muscular features of a Jeep Wrangler when Sally appears at his side.

'Jasper, you look all sort of strange. What's going on?'

'She's here Sal. My Lady Friend is back.'

Sally has no idea what happens when the snake charmer's wife makes an appearance. She has never seen a ghost or imagined that she ever would, but this really is unusual.

'Jasper, your face is glowing. Are you okay?'

'Never better,' he said.

'Perhaps you should lie down for a while.'

'Not just yet Sal. Want to see what it feels like?'

If Sally has ever experienced anything of a supernatural nature before she has never said so. And the very instant that their hands make contact, every cell in her body bursts into life.

'Oh, my God, Jasper, that is so amazing.'

'It is and I now know what it is.'

'So, what is it?' she says.

'I read about it in a book on the Kundalini. Swami Jagatpati says that holy men use the power of the Kundalini to leave their body. And apparently, they can also travel through space and time.'

'How do they do that?'

'The Kundalini is a sacred energy, Sal, some sort of universal energy or something like that. And believe it or not, it has always been represented as a snake.'

'So, your Lady Friend is a snake charmer, but of another kind.'

'Yes, I guess so, and when she appears, my Kundalini becomes active.'

'The serpent represents many things, like wisdom and creativity, but if the Kundalini ever pops up, things can happen.'

'Like what for example.'

'Well, you really know that you're alive, for one thing. I don't know whether you can walk through walls or fly to the Moon, but apparently, you can heal people.'

'If you know your bible stories Sally, you will remember that a serpent played a prominent role in the story of Adam and Eve.'

'I never did understand the point of that story, Jasper. What was all that stuff about not eating the fruit of the apple tree?'

'That's the tree of knowledge. Apparently, it was a warning to Adam and Eve.'

'Now you've lost me, Jasper. A warning about what?'

'About not succumbing to the power of the dark side, to evil in other words, but the serpent also represents enlightenment.'

'Have you ever been into a spiritual bookshop Sal?'

'Lots of times Jasper. They're all over the place.'

'The enlightenment industry is big business these days because people are searching for answers. They want to know why we are here and what life is all about and that sort of stuff.'

'So, what's that got to do with the Kundalini?'

'Quite a lot actually.'

'When the Kundalini is active, it means that you have one foot in this world and one in the next. And, you cannot only feel it, you know that it's happening.'

'At this moment, I feel as if I am about ten feet tall and as light as a feather, and when I walk, my feet don't even touch the ground.'

'However, listen to what Swami Jagatpati has to say about one of your favourite pastimes, Sal.'

*"For lovers both young and old, there is nothing that can equal a supreme state of sublime bliss and joy. It is that one indefinable moment when you and your partner become one with the universe.*

*For a few blessed moments, the physical body ceases to exist. The spirit is momentarily elevated to a higher plane, and you are transported heart and soul into the presence of the divine."*

'Really, that does sound exciting,' she says. 'Why don't we test it out?'

It only takes a moment and a feeling such as Sally has never felt before ripples through her body. And before they know it, they are lost in each other's embrace and transported to a far and distant realm.

They drift along on gossamer wings like two silver ribbons swirling in the breeze, and for a few blissful minutes, they not only transcend the physical they even have a passing glimpse of heaven on the way.

'I have no idea what just happened,' Sally says, 'but Jasper, that was so amazing.'

'I think we just became one with the universe.'

'I think you're right, Jaz, but I really do have to thank your Lady Friend for one of the most sublime experiences of my life.'

'I now understand what you mean about turning into some sort of cosmic fire-engine.'

'I am so looking forward to finding out what she wants Sally, so that she can finally rest in peace.'

'So am I, Jasper, but not for the same reasons. I now understand why her husband wanted to build a temple in her honour, if only to remember the good times.'

'I think he loved her Sally. The rest was just a bonus.'

'I am sure it was, but thank you dear lady, whoever you are.'

'Now that you have had your fun Jasper Powell, up you get. There's a house to clean because we have guests coming tomorrow.'

'I only work when I am drunk.'

'You don't work at all, Jasper. You are a wealthy young man with too much time on your hands.'

'That's true, but what about that drink.'

'Work first. Drinks later. You can start with the floor and then do the dusting.'

'Actually, I have a better idea. Perhaps you should go and talk to Bella and Paz before you do anything at all.'

## CHAPTER 72

Bella and Paz live in a little slice of Spain in suburban Melbourne, and tradition demands that a guest be offered a drink and a few homemade delicacies.

Jasper is no stranger to Spanish food, but he has never had the sort of food that a dear old lady like Bella can make.

'Jasper, your face is glowing,' she says.

'My Lady Friend popped back in this afternoon.'

'Oh, she used to do that all the time, but we never knew why. Poor old Paz nearly had a nervous breakdown after a while. He couldn't handle the strain anymore.'

'But why are you here, my boy?'

'Well, the latest news is that we have received a stash of mail from the Bank of Colombo.'

'That's where our money comes from, Jasper. We get a big cheque every month without fail.'

'Well, that makes sense, because they have had the deeds to The Phoenix for over a hundred years. But they sent me absolutely everything from their vault, including heaps of legal documents.'

'But that's not all, there's a diary as well.'

'Ooh, have you read it yet.'

'No, not yet, Bella, but we are planning to do so tomorrow, which is why I am here. We would like you to join us for lunch.'

'Sally is going to cook a roast, as well as a few other things, all of which include orange juice, from freshly squeezed oranges that is.'

'She must like them,' Paz says.

'She does, but she obviously knows a few good recipes. She's an apprentice chef, after all.'

'Then the food should be good.'

'It will be Paz and we will have plenty of good wine because I inherited my father's wine cellar. What do you say to that?'

'We will be there, Jasper, after we go to mass, of course. We wouldn't miss out on that for anything.'

Before he goes, he gets a grandmotherly kiss on the cheek from Bella, and a basket full to overflowing with a big bunch of grapes from Paz, as well as three very handsome, highly polished eggplants.

'Tomorrow at eleven then,' he says.

'That will be perfect, Jasper.'

'In that case, I will meet you at the door.'

Jasper spends the next hour wandering around with a mop in one hand and a fluffy duster in the other. His mind isn't on the job and he is just itching to read that diary, but Sally has been keeping a close eye on him from the kitchen.

'Jasper, it is not a crime to read your own mail in the privacy of your own home, you know.'

'I am dying to take a look at that diary, Sal.'

'Well, give me a few minutes, fill my glass, and get a box of tissues, just in case.'

'Do you think we should Sal?'

'Yes Jasper, we should be prepared for tomorrow.'

The diary is still on the table, and he hasn't had the nerve to touch it yet, but he so desperately wants to.

'Please be a good diary and reveal the secrets of The Phoenix,' he says.

A few minutes later Sally creeps up from behind.

'Jasper, you're all tense, I think you need a massage.'

Sally obviously knows a thing or two about the ancient art of touch therapy, so Jasper sits back and relaxes as her soft and reassuring hands release the tension from every muscle in his back.

'Feel better now Jaz?'

'Just perfect, that was beautiful Sal.'

'That is one of the simple pleasures of life, Jasper. I usually accept MasterCard for my services, but today, it's on the house.'

She pulls up a chair and sits by his side.

'Now, young man, prepare for the journey of a lifetime.'

The moment that he picks up the diary, a familiar tingling sensation ripples up his spine.

'She's here Sally?'

'She has been waiting for this for over a century Jasper. She wants someone to know her story.'

He removes the wrapper, only to discover that the diary is bound in dark blue leather with a title embossed in gold.

'Dedicated to the Memory of the Woman I Love.'

'How beautiful is that.'

'You are a romantic fool, Jasper Powell.'

'I wouldn't have it any other way. Would you?'

'Not at all. So, get on with it, lover boy.'

'Okay,' he says. 'This is dated 1885.'

*"My name is Juan Philippe Delgado, and I was born to a wealthy seagoing family in 1834 in the city of Barcelona in Spain. Up until the age of ten, I lived with my parents in a house overlooking that glorious if somewhat imperfect city. But on the streets down below it was a world of poverty and misery.*

*I knew nothing about poverty at the time as I lived a fortunate life. I had everything a boy could ask for, the love of a gentle mother and that of a devoted father. He taught me about his business, and from an early age, I often accompanied him from one seaport to another.*

*The sea, as I thought, was in my blood, but that was not to be the case. The ship on which we were sailing to Japan was wrecked in a storm and I was the only survivor.*

*At the age of ten, my life changed on the day that I washed up on a beach in the country known as Ceylon. If I had not been rescued by a passing stranger, a snake charmer called Govinda and his daughter Kashmira, I may never have survived at all. I could not remember anything for a long time after, but they nursed me back to health, and taught me their ways.*

*Kashmira called me Roshan and told me many years later that it was because of my vibrant green eyes. Over the next ten years, I mastered the art of juggling balls and doing magic tricks to entertain a sometimes-indifferent crowd.*

*Most people were too busy to stop and watch a group of passing entertainers, but I stood out, and they did notice the handsome young white boy juggling five coloured balls. The day eventually arrived when Govinda taught me how to be a snake charmer.*

*We often travelled from one place to another, but the weather was our worst enemy. In the warmer months, we found refuge under the shade of a tree. But when it rained, and it did on a daily basis, we had nowhere to hide.*

*I was entranced by Kashmira's beauty from the first day that I ever saw her. She had deep brown eyes but did not resemble her parents in the least. When I became fluent in the Sinhalese language, she told me that she had been abandoned by the roadside as a baby, and that Govinda arrived on the scene just in time to rescue her from a pack of hungry dogs.*

*Over the next ten years, we travelled extensively and were constantly improving our performance. I was now a skilled snake charmer, and Kashmira, dressed in silken veils and golden bangles would enchant an audience with the Dance of the Seven Cobras. People would flock to see us perform and the money flowed in on a regular basis.*

*We spent a few months in the city of Colombo, a city of beggars and charlatans all of whom were desperate to make a pretty penny. Word soon passed around amongst the European community of a white skinned snake charmer and his beautiful assistant, and it was not long before we were performing in front of a very different audience.*

*I had not seen a sailing ship for the last ten years, but one day I was approached by a sea captain who spoke to me Spanish. I had been speaking Sinhalese for so long that I had forgotten that it was my native tongue.*

*Captain Alvarez was an employee of the Barcelona Steamship Company and said that I bore an uncanny resemblance to the proprietor. He was certain that I was his long-lost son, and that I was the sole survivor of a shipwreck from ten years before.*

*'That shipwreck did not take the life of your father,' he said. 'He returned to Barcelona, but he never gave up hope that you had survived.'*

*'Those in his employ have strict instructions to keep a lookout for you every time we visit Ceylon.'*

*'Senor, you are your father's son in every respect, and he will be overjoyed to know that you are still alive.'*

*Before we left, Kashmira and I were married, and a few weeks later, we set sail for a foreign land.'*

## CHAPTER 73

'That was some story, but I have a feeling that it's going to go from bad to worse,' Sally says. However, we now know that your Lady Friend has a name.'

'Kashmira. That's such a beautiful name, isn't it?' Jasper says.

'But the diary was written by Juan Phillipe Delgado which means he must have returned to Barcelona and resumed his family inheritance.'

'More than likely,' Sally says.

The front balcony was once a popular nesting place for the birds, but now that Merlin rules the roost, they are no longer on the scene.

He knows that the house is haunted, and he is not about to step through those doors for any reason at all.

Jasper watches closely as he makes his way along an external ledge, but when Merlin disappears into a cavity on one side of the wall and reappears on the other, he knows exactly what it means.

'The Phoenix has other secrets and one of them is structural.'

He races over to his desk and sifts through a pile of papers searching for the plans of the building.

'They're here somewhere,' he says as he rifles through one thing after another.

'Ah ha, I found them.'

He is just about to take a closer look when Sally creeps up from behind, ruffles his hair and plants a big sloppy kiss on his lips.

'You taste nice.'

'Hungry for a bit of the action,' she says hopefully.

'Not now Jezebel, I am onto something.'

'And what would that be?'

'I was watching that psychic cat of yours.'

'Yes, and what did he do?'

'He disappeared into a passageway in the front wall and came out the other end.'

'He is a master of magic. I knew that when he adopted me.'

'He adopted you. It's usually the other way around.'

'He is a reincarnation of one of the most famous sorcerers of all time. He told me so himself.'

'Yeah, and I'll be a monkey's uncle.'

'Jasper, my boy. What's got you into such a tizz?'

'Well, just about everything Sal, as you might have noticed.'

'So, this looks important, the architectural drawings of the building. Maybe we could check them out in our own special way,' she says hopefully.

'Did you treat your other boyfriends like this Sally Velasko?'

'I have never had any other boyfriends, Jasper. I tested out the waters, tried out a few makes and models and eventually decided on you.'

'It wasn't a difficult decision. The day I saw you sitting beside that lovely old lady at the station, I knew that you were the boy for me.'

'But let's forget about that.'

She places her iPod in the speakers, hits the volume button and pumps it up as high as it will go.

'Come on Jasper. Get your dancing shoes on. It's time to dance,' she says as she entices him into her net.

No hot-blooded Latin lover could resist the scintillating sound of a hip-swaying classic which has no purpose other than to get you on your feet. And Sway is a song which can do just that.

Sally may not be as vivacious as Rita Hayworth, and Jasper may not have the sultry charms of Anthony Quinn, but they make up for in vigor what they lack in style.

And for a few intoxicating minutes they sway around the room to the syncopated rhythms of a highly erotic dance that would, under normal circumstances, only have one possible outcome.

Sway is one of those songs that you never want to end, but when it does, they collapse on the floor in an exhausted heap.

'Jasper, we should sign up for one of those Latin dancing shows. They would love all that sensuous, hot-blooded stuff.'

'Not a chance.'

Jasper is flat on his back and blissfully unaware that his virtue is in mortal danger. Sally zooms in quietly, with every intention of working her way from the top to the bottom but he catches her just in time.

'Not now Sally. Don't you have something to do?'

'I do actually, I have a cake to cook.'

She drags herself to her feet and checks out the plans on the table.

'Jasper, have you had a look at these yet.'

'No, someone ambushed me before I even got there.'

'These are not the plans of The Phoenix at all. These are the building blocks of the structure that should have been erected at the Melbourne International Exhibition.'

'I think you're right Sal, and I think we need the advice of a professional.'

## CHAPTER 74

They are up bright and early the following morning and preparing for a very big day. The leg of lamb is massaged with a fragrant orange scented oil, numerous herbs and spices and then assigned to the oven.

'Vegetables,' Sally says. 'It's peeling time Jasper.'

Their state-of-the-art kitchen has a pantry with pop out baskets and sliding drawers for every appliance known to mankind. And everything has been artfully arranged by Sally Velasko, the El-Supremo of the catering world.

The island bench even has a sneakily disguised touch-sensitive door and hidden away behind that is the dishwasher.

'Now for the magic touch,' she says, 'starting with our new tablecloth.'

It was the find of the day at the markets, a richly decorated cloth in red, blue, and gold and it's perfect for a twelve-seater table.

Sally fell in love with a romantic dinner service of uncertain origins, one that depicts two love birds in a dusky blue haze.

'Fifty dollars, Jasper, I wasn't about to leave that behind, just in case someone else snaffled it up.'

The guests are due in an hour and it's time to get into their party clothes. Apart from a collection of black velvet dresses, Sally has quite a few things stashed away in the wardrobe.

But today she has decided to wear a red and gold cheongsam, a dress that was popular with Asian women of the 1930s.

She pins her hair back in a quasi-Asian style with two ivory combs, adds a touch of ruby red lipstick, checks herself out in the mirror and prepares for her big day.

Jasper was given instructions to look his sexy best, and the moment he appears wearing black jeans and a black shirt, Sally's eyes light up with desire.

'Jasper, you look very desirable,' she says.

'Thank you, Sal, and you look absolutely beautiful, but I've gotta go,' he says as he races for the door.

It's almost eleven o'clock and Jasper has a date with his old mates, Bella, and Paz, both of whom are mentally preparing for the long hike to the summit of Mt. Everest, but for a youngster like Jasper it's no big deal to run up and down five times a day.

When you have a combined age of one hundred and sixty two, and various bodily parts are a little on the creaky side, a motorised chairlift would be a dream come true.

With her pure white hair teased to within an inch of its life, Bella looks radiant in a pale blue suit. Paz looks equally handsome in a brown Fedora hat and a starched shirt that probably took an hour to iron at the very least.

And when Geraldine appears, she looks like the mother of an Italian princess in a white cotton frock decorated with little hand stitched flowers.

'You all look very smart and very stylish,' Jasper says.

'Why, thank you,' Bella says.

But no one knows what to think when Mortisha appears in a tight-fitting blue silk dress with a matching handbag and pillbox hat.

'Dahlink,' she says as he gives Japer a kiss on the cheek. 'You have to say that at least once in your life, don't you?'

'You do,' he says. 'You look like a movie star of days gone by.'

'You can thank that busty Amazon Jane Russell for that. Or maybe it was Rosalind Russell. Actually, I think it was Deborah Kerr.'

'Fabulous, isn't it?'

'It certainly is, I agree.'

'All women have an interesting collection of clothes in their wardrobe.'

'I will believe anything you say Mortisha.'

'You are a lovely young man Jasper and Sally is a very lucky girl.'

'She knows that.'

# CHAPTER 75

A light wine is often the first drink to be served up at a typical Melbourne luncheon, but Sally is an explorer of new ideas, and she decides to serve up an exotic aperitif instead, a cocktail with a distinctive orange tinge.

'What is this magical elixir?' Mortisha says as she gazes deep into its medieval soul.

'It's champagne with a few nips of Vosomor,' Sally says.

'And what's that?'

'It's a liqueur made from bitter oranges and little flecks of gold leaf.'

Mortisha swoons as she inhales its mysterious but smoky aroma. 'Gold leaf, what an inspirational idea. I think I have died and gone to heaven.'

The real reason for this gathering is not far from their minds. But they are not about to dive into uncharted waters, not until they have dined at the newest restaurant on Brunswick Street. And now that every little detail has been sorted, Sally is ready to roll.

'Ladies and gentlemen, lunch is about to be served. Please adjourn to the dining room.'

The first course goes down like a charm, a parsnip and orange soup with a dollop of minted yoghurt. If that's any indication of what's to come, everyone is eagerly awaiting the main course.

The presentation of a meal is the thing that people notice first, so Jasper watches closely as Sally slices up the lamb and arranges each piece on a plate.

'So, what goes in the middle?'

'The crowning glory, The Golden Temple of Peace and Harmony,' she says as she whips a piping hot tray out of the oven.

'In other words, these wonderful things,'

'Amazing, but what are they?

'Sweet potatoes in the shape of a pagoda.'

'I would have worked that out eventually.'

She places each one in the centre of a plate, surrounded by a garden of miniature vegetables. And for the finishing touch she adds a trickle of orange flavoured sauce around the edge.

'Truly inspirational,' Jasper says.

His culinary skills are basically non-existent, and he isn't much of a cook but Jasper is seriously impressed.

'You are wasting your time at that restaurant Sally. I think you should open one of your own.'

'One day,' she says.

Simplicity is not the only secret to a delicious meal, a touch of the ostentatious doesn't go astray either. And as soon as she delivers her masterpiece to the table, Sally receives a hearty round of applause.

Her choice of dessert is equally inspirational, an old-fashioned idea with a modern twist. Paz gets to his feet and applauds her artistry when she delivers six statuesque parfait glasses to the table.

'Beautiful Sally, very beautiful indeed.'

'That is a veritable masterpiece,' Mortisha says. 'What is this divine creation?'

'It's sago, a favourite of yesteryear.'

'Sago,' Paz says, 'I love sago.'

'Then you will love this, Paz. It even has several extra-large sago pearls for added effect.'

Five crystal goblets filled with miniature seed pearls is a beautiful sight to behold, and as Jasper now knows, sago is the starch derived from a cassava plant.

'Ladies and gentlemen,' Sally says, 'lemon sago, with orange and lime cream, just to give it a little extra zing.'

'However, it would be a sin not to have a teensy little glass of dessert wine as well.'

'Indeed, it would,' Mortisha says.

There is nothing more satisfying than a beautifully prepared meal and everyone is impressed.

'That was absolutely delicious,' Bella says. 'I have not had a meal like that in ages. If that is an example of your skills, you are a very clever girl.'

The moment of truth is almost at hand, so Jasper clears a space on the table, and returns a few moments later with a box full of correspondence from the Bank of Colombo.

'I have something to show you,' he says as he empties the contents all over the table.

'Somewhere in there is the secret to this mystery, and it's all from the Bank of Colombo.'

'Oh my God,' Mortisha says. 'Is that it?'

'Yes, as far as I know.'

At that moment, a familiar tingling sensation ripples up his spine and he races off to the kitchen

'Sally,' he cries. 'Kashmira's here.'

'Jasper, there's nothing to worry about. She is not out to get you. She just wants to see this situation resolved. Kashmira has chosen you to do this, and she wants you to sort this problem out.'

'She does, doesn't she?'

'Yes Jasper, now get yourself together.'

After several weeks of prevaricating, Merlin finally decides to cross the uncrossable threshold. He looks Jasper in the eye and meows.

'See, he's on our side,' Sally says. 'And he probably has back up.'

'You watch too many movies.'

'The coffee is almost ready Jaz. Be a darling and put this tray on the table, and I'll be there in a few minutes.'

He returns to the dining room, only to find everyone busily reading a few of the unopened letters.

'This is just a financial statement from the 1960s,' Mortisha says. 'What have you got Bella?'

'It's a letter advising Juan Phillipe Delgado that he is now the sole beneficiary of his father's estate.'

'And who is he?'

'This could be him,' Paz says as he places a well-preserved photo in Jasper's hands.

'And this is probably his wife. What do you think?'

'Oh, my God. Sally, come and look at this.'

Kashmira really is a hauntingly beautiful woman with long black hair and almond shaped eyes. Every inch of her outfit is adorned with fabulous jewels, and she looks spectacular in a glistening belly dancer's outfit.

'Now, that's a snake charmer's wife if ever I have seen one,' Sally says. 'But Roshan really is a stunner.'

'Take a look at this Mortisha?'

'That's the very same man I saw in my dream,' she says.

Roshan has piercing green eyes, his head is held aloft, his arms are crossed over his chest, and he wears a pair of loose-fitting pants with a golden waistband.

'What a hunk he was, but I wonder what happened to Kashmira?'

'I have a suspicion that she died in the prime of her life,' Jasper says. 'As to why, I have no idea.'

Over the next few minutes, he does his best to fill them in on everything they have discovered so far.

'Juan Phillipe Delgado was also known as the snake charmer Roshan, and Kashmira was the woman he loved.'

'At the age of ten, he was the sole survivor of a shipwreck off the coast of Ceylon. He was rescued by Kashmira and her father, and they eventually became the stars of the show.'

'So, whatever is packed away in those boxes downstairs is the reason for all of this,' Mortisha says.

'Yes, I think so. Juan designed a monument which was supposed to be erected here in Melbourne but it never happened.'

'The boxes never made it to the Melbourne International Exhibition, and for some reason, The Phoenix was erected as a storage place.'

'What boxes are you talking about?' Geraldine says.

'The two floors below are full of packing crates Mum, and it could even be a memorial of some kind.'

'What sort of memorial, Jasper?'

'It's probably the size of a cathedral.'

'Okay, so what else do you know?'

'There's even more in the diary.'

'Coffee first,' Sally says.

She disappears into the kitchen and returns with an old-fashioned, three-tier cake plate and places it in the middle of the table.

'I think you might like this,' she says to Paz. 'It's a Greek recipe made from almond meal saturated with orange syrup.'

'Oh Sally, that's one of my favourites.'

'It is,' Bella says. 'How come you haven't told me about this?'

'You work hard enough, my darling. Besides, you can get it in at least three different shops in Brunswick Street.'

'If you keep serving up food like this, he will want to move back in.'

'Sorry Paz, you are way too late,' Sally says. 'I have already found the man of my dreams.'

## CHAPTER 76

Bella and Paz have been waiting for this day for as long as they can remember. This is a mystery that has haunted their lives for the last fifty years, and now they are about to find out the truth.

'Okay,' Jasper says as he settles into his favourite wingback chair. 'This diary entry is from the 23rd of October 1854.'

*"The sea journey to Barcelona was as difficult for me as it was for Kashmira. She was leaving her home, maybe for the last time but we didn't know that. We had no idea what to expect.*

*The captain was all too aware of our hesitancy and made it his business to prepare us for life in a country I had long forgotten about. But that did nothing to prepare Kashmira for the experience of entering a world of affluence on a scale she had never known.*

*My parents had never given up hope of ever seeing me again. They had suffered over the years and their health had deteriorated. My father had retired much earlier than he expected, and he handed over the control of his company to Manuel da Silva, a man that he trusted.*

*I had disappeared ten years before, but it might as well have been a lifetime. I was a different person and not the son they had known. I was a stranger in my own home.*

*My parents had to accept the fact that I was now a fully-grown man and I had married the woman I loved, but that did not make things any easier.*

*During those first few weeks, I felt as if I was living in a foreign land, one in which I did not belong. The captain advised my parents that it may not be wise to force us to their will and they made no effort to do so.*

*My family home was a luxurious mansion overlooking Barcelona. And for the first few weeks we participated in the simple aspects of daily life, but I had no idea how deeply my father felt or how he had been affected by my homecoming.*

*We had difficulty communicating and three weeks later he passed away in his sleep. We did our best to comfort my mother in her solitude, but it was to no avail. She was grief stricken and retreated into a world of her own.*

*Sadly, I was woken early one morning and advised by a member of the household staff that her body had been found at the base of the cliff on the outskirts of our property.*

*As a result, I had inherited an empire. I now had sole ownership of the family company. But I was not a businessman, and I had no interest in being one.*

*The Barcelona Steamship Company was in very capable hands and would continue to thrive, but not with me at the helm. And so, a few weeks later we packed our bags and said goodbye to Barcelona forever."*

'And that's the story so far,' Jasper says. 'I presume that they travelled the world after that, doing what they loved best.'

'I am relieved to know the truth at last,' Bella says. 'This story has been on my mind for as long as I can remember.'

'So, what happens now?' Paz says.

'Well, we have decided to consult an architect to see if he can piece together the design of this monument.'

'Perhaps you'd like to see the plans?'

'I certainly would Jasper. I am familiar with house plans, and the vital information is there, if you know how to read it.'

Jasper spreads them out on the table and everyone gathers round to hear the verdict.

'The contents of those crates are blocks of Carrara marble,' Paz says. 'That's the very same marble that Michelangelo used to create his famous statues.'

'Holee,' Mortisha says. 'This story gets more intriguing every day.'

It's the general consensus that there's a lot more to come and it leaves them with a lot to think about.

After they have escorted Bella and Paz home, Jasper and Sally decide to explore the back streets of Fitzroy.

It's a lovely afternoon to be out and about, and they end up in Brunswick Street, where even on a Sunday afternoon it's a hive of activity.

Brunswick Street is a popular shopping precinct with an old-world charm and people travel from all over Melbourne just to soak up the atmosphere.

Some are happy with a freshly brewed coffee, while others spend their time browsing through one shop or another, but no matter how he tries, Jasper cannot get that story out of his mind.

'It's such a beautiful thought, isn't it?'

'What are you talking about Jasper?'

'That Roshan wanted to create a monument to the woman he loved. It's just like the story of Romeo and Juliet or that of Orpheus and Eurydice.'

'And who were they?' Sally says.

'Orpheus was a Greek god who fell in love with a beautiful young girl called Eurydice.'

'Who?' Sally says.

'Urardeechay. It's an ancient Greek name. Have you ever heard that story Sal?'

'No Jasper, I haven't. Tell me about it please.'

'It's so beautiful Sal, but oh so heartbreaking.'

'Orpheus had never seen a girl with such beautiful eyes, and he knew immediately that this was the girl that he was going to marry.'

'Unfortunately, Eurydice was bitten by a serpent and died not long after their wedding. Orpheus, of course, was devastated.'

'I imagine he would have been, Jasper.'

'He followed her deep into the underworld where he had to bargain for her soul with Pluto, the god of the underworld.'

'That would have been a terrifying experience for anyone, but Orpheus was determined to get her back.'

'So, what did he do, Jasper?'

'Well, Pluto was in a position to grant his wish, but like all Greek gods, he was a bit of a trickster, and Orpheus had no choice in the end but to use his God-given skills.'

'And what sort of skills did he have Jasper?'

'His father Apollo, gave him the gift of music and his mother, Calliope, gave him the gift of song.'

'So, his plan was to win Pluto over with a few homespun songs. Is that what you are saying Jasper?'

'More or less Sally, yes.'

'So, one day, Orpheus picked up his lute and started to sing.'

'Pluto was bewitched by the voice of this enchanted young man, but Orpheus played and played for days on end, and after a while, Pluto had had enough.'

'There's a catch,' Sally says. 'There is always a catch.'

'Yes, of course there is.'

'Pluto eventually granted his wish, but on one condition. He could have Eurydice, but she was not to look back, and if she did, she would be his for evermore.'

'Orpheus spent ages searching the dungeons and eventually found his beloved, but she was pale and distant and had no idea who he was.'

'She died Jasper. How could she know anything?'

'She was probably in some sort of induced trance Sal. She died of a snake bite, after all.'

'Orpheus believed that if she could breathe fresh air again that she would come back to life. He carried her through one tunnel after another, and they eventually reached the outer limits of the upper world.'

'Eurydice had a glazed look in her eyes and had not said a word in all of that time.'

'She was dead Jasper. She was a corpse.'

'Well, she wasn't completely dead, I suppose, but after that, the worst of all possible things happened.'

'They were just about to cross over into the world of the living when Eurydice opened her eyes and looked back.'

'Oh no,' Sally cried. 'Why did she do that?'

'I don't know Sal, but that was the last time that Orpheus ever saw the girl of his dreams.'

'And why did you tell me that story, Jasper?'

'It's a story of star-crossed lovers Sal, that's why. They all died of a broken heart or something worse.'

'Unfortunately, Orpheus came to a very tragic and grisly end. Don't ask me about it because it's absolutely awful.'

'I will believe anything you say, Jasper.'

'Stories like that have survived through the ages, and they still have the power to tug at the heart strings.'

'Jasper Powell, do you know why I love you?' she says.

'I cannot begin to imagine.'

'Because you are a beautiful human being, and I would not trade you in for anything.'

'You wouldn't get much if you did.'

'Jasper, if I wanted to make a fortune, I would sell your soul and not your body.'

'Really, and who would you sell it to?'

'Some place where everyone could see it, like The National Gallery of Victoria. But it would have to be displayed in a specially built room.'

'Of course, it would,' he says. 'It would be like having a supernova in the bedroom.'

'It would be a hugely popular exhibit and people could see it using an electronic device.'

'But you won't do that will you, not until I have shuffled off?'

'No, I will not, my beloved boy.'

## CHAPTER 77

Their first foray into the catering business was a resounding success, and when they get back home, Sally decides to polish the silverware, but Jasper has something else in mind.

Their brand-new sofa can accommodate eight people at a pinch. It's not some yucky old pea green sort of colour but a bold statement in black and white. Jasper rearranges the cushions, and then lays back to listen to one of the most haunting songs ever written.

Esmeralda or Mary McQuaid, as she was christened was famous for just one song. Gypsy Queen came to the attention of a record producer, Charlie Moroni, who convinced her to make a recording, and after that, the rest as they say is history.

Imagine two lovers gazing at each other through the flames of a slowly burning fire, and somewhere in the background is the sound of gypsy guitars.

The next thing you hear is Esmeralda's voice rising to the surface, vibrating like a reed in a watery pond, a pale and sensuous sound like that of a fragile bird calling to its mate in the wilderness.

This song reveals the innermost desires of a gypsy woman for the man that she loves. But when Esmeralda delivers that oh so evocative first line, a romantic fool like Jasper doesn't have a hope.

He is transported to a gypsy camp on a moonlit night, where Kashmira, her heart palpitating with desire is desperate to take the man of her dreams in her arms.

But Jasper's few blessed moments of bliss and joy are rudely interrupted when his very own gypsy queen taps him on the head.

'Jasper Powell, you sweet and irresistible little thing. You're off with the fairies again, aren't you?'

'You are the only fairy-type thing I have ever met, Sally Velasko.'

'I can introduce you to a few more if you like.'

'No thanks, Tinker Bell. One fairy in this family is more than enough.'

'Jasper,' she says in her most beguiling voice. 'The Sun has set, and the Moon is shining in the night sky. What is it that your little heart desires?'

Jasper knows exactly what Sally has in mind, but he is not about to let her sabotage his magical dream world, not this time.

'Sally, my beloved queen of the night. Lay down beside me and I will show you.'

'I have been listening to a song, dearest one, but this is no ordinary song. It is alive with understated sexuality and the passion of unrequited love.'

'Oh, I do like the sound of that, Jasper.'

The very moment that she hears gypsy guitars strumming away in the background, Sally is transported to a gypsy camp on a moonlit night where a woman in red veils stands on the rise of a hill, her gaze set squarely on the man of her dreams.

It's a well-known fact that words can transport you to places you have never been before. They can make you sing, and they can make you dance, but the words of a beautifully crafted love song are the most powerful of all.

And if it had not been for an inspired lyricist, an equally inspired record producer, and the enchanting voice of a virtuoso performer, it would never have happened at all.

## CHAPTER 78

The following morning, Jasper decides to do a few stretching exercises but to his dismay, his toes are a lot further away than he would like.

Working up a sweat at the local gym is not his idea of a good time. He prefers the soothing waters of a heated pool, but he has other things on his mind, and that will just have to wait.

He is relaxing on the balcony having his first coffee of the day when Paz knocks on the door.

'Jasper, how would you like to bring those plans down to our social club?'

'You could show my mates what you've got. You never know, they might have a few ideas.'

He grabs his backpack and follows along behind. Jasper has no idea what the day has in store, but it will probably be interesting. He is about to meet some of the elder citizens of Fitzroy.

He gets home nine long hours later, and only a few minutes before Sally walks through the door.

'Sal, I have so much to tell you. What a day it has been.'

'Nothing terrible was it, Jasper?'

'No Sal, it was just the opposite. Paz took me down to his local hangout. I thought it was a den of iniquity at first, but it wasn't that bad as I found out.'

'It's a place where the old men of Fitzroy can chill out, drink tea, roll endless cigarettes and play cards until midnight.'

'And there isn't a woman in sight.'

'So, what was the point of this meeting of like-minded souls?' Sally says.

'Everyone in the area knows that this building is haunted, and no one had any intention of taking it on.'

'So, did they think you were brave or stupid?'

'When I told them about the packing crates and showed them the plans, you should have seen their faces.'

'And what did they say?'

'They sent me off to buy a few things like a big sheet of cardboard and some adhesive tape.'

'Why was that?'

'So that they could make a model, of course. Those guys are Greek, Italian, Spanish and God knows what else, but it was the most exciting thing that's happened to them in years.'

'I imagine it would have been Jasper. And did they work it out?'

'They sure did, and I even brought it home with me.'

Jasper removes the model from a black plastic bag and Sally's eyes almost pop out of her head.

'My goodness,' she cries.

'It's a spiral staircase inspired by a shell. And Rocco has calculated that it's at least three storeys high. And you can walk all the way to the top by one of four spiral staircases.'

'There's a blank walls every ten metres or so, and we believe that something special has to go there.'

'And what would that be?' Sally says.

'We don't know yet. However, at the very top, there's an open-air platform.'

'That is so amazing Jasper, but where will it go?'

'It was originally designed for the Carlton Gardens, not far from the Exhibition building on Nicholson Street. That's about the only place it could go.'

'So, what's the plan now?' Sally says.

'Well, the guys are coming over tomorrow to see what they can do. It's going to be an interesting day, that's for sure.'

'Comb your hair and brush your teeth, Jasper Powell. As soon as the media finds out about this, they will be all over the place.'

'This will be one of the biggest news stories ever, Sally, probably bigger than the exploits of the Kardashians.'

'Miracles can happen, Jasper.'

'But imagine what will happen when Hollywood finds out about it.'

'Jasper, after tomorrow, you will be the next world-famous celebrity, so, prepare yourself and read the rest of that diary.'

'Oh Sally, I don't want to be a celebrity. That's way too scary. Everyone will know more about my private parts than you do.'

'I have a feeling that I will be the first in a long line of amorous women in your life, Jasper, the first but not the last.'

'Don't say that Sally, I don't want to lose you. I have never been so happy, and we get on so well together.'

'Jasper, my beautiful, overly romantic boy,' Sally says as she tries to soothe his troubled soul. 'I am not going anywhere, not until I am pushed.'

'I would never do anything like that Sal.'

'No, but some other brazen little hussy might. However, you are destined for greater things.'

'You will have to front up to about five hundred television cameras soon. And you will have to tell the whole world about this story, whether you like it or not.'

# CHAPTER 79

Jasper's boyish heart is a turbulent ravaged mess, so they spend the time working their way through some of the correspondence from the Bank of Colombo, but his mind is not on the job.

'It's mostly financial statements,' Sally says. 'But Juan was ridiculously wealthy, wasn't he?'

'That he was,' Jasper says.

According to the diary, they spent three months of the year performing in some of the great theatres of Europe, but the temple may never have happened at all if they had not found four shells buried in the sand.

He spent a small fortune on blocks of marble from Carrara in northern Italy, after which they were transported to Melbourne on one of his ships.

They were planning to present their masterpiece to the world on the 1st of October 1880, the opening day of the Melbourne International Exhibition and had even purchased a little cottage within walking distance of the Carlton Gardens.

'Now comes the sad part, but let's have a break before we read anymore,' Sally says.

'You must be famished by now. Feel like a pizza for dinner?'

'Oh, yes please Sal.'

'It will be ready in a jiffy.'

Jasper doesn't want to do this anymore, not if it means losing Sally. He hasn't looked at another girl since she has been around, and that's a testament to his love for this sometimes crazy but wonderful creature who swept him off his feet. There are some people who give you a reason to live, and for Jasper, that person is Sally.

'I can hear you from here,' Sally says. 'You're getting all weepy again, aren't you?'

He creeps into the kitchen with his head held low so that she can't see his face.

'Jasper, nothing will ever tear us apart. Well, nothing of this world at any rate. I couldn't stand it if you were not in my life.'

'Truly,' he says.

'Really and truly Jaz, and that's God's honest truth. When the girls of the world see your beautiful face on television, they will be coming out of the woodwork. However, I have a solution.'

'And what's that, Sal?'

She slips one of the rings off her finger and places it on his. 'Just show them this.'

'A wedding band it is not, but you could say that you are happily married, and you have no intention of cheating on your wife.'

'What do you think of that idea?'

'I have a better idea, Sally. Let's do it for real?'

'If that's a proposal of marriage, my beloved boy, I accept. I think this calls for a celebration. Shall I break open a bottle of bubbly?'

'But it's late Sal and you have to work tomorrow.'

'Who cares Jasper? If I am to be the future Mrs. Jasper Powell, I won't have to work again.'

'Never again because I am loaded.'

'That I do know,' she says with a wicked glint in her eye.

They have just made a momentous, life-changing decision and Jasper's boyish heart is beating away in his skinny little chest.

The pain he felt on the passing of his father was not pain at all but love, and Sally Velasko, the girl that he cannot live without, is responsible for that.

Like a lamb to the slaughter, he follows her to bed in a slightly drunken haze and passes out from sheer emotional exhaustion.

## CHAPTER 80

Sally usually crawls out of bed around five thirty in the morning, but when Jasper wakes up just after seven, she is still fast asleep.

'Sal, you're going to be really late for work,' he says.

'I am not going in today, Jasper, and maybe not tomorrow either.'

'Excellent, but it's time to get up. Rocco and his mates will be here in an hour.'

'Okay boss, just enough time for a quick cup of coffee.'

Rocco's comrades may have diminished in size over the years, but he is still a big solid man. In a time long gone, they were stone masons and carpenters, but today they are the respected elders of Fitzroy.

They might be little on the creaky side, and the temptations of the flesh are but a long-lost dream but they are men after all. And the opportunity to meet a beautiful girl like Sally doesn't happen every day of the week.

To Jasper's dismay, she doesn't even have to turn on the charm. Sally has a dozen starry-eyed old gigolos eating out of the palm of her hand.

Rocco isn't the only one who would like to whisk her off to an ivory tower, but as Jasper reminds him, they are here for a reason.

Rocco knows exactly what he means, and with his trusty tradesmen following along behind, he heads up to the second floor to investigate the structural details of the back wall.

'Lovely old fellows, aren't they?' Sally says.

'Yes, they are, in some situations.'

'Jaz, you have nothing to worry about, just in case you didn't know.'

'Thank goodness for that,' he says.

It is an uncommonly fine winter morning in Melbourne and even the Sun is shining for a change.

For two young love birds, this is an opportunity to check out some of the charming little cottages for which Fitzroy is famous.

They wander up one side of the street and down the other and when they get back, Bella is waiting at the front gate.

'Jasper, Sally,' she says. 'Such a big day this is going to be.'

'And why is that, Bella.'

'For one thing Jasper, we will finally get to see what's in those boxes. But everyone in the neighbourhood has been talking about you.'

'Really,' Sally says.

'Oh yes, they're all talking about the love birds in the haunted house.'

'A neighbourhood has eyes and ears, and even if you change your perfume, someone finds out.'

'But worry not. From what I have heard, everyone approves of you.'

'That's good to know,' Sally says.

'But Jasper, the television people will be heading this way soon.'

'My neighbour's grandson works for Channel Seven, so don't be surprised if he turns up in the next few hours.'

'This is going to be a big story Jasper and he will be looking for you especially.'

'Have you read anymore of Juan's diary?'

'We have Bella, but we haven't got to the sad part yet.'

'Then do so as soon as possible. Everyone in the world will want to know about it. This is going to be really big you know.'

Rocco and his trusty tradesmen come marching around the corner a few minutes later, but this time he does have business on his mind.

'And is the news good,' Jasper says.

'It is Jasper. We believe that the crates can be removed through the back wall, but where will we put them?'

'We haven't got to that stage of our thinking yet, but it was originally meant for the Carlton Gardens.'

'You would have to approach the council for permission to do anything at all. But once they find out what you've got here, I think they will jump at the opportunity.'

'We will need heavy lifting equipment, scaffolding to remove a section of the wall and an oversized cherry picker.'

A few minutes later, a vehicle with a Channel Seven logo on the door pulls up near the kerb. A handsome young man in a business suit checks a message on his phone and then wanders over and introduces himself.

'Good morning,' he says. 'My name is Paul Sinopoli. Perhaps you can help me. I am looking for the house of Jasper Powell.'

'This is Jasper,' Rocco says. 'And I am Rocco Veradi, the keeper of the keys, you could say. Whereas these handsome old fellows are the grandmasters of Fitzroy.'

Paul has obviously heard of Rocco and his reputation, but for a man in his position, it is useful to have contacts in the local community.

'Jasper, Sally, and gentlemen, it is an honour to meet you. However, Jasper, I believe that you have discovered something of significance.'

'Why do you want to know?'

'Channel Seven has sent me over to investigate, and if it's true, perhaps we could discuss a few ideas.'

'About what,' Jasper says.

'Maybe we could do a news report, to start with. I don't want to waste your time Jasper, especially if it's just local gossip.'

'Well, it is true Paul. We do have something valuable on our hands.'

Paul listens closely as Jasper provides an abbreviated version of what they have in their possession.

'But there's even more Paul. There's a story associated with it, a beautiful love story.'

'That is so amazing Jasper, I have permission to negotiate, if you are interested.'

'Well Paul, our biggest problem is that we don't know what to do with it. Rocco has suggested that we approach the local council.'

'We could get the ball rolling with a news report, and after that, you will be inundated with offers from the public and private sector.'

'Something like this could change your life, Jasper.'

'I am all too aware of that Paul and I am not interested in that idea at all.'

'In which case, it would be sensible to establish a plan of action.'

'It appears that you have the support of some of the most powerful men in the area. And I have no doubt that they will play a part in whatever way they can.'

'We sure will,' Rocco says, 'but that monument belongs here in Fitzroy and that's where it's going to stay.'

'I agree,' Paul says. 'Perhaps we could discuss this over coffee?'

'We certainly can,' Jasper says.

'Gentlemen, would you be interested in a freshly brewed coffee and some homemade cake as well.'

'Lead the way,' they said.

## CHAPTER 81

After a guided tour of the first and second floor, Paul is blown away by the scale of this masterpiece. But when he sees the three-dimensional model, his ever-active mind goes into overdrive.

'That's the point of the story, but if we want to get the council on side, we have to offer something more impressive than a cardboard model.'

'It would look really impressive, especially if it was transformed by the magic of computer-generated wizardry,' Sally says.

'That is exactly what I was thinking Sally. That's the sort of thing that Channel Seven does every day.'

Paul listens closely as Jasper reveals what Juan had to say in his diary, and of how Kashmira terrorised every man who has ever lived in The Phoenix.

'In which case, we need a plan of action,' Paul says. 'Gentlemen, and Sally, of course. Let's see what you think of this idea. It's not set in stone, and it is negotiable.'

'Kashmira's campaign to attract attention to this treasure will feature prominently in the story. So too will the fact that everyone in the neighbourhood knew that this building was haunted.'

'Then there's the human element, how she enticed one young man to do her bidding. A young man who fell in love with The Phoenix from the very moment he set eyes on it. However, he had no idea it was haunted, not until he moved in.'

'Paz, you and Bella will play a major part, but this is one secret that you won't be taking to your grave.'

'Roshan and Kashmira's love story is a central element of the whole thing, and that's where we will show how Jasper was lured here by a woman in his dreams. And how you and Sally pieced the story together after reading Juan's diary.'

'But it's essential to feature the mastermind behind all of this. We will show how Juan was shipwrecked on a beach in Ceylon, and how he became Roshan the snake charmer.'

'And, of course, how he met the hauntingly beautiful Kashmira, the love of his life.'

'At some point, we will reveal the treasure that's been hidden away for over a hundred years.'

'But some excitement is essential, and that is where you gentlemen will get your five minutes of fame. We will film a scene in your teahouse Rocco and show how you created that model.'

'It will only be a short scene, but it will probably take all day to shoot. That might sound simple, but it will involve a lot of behind-the-scenes work.'

'I will email a copy of our schedule so that you know exactly what to do and when.'

'However, we must reveal this hidden treasure to the world in all of its glory.'

'Channel Seven will create a CGI version of the finished product taking pride of place alongside the Exhibition Building in the Carlton Gardens.'

'But this modern-day Taj Mahal doesn't have a name as yet, and it really needs one, especially if we want to lure the council into our net.'

'We have to make them understand that this will become a major tourist attraction.'

'But we have to find the right name first, and it has to be something of which Roshan and Kashmira would approve.'

## CHAPTER 82

Jasper wasn't interested in being pushed around by a fast-talking journalist in a fancy suit, so he told Paul only to make contact by email. At least they would have time to think before making a decision.

The problem of his anonymity is also on his mind. Perhaps an actor could play the part, an idea that he is seriously considering.

At eight o'clock the following morning, Paul's first email arrives.

*Hello Jasper and Sally*

*Attached is a draft copy of my idea. It is nothing more than that at the moment, but I will be attending a production meeting today where we plot and plan future projects. I would not be surprised if this idea takes off like wildfire. However, I need to know the conclusion to this romantic drama. Let me know what it is as soon as you have read the rest of the diary.*

*Talk soon,*
*Paul.*

*PS. Any ideas as yet on what to call this shrine to the goddess of love.*

'It's easy enough to understand,' Jasper says. 'But this looks like it's going to be a lot longer than a news report Sal.'

'It tells us a few things, Jasper, like how the scenes will be shot for one thing. But this is not the filming schedule. It's only an extended version of Paul's original idea.'

They double check every word, and even though it doesn't have any dialogue as yet, it clearly indicates the sort of thing that will be said.

'Most of the filming will take place in Fitzroy,' Jasper says. 'But it doesn't say where the shipwreck and snake charming scenes will be shot.'

'Perhaps we will get a free trip to Sri Lanka,' Sally says. 'I believe it's a very beautiful country.'

'It would be much cheaper to film it on a beach in Melbourne. They could employ actors for the snake charming scenes. That's probably what they'll do.'

'But Sally, one thing bothers me.'

'And what's that my darling boy?'

As usual, she responds in a way that Jasper has come to know so very well. Danger signal and it's only ten o'clock in the morning.

Perhaps it would be better if she did go back to work. If married life is going to be like this, Jasper could die a very young man, and it won't be from natural causes.

'Truce,' he says. 'White flag of peace.'

'Okay, what's the problem, dear one?'

'Paul said that this thing could take off like wildfire. What did he mean by that?'

'Jaz, it's obvious. Channel Seven could make a fortune from this story, but it also has Hollywood potential.'

'And he is attending a production meeting even as we speak, and he is not going to hold back, is he?'

'Never trust a sexy man in an Armani suit,' Sally says.

'And why is that?'

'They come into the restaurant at lunch time. During the day, they are mild mannered reporters, but at night they turn into voracious, unstoppable lotharios.'

'I thought you had dated a few of those in your time.'

'Two to be exact, Jasper.'

'I soon learnt how to avoid the minions of the underworld, but when I saw you at the station, I knew you were the boy for me.'

'It's because I'm a pushover, isn't it?'

'No Jasper, that is not the truth at all. Your soul shines through those beautiful eyes of yours.'

'I had to take a very deep breath before I worked up the courage to be so upfront that day. It was a gamble, but it worked.'

That's just typical of Sally. Fearless might not be the right word. Some people would say that she is downright cheeky, but the upfront approach is one way of getting your man.

'Jasper. Let's get out of here for a while. Apparently, we are famous in Fitzroy and maybe some of the locals will even talk to us.'

No one tries to molest them on Brunswick Street, but Sally ends up in a local fashion boutique and tries on one thing after another, and an hour later, she finally settles on a dark green dress with crossover backstraps.

Jasper usually hands over his bankcard whenever she's in buying mode but he doesn't mind. He always gets a kiss on the lips in exchange, followed by that oh so recognisable look which clearly says, I will repay you for your kindness later, Jasper Powell.

When they get back home, it is only to find another email from Paul Sinopoli.

*Hello Jasper and Sally*

*I have just come out of the production meeting. These guys are the front line when it comes to anything of a financial nature. But when they heard my presentation and realised what it meant, their eyes glazed over, and they saw dollars, big time.*

*It would be counterproductive to do a news report as you would be hounded by the paparazzi, and we would lose a great story. The plan at the moment is to do a one hour special, and after that, we may go for the big one.*

*I am doing my best to protect your privacy, but this is a remarkable story folks, one like no other, and you two made it happen. Have a think about the exposure this would get if you were prepared to go to the next level. However, I desperately need to know the conclusion as well as the name of this temple of love…please.*

*Regards, Paul.*

'Sally, is he going to turn this story into something else?'

'I would not be surprised, but always remember that we are in control.'

'Kashmira chose you to share her story, but without your consent, no one will ever get to see it. And Paul will have no card to play, but I have no doubt that he will try.'

'So, what do we do Sal?'

'Play the field, of course. Always remember that Roshan and Kashmira have a lot more invested in this situation than Paul does.'

'What do you mean by that Sally?'

'Everything will be revealed, especially if we read the rest of the diary. I have a feeling that there is more to this story than just a horrible tragedy.'

'Okay,' Jasper says. 'This is the diary entry from the 1st of November 1879.'

*"We have not yet decided on a name for our wonderful new creation, but it will be the stage where Kashmira and I will perform during the six months of the International Exhibition. It is a well-publicised event that will attract people from all over the world.*

*The packing crates are still at the dockside and our temple has not yet been erected. We have never seen it in its entirety, but I commissioned a small-scale model which takes pride of place on a table in our parlour. It looks like a heavenly chapel and Kashmira often sits and stares at it for hours on end.*

*This little wonder of ours has no purpose other than to allow the public to enjoy a unique performance in an outdoor setting. With the blue sky above and birds singing in the trees it will be perfect. Our performance is so much more effective in a natural setting, but we must take precautions when we perform in a theatre as fire is a primary part of our act.*

*We would not be averse to our Chapel of Love, as Kashmira calls it, being used as a wedding chapel. We have even discussed the idea that we would be the first to do so. It is not open to the elements, but you can see the world from any angle.*

*Performing has been one of the great joys of our life and we usually spent hours perfecting the finer details of a performance. Cobras are a central element of a snake charmer's act, and it is essential to train a juvenile to the point of perfection. They are venomous creatures that can strike out and kill.*

*One day, we were practicing the most critical part of our routine where Kashmira steps into the fire amidst seven writhing cobras. We have done it a thousand times before and it was the highlight of our show. But it has its dangers and one of those is that something unexpected could distract a cobra's attention.*

*What I didn't know was that a drama of a very different kind was taking place on the street outside, one that resulted in the tragedy which took the life of the woman I loved.*

*It happened the very moment that a horse and carriage was passing by. That was the very same moment that a dog decided to chase a cat across the street. The horse bolted, and the cat took the shortest path to freedom. Unfortunately, that just happened to be through our front door and the cat was followed by the half-crazed dog.*

*They ran around the room, upended the bowl of burning coals and scattered them all over the parlour floor. A timber house is like a tinder box, and as well as having lamps in the room, I often sprinkled kerosene on the coals for added effect.*

*Within moments, the house was like a raging firestorm and Kashmira, the love of my life, the woman I adored with my very heart and soul was trapped. She was caught in the middle of a blazing inferno, and there was nothing I could do to stop it. The house was reduced to cinders within thirty minutes, and there was nothing left of my beloved at all, nothing but ash and bone."*

## CHAPTER 83

'I cannot believe that such a beautiful woman came to such a grisly end,' Jasper says. 'Roshan must have been devastated.'

'I agree, but Jasper, did you notice anything as you were reading?'

'Like what?'

'Kashmira gave her memorial a name.'

'The Chapel of Love. That's just perfect isn't it, Sal?'

'But she has worked hard to see that her legacy will become a reality for all time, and the Chapel is her legacy Jasper.'

'Imagine that. A temple dedicated to the Goddess of Love, here in the heart of the Carlton Gardens.'

'That would be the perfect place for a white wedding, wouldn't it Jaz?'

'I am supposed to be the romantic one in this family, not you.'

'You certainly are, but I do have my moments, as you know. You have been a very bad influence on me, Jasper Powell.'

'I beg to differ. Apparently, I saved you from a fate worse than death.'

'So, you did Jaz, from those lotharios in expensive Armani suits.'

'I wouldn't mind an Armani suit, and white would be the perfect colour for a wedding in the Chapel of Love.'

'It definitely would, my dearest boy, and you would look so very handsome,' Sally says. 'But we have to make sure that the Chapel sees the light of day and finds its place in history.'

'Now you're talking Sal. Let's get proactive.'

'Okay, your place or mine?'

'Sally Velasko, you are an incorrigible tease, just in case you didn't know.'

'I do know that Jaz. It's an art form I have developed to perfection. That's because I have two annoying brothers, Jacob and Jarrod. They were game players extraordinaire who did their best to make my life a misery.'

'But they had no idea who they were up against, and, over a period of time, I showed them a thing or two about girl power.'

'However, I am a trailblazer who has single-handedly reinvented the woman of the future.'

'Only time will tell,' Jasper says.

'In the meantime, Wonder Woman, I think we should contact the local council, drag them down here by the bootstraps and show them what we've got in the bowels of this building.'

'We will need reinforcements in that case. It's time to make a call on that den of iniquity and talk to those naughty old tradesmen.'

'That's good thinking Sal.'

They take a short cut down a few back alleyways, hoping that Rocco and his mates really do have contacts in the local council.

'So, what's this place called, Jasper?'

'I don't think it has a name. It's just the front room of an old cottage. It might even be Rocco's place. It's not much to look at, faded walls, tables with smelly ashtrays, and it reeks of tobacco smoke as well.'

'If it hasn't killed them yet, it's never going to.'

'Not a chance Sal. These guys are big time smokers. You may not believe this, but Rocco is the President of the Fitzroy Branch of the Celibacy Society, and he even tried to sign me up.'

'He doesn't look like the celibate type to me, Jasper. An old lecher maybe.'

'Well, he is. No one else would take the job. As he said, it pays to have your finger in as many pies as possible.'

'So, what did you say?'

'I told him that I have a happy love life.'

'It's not a very popular club and hardly anyone ever goes to the meetings.'

'I can understand that Jasper, especially in this area.'

The inhabitants of Fitzroy are nothing if not diverse. Most people are regular upstanding citizens and typical happy families. But it also has a healthy collection of musicians and bohemians, and a cross-section of the gay community as well. They would not think twice about a life of celibacy, not unless they had to.

Other than Rocco who is busily rolling a cigarette, and an old fellow called Franco who is polishing the glasses, the teahouse is deserted.

'Jasper, Sally. This is a surprise. Come on in and take a seat.'

'Franco. Two more glasses, please.'

'So, why do we have the pleasure of your company?'

'Has something gone wrong Jasper? Did Paul Sinopoli back out of the deal?'

'No, he didn't Rocco, but he is playing the waiting game.'

'So, what do you want to do?'

'We have to get the Chapel of Love out of storage as soon as possible.'

'Is that what it's called?'

'Yes. That's what Kashmira called it.'

'In that case, we had better get moving. Leave this to me my youthful friends. The Fitzroy mafia is alive and well, but don't spread that around, will you?'

## CHAPTER 84

That old saying is true. It's not what you know, it's who you know. Rocco obviously has contacts in places other than the Fitzroy underworld, and before the day is over, he alerts them to the fact that his mission has been successful.

Two days later, five government officials appear at their door and Daniel Steel and his associates are awestruck at the scale of this creation.

'Jasper, this really is a monument of historic importance.'

'It is Daniel, and it belongs in Fitzroy, and that's where it's going to stay.'

'I agree wholeheartedly, Jasper, and the Carlton Gardens would be the perfect place for such a masterpiece, and like all public parks, it comes under the jurisdiction of the government.'

'Leave this in our hands Jasper and expect to hear from me very soon.'

A few days later, a team of government engineers assess the situation and not long after they receive an email from Daniel Steel.

'Sally, we did it,' Jasper says. 'Kashmira's monument will soon become a permanent feature of the Melbourne landscape.'

Paul Sinopoli is a little peeved that Jasper didn't keep him in the loop but he's in no position to argue.

'Paul, this will be an opportunity to get in first,' Jasper says.

'Can I bring a camera crew over? This is an historic event Jasper and it should be documented?'

'I agree Paul, but it would be best to do so as soon as possible.'

Over the next two weeks, the world watches with bated breath as the first in a series of events become headline news on television.

Word soon passes around that the packing crates are about to be removed from their resting place. Everyone in the neighbourhood is out in force, and are eagerly awaiting the best show in town.

A team of men are about to remove a section of the rear wall with heavy lifting equipment, and it will all take place in a back alleyway.

Jasper has to face a barrage of questions from dozens of inquisitive reporters, but Sally holds his hand from beginning to end.

It might not be important to anyone else, but he wants to send a clear message that he is in a relationship with a girl that he loves, and he is not up for grabs.

It takes three days to remove the crates from The Phoenix, after which they spend the next two weeks at the Carlton Gardens.

The discovery of a hidden treasure captivates the hearts and minds of everyone in the world, but Roshan and Kashmira's love story is headline news and everyone is talking about it.

Over the next two weeks, the streets are packed with sightseers, all of whom are eagerly awaiting the moment that the blocks are removed from the crates. Even the council comes to the party and provides chairs for those who just want to sit and watch.

Jasper and Sally meet more people than they have ever met in their lives. They are familiar faces on every television network around the world, and whether they like it or not, they are now world-famous celebrities.

This is an opportunity to get that most prized of all possessions, and everyone wants a selfie with Jasper and Sally. And a few minutes later, they appear like magic on The Jasper and Sally Facebook Page.

A distinct sense of excitement is in the air, and the Carlton Gardens is the place to be. Some people bring picnic baskets, while those of an entrepreneurial nature set up food stalls.

Mortisha makes a daily appearance, dressed as one Hollywood femme fatale or other. And as always, she looks glamorous in a fabulous hat and diamante sunglasses.

'You never know,' she says. 'A well-disguised Hollywood producer might be on the lookout for the next reincarnation of Elisabeth Taylor.'

'Queen of the Witches she might be,' Jasper whispers to Sally. 'But flamboyance is her middle name, of that I am certain.'

Jasper even gets to spend a day with Sally's mother and father. Stella and Marco are an attractive couple in their mid-forties and the parents of three grown children.

Stella is a typical European mother who has been slaving away in the kitchen preparing a smorgasbord of Polish treats and delicacies.

And as soon as she meets Jasper, she takes him in her arms and plasters him with sloppy kisses.

'You are so adorable,' she says. 'I want to wrap you up and take you home.'

'Well, you might have to speak to Sally about that, but don't hold your breath.'

'Yes, that could be a problem.'

Jacob and Jarrod are now strapping young lads, and are obviously very proud of their big sister. They have long since relinquished their role as serial pests, but they still have a mischievous sense of humour.

This is heaven for two young studs, and they take every opportunity to chat up any young girl who catches their eye. If they are anything like their sister, their love life will be nothing if not busy.

## CHAPTER 85

The big day finally arrives, and the blocks are about to be placed side-by-side. This is a huge undertaking that involves hundreds of tradesmen, but on the fifth day, Jasper and Sally are called to a meeting with George Tatopolous, the engineer in charge of the operation.

'I have encountered a problem,' he says. 'We have every piece of the puzzle sorted Jasper, but the base is missing.'

'According to the plans, the chapel is supposed to sit on a platform, a layer of marble blocks, but they are pieces that we do not have.'

Sally and Jasper look at each other and the penny suddenly drops.

'The ground floor was sealed up after The Phoenix was built and no one has ever seen what's inside' Sally says. 'If the blocks are anywhere George, that's where they'll be.'

They set off immediately, accompanied by a team of men with hammers and chisels. The front door and windows are on the footpath, and the only option is to go through the rear wall.

The men remove one brick at a time, a task that takes almost an hour, and as soon as they have finished, George steps through to investigate.

'You were right Sally. The blocks are here, but that's not all. We have hit the jackpot.'

The basement is a vast open chamber and the storage place for hundreds of packing crates. And even in the muted light it's possible to see two beautifully carved statues. One is obviously Roshan and the other is Kashmira, dressed in their snake-charming outfits.

'Oh my God, that is so extraordinary,' Jasper says, 'but where will they go?'

'Probably in the chapel, but all will be revealed.'

'But what about those other boxes?' Sally says.

'They look like the sort of packing crates which are used in art galleries,' George says. 'And that could be a clue as to what they contain.'

'I think we should open one up just in case it requires specialised attention.'

The crates were designed to survive manhandling at the wharves and damage during a potentially dangerous sea voyage.

George removes one nail at a time, a task which takes a good thirty minutes. And when he finally removes the lid, it is only to find that the contents are wrapped in layers of canvas, bonded together with some sort of 19th century superglue.

'This could take a while,' he says.

It's a delicate operation that takes over an hour as he has to peel away one layer at a time. And when the canvas is finally removed, he can hardly believe his eyes.

'It's a solid glass painting.'

This is not the work of an amateur, but a highly decorative image with jewel-like colours in orange, reds, and blues, in a style reminiscent of Indian paintings of the 16th century.

The subject matter is the beautiful Kashmira dressed in a colourful sari, and in her hands, she holds a pair of pure white doves.

'Her feminine charms are obvious, that's for certain. She really was a beautiful woman, wasn't she?'

'She certainly was Jasper, but I now understand the purpose of those blank walls on either side of the staircase. I was wondering what they were all about.'

'To think that they have been hidden away for over a hundred years, and no one even knew they were here.'

'But we will need the advice of a specialist before they are installed,' George says. 'We must ensure that they are never damaged by natural forces or brutalised by vagrants with a can of spray paint.'

Following the death of Kashmira, Roshan placed her ashes in a cemetery behind their home in Galkissa. Many years later, he returned to Melbourne with every intention of erecting the chapel as a permanent feature of the Carlton Gardens.

After visiting the warehouse, Roshan did not have the heart to go ahead with that plan. So, over a period of months, he devised another much more elaborate plan for someone to do what he could not.

The Phoenix was designed as a storage place for his masterpiece, and before it was finished, he travelled to the island of Murano in Venice to engage the services of a master craftsman.

His task was to create a series of solid glass paintings that depicted scenes from their life in the style of Indian murals. And just before he died, he established a trust fund and placed his finances in the hands of the Bank of Colombo.

His last words were these.

*"I know that one day in the future, someone will discover this treasure and realise what it is. Hopefully, they will also find this diary and understand its importance. I sincerely hope that whoever does so, honours it in the way it is meant to be honoured. The Chapel of Love was something I wanted to share with the world. I can only hope and pray that the universe intervenes, and that this shrine to the memory of my beloved finds its place in history.*

*If you are the person reading this diary, you are also the owner of The Phoenix. It was named for that fabled creature that rises from the ashes and lives once again. If you have successfully erected the tribute to the love of my life, it is now one hundred years later, and it is the year 2014.*

*If you have completed the task that I could not, and the Chapel of Love is now a reality, I say to you my beloved friend, thank you from the bottom of my heart, and may God bless you for all eternity.*

*Before I take to my bed for the last time, I have one more thing to say. Hidden away in the back of this diary is a key to a vault in the Bank of Colombo.*

*If you have done as I could not, I have left a token of my thanks for your efforts. Blessings be upon you, for you are a good and honest soul. What you find in my adopted land will be a reward for your efforts.*

*I will not be for this life much longer, but I will be watching, hoping, and praying that one day, I can look down from heaven and see Kashmira's Chapel in pride of place in that beautiful garden.*

*I will sign off now, but I will be calling to you from afar, of that you can be assured.*

*Juan Philippe Delgado, also known as Roshan the Snake Charmer, husband of the beautiful Kashmira, the love of my life and the Snake Charmer's Wife."*

## CHAPTER 86

Amateurs and professionals and anyone with a camera have their sights trained on the construction of the newest version of the Taj Mahal, and the world watches in anticipation as it is pieced together stone by stone.

Three weeks later, Roshan's monument to the woman who stole his heart is finally finished. It will become a world class tourist attraction and a major source of revenue, and in their wisdom, the Victorian government surrounds it with a fence and a translucent glass dome.

The Chapel is three storeys of pure white marble, and it's essential to protect it from vagrants, not to mention several thousand birds.

Given half a chance they would build a nest in every nook and cranny and then leave a reminder that it's also a public toilet.

Things eventually settle down for Jasper and Sally, and they are no longer ignored when they wander down Brunswick Street, but they have met just about every kid in the neighbourhood.

If it had not been for them, they would never have been invited to be guest readers on storybook day at a local primary school. And when they appear at the school yard gates, they are ambushed by hundreds of screeching little angels.

'Sally, Sally, Jasper, Jasper,' they scream.

As they now know, little kids are really good at screaming. In fact, they have mastered the art of high-pitched screeching to a never before known level. But when they sit down to read a story, which is all they have to do, they are like putty in their hands.

So many extraordinary things have happened over the last few months, and Jasper was inspired to start writing in earnest. So, he came up with an idea for a children's version of this now famous story. He decided to become a self-published author, and within days, he had sold over 100,000 copies.

*The Little Snake Charmer* not only became a publishing phenomenon; it went absolutely ballistic, and at ninety-nine cents a copy, Jasper made enough money to buy a dozen Jeep Wranglers.

The pub now has a new wooden floor, beautiful new windows, and a very handsome front door.

Sally eventually agreed to open a restaurant and spends her time comparing colour charts and numerous other things.

And from Jasper's perspective, that is not just good, that is excellent. At least it keeps her out of his hair.

One night, Sally told her mother that she and Jasper were planning to be married. Stella knew it was on the cards as soon as she saw them on television.

Being as she is of European heritage; Stella has been plotting and planning and God knows what else. But when Sally told her that they were going to be married in the Chapel of Love, well, Stella didn't know what to say. Everyone on the planet will be watching that wedding and what could she do.

'It will be bigger than the wedding of Prince William to Cate Middleton.'

After that, Stella wanted to know absolutely everything. 'So, how did you meet Jasper?' she said.

'The first time I saw him was at a railway station, but Mum, I just couldn't help myself. When I saw those beautiful green eyes, well, I was lost, heart and soul.'

'I know what you mean,' Stella says. 'Marco had the same effect on me. He and Jasper are so similar.'

'You were a delight as a child, but I have no idea where Jacob and Jarrod came from. They were little terrors, but I love them even so.'

'But Jasper is rich too, isn't he?'

'He inherited a lot of money after his father passed away, and he has made enough from The Little Snake Charmer to feed the starving people of Africa.'

'Nobody knows this yet, but he is probably going to inherit even more soon.'

'Really,' Stella says. 'And how is that going to happen.'

'Not long after we moved into The Phoenix, we received a diary in the mail. If it had not been for that, we would never have worked out what was going on.'

'But in the back of the diary, Juan left a key to a bank vault in Colombo.'

'Oh, my God,' Stella says. 'What do you think it is?'

'We have no idea Mum, but it's probably all sorts of priceless treasures.'

Very few things have the capacity to leave Stella speechless but that did for a few passing seconds.

'I have only one word of advice Sally. Just pray that your children are like Jasper. If you end up with the progeny of Satan…just run the other way.'

'I don't think we will, Mum.'

'Your life will be so much simpler if you have a little Jasper, otherwise you could end up with a Jacob and Jarrod.'

'God forbid.'

## CHAPTER 87

As he was wandering up the stairs one day, Jasper stopped to contemplate the view. The fact that he couldn't see anything at all gave him an inspired idea. So, he decided to have a section of the rear wall replaced by a plate glass window, and now they have an uninterrupted view of the Chapel.

Long gone are the days when they have to sit on a freezing cold balcony and watch the trams waddle down Brunswick Street. Now they can cuddle up on their black and white sofa and gaze out over the Gardens as the sun disappears over the horizon.

Unbeknownst to Stella, they have set a date for the wedding, but before church bells ring out through the streets of Fitzroy, they are going to pack their bags. But they will not be heading off to the jungles of Sri Lanka, they are going to Colombo.

Ever since she read the last page of Juan's diary, Sally has been dreaming about Sri Lanka, and she is just itching to find out what's in that vault.

This has been a very interesting year for these two lovebirds but it's not over yet. It's the middle of winter and that's a perfect excuse to fire up the central heating system.

It can be bitterly cold on some days but once you step out the door, you must be prepared for anything. On any given day in Melbourne, it can rain, or it can shine, and the wind factor can chill you to the bone.

An old-fashioned fireplace for a huge apartment like Jasper's was absolutely useless, and he was happy to invest in a hi-tech central heating system. And now, when he gets out of bed in the morning, the house is as warm as toast.

Winter has settled in, and they have no choice but to cuddle up in their oversized bed in their Queen of Sheba boudoir.

Before he falls asleep, Jasper always has one more thing to say. And after six months of hearing the same old thing, over and over again it's starting to get on Sally's nerves.

'Good night my beautiful girl,' he says.

'Jasper Powell, how many times have I told you, that's my line?' she says, pretending to seethe with anger.

'I say girl, you say boy,' is Jasper's usual reply.

'That makes approximately seven times this week.'

'You were a nice boy when I first met you, but now you are getting too big for those size ten shoes of yours.'

'Nine and a half, if you must know,' Jasper says.

Sally smiles the smile of a contented goddess, gives Jasper a goodnight kiss and drifts off into dreamland. Her destination is Sri Lanka, that most exotic of all places.

Sally is a woman on a mission, and she is determined to solve the mystery of the mysterious bank vault. And as Jasper knows, Sally always gets her way.

## CHAPTER 88

## THREE MONTHS LATER

As he gazes out over the rooftops of Fitzroy, Jasper reflects on the events of the past few months. He is not the man of the decade as one news report has said. He might have played a role in the discovery of a treasure of historical and cultural significance but he wasn't the only one.

If his apartment had been haunted by anyone other than Kashmira, it could have been a lot worse. She tried to attract the attention of three other men, but all she succeeded in doing was scaring them away.

And then she found Jasper Powell, romantic fool, and part-time dreamer, but it would never have happened at all if it had not been for a young woman called Sally Velasko.

Kashmira's Chapel is now a world class tourist attraction and people from all over the world were glued to the television as a new architectural wonder took shape and form.

It was hailed as a work of genius and a modern-day masterpiece, and as a result, the city of Melbourne is now the proud owner of a temple dedicated to the Goddess of Love.

Sally is downstairs talking to another kitchen specialist at the moment, and even though she has not decided on a name for her restaurant, Jasper has a sneaking suspicion as to what she has in mind.

Sally loves oranges and puts them in every dish she makes, and if Jasper hadn't got in first, she would probably have married one. He could not bear the thought of living without his Sal, and in a moment of madness, he asked for her hand.

She abandoned a perfectly good career as an apprentice chef in a high-class restaurant and agreed to become the future Mrs. Jasper Powell.

And even though she is not a witch and has no idea how to cast a spell, she does know the secret ingredient of love potion number nine. And as Jasper now knows, that is freshly squeezed orange juice.

He has been pecking away on the draft of a novel called, Gypsy Queen, a story loosely based on the song made famous by that vocal virtuoso, Esmeralda.

Gypsy Queen oozes sensuality in every line, and in a nutshell, it's about old-fashioned lust. A seriously handsome man oozing buckets of masculinity would be a temptation for any hot-blooded gypsy woman looking for a good time.

But the last line is enough to make a boy's heart go all a flutter. Some things have the power to transport you to another world, and that song does it for Jasper every single time.

He is a million miles away, lost in his own hazy world, but his few precious moments of navel-gazing dissolve into thin air when he hears the love of his life coming up the stairs.

'Jasper, Jasper Powell,' Sally says in that oh so recognisable tone of voice.

It's only three o'clock in the afternoon and he braces himself.

'Yes Sal,' he says tentatively.

'Have I come at a bad time, Jaz?'

She ruffles his hair with her lovely hands, but what can he say? He just has to tell a barefaced lie.

'No, my gypsy queen, you have not.'

'So, how's the story going?'

'Slowly, but it's getting there.'

'Has that Mata Hari got her wicked way with the hero yet?'

'She's a bit like you Sal. She always gets her way.'

'Sound more like erotic fiction than a love story Jasper.'

'It's a bit of both Sal, but it can and does happen, as you know.'

'That I do know, but look what I found in the mailbox,' she says.

Sally's eyes are alive with excitement as she waves a white envelope in the air.

'It's from the Bank of Colombo of all places, and I think I know what it is.'

'It's probably just another financial statement.'

'Just open it Jasper, I can't stand it any longer.'

'Okay, hold your horses,' he says. 'Now where did I put that letter opener?'

'Forget the letter opener Jasper. Just give it to me.'

She inserts a fingernail under the flap with the surety of a woman who knows the value of having a sharpened dagger at the ready.

'There,' she says.

'No, you read it. It's probably just another boring old bank statement.'

'Whatever you say, Master.'

*Dear Mr. Powell.*

*I hope you received the correspondence relating to the estate of Juan Philippe Delgado. The Bank of Colombo has had the honour of attending to his business for over one hundred years. It's a very long-standing arrangement and Senor Delgado is one of our oldest clients.*

*The personnel of the bank had no idea as to the contents of your building, but like everyone else in the world, we do now.*

*You might be interested to know that we are the trustees of a bank vault in Senor Delgado's name. And according to the instructions left by the departed, it is our duty to advise you that this vault is now your property.*

*According to our records you should be in possession of a key. If that is so, and if you and your friend, Miss Velasko, are planning to visit Sri Lanka sometime soon, the Bank of Colombo would be happy to make all arrangements for travel, accommodation, and entertainment.*

*I can assure you, Mr. Powell, that you have many fans in Sri Lanka, including the employees of this bank.*

*We look forward to meeting you sometime in the near future. Please, do not hesitate to contact me if you decide to visit this fair country of ours.*

*Regards*
*Dilvan Kumara Singhe*
*Assistant Manger*
*Bank of Colombo*
*Sri Lanka.*

'Boring old bank statement indeed,' Sally says. 'That's so exciting, Jasper.'

'Please say we can go Jaz, pretty please.'

'Okay, pack your bags and I'll meet you downstairs in ten minutes.'

'Truly, Jasper.'

'Of course, Sal. Would I lie about a thing like that?'

'But we don't have a passport yet, silly boy.'

'Not yet Sal, but I picked up two application forms from the post office last week.'

'Jasper, you little sneak. You have been planning this all along, haven't you?'

'I had no choice. You have been talking about it in your sleep, just in case you didn't know.'

'Then it has to be important Jaz, doesn't it?'

'It's probably a packet of moth-eaten old sandwiches or something like that.'

'Jasper, how could you say something like that? After all those beautiful things Juan said in his diary. He trusted you Jaz, and he is forever in your debt.'

'I am sure he will forgive me for one little indiscretion.'

'Maybe he will but I am not so sure about Kashmira. She will probably come back to haunt you.'

'No, she won't. They have wandered off to greener pastures, content in the knowledge that the Chapel of Love is there for all the world to see.'

'Jasper Powell, you are turning into a little trickster, and all this writing business is going to your head.'

'You have too much time on your hands to think up smarty pants lines and fantasize about voluptuous women in silken veils.'

'That's not all I think about, Sally Velasko.'

'You can be a big tease sometimes Jasper Powell, but I wouldn't have it any other way.'

## CHAPTER 89

Most of Sally's plans had to be put on hold. Well, not all of them, of course, as there are some things that she can't live without. She picked up a couple of brochures from the travel agent and has been compiling a list of things on a daily basis.

'I will have to buy a whole new wardrobe, Jasper, like formal wear and cotton frocks.'

'You will wow them Sal, but I think it's time to do a bit of serious shopping. I have a feeling that an Armani suit and five hundred new dresses might come in handy.'

'But where are we going to put all that stuff, Jasper?'

'Well, I think it would be a good idea to have the other two apartments refurbished. One could be a walk-in wardrobe for your clothes, and one could be for mine.'

'Jasper Powell, you are becoming cheekier every day. However, I will need both apartments to store such valuable possessions.'

Mr. Kumara Singhe, or Dilvan, as Sally prefers to call him, is delighted that they have agreed to accept his offer, and he even has a few suggestions as to what they could do.

'He sounds like such a nice man,' Sally says. 'Nice men in business suits are such a rare breed these days.'

'He is probably a Sri Lankan stud who owns nothing but Armani suits,' Jasper says.

'Well, that's not a crime, Jasper. After all, you are planning to get one.'

'That's what you call one of the perks of celebrity, and I vowed not to stoop to that level.'

'Save your moralising for someone who cares, Jasper. This was meant to be, but I would not be surprised if Roshan and Kashmira have something to do with this.'

Two days later, they receive a five-page itinerary from Dilvan. The details as he said are negotiable, and he asked if they could give it their considered opinion.

'He's a fast worker, isn't he?'

'I have no doubt that an assistant bank manager has ten people at his beck and call, and he knows everyone of importance in Sri Lankan society.'

According to the itinerary, they will fly first class with Sri Lankan Airlines and be met at the airport by a delegation of people from the bank.

'This isn't going to be a private trip from what I can see,' Jasper says. 'In fact, it's just the opposite.'

'Jasper, it will be wonderful whatever happens.'

'But we will be travelling from one venue to another in a bullet proof limousine and be accompanied by policemen on motorcycles.'

'The Royal family does it all the time Jasper, and so do lots of other people.'

'But Sally, there's a terrorist threat going on at the moment, and those extremists are out to get anyone in the Western world.'

'Why would they be bothered with us?'

'Because we are celebrities now, that's why. They pick their targets, and if they get wind of this, they could use it as an opportunity to take a few hostages.'

'Jasper, you are starting to scare me. Perhaps we should talk to Dilvan before we make any hasty decisions.'

Jasper was just stating the case. The terrorist threat is the news of the day. As to what Sally has been dreaming about, he has never bothered to ask.

She collapses on the couch and buries her head in a pile of pillows. Jasper's revelation has obviously opened up a hornet's nest.

Sally usually has a hide like an African elephant, but as he discovers on that cold September afternoon, that is not the case at all. He has a sneaking suspicion that there's something else going on.

'Sal, tell me about your dreams.'

'They have all been so lovely Jaz, except for one about a boy. He was a prisoner on some filthy old boat on some stinky old river, but the creepy thing is that he looked just like you.'

'That does sound creepy, but did you have any good dreams?'

'Yes. In one dream, we were staying at a big hotel not far from the beach and decided to take a stroll along the esplanade.'

'And you may not believe this Jasper, we met a snake charmer, a little boy and his sister.'

'Really, like a little Roshan and Kashmira.'

'They probably were, and as we stood there watching, he charmed a little cobra from his basket.'

'You should have seen the look on his face Jaz. He was so thrilled as if it was the first time it had ever worked at all.'

'But one morning after breakfast we set off on the next leg of our journey when the car stopped in the middle of nowhere.'

'The driver pointed to a series of steps that wound their way up the side of a mountain and said, 'This place you must see. This is the Golden Temple.'

'I have checked it out on the internet Jasper, and the Golden Temple of Dambulla really does exist. It's a series of magnificent caves with statues of Buddha all over the place.'

'And just as we were about to leave, I looked up at a seated Buddha, and you may not believe this Jasper, his lips were moving, but that wasn't all, he was nodding at me as well.'

'I grabbed you by the arm and said, 'look at that Jasper. Can you see what I can see?'

'And what did I say?'

'You just stood there with your mouth open and had no idea what to say.'

## CHAPTER 90

Even at the ripe old age of nineteen Jasper doesn't know much about the mysteries of the world, but at the age of eighteen he knew even less.

As to the meaning of those dreams, he has no idea, and the only person who could shed some light on this situation is Mortisha.

They are having second thoughts about the trip, and if it is going to be dangerous, well, they just won't go. Whatever Roshan has stashed away in the bank vault can wait. It's been there for a hundred years, and it can wait a little longer.

Mortisha looks positively radiant when she opens the door, and if she is older than she looks, then she obviously knows how to tinker with the equipment.

'My darlings,' she says. 'You look as if you have seen a ghost. Kashmira isn't haunting the house again, is she?'

'No, she's not,' Jasper says.

'Come inside and tell Aunty Mortisha absolutely everything.'

To those in the know, Mortisha's home is a temple dedicated to the goddess of sorcery and witchcraft. Anyone who dabbles in magic would also know that the Supreme and Powerful Queen of the Witches is the Almighty Hecate.

And when she is not advising her acolytes on how to do this that or the other, Hecate's idea of a recreational pastime is to roam through the forest with a pack of highly trained hunting dogs.

'Now, take a seat,' she says, 'and I will treat you to a mid-day aperitif.'

She returns a few minutes later and places three long-stemmed glasses on the table, all of which are fizzing away like little volcanoes.

'Mortisha, you didn't spike them with something, did you?'

'Jasper Powell, I only do that to very bad men who cross my path on a very dark night so to speak.'

'No, I just added a touch of baking soda, but it does look rather impressive, doesn't it?'

'So, you don't have to be a witch to work out that something is bothering you two love birds.'

'Why do you look so forlorn?'

This is not what you would call a major drama as nothing has even happened yet. But Mortisha sits up and takes notice when Jasper reveals the little-known fact that Juan Philippe Delgado left them a key to a bank vault in Colombo.

'What a lovely old man. Do you have any idea if it's gold bullion or a treasure chest full of priceless jewels?'

'Haven't a clue, but it is a token of his appreciation. After all, he was a wealthy man.'

'So true. Even Prince Harry would think twice about a holiday planned by a bank manager, especially with all this terrorist stuff going on.'

'If it didn't involve such high-level security, it would be okay Mortisha, but we will be on every television network in the world, and we will be sitting ducks wherever we go.'

'Such a shame, you would be treated like royalty and get to meet so many lovely people.'

'Have you expressed your reservations to Mr. Bank Manager yet?

'No, we haven't but there's more. Sally has been having dreams about this trip for months. Good dreams mostly, except for one, that is.'

'Really Sally, tell me about them,' she says. 'But give me your hands first, my dear.'

'There is nothing better than going to the source of a problem in some situations.'

'One day, we visited the ruins of an ancient city. It was a very humid day and it started to rain, so we took refuge in a temple beside a statue of Buddha,' Sally says.

'The storm lasted for ages, but as I was looking at the face of the statue, I realised that it looked just like Jasper.'

'Not long after, an old lady offered to give him a massage. Every muscle in his neck was constricted but she was very skillful, and it took several minutes of pounding before he even exhaled.'

'Very good,' she said. 'You be feeling much better after this.'

Jasper paid her handsomely for her services and she was happy to accept the money.

'Not go hungry tonight,' she said. 'But before we left, she had a warning.'

'And what was that?'

'Must not go near water. Very bad men near water.'

'What did she mean by that?'

'I don't know, Mortisha, but one night we were strolling alongside a very squalid canal, and I thought I heard someone crying out for help.'

'The only place it could have come from was an old junk moored in the harbour. But it was then that I had a vision of a young man who looked just like Jasper.'

'He was a prisoner on a filthy old boat and his body was covered in ugly green sores, but the worst thing of all was the look in his eyes.'

'Hmm,' Mortisha says as she releases her grip on Sally's hands, 'that is all very interesting.'

'You are a very connected young woman, Sally. Did you ever notice if you had company during those dreams?'

'I often had a feeling that I could see Roshan and Kashmira out of the corner of my eye.'

'What does that mean?' Jasper says.

'It means they have unfinished business, my boy.'

'I don't understand, Mortisha. What sort of business?'

'I have no idea, but they obviously do, otherwise they would not have been there.'

'So, what are we to do, Mortisha?'

'I suggest that you go ahead with your trip, and if you wish, I will be happy to accompany you.'

'Really, are you going to bring your crystal ball and wand along as well?'

'No Jasper, it would take five men with heavy lifting equipment to move that thing, but I will be taking my little travelling wand.'

'Is it anything like Harry Potter's?'

'Harry's wand was a fictitious creation, Jasper, but mine is the real thing.'

## CHAPTER 91

The following day, they apply for a passport, and then do a spot of shopping in the city.

'Jasper, we've got your suit, three pairs of trousers and six shirts. Do you have enough underwear?'

'I think so Sal. I have at least twenty-five packets in the wardrobe. Will that be enough?'

'Probably, but Dilvan did say that laundry will be taken care of.'

Sally does her best to find a wardrobe suitable for such a venture and Jasper thinks that she looks gorgeous in anything that she tries on.

Rather than loitering around in the lingerie department of an all-girl's boutique, he decides to wait outside instead, but Jasper is not the invisible man anymore.

A few people recognise him immediately, especially a gaggle of boys from a local high school.

'Look, it's Jasper,' they cry. 'Hello Jasper.'

One young woman turns around, marches back and plants a juicy kiss on his mouth, then wanders off with a contented smile on her face. The boys go ballistic, and one even gets a happy snap.

'Jasper Powell, that sort of behaviour will get you a very bad reputation,' someone says.

Jasper turns around, only to discover that this is no casual comment from a passing stranger. It's Fabian Stella-Marcus, PE student extraordinaire and red-headed heartthrob, accompanied by his best friends, Declan Smith, and Mark Jacobsen.

'I already have a reputation, Fabian, but not for that.'

'Pity, I thought you were giving them away for free.'

'Sally would kill me, but please, whatever you do, don't tell her.'

'So, the Three Musketeers to the rescue.'

'It's good to see you guys again. So, what are you up to?'

'Nothing much, just going to see a movie,' Mark says. 'What about you?'

Jasper explains that they have to go to Sri Lanka to finalise the details of Roshan and Kashmira's estate, and it's then that he has an inspired idea.

'How would you like to come with us?'

'That depends on what you have in mind,' Fabian says.

'I am asking if you would like a job, Fabian, a very well paid one.'

'Tell us more, in that case.'

'Okay, I'll let Sally know what's going on and I'll be back in a few minutes.'

They make themselves comfortable in a nearby coffee shop while Jasper explains the problem.

'We are concerned because we are so well-known, and Sally even had a dream about being kidnapped.'

'That would be enough to put you off,' Declan says. 'So, what's the plan, Jasper?'

'How would you like to be our bodyguards?'

'Keep going,' he says.

'Undercover bodyguards, that is. I presume you have martial arts training.'

'We sure do.'

'Hopefully, you will never have to use those skills, but if you guys are with us, we would feel so much better.'

'And as I said, the money will be good.'

'Like how much are you thinking?' Fabian says.

'I could transfer two thousand dollars into your account for initial expenses, but it would be a good idea to buy a suit. You never know, it might come in handy.'

'Does that sound interesting?'

'It certainly does,' Fabian says. 'Is there anything else we should know, Jasper?'

'Yes, I will happily pay you three thousand for the week that we are there.'

'Count me in,' Fabian says.

'That is seriously good money,' Mark says. 'What do you think Declan?'

'You count me in too,' he says.

'Thanks guys. Sally will be relieved to hear that, so I will transfer the money immediately.'

'But it would be a good idea to come over and meet Sally and my friend Mortisha sometime, like for lunch or dinner or something like that.'

'Sure thing, boss,' says a cheeky Fabian.

'Naughty boy, Fabian. It's good to see that you know your place.'

'I will do anything you ask of me, Jasper.'

'Declan, you have my permission to give him a slap across the wrist.'

'He needs more than that Jasper. Medication is what he needs.'

'I do not,' Fabian says. 'Well, not the sort that you are thinking about anyway.'

'Whatever you do, please don't bring it with you,' Jasper cries.

'I might act like a certified idiot, Jasper, but I am not stupid.'

'At least we agree on something,' Declan says as he gives him an affectionate slap over the head.

## CHAPTER 92

What a stroke of luck, the Three Musketeers disguised as the Three Stooges, or was it the other way around. Either way, they will all feel so much safer.

Fabian will no doubt keep Mortisha amused, but she will probably take a fancy to Mark. If she thought Roshan was a hunk, she won't be able to control herself once she gets an eyeful of him.

Jasper contacts Dilvan regarding their concerns and he agrees to lower their profile. But he also advises Jasper that the bank has another letter penned by Juan Philippe Delgado.

This one clearly states that the person in possession of the key must answer several questions before the vault can be opened. If the answers are not acceptable, the contents will revert to the trust fund.

'Sally, Dilvan says that I will have to answer questions before the vault can be opened. What's the point of going if I don't know them?'

'They are likely to be questions of a personal nature, Jasper. What else could they be?'

'Juan didn't mention anything like that, did he?'

'I have no doubt that you already know the answers Jasper, but you have plenty time to read the diary again. Besides, we won't be going anywhere, not until the boys have finished their exams, and that's over a month away.'

Whether they like it or not, it's going to be Sri Lanka during the hot season. This is Sally's first overseas trip, and she has everything planned down to the colour of her lipstick.

Jasper has a suspicion that it's probably gold bullion or something just as valuable. His financial situation is brilliant for someone of his age.

He has invested his money wisely and is planning to sublet the other two apartments. He has a steady stream of money coming in from The Little Snake Charmer and they will eventually make a fortune from Sally's restaurant.

'Sally, what could be in that vault?'

'I have no idea, Jasper.'

'Roshan didn't say anything about that in the diary, did he?'

'Not that I noticed but read it again and read between the lines this time. The answers will be in there somewhere.'

'However, I was looking at a map of Sri Lanka yesterday and it has a few very tricky place names.'

'Perhaps it would be a good idea to do a bit of *research*, say, in five minutes or so.'

The very mention of that word is enough to send shivers up Jasper's spine.

It all started at the train station one afternoon after school. Jasper had been on Harriet Mendelsen's radar for quite some time, but on that day, she zoomed in for the kill. She seemed charming enough at first, but unbeknownst to little old Jasper, Harriet had a well thought out plan.

She wasn't his first experience with the opposite sex, but Harriet Mendelsen was the most terrifying of them all.

She lured him into her net on the pretext of collaborating on a science project, but her idea of *research* was more of a biological nature.

The moment she had him in her grasp, she locked the door and hid the key. Unfortunately, her parents arrived home a little earlier than usual and Jasper was trapped in her bedroom. Harriet had a new toy to play with and she was determined to keep it for as long as possible.

Before she could suck the life from his body, Jasper escaped through a window and shimmied down the drainpipe. He hobbled all the way home, one excruciating step at a time, dragging his school bag along behind. But no matter how he tried, he could not get that experience out of his mind, and to his horror, the spectre of Harriet Mendelsen haunted his dreams for the next three weeks.

# CHAPTER 93

According to Dilvan's plan, they were to arrive in Colombo under the cover of darkness. Unfortunately, Sri Lankan Airlines arrives at midday and that idea had to be scrapped, but they were happy to fly with Emirates.

It's a twelve-hour flight with a stopover in Singapore, and it's just after midnight when the plane finally lands at Bandaranaike International Airport.

Anonymity is the key issue and Jasper's disguise is a baseball cap and sunglasses, whereas Sally just slaps on a bit of extra make-up.

After all, this is an airport and a security camera monitors their every move, but they also have to present their passports to a vigilant officer at the Customs and Immigration desk.

Dilvan is waiting for them as he said he would be. As to why he is wearing a pair of wrap-around sunglasses in the middle of the night, Jasper has no idea. He obviously has a sense of the absurd, and if he does, that has to be a good sign.

Dilvan is a good-looking young man who speaks English with a discernible Sri Lankan accent. As to whether he is a Sri Lankan pin-up boy is yet to be seen but Mortisha is seriously impressed.

'This may not be so bad after all,' she says to Sally. 'For a woman of my age to meet one hunk in her life is rare, but to meet four of them at once is almost unheard of.'

'I would have to book myself in to a rehab clinic just to recuperate.'

After a very speedy introduction, Dilvan sweeps them out the door and into a very unassuming-looking vehicle.

'Your bags will meet you at the hotel,' he says.

The hotel is not the sort of place that the media would expect them to stay, but Jasper has his doubts. The boys have probably blabbed to everyone they know. As Dilvan pointed out sometime later, the grapevine is alive and well, especially in the airline industry.

Because they have access to Roshan's trust fund, The Bank of Colombo will be picking up the tab for this trip but there are guidelines as to what they can and cannot do.

Roshan encountered extensive poverty in his travels and he established a trust fund to help the poor and needy. The bank employs a team of professionals to ensure that his money is spent wisely.

Children in outlying areas now have access to education. Labourers working their hands to the bone in remote villages, and people living on the breadline have a safety net to fall back on.

Jasper made a point of saying that he did not want the contents of the vault to be the reason for their visit. He preferred a semi-formal itinerary with a bit of sightseeing on the side, but what he really wants to see is a snake charmer and maybe meet a few of the local gypsies.

Dilvan joins them for breakfast the following morning, and when they step out the door the temperature is somewhat warmer than they are used to. But they are relieved to see that they will be travelling in a brand new, air-conditioned minibus.

The boys are dressed in shorts and T-shirts, and the girls wear lightweight summer dresses. And even though she probably gave it a little bit of serious thought, Mortisha has chosen not to wear her favourite diamante sunglasses. They don't want to look as if they reek of money particularly as this is an Asian country.

Sri Lanka is not technically Asian, but the population is varied, Indians from India, Tamils, Malays and Arabs, and people from other countries as well.

Colombo is a fusion of people, cultures, and religions, and it is not unlike any other Asian city where everyone lives on the street and the floodtide of humanity goes on and on forever.

Most people are engaged in the oldest activity of all, but hotels and boutiques are making a fortune, and it all happens in a haze of fuel-congested roads, streets stalls, and markets.

They eventually leave Colombo far behind, but this is a whole new world. Melbourne is very different and there is nothing they can do except sit back and take it in a little at a time.

The boys spend most of the time gazing out the window or arguing about whether Australia or Sri Lanka is the superior cricket team. It's an issue which they never resolve but it was getting on Mortisha's nerves.

'Juan was the owner of numerous properties, but we are going to see his house at Mt. Lavinia Beach,' Dilvan says. 'It is still in immaculate condition and that will be our first port of call.'

'Now, we will soon be passing through Mt. Lavinia Beach. It's a popular tourist resort but it also has a rather unique history.'

'It was the home of the Governor of Ceylon, Sir Thomas Maitland in the early 19th century, but now it's known as the Mt. Lavinia Hotel.'

'It was also the site of a gypsy village and the spot where a ship was wrecked in the mid-1800s.'

'Which means that it was probably the place where Roshan was rescued as a boy, and where Kashmira was born,' Sally says.

'That is possibly true Sally, but there is another equally interesting local legend, and it is not unsimilar to that of Roshan and Kashmira.'

'It's the story of Thomas Maitland's love for a gypsy girl called Lovinia. He had no choice but to smuggle her through a tunnel in the dead of night, so that he could see her on a regular basis, of course.'

'His house is now a monument to Lovinia, but he also had a statue made in her honour. It still stands to this very day and is the centrepiece of a fountain at the front of the Mt. Lavinia Hotel.'

'How interesting,' Mortisha says. 'But everyone in the world knows about Roshan and Kashmira.'

'They certainly do Mortisha but no one knew anything about them until a few months ago. Which is what Juan wanted, and it is also why no one has ever been aware of their home.'

'He probably built it here because this is where they met as children,' Sally said.

'I do agree, but we are almost at our destination, and you will be able to see for yourself why Juan had no interest in his home becoming a tourist attraction.'

'And why is that?' Mortisha says.

'Have you heard that old saying, that a man's home is his castle, or something like that, well, theirs is a temple.'

## CHAPTER 94

The property is surrounded by a ten-foot fence but the bus has to pass through two security gates, the first of which is remote controlled and the second has a sentry box manned by a security guard.

Roshan and Kashmira's home sits on the rise of a hill surrounded by a lush and tropical rainforest, but this is no ordinary home as they can see, it really is a replica of the Taj Mahal.

'That is what you call classically beautiful,' Fabian says.

As soon as Jasper steps off the bus, a familiar tingling sensation ripples up his spine.

'They're here Mortisha, aren't they?'

'They certainly are Jasper, and they have a little boy with them as well.'

'Oh Jaz, I wish we could see them,' Sally says.

Accompanied by three ghosts in their finest clothes, they follow Dilvan through an archway that leads to an open-air courtyard.

It's as peaceful a place as you could ever wish to see, surrounded by a garden of flowering shrubs. The aroma of orange blossom wafts through the air, and taking pride of place in the very centre is an ornate marble fountain.

'This is a temple of peace and harmony if ever there was one,' Mortisha says.

This is no austere home of stark lines and features, but a retreat for the soul where every little thing has been thought out in detail.

And while everyone else sits around soaking up the atmosphere, Fabian listens to the smoky voice of Nat King Cole singing *Stardust Memories*.

'Now, we are here for two reasons,' Dilvan says. 'Firstly, we are going to see an art gallery, and secondly, it is to pay our respects at their final resting place.'

'Follow me and prepare for the experience of a lifetime.'

The gallery is a repository for an extraordinary collection of treasures which any museum would love to get their hands on but Jasper is immediately attracted to the paintings on the walls.

'These are the original versions of the paintings that are now a feature of the Chapel of Love,' he says.

'That I did not know,' Dilvan says. 'Are they like stained glass windows perhaps?'

'No, they're solid glass paintings from the island of Murano in Venice. Juan commissioned twenty paintings depicting scenes from their life.'

In one painting, Roshan and Kashmira are performing in front of an audience in a local marketplace. One of the most poignant images of all is that of Kashmira gazing into the eyes of a boy lying on a beach. And in the background is the shattered hull of the ship on which he almost lost his life, but the most intriguing image of all is a painting of a young boy.

'Jasper, he looks just like you,' Sally says.

'He certainly does,' Mortisha says. 'That is interesting.'

If he didn't know any better Jasper would swear that this was a portrait of himself.

'That's a bit weird,' he says.

They follow Dilvan up a winding staircase to the master bedroom, and once they step through the door, it's like stepping into a scene from *Tales of the Arabian Nights*.

Persian rugs are scattered across a marble floor. A huge chandelier hangs from the ceiling, and soaring high above is a dome decorated with an Indian mural. The bed is the focal point of the room and a masterpiece of Indian ingenuity adorned with exotic silken veils.

'Now for the best part,' Dilvan says, 'a cemetery to rival that of any prince of the realm.'

They venture outside and wander through a beautifully manicured garden with lacework pergolas, bubbling fountains, and sculptures from many different lands.

The cemetery is some distance away behind a grove of old fruit trees, but what they had not expected to see is a replica of the Parthenon in Athens.

'Yet another example of Juan's devotion to detail,' Mortisha says.

'He certainly knew how to do things in style, didn't he?' Fabian says.

'He certainly did but Juan chose to be cremated,' Dilvan says, 'and his ashes were placed in an urn alongside those of Kashmira.'

'But what about that other one,' Sally says, as she inspects a marble casket decorated with a garland of leaves and flowers.

'It looks like a child's coffin.'

'I wasn't aware that they had children,' Dilvan said.

Jasper steps up to take a closer look. 'There's something written on it.'

*'The restless sea thy body may consume, but the love in our hearts will only increase with time.'*

'That's so beautiful, isn't it?'

'How do you know that?' Fabian says. 'It's written in ancient Sanskrit or something like that.'

'I am just guessing, Fabian, that's all.'

'Jasper Powell, I am having second thoughts about you. Were you a Brahmin priest in a previous life?'

'Not that I know of Fabian.'

This is not the time to discuss things of an otherworldly nature, but Fabian is not convinced. He inspects the coffin closely and takes a couple of photos as well. He will no doubt investigate this mystery at a later stage. Fabian has never been one to leave any stone unturned.

'There is one room that no one has ever seen before,' Dilvan says. 'And unfortunately, we do not have the key to the door.'

'That sounds interesting,' Fabian says. 'Has anyone ever tried to open it?'

'Not that I know of.'

While everyone else races around taking photos, Jasper is drawn to the mysterious room. Mortisha is equally curious and just happens to notice the look on his face.

'Jasper, you're on fire. It's the Kundalini again, isn't it?'

'Yes Mortisha, Kashmira's here. You said so yourself.'

'Jasper, Roshan is standing at the door of that room, and I think he wants you to take a look.'

'But it's locked Mortisha and we don't have a key.'

'There might be a way around that problem,' she says as she rummages around in her handbag.

'Oscar is in here somewhere.'

'And who is Oscar?' Fabian says.

'My wand, of course. What else would I be talking about?'

'You call your wand, Oscar.'

'I misplaced it once and couldn't find it for days, so I placed a simple spell on it.'

'And now, all I have to do is call out, Yoo hoo, Oscar, where are you, and he lets me know immediately.'

'Brilliant, isn't it?'

'Ah, there you are you little scallywag. Come to Mama. You have a job to do, my boy.'

'It looks like an ordinary old coloring pencil to me,' Fabian says.

'This is no coloring pencil, as you will soon see. This is a magic pencil. And no peeking either, Fabian. This is secret witch business.'

With her lips moving imperceptibly, Mortisha intones a simple spell, touches the lock on the door, and to Fabian's amazement, it releases the locking mechanism.

'Excellent, that idea worked,' he says. 'So, let's have a look, shall we?'

'Unfortunately, Fabian, you are not going in.'

'And why is that, Mortisha?'

'Because Roshan is barring the door, that is why. In other words, it's out of bounds to everyone except Jasper.'

'I have no idea what this is all about,' Jasper says. 'But be ready to act if you have to Fabian.'

'I will Jasper, but you will be careful, won't you?'

'I'll do my best, Fabian.'

## CHAPTER 95

The room is dark and forbidding and hasn't seen the light of day for over a hundred years. The very sight of it chills Jasper to the bone and he is having second thoughts about this idea.

'Sal, please come with me.'

'Do I have to Jaz?'

'No, but I want you to. I have a feeling that there's something in there for both of us.'

'Okay, but if anything happens Fabian, you will come and get us, won't you?'

'You can count on it,' he says.

The windows are boarded up. The bedroom is in darkness and it's impossible to see anything at all. Only moments after they cross the threshold, the door slams shut and the lock falls into place.

'Mortisha, what's going on?' Fabian cries.

'I'm not sure Fabian.'

Fabian is not about to stand by and do nothing, Jasper is paying good money for his services. Not knowing what else to do, he gets down on his knees, and with one ear to the door, he listens closely.

Mortisha paces back and forth, her anxiety levels increasing with every passing minute. Fabian is all but ready to break down the door when he hears Sally screaming out for help.

Mortisha activates her wand and releases the locking mechanism, only to find Sally on the floor cradling Jasper in her arms.

'Oh, my goodness Sally, what happened?'

'I don't know, but Jasper has passed out.'

The ever-dependable Fabian picks him up, lays him on a bench in the garden and proceeds to check his pulse and vital signs.

'His temperature has dropped. We need blankets. Dilvan, can you get some from the bus?'

Jasper is out cold, so Fabian wraps him in a blanket, places one under his head and another beneath his feet and then kneels at his side.

'Come on Jaz. You can do it.'

Jasper wakes with a start and releases a long and soulful sigh, but he has a strange and vacant look on his face.

'You're okay. Just take it easy mate. It's all good.'

'What happened in there, Sally?'

'I'm not sure Fabian. I can't remember anything at all.'

If she had the words, Sally would have said that they crossed over from the world of the living to the world on the other side. She has just experienced something of a supernatural nature and that experience is still flowing through her veins.

'It was something out of the ordinary, of that I am certain, but I think we saw Roshan and Kashmira.'

'Well, that makes sense. He was waiting at the door,' Mortisha says. 'But the shock was all too much for Jasper.'

She takes his face in her hands and says, 'Just let it out, my boy. Just let it go.'

'Tissues, has anyone got any tissues?'

'I do,' Fabian says. 'I keep then handy for special occasions.'

'Don't tell me anymore, Fabian. Just pass them over.'

It takes a while before Jasper settles down, but it could have been a lot worse if not for dear old Fabian.

He was getting a little twitchy with all the waiting around, so he decides to do a few basic stretching exercises, but when he realises that he is the focus of attention, Fabian has one of his inspired ideas.

'Okay boys, up you get,' he says to Mark and Declan. 'It's time to earn your keep.'

'Little old Jasper needs a good laugh. He is paying us good money, after all.'

'This particular exercise is one of my own inventions,' he says.

Fabian, it seems, is quite the showman at heart and happily thrusts his pelvis back and forth and wriggles his backside from one side to the other.

'It's called the Bum-Wobble, Jasper, and it is excellent for getting rid of those flabby bits that creep up when you're not looking.'

'Feel like joining in, perhaps.'

'Not just yet Fabian. You are doing an excellent job.'

'That's because I am an expert Jasper and trained to the highest standards, but we are especially good at ballroom dancing, aren't we boys?'

'Would you care to dance?' he says to Sally.

'I would love to Fabian.'

For a few enchanting minutes, they pirouette around the garden to the strains of an imaginary orchestra playing away in the background.

'People rarely do these dances anymore, but they are actually very graceful.'

'I have always wanted to do the Pride of Erin,' Sally says, 'but not in the garden.'

'In that case, I will make it my mission to teach you everything I know, because I am an expert, after all.'

'And an artist of the highest calibre,' Declan says. 'As to what sort, Sally, I am sure you can work that out for yourself.'

## CHAPTER 96

'So, Jasper,' Fabian says. 'Did you see Roshan and Kashmira?'

Fabian is doing his best to be patient, but he is just aching to find out what happened in the bedroom.

'I can't remember,' Jasper says.

He really does know, but he is not about to tell Fabian or anyone else at the moment.

'However, when I do remember, you will be the first to know.'

'Spoilsport,' he says. Jasper is holding back vital information and Fabian knows it.

'Dilvan, I don't care what you've got planned for the rest of the day,' Jasper says, 'but I don't want to do it.'

'Okay, so what do you want to do?'

'I have to immerse myself in water, and I am in serious need of a drink, but not at the hotel or a public beach.'

'In that case, my place will be perfect. I have a beautiful house that overlooks the Indian Ocean, and it has a pool as well.'

'That will be perfect,' Jasper says.

'Fabian, I hope you packed your boardshorts.'

'Jasper, men with bodies like ours do not wear board shorts in the pool.'

'Then what do you wear?' Dilvan says.

'Budgie smugglers.'

'And what are they?'

'Well, they're a bit like Tarzan's lap-lap but with a lot less material.'

'He means Speedos,' Sally says. 'Those tight-fitting, Australian made, hip-hugging things that show just about everything a man owns.'

'I know what they are,' Dilvan says. 'I've got a dozen of those things.'

'Then lead the way,' Fabian says.

'This should be interesting, very interesting indeed,' Mortisha says.

They creep back into the hotel, an undertaking that has all the attributes of a midnight raid. The staff have obviously been given instructions to respect their privacy, and they pass through reception without so much as a second look. They pack a bag of essential items, and an hour later, they arrive at Dilvan's beach house.

This is obviously a retreat from the wild world of high-level finance, a refurbished villa from the colonial era. And its main claim to fame is that it has a classic view of the Indian Ocean.

This is as tropical a place as you could ever wish to see, a low maintenance landscaped garden with two attractive swimming pools, one of which has no practical purpose at all. Dilvan's garden is no leafy green rainforest but it does have numerous palm trees swaying in the breeze.

'My modest bachelor pad,' he says.

'I thought so,' Mortisha says. 'The odds were in his favour.'

'Which means that you only have one mountain to conquer now and not two,' Sally says.

'A woman of my age doesn't have a chance if the odds are stacked against her, my dear.'

Sally spent ages selecting her swimwear of choice, and she looks vivacious in a red and gold one-piece suit.

As could be expected, Mortisha looks fabulous in a designer sunhat with a woven handbag draped casually over one arm. Her dress of choice is a stylish but sensible dark red caftan.

As to whether it was manufactured in India doesn't really matter but it is decorated with a motif of miniature flowers and tendrils. And just because she can, she is also wearing her favourite diamante sunglasses.

She requisitions a banana lounge and then lays back to luxuriate in the moment. Two glasses of wine are not enough to get her motor running, but when the boys appear on the catwalk wearing almost nothing she sits up and demands a third.

'They're almost naked,' she cries. 'That sort of thing should be illegal.'

With physiques like Spartan soldiers, the boys are the quintessence of the stereotypical bronzed Aussie with loaded six packs and sculpted pecs.

'I can see just about every muscle in their muscular system,' Mortisha says. 'Call the cops. I can't take any more of this.'

'Just hit the music button Jasper and take me out of here. Anything will do, but not that mealy-mouthed siren with skinny legs.'

To Mortisha's dismay, the entertainment for the afternoon is volleyball and the boys spend the afternoon frolicking about in the pool.

And when they are not doing that, they are dancing away to anything on Fabian's playlist, but they do take time-out at regular intervals to replenish their drinks.

Fabian does his best to entice Jasper down their end of the pool but he politely declines. He is not about to endanger his life in the Roman arena. One traumatic experience a day is more than enough for anyone.

Three long hours later, the boys eventually crawl out of the pool, and to Mortisha's relief, they even put their clothes back on.

But it's late afternoon and visible on the horizon is one of the most dramatic of all natural attractions.

'Okay folks, grab your cameras and follow me,' Dilvan says.

'Where are we going?' Jasper says.

'To see the best show in town, of course. You haven't lived until you have seen the sun set over the Indian Ocean.'

'You are in Sri Lanka after all Jasper, and that is a sight which should not be missed. This is Mother Nature at her most excellent best, and for some unknown reason, she does the same thing every afternoon without fail.'

'It's a perfect opportunity to get into her most extravagant party clothes for one thing.'

'What a show-off,' Fabian says.

'A woman must look her best,' Mortisha says, 'especially when she is about to step out for the evening.'

'So true,' Dilvan says.

'But now, you can say that you have seen a sunset on a foreign shore, overlooking the formidable Indian Ocean.'

'And we even have the photos to prove it,' Fabian says.

# CHAPTER 97

Darkness is closing in and it's almost dinner time, so Sally decides to investigate Dilvan's pantry. Food is food wherever you are, and a cupboard full of Sri Lankan goodies would be a challenge to a lesser mortal but Sally is not fazed in the least.

'Dilvan, it's time to get some food happening, which means that we will need reinforcements.'

'In that case, I will assemble the troops,' he says. 'Okay, everyone in the kitchen. Sally has a plan for dinner.'

'I think we should whip up a curry,' she says. 'Dilvan, we will need fresh chicken filets. Is that a possibility?'

'I will pop down to the markets and get some. Do you need anything else?'

'Yes, several eggplants, a kilo of potatoes and some roti bread. And maybe a watermelon as well. It's excellent after a curry.'

'Okay boys, and Mortisha, of course. Are you domesticated?'

'That means what?' Fabian says.

'Can you cook? How would you rate your skills in that department, Fabian?'

'Excellent,' he says.

'And you, Mark?'

'Not too bad, Sally.'

And you, Declan?'

'I can follow a recipe if that's what you mean.'

'And you, Mortisha.'

'My skills are legendary, Sally.'

'That's good to know, Mortisha.'

'What about your culinary skills, Jasper dear?'

'I can boil an egg and make toast and I am pretty good at pizzas.'

'A trained monkey could do better than that,' Fabian says.

Jasper is just about to give him the finger, an internationally recognised gesture that is usually accompanied by two famous words, but he has a better idea, Fabian's humiliation can wait until later.

'Now Fabian, be nice,' Sally says. 'Not everyone is super-human, and for that I am very grateful.'

'In that case, Jaz, you can dice the onions.'

'The stinky job,' he groans. 'I always get the stinky jobs in the kitchen.'

'You will survive, my dear and beloved boy.'

'Okay folks, check out these recipes on your phones and then sort yourself out.'

It takes less than two hours to create a banquet fit for Sri Lankan royalty, but music is essential in the production of any masterpiece. It's a crucial ingredient in most recipes. It says so in the fine print.

But the songbird within cannot be contained, and Fabian nominates himself as DJ for the day. He has an extensive playlist on his phone, and he just has to join in as the great divas of Motown belt out one classic hit after another.

Jasper has been waiting for an opportunity to give the great and glorious Fabian a taste of his own medicine, so he prances around the room and takes great delight in proving that anyone can do the Bum-Wobble.

This is war in Fabian's mind. As manslaughter is out of the question, the only option is tea-towels at five paces.

He chases Jasper from one end of the house to the other, and eventually corners him in the pantry, after which he smiles the smile of the victor.

'I have you at long last,' he says with a wicked glint in his eye.

Jasper does his best to wriggle out of a big fat bear hug but it's a waste of time. After which, Fabian deposits him at the kitchen bench.

'Did you enjoy that, Jasper?'

'I am thinking about it, Fabian. I'll let you know when I have recovered.'

What can he say? If it had been anyone else, he would have been whipped, scourged, and brutalised, his chastity defiled, his virtue not to mention his life would have been in mortal danger.

Dicing fifteen onions takes a lot longer than it should, and Jasper is suffering, but nobody takes the slightest notice.

An hour later, several platters of steaming hot food are placed on the table, but before they dig in, it's essential to document a triumph of this nature.

After taking a few too many selfies, they are ready to indulge in an array of appetising Sri Lankan treats and delicacies.

'We have created a culinary masterpiece, and in record time,' Sally says.

It's a veritable feast, chicken curry, chicken in peanut sauce, accompanied by eggplant and potatoes, mint relish, pan-fried roti, an onion sambal, mango chutney, assorted spicy relishes and a huge bowl of scented rice.

'It looks absolutely delicious,' Jasper says. 'But it would never have happened, if not for my onions.'

'It's a wonder you got them done at all.' Fabian said. 'The only reason this meal is here is because of my music.'

'So true,' Sally says. 'Ladies and gentlemen, take your seats and enjoy the fruits of your labours.'

They are justifiably proud of their efforts and Sally's skills are applauded several times over. It turns out to be a very pleasant if not intoxicating evening, especially for Jasper.

'If I may be so bold,' he says as he stumbles to his feet. 'I would like to say a word or two.'

'Spit it out,' Fabian says, 'before you topple over.'

'I will, Fabian. Just give me a minute.'

'Sally and I would never have achieved anything at all, not without the support of friends and loved ones, and that means all of you, of course.'

'Mortisha, why I don't know why but you accepted us without reservation.'

'Jasper, I know good people when I see them, and you and Sally are two of the best.'

'Thank you, Mortisha. We appreciate that. We really do.'

Jasper is about to launch into a full-blown monologue, but his body has something else in mind. And only moments before he takes a nosedive onto a table full of left-over food, Fabian comes to the rescue.

'And you Jasper should go to bed right now, but before you do, I have something to say.'

'And what is that, Fabian?'

'Thank you for inviting us into your life, young man. We are having a wonderful time, but we will talk about this tomorrow.'

The very moment that his head hits the pillow, Jasper is out like a light. And according to a rumour which is yet to be verified, Mortisha may or may not have got her wicked way with Mark.

As to whether Fabian and Declan had an equally exciting night with Dilvan Kumara Singhe is a mystery that will never be solved.

## CHAPTER 98

Sally is up bright and early the following morning and preparing for another big day, but Jasper is dead to the world, a result no doubt of an overly traumatic experience and way too much to drink.

As to whether he is dreaming about the girl that he loves, Sally has no idea? As she gazes at his sleeping face, she knows that she has made the right decision.

Something wonderful happened the day that she saw those beautiful green eyes, and like a boat without a sail, she drifted helplessly into his arms.

Wakey, wakey, my sweet Prince. Jasper, it's time to get up.'

'Yes, my Princess, I am awake, but I just had a dream about that boy on that awful old boat.'

'You mean the boy that looks like you.'

'Yes Sal, but it wasn't me.'

'Then who was it, Jasper?'

'You may not believe it, but I think it was Roshan and Kashmira's son.'

'Really, so why was he there Jaz?'

'I think he was a sex slave for some nasty old pirates.'

'Oh, that's so horrible, Jasper.'

'Nothing much has changed, has it?'

'It certainly has,' she says, as she reproaches him for what she considers to be a tasteless remark.

'It has in every way, and you know it, Jasper. But Roshan never mentioned a son, did he?'

'I don't think so, but they had a boy with them at Mt. Lavinia.'

'But what happened in that bedroom Jasper? I don't remember anything at all, do you?'

'Yes Sal, I do, and I will tell you about it one day, but not until this is all over.'

'So, we really did see them.'

'We did Sal and it's a shame you can't remember.'

'But Sal, how did I get to bed last night?'

'Fabian carried you in his arms, sweet Prince.'

'And who took my clothes off?'

'Fabian did that willingly, of course, but his eyes were closed as he delicately removed your boardshorts.'

'Oh no, Sally. Why did you let him do that?'

'What else did he do?'

'Well, he gave you a good night kiss.'

'Where, on my lips or somewhere else?'

'Jasper, there is no need to get paranoid.'

'He gave you a gentle peck on the forehead. Fabian was the perfect gentleman but that's because I was watching everything he did.'

'I have no doubt that he has seen more naked men in locker rooms than anyone on the planet.'

'I guess so,' Jasper says.

'Rise and shine and get into the shower, as we have another interesting day ahead.'

Everyone is sitting around the kitchen table, and some are already onto their second cup of coffee when Jasper appears at the door.

It's like a scene from a movie where the camera scans the face of one character after another looking for the guilty party, but they never do tell you who did it, not until the end.

'So, how's the head?' Fabian says.

'It's good Fabian, I don't suffer from melancholia, morning sickness or…'

'A hangover,' he says.

'That either, Fabian, luckily.'

'So Dilvan, what's on the agenda for today?'

'I have organised a day trip Jasper, a helicopter flight, in fact. It will be a sightseeing tour of this beautiful country as seen from the air.'

'I love that idea,' Mortisha says. 'I have never been in a helicopter before.'

'After that, you will have the afternoon at your leisure to catch up on your beauty sleep. But tonight, I thought we might sneak out onto the streets and check out the famous Pettah Markets.'

'Lots of interesting things to spend your money on ladies,' Dilvan says with a twinkle in his eye. 'And lots of tasty things to eat as well.'

'I will vote for that,' Sally says.

'And for tomorrow, your special request, Jasper. You said you would like to meet a snake charmer, didn't you?'

'I certainly did Dilvan, and I still want to.'

'That's good, but the day after is your big day with the Board of Trustees.'

'Yes, I do know that Dilvan.'

'An event to which you are all invited, of course.'

'Now, about breakfast. There are quite a few places on the beachfront but you might like to try a traditional Sri Lankan breakfast, since you are here.'

'That sounds interesting,' Jasper says. 'I will try anything once.'

'That's good to know,' Fabian says. 'I shall keep that in mind.'

## CHAPTER 99

Just about every dish on the Sri Lankan breakfast menu is meant for the Sri Lankan digestive system. It is not usually the breakfast of choice for lily-livered westerners, not unless they like chili as a first course. And according to Dilvan, green porridge is another option.

'It's made from herbs and it even has medicinal qualities, or so I have heard, but it is green. However, there is one item on the menu you may not be familiar with.'

'And what's that,' Jasper says.

'It's a hopper.'

'A grasshopper, do you mean?'

'No Jasper, hoppers are made from rice. One is saucer shaped, one looks like a ball of string, and another looks like an egg roll. Check out the pictures on the menu.'

'Interesting,' he says.

A pineapple curry would probably be delicious but it's a bit too early for any sort of curry at all. Luckily, the menu has little pictures on the side with a brief description for the uneducated traveller.

'I think I might have a go at the saucer shaped one,' Jasper says.

The proprietor is a lovely, grey-haired old lady in her senior years, and she recognises Jasper immediately. She takes his hand and gives him a grandmotherly kiss on the cheek.

'There are obviously benefits to being a celebrity,' Declan says.

'Yes, old ladies molest you in the middle of street,' Fabian says. 'And then give you a big sloppy kiss on the lips.'

'They wouldn't dare do a thing like that,' Jasper says. That's the last thing he wants Sally to know about.

Fabian can be a big tease and has a roguish sense of humour, but he obviously has a dark side as well.

'I would have to kill them,' Sally says. 'And then hide out in a cave for the next ten years.'

'What a miserable idea,' Fabian says.

Dilvan selects a Sri Lankan favourite, a rice pudding with coconut milk, while everyone else chooses a bowl of seasonal fruit with a colourful passionfruit dressing.

And when his breakfast appears at the table, Jasper is surprised to see that it looks like a bird's nest with a half-cooked egg in the middle.

'This very hot,' the old lady says as she places a side dish on the table.

'That looks positively lethal?' Jasper says as he scrutinises a dark red paste with a distinctly forbidding appearance.

'What is that?'

'That's a sambal, a chili relish in other words,' Dilvan says. 'The idea is to shred the crust and mix little bits of relish with the egg.'

'However, be warned Jasper, the sambal is a little on the fiery side.'

Everyone watches closely as he dips the crust into the sambal and then pops it into his mouth. But that, as he discovers, is like a match to a flame. His face starts to glow and he starts gasping for breath.

'Do something,' Dilvan cries. 'He's choking.'

Fabian grabs him around the abdomen and initiates the lifesaving Heimlich Maneuver. And with a few deft movements, he thrusts Jasper's stomach in an upward motion until the offending item pops out of his mouth and onto the plate.

It's a hair raising few minutes and everyone heaves a sigh of relief when he finally gets his breath back. Fabian sits him down, mops his brow with a napkin and gives him a reassuring hug.

'Silly boy, we nearly lost you.'

Fabian would never say so, but he has become quite fond of Jasper.

'Thank you, Fabian. You're always there when I need you.'

'It's my pleasure Jasper. Besides, we don't want to get rid of you just yet.'

'I could have choked to death and died you know.'

'I would never let that happen, Jasper. I am an expert at mouth-to-mouth resuscitation, and I would happily have given you the kiss of life if I had to.'

'Saving lives is a part of our training as PE teachers. But you did say that you would try anything once.'

'Next time, you should read the fine print. After all, the menu describes the honey-flavoured hopper as an appetising variation.'

When no one is looking, Jasper covers the sambal with a paper napkin and pushes it to the far side of the table.

# CHAPTER 100

Fabian is doing an excellent job as Jasper's highly paid bodyguard. And if anything was to go wrong, he would be there with his Spartan sword and shield, his laser, taser and Captain Kirk's phaser, and anyone who stood in his way would be hospitalised for the next five years.

A few hours later, they are winging their way through Sri Lankan airspace in a very sleek blue and green helicopter, one that can accommodate ten people at the very least.

'The pilots have been given strict instruction not to say anything about their passengers,' Dilvan says. 'Or they will not be paid for their services.'

Sri Lanka is not the biggest island in the world, but it has been inhabited by a succession of empires for over three thousand years. It also has an abundance of natural and historical attractions, which is a temptation to tourists from all over the world.

'To see Colombo from the air is like viewing an ant's nest through a magnifying glass,' Dilvan says. 'As you can see, there is nothing leisurely about life on the streets. It never stops.'

'This is a classic opportunity to see some of our famous attractions. And if we had travelled by bus, it would have taken hours to reach our first destination.'

'Habarana is the place to go if you want to see elephants at close range, and you can even have an old-fashioned, safari-style experience.'

'Doing what?' Fabian says.

'Riding an elephant, of course, but if you look down there, you can see them in their natural habitat. However, Habarana also has an elephant nursery.'

'Is that because of ivory poachers?' Jasper says.

'No, it's not Jasper. The Pinnawela Elephant Orphanage is a refuge for baby elephants that were abandoned or injured, for one reason or another.'

'I don't know why anyone would want to harm such gentle creatures, especially when they are on the endangered species list.'

'The days of the great white hunter have long gone Jasper, but not far from here is our next destination and that really is a world class classic.'

'You will be pleased to know that it only takes about twenty minutes to get there by helicopter, but it would take at least eight hours by road.'

'And what is this classic destination?' Fabian says.

'It's one of Sri Lanka's most awesome tourist attractions, of course, the mountain-top fortress of Sigiriya.'

'I have never heard of it,' Fabian says,

'Perhaps you should look it up.'

'Okay folks, the all-knowing Google says that Sigiriya is a heritage listed site, a huge mountain of solid stone and it's almost 700 feet high, but get this, it even has an ancient fortress on the top.'

'There it is,' Dilvan says.

'Oh, my God, you were right,' Fabian says. 'That is awesome.'

Sigiriya is just one of many monolithic stone mountains scattered around the world. Uluru or Ayer's Rock in Australia is the biggest of them all, but it's not the only one.

There are numerous others, including the equally impressive Rock of Gibraltar in Spain, Sugarloaf Mountain in Rio, and Mount Zuma in Nigeria.

'There are many advantages to sightseeing in a helicopter,' Dilvan says. 'And one of those is that you don't have to climb all the way to the top.'

'But you will get to see the famous Lion Gate up close. Unfortunately, you won't be able to see the ancient frescoes, but you can find them online and in every art book in the world.'

'Now, for a brief history lesson. Sri Lanka has been ruled by many dynasties over the centuries.'

'Sigiriya was our capital for a very brief period during the 5th century, but the next place on our agenda is the ancient city of Polonnaruwa.'

'Fabian, what does Google have to say about Polonnaruwa?'

'Okay, give me a minute,' he says.

'Polonnaruwa was the capital of Ceylon during the 11th century, and it is here that you will find colossal images of the Buddha. And even though Polonnaruwa is now in ruins, you can still see the evidence of its former glory.'

'It is literally acres of palaces, temples and stupas, amongst other things,' Dilvan says. 'And once upon a time it was the custodian of one of our most sacred relics.'

'And what was that?' Jasper says.

'Buddha's tooth, of course, what else?'

A temple was built to protect the tooth in one place or another, and over time it became a symbol of a monarch's right to rule. After Polonnaruwa fell into disrepair, the tooth moved around from one kingdom to another for nearly 600 years.

'In the 16th century, it found a permanent home in the city of Kandy and can now be seen in The Temple of Buddha's Tooth.'

Located high up in the mountains, Kandy was the last stronghold of the kings of Ceylon, but today it is renowned for its cool climate and its many historical attractions.

'Is that for real,' Jasper says. 'Is Buddha's tooth still around after 3000 years?'

'According to legend, it was smuggled into the country by a royal princess,' Dilvan says.

'But I have to say yes to a question like that Jasper. It would be unpatriotic and not very good for business if someone decided that it was a fake.'

'There's nothing wrong with fakes,' Fabian says. 'They can be good for business too.'

'So true,' Dilvan says. 'And you will see quite a few modern fakes in the Pettah Markets this evening.'

'Okay, now we are heading up into the mountains to Nuwara Eliya, one of our major tea growing plantations. That's pronounced as New Ralia just in case you were wondering.'

'Tea, as you no doubt know is a commodity for which we are world famous, and it grows abundantly in moist conditions at high altitudes.'

'Nuwara Eliya is over 6000 feet above sea level, and in this area alone, there are over twenty plantations.'

'It's never-ending, isn't it?' Mark says.

'A typical plantation covers an area of 50 acres, but this is the central highlands, and as you can see, it is a magnificent spectacle.'

'Sri Lanka really is a paradise,' Sally says, 'and unbelievably beautiful.'

'It certainly is Sally, and you can thank Mother Nature for that, but the last place on our tour will be a wildlife sanctuary.'

'Its original name was Maha Eliya Thenna, but the English christened it the Horton Plains.'

'That doesn't sound nearly as romantic,' Sally says.

'It's not a very romantic name in Sinhalese either, but it is the home of the Sri Lankan elephant and numerous birds, reptiles, and mammals.'

The Horton Plains is a wild stretch of country, a vast and beautiful highland plateau 2000 meters above sea level.

It's not possible to see everything from a fast-moving helicopter, but they do get to see one of Sri Lanka's major attractions, a cliff at the southern end that plunges 4000 feet down into the valley below.

'What is that place?' Fabian says.

'That is known as World's End, and it has one of the best views in the country. But you have to make a three-hour trek along a very dangerous path, and on a good day, you can even see the Indian Ocean.'

Four hours pass in the blink of an eye, and when they finally get back to the airport, everyone has a glazed look in their eyes.

'Dilvan, that is the only way to see the highlights of a country,' Jasper says.

'I agree and if we had travelled by bus, it would have meant endless miles of driving and two weeks on the road.'

'And we would have encountered people everywhere we went,' Fabian says.

After an experience of that nature, everyone is lost in a world of their own but Fabian has questions.

'Dilvan, how much does a trip like that cost?'

'About one thousand dollars per person,' he says.

'Did Jasper pay for it?'

'No Fabian, he did not.'

'Senor Delgado established a trust fund that is now worth several billion dollars and his estate makes a small fortune on a daily basis.'

'He came up with a plan so that the Chapel of Love could find its place in history. And he left a reward for the person who could make his dream come true.'

'As to what that is, we have no idea but in two days, we will all know about it.'

'Jasper has to appear before a Board of Trustees who will ask six questions from a sealed envelope.'

'And if he knows the answers, he will become a juvenile version of Nelson Rockefeller.'

# CHAPTER 101

The Pettah Markets are not unlike any other markets in the ancient cities of the world. And as they are about to find out, they are not for the feint hearted.

When in Rome, as the old saying goes, do as the Romans do, but when in Colombo, you have to travel by a three-wheeled, two-person transport vehicle, a motorised rickshaw commonly known as a tuk-tuk.

And as soon as they step out onto the streets, they are overwhelmed by the noise, the fumes, and dozens of tuk-tuk drivers, all of whom are eager for their business.

'Now you have to make the first big decision of the day,' Dilvan says. 'Do you want to live a long and happy life or travel in a tuk-tuk.'

'Let's just do it,' Declan says.'

You would have to be half blind not to notice the remarkable feats of derring-do as these highly skilled drivers weave their way through the traffic in these multi-coloured missiles.

They have no idea what they are letting themselves in for, and a few minutes later they are zooming through the traffic in five little tuk-tuks.

A quiet ride along a country road this is not. It's a race against time through peak hour traffic at breakneck speed, but for a few desperate minutes, their lives hang by a fragile thread and the only thing to do is hang on tight and just hope for the best.

But it's just as chaotic when they get to the markets. As to whether Dilvan can protect them from the floodtide of humanity is yet to be seen.

He wriggles his hands in the air, whispers an enchantment in Sinhalese, and for a few blessed moments, they have a chance to take a breath.

'Sinhalese magic. It works miracles in some cases,' he says. 'So, are you ready for a new adventure?

'After that, I am ready to go home,' Fabian says, 'by helicopter preferably.'

'Scaredy cat. The fun hasn't ever started yet.'

'That there,' he says as he points to a clock tower in the middle of a roundabout, 'is the doorway to another world.'

Dilvan had warned them not to wear valuables or carry a wallet, but he did suggest that they keep their money close to their chest.

'That sounds a bit scary,' Sally had said.

'Not with bodyguards like these guys.'

'Besides, I have been here a hundred times before, and I will be keeping a close eye on everything.'

'However, buyer-beware. Just about all of the high-class goods are fakes but the ambience is not, and that is why we are here.'

'This will be an experience you will never forget, if you survive to tell the tale, that is.'

'How very reassuring,' Mortisha says, 'but I have Oscar at the ready in case of an emergency,'

'Then use it now,' Fabian says. 'Freeze this situation in time so that we can swim to an island of safety.'

'There is no such thing in the Pettah Markets,' Dilvan says.

If something takes their fancy, it involves the fine old art of haggling. These guys have five thousand years of experience, and as they are obviously tourists, that has an impact on the sale price.

It is not an untruth to say that Fabian has an eye for the unusual, but what he intends to do with a collection of garish key rings which look like fingers that have been amputated by a rusty old bread knife is anyone's guess.

'Witchdoctors put things like that on voodoo dolls,' Jasper says.

'Don't put ideas into my head Jasper, but now that you mention it, I know a few people who could do with a good scare.'

The spice market is row after row of mysterious ingredients in every shade of red, orange, and brown, and for those who are partial to seriously hot food, this is tastebud heaven.

In the produce market they see quite a few things which may or may not have been identified by scientists on this or another other star system.

'What are those things?' Jasper says as he inspects what appears to be a basket of wooden balls.

'They are called wood apples, a fruit that smells like a Durian,' Dilvan says. 'And if you have ever had a whiff of a Durian, then you would know to avoid it at all costs.'

But the thing that sends Mortisha into a spin is a long green vegetable called a bitter melon.

'That's the sort of thing you'd see in an adult-only shop,' she says.

The melon is similar in appearance to a continental cucumber, but this is not the smooth skinned variety. It is lumpy and bumpy, and of course, Fabian has something to say about it.

'If I didn't know any better, I would say that thing has a bad case of vegetable herpes. However, now that I come to think of it, I have seen something like that before.'

'It wasn't the edible variety, and it wasn't battery-operated either, but it was leather, and it was rechargeable.'

'That doesn't surprise me in the least,' Sally says. 'It was in your bedroom, wasn't it?'

'What do you take me for Sally Velasko, some sort of sex fiend?'

'If the shoe fits, Fabian.'

'I will have you know, Sally Velasko, that I am as pure as the driven snow.'

'Snow does come in black, Fabian, especially on Devil's Mountain.'

'You all hate me, just because I am different.'

'I don't,' Jasper says. 'I will be your friend, as long as you don't try to kiss me.'

'I would never do that, Jasper, not while your eagle-eyed girlfriend is around.'

Sally takes Fabian by the shoulders as if she is about to whisper something in his ear and plants a juicy kiss on his lips.

'What did you do that for?' he cries.

'Just to let you know that we do love you, Fabian. And to see how you'd look with cherry red lipstick.'

'Jasper, get out of here now before she corrupts your innocent soul.'

'It's too late for that Fabian. The process is already underway.'

He wanders off in a huff and pretends to be mortally offended, but it would not be the same without dear old Fabian.

The ever-present aroma of market-style food permeates the atmosphere. Sri Lankan food smells great and looks very appetising, but Fabian is not impressed when a stallholder scoops a cup of water from a bucket and pours it into a flavoursome soup.

'I vote that we eat back at the hotel,' he says. 'At least they have to abide by international hygiene laws.'

The dining room has a smorgasbord of culinary delights to choose from and not even Fabian has any complaints.

To a passerby, this may look like an innocent dinner table but there's a lot more going on, other than small talk. And not long after she has finished her meal, Sally decides to call it a day.

'Please excuse us,' she says. 'It has been a very long day and I am in desperate need of my beauty sleep.'

'I don't think they believed a word of that,' Jasper says as they are heading up the stairs.

'Didn't you notice the way those boys were trading glances across the table.'

'Yes, I did, but Mark and Mortisha were holding hands under the table.'

'That naughty green-eyed dragon is up to its old tricks again.'

'I have heard of the green-eyed monster Jasper, but what's the green-eyed dragon?'

'The green-eyed monster feeds on the broken-hearted, whereas the green-eyed dragon fans the flames of lust and desire, so to speak.'

'In that case, I know exactly what you mean, but on this planet, it probably never sleeps.'

'Don't think it does Sal, day or night.'

# CHAPTER 102

They are about to see a real live snake charmer in action, and after breakfast, they take their seats on the bus and head north to the city of Negombo.

The Portuguese were the first to establish a foothold in Sri Lanka, and they left their mark in the form of public buildings and Christian churches, but Negombo is no longer just a fishing village. Today, it's a popular tourist destination.

'Snake charming is a dying occupation,' Dilvan says. 'It is still acceptable to own one in Sri Lanka but it's illegal in India.'

'Snake charmers are usually accompanied by a trained monkey and a gypsy woman who reads your palm. It's not the real deal, of course, just a way to make a bit of money on the side.'

'However, we have tracked down the best of the best. This particular troupe is a family concern Jasper, and I think you will be impressed by their performance.'

'I am looking forward to it Dilvan.'

'The people you are about to meet are of Moorish descent, and one of the acts in their repertoire is a snake charming act with a difference.'

Abdul and his wife Fatima and over a dozen members of their family have been eagerly awaiting the arrival of their distinguished guests.

The women are dressed in belly dancing outfits, whereas the men wear a pair of loose-fitting pants with a chain of gold around their necks.

Accompanied by the sound of flutes and drums, they escort their guests through an avenue of palm trees and into their Palace of Dreams.

And as soon as they step through the door, it is only to find themselves in a richly decorated room festooned with elegant wall hangings.

Brass lamps hang from the ceiling. Colourful pillows are scattered over the floor and permeating the atmosphere is the familiar aroma of incense.

'This is going to be really good,' Fabian says.

Jasper and Sally are whisked away only moments later, and when they reappear, they are dressed like the king and queen of Persia.

To the sound of a drum roll, Princess Salome appears in glittering veils and a golden headdress, but her lord and master looks equally regal in a black and gold turban, loose fitting pants, and a golden sash around his waist.

They take their places on two golden thrones, the lights are dimmed, and the distinctive sound of gypsy guitars can be heard in the background. And the moment that Fatima starts to sing, everyone is transported to a gypsy camp on a moonlit night.

The curtains open and a woman in red silken veils appears on the rise of a distant hill. She has travelled far to find this man, but this is no snake charmer, and he is no gypsy king. This is the cobra king, a conjurer of dreams and lies, his soul blackened by lust and power.

He stirs the embers of a dying fire, and removes the hood from his long black cloak, only to reveal a crown of writhing serpents on his head.

The sky turns to an inky black and Fatima makes her way down the hill on the heels of a howling wind.

The cobra king knows instinctively that a woman with raven black hair and flaming red eyes means trouble. He throws a handful of powder onto the fire, and a nest of green-eyed serpents rise from the flames, hungry for the taste of mortal flesh.

The sound of Fatima's voice echoes through the midnight sky, a shrill, high-pitched noise like that of hailstones exploding on an old tin roof.

With a razor-sharp blade in each hand, she leaps into the flames, and with the skill of a seasoned executioner, she eradicates one viper after another, and then turns her gaze on the cobra king.

'Your power shall not prevail,' she cries.

The carnage that ensues is swift and lethal, and when the smoke finally clears, the very life has been sucked from the cobra king's soul.

Fatima stands alone but triumphant amidst the embers, the cobra king is nowhere to be seen, and on her head, she wears a crown of stylised serpents. It was a powerful and stirring performance for which she receives a resounding ovation.

Music can soothe a savage beast, but a beautifully crafted performance not only opens the heart, it can also stir the soul.

Jasper wipes a few stray tears from his eyes, but he is not about to get back on the bus, not until he has spoken to Abdul and Fatima in person.

'That was truly extraordinary. Thank you.'

'It was an honour to perform for you,' Abdul says. 'But it is we who should thank you Jasper. Because of you and Sally, there is a renewed interest in our act.'

'I think you should thank Roshan and Kashmira for that. They had more to do with it than we did. They had something to share and they found a way.'

'But where did you get the idea for that performance? Was it from Esmeralda's song?'

'To some extent,' Fatima says. 'Because of that song, an age-old tradition will survive but in another form.'

'Snake charming is a tradition that has been passed on from one generation to another, but our routine changed, especially after we discovered that song.'

'It really is amazing, and it works like a charm.'

'It certainly does,' Abdul says.

'I don't suppose you perform in other countries as well, do you?'

'No, we are only local performers. Why are you asking Jasper?'

'I presume that you have heard of the Chapel of Love in Melbourne.'

'Everyone in the world knows about that, but we were amazed to find out about Roshan and Kashmira as well,' Fatima says.

'They must have been great performers to perform with seven cobras. One cobra is more than enough for anyone.'

'But you just did, didn't you?'

'Our performance is all smoke and mirrors. Our snakes are animatronic Jasper, brought to life by the wonders of modern technology.'

'But they look so real.'

'Yes, they do but if we want to make a living we have to change with the times.'

'So true,' he says.

'Sally and I are planning to be married in the Chapel sometime soon. And if you would like to perform for our guests, I will happily pay your expenses. Is that a possibility?'

'It will be televised, of course, after which you will probably be inundated with offers to perform all around the world.'

'If you decide to take up my offer, just let me know.'

'We will talk,' Abdul says. 'I have no doubt that my family will be happy to perform at your wedding.'

## CHAPTER 103

Jasper takes his leave but does so with a heavy heart. He is about to say goodbye to the world that Roshan and Kashmira once called their own.

For a few passing minutes he had an opportunity to experience something extraordinary, but when he gets back on the bus, no one other than Sally even notices. The boys are away with the fairies, listening to a song on their iPods.

'Sally, what's going on?'

'They were desperate to hear the original version of that song.'

'Gypsy Queen, you mean.'

'Yes Jasper, of course.'

This is too good to be true, so Jasper sneaks down to the back and gently removes Fabian's headphones.

'Give those back, you naughty boy. Why did you do that Jasper?'

'Just felt like it. So, did you like the show?'

'Jasper, that was the second most amazing thing I have ever seen, but Gypsy Queen has to be the most sensual song I have ever heard in my life.'

'I hope it doesn't put you off your sleep, Fabian.'

'Not likely. If anything, it will…'

Jasper holds up his hand. 'Too much information Fabian. Save it for someone who cares.'

'So,' Dilvan says. 'Was that what you were hoping to see?'

'That was a thousand times better. Thank you, Dilvan.'

'It was my pleasure, Jasper.'

'However, I asked Abdul and Fatima if they would be interested in performing in Melbourne next year and they said yes.'

'That's an excellent idea,' Fabian says. 'Any reason why.'

'As a matter of fact, there is. Sally and I are going to be married in the Chapel, that is why.'

'Did you hear that,' Fabian cries. 'Jasper Powell is going to marry Sally Velasko.'

'That is the best news I have heard in ages. Please accept my congratulations and may you both live happily ever after.'

The boys are over the Moon with excitement and Jasper happily endures a few too many handshakes.

'Sally, please let me give him one tiny little kiss,' Fabian says.

'As long as it's not a sloppy one Fabian. That is a privilege to which I alone have the rights.'

'You have to catch me first,' Jasper says.

He makes a mad dash for the front of the bus, leaps into the seat beside Sally and takes refuge under her arm.

'Coward, a little peck on the cheek won't do any harm.'

'If I know Fabian, he won't be aiming for my cheek.'

'I have a major in archery,' Fabian bellows. 'My aim is true Jasper and I always get my man.'

'Not today you won't, Robin Hood.'

Jasper has never excelled at the fine old art of repartee, but he gets a perverse sort of pleasure out of teasing Fabian.

The indefatigable Fabian is by far and away the master of that particular art form and Jasper is just a Padewan learner.

Before deciding on where to have lunch, they take a leisurely stroll around the streets. Negombo's claim to fame is not its architectural heritage but its beautiful beaches.

A few lucky tourists are frolicking about in the clear blue water, while some enjoy a boat trip along the canal, and it's enough to make Fabian green with envy.

'This place is to die for, isn't it? I would love to spend a few days here. There is so much to do.'

'There sure is,' Dilvan says. 'This is water sport heaven, and you can also do a fishing trip or go diving on the reef.'

'Sounds good to me,' he says.

It's a beautiful day. In fact, it is picture postcard perfect and the magnificent Indian Ocean beckons.

As they wander along the beach dreaming of what could be, they encounter a group of people cooking up a seafood extravaganza. Total strangers welcome them with open arms and invite them to share their midday meal.

It turns out to be a pleasant afternoon feasting on freshly caught prawns and lobster, enhanced by a selection of flavoursome Sri Lankan herbs and spices.

But word soon passes around that Jasper and Sally are on the beach and people come from everywhere.

They thank their newfound friends and make a speedy retreat, but everyone gets a few happy snaps before they disappear over the horizon.

## CHAPTER 104

In an effort to avoid the bloodhounds of the media they decide to spend the rest of the day at Dilvan's beachside retreat.

Mortisha has no choice but to turn a deaf ear to four high-spirited athletes battling it out in the pool. She would rather lay back and soak up the incomparable view that is the magnificent Indian Ocean.

'Dilvan, I am in love with Sri Lanka,' she says. 'It is such a beautiful country.'

'It is Mortisha. It certainly is.'

'You have been so generous of your time young man, and I for one am very appreciative of your hospitality.'

It is then that Dilvan launches into the behind-the-scenes story.

'I couldn't sleep after I saw Jasper and Sally on television, so I decided to do a little investigating.'

'I wanted to contact them in person, but I followed protocol, prepared my brief and presented it to the Board of Trustees.'

'I discovered that there are more secrets in our dungeons than the bank was aware of, and thankfully, they listened to what I had to say.'

'And what did you find?' Fabian says.

'Letters, bank statements, you name it, a stash of correspondence from the last one hundred years, none of which had ever been opened.'

'But there was one other thing as well, and for a few precious moments, I held Juan's diary in my hand, but I just had to take a quick peek. I opened it to the last page and read the last paragraph.

*"I know that one day in the future someone will discover our treasure and realise what it is, and hopefully, they will also find this diary and understand its importance.'*

*'I hope that whoever does so, honours it in the way it is meant to be honoured. The Chapel of Love, as Kashmira called our beautiful temple, was a labour of love for me, and I wanted to share it with the world.*

*I can only hope and pray that the universe intervenes and that this shrine to the memory of my beloved finds its place in history.'*

'Those words will be forever imprinted on my soul, but that wasn't all. Juan also said that the person who completed his project would receive a reward for their devotion and persistence.'

'So, I decided to contact you by mail, and to my undying relief, you replied.'

'The rest as they say is history. You followed your instincts, and now, here you are on the verge of a major discovery.'

'So, you obviously knew that there was a key in the back of the diary,' Jasper says.

'I did and even though I am a banker, I am also an honest man.'

'So, what's in that vault?'

'That is the biggest vault in our dungeon, Jasper. There is every possibility that it's just like Ali Baba's cave.'

'And even though I am dying to see what it contains, I really wanted to meet you and Sally.'

'I think we knew that Dilvan, and we know that you are an honest man, even though we have never seen you in an Armani suit,' Sally says.

'What does that mean?'

'I once worked in a high-class restaurant where most of our clients were suit-wearing businessmen. I tested out a few and I was not impressed in the least.'

'I know the sort that you mean,' Dilvan says. 'They're everywhere in a big city.'

Dilvan is having the time of his life playing host to two world famous celebrities, but on that afternoon, they get to see another side of his life.

Hidden away in a cupboard are albums of his boarding school days. Dilvan Kumara Singe comes from a wealthy family but he barely knew his parents.

And even though he has hundreds of photos, he has very few of his mother and father. He puts them to the side, refills their glasses and pulls up a chair.

'So, what about you?' he says. 'You know almost everything about me, but I would love to hear about your lives.'

'Mortisha, how do you become a practicing witch?'

'Well, it's in your genes for one thing, but the essential knowledge is passed on through the generations.'

'But you look more like a Hollywood glamour queen.'

'I was hoping to be a fashion designer, until the day my grandmother revealed the secret of my ancestry. She taught me everything she knew, but she did have one word of advice.'

'And what was that?' Dilvan says.

'Be gentle with you friends and even gentler with your lovers, because a power such as ours will scare them away.'

'That is good advice.'

'So, Fabian, now it's your turn. What strange and mysterious power guided your path in life?'

'Well, I was a pain in the neck until the day that I met the love of my life after a football game. I asked Declan if he wanted to share a pizza and he agreed.'

'Everyone hated Fabian because he had such a vicious tongue,' Declan said. 'Anyone else would have made a fast getaway but Fabian took it oh so very slowly.'

'So, he seduced you,' Sally says.

'Yes, he did, and I have been trapped in his spell ever since.'

'And you Mark, you were the filling in the pie.'

'Well, sort of Dilvan, I grew up with these guys. We did everything together. Well, not everything, but we played just about every sport a boy could play.'

'And did Fabian make your life a misery too?'

'No, he did not, and believe it or not, he never tried to hit on me, not once.'

'And why was that?'

'Because Mark was the brother that I never had,' Fabian says. 'And when I had a problem, which was every second day, I only had one shoulder to cry on. And if it hadn't been for him, I could have turned out a lot worse.'

'Fabian's father didn't really like him,' Mark said. 'He probably knew what he was from day one, even though he had always excelled at sports.'

'Okay, that is interesting,' Dilvan says.

'Sally, I imagined that you would have gone for a somewhat different type of man.'

'Not a chance Dilvan. My family is of European descent but I have the most annoying brothers in the world, both of whom came fully loaded with more testosterone than the Terminator on a bad day.'

'They were little terrors until I decided to bring them into line. That took a few years, but I was the victor in the end.'

'After that, I checked out a few reprobates in Armani suits and then found the love of my life at a railway station.'

'And that was me,' Jasper says. 'An innocent young boy who didn't have a clue what he was in for.'

'So, you were as pure as the driven snow?' Fabian says.

'No, I was not Fabian. A few girls had their wicked way with me, for a fleeting moment or two.'

'And then what happened?'

'Sally stole my heart and we have never looked back.'

'That's exactly what I saw on television and so did everyone else,' Dilvan says. 'This is all very interesting but what would you like to do this evening?'

'Dance,' Sally says. 'I would love to do all of those old-fashioned dances, like the Pride of Erin and the Foxtrot.'

'In that case,' Fabian says, 'you have come to the right place because we know them all.'

'But we have odd numbers, Fabian.'

'That's easily fixed Sally. I will play the part of the dance instructor, bark out instructions, slap you around the ankles with my trusty cane, and you can be my servile minions.'

'I like the first part of that idea but if you try beating me around the ankles Fabian, I will have to make you suffer for a very long period of time.'

'Okay, I will retract the part about being a Gestapo prison guard, if that's to your liking, Madam Hitler.'

'You will soon learn who holds the reins of power in this family, Fabian.'

'Run Jasper, run, before she slips that ring on your finger.'

'It's too late for that Fabian, I am addicted to pain, but not the sort that you like.'

'Jasper Powell, you are a very naughty boy.'

'Is he always like this, Sally?'

'No, he isn't, but he's getting cheekier every day.'

'I agree,' he says.

'Okay, ladies and gentlemen, take your partners for the Pride of Erin Waltz.'

Fabian is a self-professed expert in a variety of fields, and over the next few hours, he instructs his minions in the fine art of ballroom dancing.

It was an inspired idea on Sally's part as it keeps them off the streets for one thing. To those who have little or no experience of ballroom dancing, The Pride of Erin involves coordinated legwork.

'The first thing you have to do is the promenade,' Fabian says. 'That's a dance walk, in other words, which means you have to sashay both forward and backwards.'

Once they have mastered that little routine, they then have to do the same thing in reverse. But that's when things get a little pear-shaped, and Fabian is not impressed in the least.

'Jasper, what don't you understand about changing legs. Let's try that again.'

The routine responsible for more than a few groans of frustration is the point and dip, a series of leg movements performed by the female partner as the dance is in motion.

'Ladies, place your weight on your left foot, and then bring your right foot around and point your toe.'

'Move your leg to the rear and dip while bending your knee, and then turn away from your partner.'

After about the sixth time, Jasper and Sally lose it completely. Dear old Fabian does his best not to go ballistic but his patience is wearing thin.

There is every possibility that unspeakable profanities are balancing on a knife-edge at the forefront of his mind. And even though he is tempted to give them the beating they so justly deserve, he mutters a few caustic words to himself and does his best to be as civil as possible.

'Get up off the floor this instant,' he says.

'Or what,' Sally says as she gives him the evil eye.

'Or I will have to help you up.'

Fabian is doing an excellent job, and his servile minions have no choice but to practice over and over again.

Two hours later, they finally get to show off their newly mastered skills to the sound of music. Not the famous Julie Andrews song, of course, but The Pride of Erin Waltz, and Fabian is impressed.

'Whatever you do, Jasper, do not give up your day job.'

'He doesn't have one,' Sally says. 'He is independently wealthy, and he is going to be even richer tomorrow.'

'In that case, you will need a private secretary to take care of this, that and the other.'

# CHAPTER 105

At ten o'clock the following morning, they have a date with the Bank of Colombo, and as any city dweller knows, that means the dreaded battle with peak hour traffic.

After breakfast, it's time to dust off their suits and polish their shoes as they are about to have their first ever brush with the world of high-class finance.

After he has had a shower, Jasper lays out his suit in preparation for its first ever christening. Sally knots his tie, gives him the seal of approval, and hustles him out of the room.

'You look gorgeous,' she says.

Thirty minutes later, she makes an appearance and looks dazzling in a dark green dress with crossover backstraps, accentuated by the earrings that she bought at the Pettah Markets.

'You look so beautiful,' Jasper says.

'Thank you, my darling boy.'

But when Mortisha emerges from her boudoir, no one knows what to think.

'You look absolutely stunning,' Sally says.

Mortisha is wearing yet another classic outfit inspired by a Hollywood actress of the 1960s, but this ensemble was not made famous by Sophia Loren or Lauren Bacall.

Only a dyed-in-the-wool Audrey Hepburn fan would recognise the tight-fitting black dress, the infamous mushroom-shaped hat, the oversized sunglasses, and the chunky pearl earrings.

Fabian is not about to miss out on an opportunity like this, and with Mark and Declan humming away in the background, he launches into an A Capella version of Moon River, the theme song from the movie, Breakfast at Tiffany's.

'I think you've got a fan club,' Sally says. 'And they're doing a pretty good job as well.'

'It appears that our muscle-bound heroes have hidden talents,' Mortisha says.

The boys receive a hearty round of applause for their efforts, but Mortisha is not about to let them off so lightly. She has a wicked idea and decides to engage in a little bit of innocent fun.

'Watch this,' she says to Sally and Jasper.

She saunters up to Fabian as casually as a cat on the prowl and removes Oscar from her handbag.

'You were singing out of tune,' she says as she places Oscar to his throat. 'I think I can fix that.'

'No,' Fabian says. 'Put that thing away. We did a perfectly good rendition of that song, and I was not singing out of tune.'

'I agree,' she says. 'You were very good.'

She looks him up and down, removes an invisible speck of lint from his jacket, places it on her lips and dispatches it to the ethers.

'Such handsome men you are,' she says. 'You'll do.'

'Is that all you've got to say,' Fabian says. 'I think we look positively electric.'

'But you ladies will definitely turn a few heads at that stuffy old bank, that's for certain.'

'It's not that bad,' Dilvan says.

Up until this moment, they have seen no evidence of the bank manager within, but Dilvan looks the part in an Armani suit in a temperate shade of grey.

'The Board takes their role seriously.'

Now that they are satisfied that they look their stunning best, they take a seat on the bus knowing that this could be a long and frustrating journey.

Twenty minutes later, they are stuck in peak hour traffic but it could have been a lot worse, if not for the irrepressible Fabian.

'I have an idea. Why don't we play a game? It will help to pass the time for one thing.'

'What sort of game do you have in mind?' Jasper says tentatively.

Knowing Fabian as he does it will probably be one his favourite topics, and the last thing he wants to think about at this time of day is anything of an unpalatable nature.

'We will be the Board of Trustees, and you, Jasper, can be the guinea pig.'

'I hate being the guinea pig.'

'Worry not Jasper, this will not be a surgical operation, and we will not remove any of your vital organs. This is just to get you into the mood for the interrogation.'

'It won't be an interrogation,' Dilvan says. 'Jasper just has to answer a few questions, and if he gets them right, well, it will be history after that.'

'So Dilvan, do you have any idea what the questions will be?'

'No Fabian, but they will probably have something to do with Roshan and Kashmira in one way or another.'

'Okay,' Fabian says. 'In that case, I will go first.'

'Jasper, when was Juan born?'

'In 1834, that was in his diary?'

'Where was he born?'

'Barcelona, another diary entry.'

'What sort of snakes did they use in their performance?'

'Cobras,' Jasper says. 'Diary entry, another easy one.'

This routine goes on for the next ten minutes, but Jasper is not about to tell them that he really does know the answers to Juan's questions. If it had not been for his experience at Mt. Lavinia, the outcome might have been very different.

Thirty minutes later, they arrive at the front door of the grand establishment known as the Bank of Colombo, and it does not go unnoticed, especially by Fabian, that it has an uncanny resemblance to an overly decorated wedding cake.

Nevertheless, it's a superb example of 19th century architecture which makes a statement that this is a reputable institution.

The staff is eagerly awaiting their arrival, but they don't have time to dilly dally, not just yet. The first thing on the agenda is to meet the Manager, Mr. Chaminda Vaas da Silva.

He is an amiable but distinguished man in his sixties, and he has been looking forward to meeting Sally and Jasper for the last two months.

'I hope you are enjoying your visit, Jasper.'

'I certainly am, Sir. Sri Lanka is a very beautiful country.'

'I agree and that is excellent news. Now, Jasper, you are not nervous, are you?'

'No Sir, I am confident that I will pass the test.'

'That is what I like to hear, a man who is not afraid to put his hand into a spider's nest. That takes courage, but this is not a spider's nest, and the members of the Board are not venomous. They are simply doing their job.'

Dressed in their new Armani suits, the boys look like high-class fashion models, and they are the first to step forward and offer Jasper the best of luck.

He gets a reassuring kiss on the cheek from Mortisha and Sally, but Jasper braces himself as Fabian is the last in line.

'You are not going to the gas chamber, Jasper. This will be a piece of cake.'

'Thanks Fabian. That is reassuring.'

To his relief, Fabian really does know how to behave in civilised society.

# CHAPTER 106

Mr. da Silva escorts Jasper through corridors decorated with vintage 19th century furniture and adorned with portraits of financiers of days gone by. Several minutes later, they arrive at two beautifully carved oak doors.

'Good luck Jasper, I know that you will do brilliantly.'

'Thank you, Sir.'

'Now, go in there and give it all you've got.'

Jasper takes a seat in a rather grand boardroom in front of six members of the Board of Trustees. They are middle-aged, courteous, and respectable members of Sri Lankan society, two women and four men with names that he will never remember.

Sally manicured his nails and even managed to do something with his hair. Jasper's fringe usually has that casual ripped and torn look, but she helped it along with a touch of aromatic hair gel. And after a few minutes of general chit-chat, the President is ready for business.

'Jasper, the questions compiled by Senor Delgado have been sealed in a secure vault for over one hundred years, and this is the first time that they have seen the light of day.'

'Are you ready Jasper?'

'Yes Sir, I am.'

'Now, we have no idea what the questions will be, but according to Senor Delgado's instructions, they should be accompanied by the correct answers.'

'Question number one is this, Jasper. How many children did Roshan and Kashmira have?'

'One,' he says.

'Correct Jasper, that is true.'

'Now, for the second question. Was their child a boy or a girl?'

'It was a boy,' he says.

'That is also correct, Jasper.'

'Now, what was the name of this boy?'

'It was Donatello.'

'That is so amazing, Jasper. Even we were not aware that they had a child.'

'Question number four is this, Jasper. What happened to Donatello?'

'He disappeared while fishing on the beach at Mt. Lavinia and was never seen again.'

'That is so sad but the answer is correct,' the President says. 'You are doing brilliantly Jasper.'

'Now, for question number five. What did Roshan and Kashmira find on the beach? And could you describe it please?'

'They found a golden locket with a portrait of Donatello and his parents.'

'Oh, that must have been so heartbreaking to lose their only child. They must have been devastated.

'I imagine they were,' Jasper says. 'I lost my father recently and that just about killed me.'

'Yes Jasper, to lose a loved one is one of the most difficult experiences in life.'

'However, Jasper, the sixth and final question requires you to describe Donatello. And if your answer is correct, we will be able to confirm it, as Senor Delgado has provided a miniature portrait of his son.'

'Donatello has green eyes and dark hair,' Jasper says. 'And he could very easily be my twin brother.'

The members of the Board pass the portrait around and compare it to his face. And when they are satisfied, the President nods his head in agreement.

'I have no idea how you knew that Jasper, but you are correct. Well done, my boy. Please accept our congratulations.'

'So, what do you say to a glass of champagne to celebrate this momentous achievement?'

'That would be excellent, Sir.'

If a quiz show contestant doesn't know an answer to a question they may choose to pass. But in a show from the recent past you could even ring a friend.

Jasper had a lifeline of a different kind and if it had not been for Roshan and Kashmira, he would never have passed at all.

What would he tell the Board if they asked how he knew the answers to those questions? That issue has been bothering him for the last few days.

'Why not say that Kashmira has been appearing in your dreams,' Sally said. 'And that she revealed these things over a period of time.'

'That doesn't sound any better than saying I saw a ghost in the middle of the day in a locked room in a beach house. Luckily, they didn't ask.'

The staff has been waiting patiently for this moment, and even if Jasper failed the test, they were going to celebrate anyway.

They peck away at a delicious array of Sri Lankan treats, and as soon as everyone has a glass in their hands, Dilvan steps forward to say a few words.

'When I first saw Jasper and Sally on the television, I knew that they were very special people. And now that I have spent a few days with them, I can assure you that it's true.'

'Ladies and gentlemen, Jasper and Sally are accompanied by four of the loveliest people you could ever wish to meet. And if you are interested, I know they will be more than happy to talk to you.'

They have no choice but to spread themselves around. And even though everyone is dying to speak to Jasper and Sally, they have serious competition from Audrey Hepburn and three seriously attractive men in Armani suits.

Their thirty-minute time frame is over before they realise it, but before they head off to investigate the contents of the vault, they have something equally important to do.

The very moment that Dilvan announces that it's time for a photo-shoot, phones of every make and model appear out of thin air.

'Please, do not post them on any social media sites,' he says, 'not until they have left the country, for security reasons, of course.'

They spend the next ten minutes lining up beside one smiling face after another so that their newfound friends can get that all-important selfie.

'Oh, the Sri Lankans are such lovely people,' Fabian says, 'aren't they?'

'They definitely are,' Jasper says.

'I could get used to this lifestyle. Are you planning another overseas trip in the near future?'

'You never know, Fabian.'

'In that case, you will definitely need a bodyguard.'

'Make that three,' Declan says.

'No,' Dilvan says. 'Make that four.'

## CHAPTER 107

The big moment has finally arrived, so they follow Mr. da Silva down one corridor after another, and eventually arrive at the first of two electronically controlled doors.

Jasper's little heart is pounding away as he makes his way down three flights of stairs, but when he steps through the door it's like stepping back in time.

This is a storeroom for hundreds of bank vaults, but it could also be the armoury of an interstellar warship.

'Vaults are for customers who prefer something other than a strongbox,' Dilvan says. 'This is a facility in which to store valuables in the event of a personal or natural disaster.'

'But we are here to see this one in particular. This is the oldest vault in the facility, and it is also the most ostentatious.'

Juan's vault is solid concrete reinforced with steel and is obviously a product of 19th century technology. The door has a gilded pattern around the outer edge and weighs at least a ton, and it is still in immaculate condition.

'Modern vaults are armed with anti-theft devices, but this one has a combination lock, and that's what we have to open first.'

'After which, it will require muscle power to turn the wheel, and that, Jasper, is where your bodyguards will come in handy.'

'But before we get to see what's inside, we have to crack the combination lock.'

'Jasper, the code is on your key. I hope you brought it with you.'

'I did,' he says as he fishes it out of his pocket.

Dilvan memorises the sequence of numbers and then turns the dial back and forth.

'It's a clicking sound we want to hear, ten of them in fact.'

They listen closely for one audible clicking sound after another, and when the last number finally falls into place, they let out a resounding hurrah.

'Well done,' Mortisha says.

'Now, you guys, get over here and earn your keep,' Dilvan says.

'At least someone appreciates our hard work,' Fabian says.

'I do too, Fabian, but I don't want to see any more of the finished product.'

'Jasper, we are what you would call a work of art.'

Mr. da Silva is doing his best to keep a straight face, but with someone like Fabian around, that is virtually impossible.

'Stop hedging, Fabian and put your back into it man.'

'Yes Master.'

It takes two muscle-bound men to turn the wheel, and everyone is waiting on tenterhooks for the revealing moment.

'If this is the sort of vault that I think it is, it should be ten-foot-long by six-foot-wide,' Dilvan says. Ali Baba's cave, in other words.'

'All done,' Fabian says. 'The door of the cave is ready to open. Will there be anything else, Master?'

'Jasper, it's a good thing that you have such obedient servants,' Dilvan says, 'but it's essential to use a spell-breaker.'

'And why is that Dilvan?'

'Jasper, my boy. Everyone dreams of finding a cave riddled with jewels and gold bullion, but you were given the key to one.'

'Make this count Jasper. Do a Meryl Streep and give your one and only Oscar winning performance.'

'Okay,' he says. 'Here goes.'

Jasper has never seen a real magician in action but in this day and age, Gandalf the Grey is the most famous wizard of all.

Everyone knows that scene from The Lord of the Rings where he stands on a narrow bridge, the only barrier between the forces of good and the power of the dark side.

And when he raises his staff into the air, he says the words that everyone on the planet knows off by heart, 'You shall not pass.'

Jasper raises an invisible staff into the air, and with his head held high, he utters the words that will finally break a one-hundred-year-old spell.

'Oh, Great Lord of the bank vault, hear my plea, Oh Dread Lord, and on my command, open the door of this cave and reveal its treasures to the world.'

'Open Sesame,' he cries in a voice that even has the power to shock the unshockable Fabian.

'That was very impressive Jasper. Are you sure that you are just a normal human being?'

'I was the last time I looked, Fabian, but that felt so good, and it even worked.'

'Yes, Oh Mighty Master, it did indeed.'

## CHAPTER 108

'Be prepared to be amazed,' Dilvan says as he opens the door a little at a time.

'Tra-la. The treasure house of Juan Philippe Delgado.'

'Oh, my goodness,' Fabian says. 'That is not just awesome, that is totally mind-blowing.'

This is the moment they have been waiting for, the moment they finally see treasures that have not seen the light of day for over one hundred years.

The vault is packed with caskets of jewels, beautifully carved ornaments of marble and gold, as well as priceless objects from foreign lands. And taking centre stage against the rear wall is Kashmira's pride and joy, a replica of the Chapel of Love.

'There is it,' Jasper says. 'How beautiful is that.'

'Jasper, there's a scroll on the table,' Sally says. 'I think you should read it before doing anything else.'

He eases his way in and holds it to his heart, all too aware that Juan was the last person to have ever touched it.

He unfolds it carefully, only to discover that it has a filigree pattern around the outer edge and every letter is decorated in flowering tendrils.

'It looks like a page from an ancient manuscript. It's beautiful, isn't it?'

'It certainly is,' Mortisha says, 'but what does it say Jasper.'

'This is the Last Will and Testament of Juan Philippe Delgado.'

*My Dear and Beloved Friend, if you have made it this far, you are the one who has listened to that gentle voice within. And you would not be standing in this vault if you had not completed my life's work.*

*And you would not be the beneficiary of my passion as a collector of all things beautiful. But if you are holding this scroll in your hands, you have answered the questions that have opened the door to this little treasure house of ours.*

*Within this room are things that my wife and I collected on our travels. They are now yours to do with as you please. But if you are one of those rare souls with vision, please do not sell them or give them away.*

*There are many valuable treasures in this room, but in one box you will find the deeds to properties in many different lands. These are now yours to do with as you see fit.*

*According to my instructions, they must always be maintained in perfect condition, and when you eventually see them, I hope you find them in a habitable condition.*

*If you have someone special in your life, I would like you to give her one of Kashmira's many beautiful jewels. You will find it in a silver box on the shelf close to the door.*

*As to what you choose to take for yourself, that is up to you, but if you are a man of heart, as I believe you to be, I have one request.*

*Please donate these treasures to a gallery or a museum, and along with the paintings in our house at Mt. Lavinia Beach, they should tell a pretty tale.*

*The clock is ticking and I still have a few loose ends to tie up, but more than anything, I would love to sit down and talk about your life, but alas, that is not possible.*

*Whoever you are, you deserve all this and more for what you have done. Please call upon myself and my wife at any time that you so desire, and we will be there by your side.*

*Blessings be upon you for today and every day of your sweet life to come.*

*Juan Phillipe Delgado, also known as Roshan, the Snake Charmer*

Poor old Jasper is a blubbering mess, so Sally gives him a reassuring cuddle and wipes the tears from his eyes.

'What a lovely man,' Mortisha says, 'and such a beautiful soul.'

'That he was,' says a very tearful Jasper.

To see treasures that have not seen the light of day for a century is something that most people dream about but it was worth the wait.

While Dilvan and Mr. da Silva discuss the legalities of taking a few photos, everyone else is eager to see what Juan has left for Sally.

She removes the cloth, only to discover a silver box decorated with semi-precious stones. And even though the patina has tarnished over time, it is probably worth a small fortune in its own right.

'This is going to good,' Fabian says, 'I just know it is.'

Sally gives the box a quick polish and opens it carefully. 'Oh, my goodness,' she cries. 'It's a necklace.'

'That's the sort of thing the queen would wear,' Fabian says.

The central stone is a pear-shaped emerald enhanced by a cluster of old cut diamonds but the collar is hundreds of miniature emeralds.

Sally's necklace is a masterpiece of 18th century ingenuity, the work of a highly skilled craftsman and a jewel such as you would only see in a royal collection.

'Jaz, it's so beautiful,' Sally says. 'I never dreamed I would own something like this.'

If she had never met Jasper, Sally's life would have been so different, and as she gazes into his eyes, she knows that she has been blessed.

'Jaz, I really do love you, my dear and beloved boy.'

'Thank you, Sal, and I love you too, but we could never have done this alone, could we?'

'No Jaz, that's true.'

'Mortisha, you have been with us every step of the way, and for that I thank you from the bottom of my heart.'

'I would not have swapped this experience for anything in the world.'

'And you, you wonderful, wonderful boys. If it had not been for your support, none of this would have been possible.'

'Think nothing of it,' Fabian says.'

'Not for one moment will I ever forget what you have done Fabian. You were there when we needed you, and for that, you will always have my undying gratitude.'

'But this is not just about us. It is about the legacy of two star-crossed lovers and a love that will never end.'

'So true,' Fabian says.

They take one last look at the vault, and with Dilvan's consent, they take one photo each, but before they leave, Jasper places the will in Mr. da Silva's hands.

'I believe that this is your area of expertise.

'It is Jasper and we will take care of the details.'

'If I have to sign anything, I will be here for a few more days.'

'Leave it with me, my friend. Juan's wishes will be adhered to.'

## CHAPTER 109

As to when he will reveal what happened in the bedroom at Mt. Lavinia, Jasper has not yet decided. Fabian has proved himself many times over and it is only fair that he should know the truth.

It was an experience that will probably find its way into one of his novels. It was like a dream come true he will probably say, and for a few glorious moments, the impossible really did happen.

Sometimes, it just drifts in unannounced, simply because it can. For such a thing to happen, everything must be in alignment, and a door that is rarely visible, opened for a few fleeting seconds.

The moment after they crossed the threshold, it was as if they had stepped into a heavenly realm. But the last thing they expected to see was Roshan and Kashmira dressed in all their finery.

As to where they came from, they could not imagine, but they were so radiantly beautiful, so elegant in appearance and so glorious to behold. And as he was gazing into their eyes Jasper had so many questions."

'Is it really you,' he said.

'It is, indeed, my boy. I promised that I would be calling to you from afar,' Roshan said.

'Yes, you did.'

'We would like to thank you and Sally for what you have done,' Kashmira said. 'We are indebted to you for so many reasons. And it is because of you that our beautiful Chapel is there for all the world to see.'

'But what is the meaning of this? Why are you here?'

'This was the room of our only child, but it was also your bedroom Jasper.'

'Oh, Jaz,' Sally says. 'It all makes sense now.'

'Donatello was a beautiful boy, but unfortunately, he died at the age of twelve.'

'He often went fishing on the beach, but one day he did not come back at all. We saw signs of a struggle, but found no sign of our son, nothing but his golden locket.'

'We found out that he had been kidnapped by pirates. He spent a few weeks on a slave ship in the Far East and we eventually tracked him down, but he died not long after.'

'That was the dream I told you about Jasper.'

'Yes, Sally, it was,' Roshan said. 'And we have kept this room as it was, but the key to the vault is also the key to this room, and it is now yours Jasper.'

'However, as you know, you must answer several questions before it can be opened. Donatello's story holds the clue to those questions.'

This is not just a room, it is a sacred chapel, one that dust nor time has ever disturbed. Donatello's portrait hangs on the wall above the bed, and above that is a little crucifix. And on the bedside table is a wooden rattle, a hand painted doll, a little pair of boots and his golden locket.

Jasper opens it tentatively and shows it to Sally. 'He really does look like me.'

'He was such a good-looking boy, wasn't he?'

'That he was,' Kashmira says, 'as you know so very well of your own beloved boy.'

'That I do know.'

'One day, you will be the mother of your own little boy, Sally, and I would like to think that his name will also be Donatello.'

'I can assure you that it will be,' Sally says.

'However, our time is almost up, and we must be going,' Roshan said, 'but there is one more thing Jasper.'

'We know that you and Sally are planning to be married in the Chapel sometime in the future.'

'We definitely are.'

'Kashmira and I were hoping to renew our vows, but unfortunately, we never got around to it. And on the day that you take your vows as husband and wife, we will be standing by your side.'

'That will be very beautiful indeed, Roshan.'

They are about to vanish into the ethers, but before they do, they take one last look at Donatello's room. A few childhood trinkets are all that remain of their one and only son, the only evidence that he passed this way at all.

'What he must have endured does not bear thinking on,' Sally said. 'But for a few blessed years, he had the love of a gentle mother and that of a devoted father.'

'That he did, but we have waited a long time for this day,' Kashmira says.

'We will always be close by, and if you ever need our help, do not hesitate to ask.'

## CHAPTER 110

They have had an extraordinary time, and in the process, they discovered the beauty of Sri Lanka, but they were not prepared for the warmth and generosity of so many lovely people. Five days later, the journey of a lifetime is almost over.

'So, Jasper,' Fabian says. 'What do we do after an experience like that?'

'I have no idea, Fabian.'

'I do,' says the ever-reliable Dilvan.

'An adventure is in order but a change of clothes would be a good idea first. Very casual in fact. Shorts and T-shirts will be perfect or something like that.'

An hour later, the bus pulls up at the front gates of the Royal Botanical Gardens.

'Now, this is the domain of Mother Nature,' Dilvan says. 'Her Imperial Majesty has been whispering in my ear and she told me that you deserve a special treat.'

'And what would that be Dilvan?'

'Firstly, Fabian, there is a little stall not far from here that makes freshly squeezed fruit juice.'

'Now, this man Barbar has been doing this city a service for the last thirty years. He is my grand uncle three times removed, or that's what my mother told me when I was a boy.'

'Barbar's stall caters to thirsty travellers, and there is quite a lot to choose from. However, you can also add a variety of delectable ingredients to your drink if you so desire.'

'Superfoods you mean,' Fabian says.

'Yes, and if you ask nicely, Barbar might even throw in a flavoursome little herb, and one which I know for a fact that you like.'

'Dilvan Kumara Singhe,' Fabian says. 'I am a reformed man. My master has given me strict instructions to behave myself while in this country.'

'Fabian, Oh Mighty Lord of all that he surveys, that is good to know, but this is Sri Lanka, and we love our herbs and spices.'

'Tell me more,' Fabian says as he takes Dilvan by the arm to investigate the authenticity of his claim.

Everyone takes a seat under a shady tree, while Dilvan wanders back and forth with one icy fruit juice after another.

'If you haven't made up your mind, I recommend orange, apple, watermelon or pineapple but not Durian.'

'Do not go anywhere near that thing, not unless you like the aroma of three-day old socks.'

'You weave a convincing argument against that poor maligned fruit,' Mortisha says.

'And for good reason Mortisha, it really does stink. However, folks, there is more to come.'

'Like what? Fabian says.

'There is, in these very gardens, a young magician, and he is called of all things, Merlin.'

'It's probably Sally's cat in disguise,' Jasper says.

'I told you he was a shape-changer, but you didn't believe me, did you?'

'Well, if it is your cat, Sally, he is a very clever cat, and like Leonardo da Vinci, he is also an inventor extraordinaire.'

'Are you interested, perhaps?'

'Lead the way,' says the ever-curious Fabian.

Standing in front of a colourful little tent is the man himself. As to whether this is the one and only Merlin of great fame and acclaim, they have no idea, but he looks the part in a black robe and magician's hat. And he even has a wand hanging from the belt around his waist.

The tent is somewhat bigger on the inside than it is on the outside, an undeniable clue that this really could be the great and wonderful Merlin.

'So, Mr. Merlin, what is this mysterious invention?' Fabian says.

He slips his hands into his pockets and withdraws one yellow ball after another.

'I have one of these for each of you,' he says.

'So, what are they?'

'They are inflatable bodysuits that have been compressed into a portable size. They are flight suits in other words, the sort of thing that an astronaut would wear.'

'So, are we going to the Moon? Is that what you are saying?'

'Perhaps not that far, my friend, but believe it or not they are perfectly safe.'

'The first thing you have to do is press that little button on the side and the suit will self-inflate.'

'I am impressed Mr. Merlin, but how does it work?'

'With a remote control, of course. What else?'

'This is the coolest invention ever,' Jasper says. 'How come we have never heard of it before Mr. Merlin?'

'This is not the sort of thing a government would approve of Jasper. Too many issues involved for one thing.'

'So true,' he says.

# CHAPTER 111

With a simple press of a button, the balls inflate and expand to the size of big yellow bodysuits, but it takes a bit of shuffling back and forth to get them on. And when they finally do, it does not go unnoticed by Fabian that they all look like a character called Laa-Laa from a television show called the Teletubbies.

'However, she a was girl, so you can call me Tinky-Winky.'

'Dipsy might be more like it,' Sally whispers quietly.

'So, are you ready to free wheel it through the air?' Dilvan says. 'If so, press the red button on the remote.'

As to whether it was accidental will never be known, but Fabian takes off like an out-of-control balloon.

'The idea is to take it slowly,' Dilvan cries. 'You silly boy, Fabian. You just have to be the life of the party, don't you?'

'Come on, let's go and get him before he disappears off the radar and is never seen again.'

By the time they catch up, it's obvious that Fabian is a little flustered and has not yet recovered from the shock.

'Going somewhere?' Declan says.

'Nah, just testing out the equipment. After all, I do know my way around a remote control.'

'You naughty bad boy, Fabian. You could have ended up in Siberia,' Jasper says.

'It's a good thing I didn't. The KGB would lock me up and throw away the key.'

'More than likely,' Dilvan says.

'So, folks, look at that view. It is absolutely breath taking, is it not?'

'It sure is,' Jasper says.

'You can thank Mother Nature for that. She is a bit of a show-off as you know, but she does go out of her way to impress.'

From the air, Sri Lanka looks like a glistening jewel, but there is so much more hidden away high above the clouds.

And it is here that they have their first experience of endless miles of magical mountains, but this is no ordinary landscape. This is a fairy-tale world of soft fluffy clouds, soaring bridges, gaping chasms, and at least ten fairy-tale castles with domes that glisten like tinted ice.

Floating through the air is a little daunting at first, but once he gets used to it, Jasper is happy to just drift along.

But the last thing he expected to feel is a familiar energy rippling up his spine and he knows immediately that Kashmira is nearby.

'Jasper, Jasper Donatello Powell,' she says. 'Where are you?'

'I'm over here Kashmira.'

Like an angel alighting from heaven, she steps through a glistening portal and looks radiantly beautiful as always.

'Jasper, it's so lovely to see you again.'

'But what are you doing here Kashmira?'

'This is my territory, Jasper. I am a spirit after all. But before you go, I have something I would like to show you.'

'What is it, Kashmira?'

'Follow me and you will see.'

'So, where are we going?'

'To Italy, to that most gorgeous of all places, to Napoli, of course.'

'But why Kashmira?'

'Because we can Jasper. I want to show you something very special.'

Kashmira obviously knows the secret of inter-dimensional travel, and before he knows it,

Jasper is soaring through the air and heading for a doorway that glistens like gold.

Under normal circumstances, he would be a little worried, but not when you are in a state of Kundalini-inspired bliss.

As Swami Jagatpati once said, a holy man can walk on water and they can even travel through space and time.

A few moments later, Jasper steps out the other end, only to find that he is in a little square in the back streets of Naples.

'Oh, this is so beautiful, Kashmira, but why are we here?'

'Look over there, Jasper.'

Sitting on a chair against the wall of a derelict building is a lovely old man strumming away on an old mandolin, and even though it's a little battle-scarred, it is still in perfect order.

'Giuseppe sings the same song three times a day,' Kashmira says, 'and the tourists come from everywhere.'

'Really, just to hear him sing.'

'Yes, and he is about to do so again. Let's move in a little closer because something special is about to happen.'

The moment that he hears the first few chords of Giuseppe's song, Jasper recognises it immediately.

'That's a Vito Fontana song.'

'It certainly is Jasper, but what the tourists don't know is that Vito often makes an appearance and sings along in the background.'

'Really, Kashmira, his ghost you mean.'

'Yes, Jasper, call it what you will, but it is Vito.'

The very instant that Giuseppe starts to sing, Vito's ghost really does appear at his side. Vito was renowned for his easy-going style and happily joins in.

Giuseppe has a rich and vibrant voice, but he also has a heartbreaking tale about a man who once met a lady fair.

For a few delirious weeks she was the love of his life and the woman who stole his heart. Unfortunately, she ran off with someone else, and now, all he has left are a few memories and his little mandolin.

Even the old tour guide who has seen this performance a hundred times before has tears in his eyes. But for those of a romantic disposition, it is a touching experience in every way.

Several dozen over-emotional tourists happily throw their unwanted lire into Giuseppe's battered old cap. But if he had known that he is always accompanied by the inimitable Vito Fontana, Giuseppe would have been a millionaire years ago.

'What did you think of that Jasper?'

'That was beautiful Kashmira.'

'That is one of your options when the Kundalini is active, and you can go places and do things like this.'

'However, we must get back because Sally is looking for you. But before we do that, I want to take you to one more place.'

Jasper follows her through the portal and a few seconds later, he finds himself on the outer edge of a beautiful garden. And in the distance is a ghostly house that resembles their home at Mt. Lavinia.

'Where are we Kashmira?'

'This is the garden of our home, Jasper. This is where we live with our son Donatello and a few close friends.'

'Really,' he says. 'Dead people.'

'Deceased, Jasper, those who have passed on. They are people we have known for a very long time.'

'We have worked long and hard to see our dream come true. We achieved what we set out to do, and now, our work is done.'

'But you are now a part of our lives, and I just wanted to remind you of that.'

Jasper would love to take Kashmira in his arms, but alas, alack, that is not possible. He is a physical being in an inflatable flight suit and Kashmira is nothing but a semi-transparent wisp of air and vapors.

'You are welcome to visit at any time, Jasper. However, there is another reason for my visit.'

'And what is that Kashmira?'

'I have everything organised for our wedding.'

'You have, like what?'

'Well, you name it, and I've got it sorted.'

'We have invited over two hundred friends. They were well-known entertainers in their day, but they have all passed on now, of course.'

'Such as whom, for example.'

'Pick a name and they will be there. Vito loves a good party, and he wouldn't miss out on a wedding for anything.'

'That sounds pretty impressive,' Jasper says. 'In that case, we will have to get things moving.'

'If you need any help, all you have to do is ask Jasper, and I will be at your side in an instant, of that you can be assured.'

'Thank you Kashmira?'

'You look so adorable in that suit Jasper, but I think you should get back, because Sally is beside herself with worry.'

'But how do I get out of here, Kashmira?'

'Your imagination is the key Jasper, and it is even more powerful when the Kundalini is operating at full potential. Your imagination is the only key that you will ever need.'

A few seconds later, Jasper is standing on the battlements of a fluffy white fairytale castle. And for a few blissful moments, he is the master of all that he surveys, but he is back in the real world and Sally is almost frantic.

He would love to make an entrance in a blaze of glory, accompanied by a fanfare of trumpets but that isn't going to happen. He will have to save that idea for another day.

'Jasper,' Sally cries. 'Where have you been?'

'I just popped off to Naples to have a quiet chat with Kashmira, that's all.'

'You're serious, aren't you?'

'Yes Sal, I certainly am.'

'I have been looking everywhere for you.'

'But I am here now Sal and I have a brilliant idea.'

'And what is that?'

'I think we should get into our best clothes and christen the Chapel of Love with a wedding that no one will ever forget.'

'What do you think of that idea?'

'Jasper, truly,' she cries.

'Yes, my Princess.'

## CHAPTER 112

Sally's mother is the mastermind behind this wedding, and if Stella has anything to say about it, this will not be just any old wedding, it really will be a wedding to remember.

Sally's dress will be designed by the celebrated fashion designer called Josephine Gilbert, a talented young woman from Central Australia who has made a name for herself on the Australian fashion scene.

Sally will be accompanied by four beautiful bridesmaids, two of whom are cousins and two of whom are old school friends.

Jasper will have four best men, three of whom are PE students, while the fourth is an assistant bank manager from Colombo. And as Jasper now knows, Dilvan never was a Sri Lankan pin-up boy.

'But you will all look drop-dead gorgeous in Armani suits,' Stella says.

Fabian is not about to complain as he will finally get his five minutes of fame. Mortisha agrees to be Matron of Honour but only if she is accompanied by an entourage.

'You are not thinking of witches on broomsticks,' Stella says.

'No, I am not, Stella, but that is an excellent idea. I would like to be accompanied by the elders of Fitzroy, all of whom should have the option to renew their vows, if they so desire.'

'That is such a beautiful idea,' Stella says.

Being the old love birds that they are, Bella and Paz agree wholeheartedly.

'I still have my wedding dress but it gets smaller and smaller every time I look at it,' Bella says. 'I must have been the size of a string bean in those days.'

'No, my darling, you were absolutely gorgeous,' Paz says.

'Oh, you are naughty Paz, but with a few alterations here and there it will be just perfect.'

Stella can't get her head around the idea that Roshan and Kashmira will also be making an appearance, and as far as she is concerned, that's a major problem.

'They're dead people. They're spirits or something like that. No one will be able to see them, but that's what everyone will want to see.'

Stella approaches Paul Sinopoli from Channel Seven and he jumps at the opportunity. If they can work out a way to film spirits from the non-physical realms, Channel Seven will make a fortune.

As far as Paul is concerned, this will be the scoop of the decade. The technical wizards at Channel Seven spend a few solid weeks working on the problem, and to Stella's relief, they eventually work out a way to do it.

Jacob and Jarrod will lead the procession, followed by a contingent of elderly citizens and the students of Fitzroy Primary School. And even though she is horrified at how much it will cost to dress fifty kids in white suits, Stella throws caution to the wind and does it anyway.

Jasper and Sally have to do their bit as well, and over the next few weeks, they appear on every current affairs show in Melbourne.

'The stars of the show are coming to town,' Jasper says. 'Roshan and Kashmira have invited a few close friends to celebrate their special day.'

'They were some of the most talented performers of the twentieth century, and they are still around in some form.'

'Performers such as Vito Fontana, Esmeralda, Lee-Lee Pasolini, Sylvester Slovakian, Athena Donaldson, and hundreds of others will be in attendance.'

# CHAPTER 113

Accompanied by just about every media organisation in the world, the people of Melbourne are out in force on the day of the wedding. And even Mother Nature contributes with a gentle breeze and a moderate summer temperature.

Spectators line the streets all the way from the parliament building at the top of Collins Street to the Exhibition Building at the Carlton Gardens.

Jasper and Sally look radiant as they roll along in a white carriage pulled by six white horses. They have a police escort at the front and one at the rear, but they also have a bodyguard concealed on the floor of the carriage, and he has an arsenal of weapons to prove his point if he has to.

As the carriage makes its way down Nicholson Street, they are inundated by a pool of floral garlands.

The excitement is mounting and people all over the world are watching this spectacle on one device or another, but the question on everyone's mind is will the impossible really happen?

Kashmira and her entourage are about to make an appearance, but Jasper is the only one who knows what they have in mind.

He has a direct line to Paul Sinopoli at Channel Seven studios, and the moment he gives the word, the cameras will start to roll.

'Paul, it's time to activate the Ghost-Cam. They're on the way.'

'Oh Jaz, I wish I could see them,' Sally says.

'Take my hand Sal and you will. Look, there they are up there,' he says.

The last thing that Sally expected to see is a spiral staircase in the sky, and after six long months she finally gets to see the face of the hauntingly beautiful Kashmira.

'Oh Jaz, she looks absolutely magnificent.'

This extraordinary spectacle is visible on huge screens all around the Gardens, but it is also streaming live to hundreds of television networks around the world.

This is an historic moment for the people of Planet Earth, and an age seems to have passed before they even take a breath.

Followed by Roshan in a suit of gold, Kashmira looks radiant in a spangled silver gown. She glides down the staircase with the grace of a disembodied spirit, and the very moment that her feet hit the ground, she walks up to Jasper and takes him in her arms.

'Jasper, my beautiful boy. You look so handsome,' she says. 'And Sally, my dear, you look absolutely radiant.'

She turns to face the cameras and it's apparent that this is a very emotional moment. Kashmira is a trooper from way back, so she takes a deep breath and bows to one and all.

'Ladies and gentlemen, boys and girls, people of Planet Earth, I have wanted to do that ever since Jasper was a little boy.'

'As you know, this young man is Jasper Powell, accompanied by his beautiful girlfriend, Sally Velasko, the two people who made all of this possible.'

'My name is Kashmira, and I was born in the country now known as Sri Lanka. I died in this very suburb in a house fire in the year 1880, just over a block away from here.'

'But enough about me. Allow me to introduce my family.'

'This handsome man on my left is my husband, Roshan. And this handsome young man on my right is our beautiful son, Donatello.'

'We are here for a reason, but we are not alone as you can see. We are accompanied by a few close friends.'

'You have probably heard of most of them, but if you haven't, you will find out about them soon enough.'

'We are here on this day because Roshan and I never had a church wedding, but today, all that is about to change.'

'We promised Jasper that we would be at his side when he and Sally took their vows as husband and wife.'

'And as a consequence, we are about to do so in the beautiful temple that I long ago christened, The Chapel of Love.'

## CHAPTER 114

Kashmira won hearts all over the world. She was beautiful, she had grace and style and that indefinable something called charisma.

She had orchestrated one of the greatest feats of all times. And after one hundred years of trying, she eventually found someone who could make The Chapel of Love a reality.

The celebrant is a seventy-year-old woman called Patrizia Santos, an old friend of Bella's who has lived in Fitzroy all of her life.

Patrizia was delighted to officiate at Jasper and Sally's wedding, and over a period of weeks, she finetuned the details of an event which she knew would be both beautiful and special.

Patrizia has officiated at more weddings than the local priest, but what she says comes from the heart. And from the moment the ceremony starts, she hits all the right notes and there is not a dry eye in the house.

As the bridal parties makes their way through the gardens and up to the chapel, Tika Lakani does a stirring rendition of that well-known anthem, *Eternal Love*, and she does so with both reverence and humility.

As they walk down the aisle, the music that heralds the arrival of the bride is performed by none other than the maestro of the keyboards, Sylvester Slovakian.

He appears on a cloud of light playing a baby grand piano but Sylvester does not try to steal the spotlight, not this time. This is Roshan and Kashmira's special day and he plays his part with grace and style.

And as they take their vows, they are accompanied by one of the great divas of the opera world.

Athena Donaldson was an acclaimed mezzo-soprano who sings the classic song, *To Thy Love Be*

*True*. It is one of the most soul-stirring songs of all time, and even those with the most hardened of hearts are moved to tears.

Stella has worked long and hard to make sure that this really will be the wedding of the century, and it turns out to be everything she had hoped for.

Beyond anything else, it was beautiful, it was heartfelt, and it was sincere. But the thing that did not go unnoticed were the tears in Jasper's eyes as he accompanied Sally to the altar.

This is a day to remember for many reasons, but it is also the day on which two spirits from a non-physical realm finally renew their vows.

Roshan and Kashmira's love has survived the test of time, and it is as strong today as it was on the day they met.

# CHAPTER 115

Eight months later, Jasper and Sally become the proud parents of a beautiful little boy called Donatello.

Sally doesn't have the time to think about opening a restaurant as she is a busy and loving mother. Jasper is an equally devoted father, but to see that beautiful little face looking back at him is almost too much to bear.

Unfortunately, he never did get around to finishing his novel, Gypsy Queen, and eventually abandoned it as a lost cause.

Inspired by the gypsy king in Fatima's performance, he came up with another idea and had even decided on a title, *The Conjurer of Dreams*, but try as he might it just wasn't happening.

He had trouble imagining the life of a gypsy, let alone that of a gypsy king, and he had no choice but to ask for Kashmira's help.

And over a period of weeks, they travelled extensively, observing life in gypsy camps from times gone by, in places such as India, Ceylon, and Eastern Europe.

It was an opportunity to soak up the atmosphere and gaze at the flames of a slowly burning fire on a moonlit night. But in all of the excitement, Jasper had forgotten about Swami Jagatpati's warning.

If a Holy Man is exposed to the power of the Kundalini over an extended period of time, there will be repercussions.

For two whole weeks after that, Jasper wandered around in a state of Kundalini-inspired bliss. But to Sally's horror, he didn't eat and to make matters worse he didn't sleep.

He would disappear in the middle of the night and wouldn't come back for several days at a stretch, but one day, Jasper did not come back at all.

Two long and agonising weeks later, there is no trace of him at all. Once again, Jasper is the biggest news story of the day but for a very different reason.

Every search and rescue agency in Melbourne is out in force trawling the back streets and alleyways but it's to no avail. The police make an announcement that Jasper is now a missing person.

Sally is devastated and even though she has the support of friends and family, she cannot quell a rising tide of fear. She can only hope and pray that she will see her beloved boy again.

Two weeks later, Jasper is found in a park not far from the Yarra River in Melbourne. And according to the authorities, he is in perfect health, but he is in some sort of self-induced coma. A medical consultant makes a statement that Jasper is in a state of suspended animation.

Accompanied by Stella and Fabian, and anyone who can spare the time, Sally spends the day at Jasper's bedside. Mostly, she just holds his hand and sometimes she lays little Donatello in the crook of his arm.

'Jaz, if you are there,' she says. 'Please say something.'

One day as she is wiping his face, Jasper opens his eyes and looks around the room, but he doesn't notice Sally or even say anything.

He sits up, crosses his legs, assumes the position of a meditating guru, and just gazes out the window, his eyes focused on a far and distant star.

'Mum, what's going on?' Sally cries.

'I don't know my darling, but he's still with us.'

Experts the world over are baffled and have no idea what to think. Jasper is headline news, and everyone is following his progress.

Swami Jagatpati makes a statement that Jasper is experiencing a condition which is common to the Holy Men of India.

'Jasper is not going to die. He has been exposed to the energy of the Kundalini. He is in a state of suspended animation and he could stay like that for days, months or even years, but he will recover in time.'

Two months later, Jasper's condition has not changed but his aura is clearly visible.

Sally once said that if he ever passed away, she would donate his soul to the National Gallery of Victoria, and not knowing what else to do, she decides to donate his body instead. As a consequence, Jasper is now on display in a purpose-built gallery.

Holy Men are not unknown in India but they are an unknown quantity in the western world. The curious and faithful flock to Melbourne in their thousands, and when they enter the gallery, they know that they are in a sacred space.

Jasper's aura is a light of such brilliance that it can only be seen with an electronic device, but it is possible to communicate with him, and on the odd occasion he even answers back.

One little girl made headline news when she asked Jasper a question, but no one would have known anything about it if a television reporter had not been standing at her side.

'Jasper,' she says. 'Are you an alien?'
'No, I am not. I am an angel.'
'Really.'
'Quickly, ask another question,' the reporter says.
'What will I say?'
'Ask him why he is doing this?'
'Jasper, why are you doing this?'
'Doing what?' he says.

'The things that you have been doing with Kashmira.'

'I agreed to complete the task that she could not.'

'Will you ever be normal again?'

'I will be soon, but I would like you to do me a favour please.'

'And what is that?' the little girl says.

'Tell my wife that I will be home for Christmas.'

Jasper Powell is not the only heartbreaker who has ever walked this Earth. He is one of those people who just drift down from the clouds and does something that everyone remembers for a long time after.

The line-up of famous faces at his wedding was a star-studded cast of some of the great performers of the 20th century.

The vocal enchantress Esmeralda was delighted to perform her famous song. And accompanied by the incomparable Lee-Lee Pasolini, she stepped up to the stage, and together they did a haunting rendition of Gypsy Queen.

Another favourite was the irascible and delightful Vito Fontana. He was the Master of Ceremonies and he delivered the goods in style. Vito was renowned for his silky-smooth voice and happily crooned away to some of his biggest hits.

But the most poignant moment of all, and the thing that still brings a tear to many eyes was the bridal waltz.

*If Only for a Time* is a touching song about a young girl who falls in love with a handsome prince. But one day, he disappears and is never seen again. That was the last thing that Sally wanted to think about on her wedding day.

## CHAPTER 116

Now dear reader, you are probably wondering what could possibly happen next, and you have every reason to expect an answer.

Jasper recovers from his Kundalini-induced trance on the 30th of November 2014, and on the following evening, after the gallery doors have been locked, Sally is waiting to welcome him back to the world of the living. And no matter how she tries, she cannot hold back a floodtide of tears, but she has three muscular angels at her side.

If the media ever found out what they were up to, they would never hear the end of it. So, they slipped out the back door and into a waiting car, but they were not going home, they were heading for the airport.

Geraldine placed a sign on her shop saying that she had something important to do. And along with Mortisha and Stella, she spent every day at the gallery.

They were making a fortune from Jasper, and they even went so far as to create a private chapel where visitors could light a candle or whisper a heartfelt prayer.

Stella was beside herself with worry, but it could have been a lot worse if not for Marco. He barely left her side, and even Jacob and Jarrod rallied to the cause.

And now, they are all waiting on the tarmac, alongside friends and loved ones, waiting for the moment when they see Jasper again.

And the very moment that he steps out of the car, his mother rushes up and takes him in her arms.

'Oh, Jaz, you have no idea how I have missed you, my boy.'

'But I am here now Mum, and this time I intend to stay.'

'Jaz, please don't do anything like that again.'

'I won't Mum, I promise.'

'We gave it everything we had,' Mortisha said. 'We have been praying for your soul every day for the last five months. We were not about to let you go Jasper, not if we had anything to say about it.'

Jasper has no idea how to explain what he has been through, and in one way, he is not even sure what happened.

He was out there somewhere, drifting about in an ocean of eternal bliss, but every now and then, he could hear voices calling to him from afar, and sometimes he even made the effort to respond.

'Jasper, you are a naughty bad boy,' Fabian says, 'running off like that and leaving your baby in the bathwater.'

'I didn't, did I?'

'No Jaz,' Sally says. 'Fabian is joking, as usual.'

Fabian can be a bit of a pushy know-it-all sometimes, but he is proud to say that he has saved Jasper's life on several occasions.

When he realised that Jasper was coming home, he came up with an inspired plan to whisk him away. It was an expensive solution but Sally didn't care less, she just wanted her husband back.

'This plane is not going anywhere, not until we have had a group hug,' Fabian says. 'New friends and old, gather round, and remind this little traveller where he belongs.'

'Jasper, it would be a good idea if you held your baby in your arms. You are a father now Jasper and you have a very big responsibility.'

'Oh, where is he Sal?'

'He's in the bassinet, waiting to see his Daddy.'

Little Donatello has the same smile as his father, the same dimples around the mouth and the same glistening green eyes. Jasper takes his little boy in his arms and he cannot believe how much he has grown.

'Oh Sal, he's so beautiful, isn't he?'

'Just in case I haven't said so before, thank you for everything that you have done.'

'So, where are we going, Fabian?'

'To Sri Lanka, of course, where else?

'We found a wonderful place just north of Negombo, a villa that once belonged to an American movie star. He died of unnatural causes of some kind but we got a bargain Jasper.'

'It's right on the beach. The ocean is at your front door, and it has a beautiful pool and more toys than you can possibly imagine.'

'That sounds excellent,' Jasper says. 'In that case, let's get going.'

'Okay folks, take a seat and buckle up,' Fabian says, 'because our destination is paradise.'

# CHAPTER 117

As Jasper discovers, he is the owner of that beautiful if somewhat ostentatious villa to the north of Negombo, and he could not be happier, but Stella keeps a close eye on him at all times. The last thing she wants is for her son-in-law to drift away, never to be seen again.

One evening, as he is watching the waves roll onto the shore, she appears at his side with a handful of tissues wrapped around a blood-soaked finger.

'What happened?' he says.

'I had a close call with a kitchen knife.'

'Let me take a look.'

'It's only a shallow cut but it'll be fine.'

'I can fix that,' Jasper says.

'And how will you do that?'

'Like this,' he says.

As Stella finds on that quiet summer evening, miracles are not the exclusive domain of saints and sinners.

Jasper takes her hand and holds it to his heart, and for a few blissful moments Stella has an experience of a very different kind.

'There, it will be fine now,' he says.

To Stella's amazement, her finger is no longer bleeding and even the wound has healed.

'Don't tell anyone, promise me Stella.'

'I won't Jasper, but I want you to promise me something.'

'And what is that?'

'I want you to enlighten me. You obviously know things about things, and I don't know anything at all.'

Jasper would dearly love to say that he has no idea what she is talking about, but that is not entirely true, not anymore. After an experience of that nature Stella would not believe him even if he did.

For someone without any career prospects, Jasper has notched up a pretty impressive resumé over the last year. He played a central role in the discovery of The Chapel of Love. His wedding guests were spirits from the non-physical realms. And then he pulls a rabbit out of the hat and becomes a modern-day holy man.

Stella is not convinced.

The exhibit at the National Gallery of Victoria no longer exists, but they have the evidence to prove that Jasper passed their way.

The floodgates to wealth and riches opened the day that he said that he was an angel. Jasper became an overnight marketing bonanza on a global scale, and he was a Godsend for budding entrepreneurs with an itch to get rich.

The *Jasper the Angel T-shirt* and the glow-in-the-dark bed lamp are not the only things that have been selling like hot cakes.

This is the 21st century, the era of digital technology and you can even download an exciting new game called *The Adventures of a Modern-Day Holy Man*.

The Chapel of Love has become a pilgrimage site to people from all over the world, but it is not just dedicated to Kashmira, it is also a shrine to Jasper.

There is nothing more potent than the power of love, and little old Jasper Powell, part-time dreamer and romantic fool is up there with the best. He is not the only one, of course, but for a brief period of time he touched the hearts of so many, and for that he will never be forgotten.

THE END

# The Gods of Space and Time
*A series of fantasy fiction stories.*

## THE ETERNAL OPTIMIST
## BOOK ONE

Unlike his brother who is cautious and irritable, Addric has a bit of a reputation. He not only believes in miracles, he believes in the impossible.

Their holiday plans are sabotaged from the first day and they barely survive one life threatening situation after another. The stakes are high, and they have to succeed. A card-carrying member of the dark side is out to get his revenge, but they can't allow that to happen. Addric rises to the challenge and shows what he is made of.

He proves to everyone that he is both brilliant, and audacious. Fearless is a rollercoaster ride through an inter-dimensional realm, a place where unusual things can happen.

A drama set in motion long, long ago is about to unfold. All they wanted was a boy's own holiday. They had no idea what sort of holiday they were in for.

This story was selected as a finalist in The 2020 Book Excellence Awards.

# THE OCEAN OF INFINITE MYSTERY
## BOOK TWO

Allow your mind to roam further than it has ever done before, to the outer perimeter of Alpha Centauri. It is here you will find a galaxy called the Khavala, an inter-dimensional realm, where many worlds exist side-by-side, a world of strange beauty, hidden power, and wondrous mystery.

The Khavala is a self-conscious entity, but when danger threatens the most sacrosanct of all domains, she calls upon the assistance of her most powerful creations, an invincible task force that includes Yumi Masters, and Warrior Angels.

To resolve this problem, they must travel deep into the heart centre of the Khavala, to a place of legend, to the domain known since time immemorial as The Ocean of Infinite Mystery.

## THE LAST DAYS OF LEMURIA
## BOOK THREE

Elisabeth Trundle's life changes on the day that she meets two attractive young men in The Great Library of London, but these guys are not Earthlings as she eventually finds out. Elisabeth has been having dreams about the lost continent of Lemuria, but the last thing she expected is that she would actually get an opportunity to go there. And that would never have happened if the chronometer of a passing spaceship had not malfunctioned. Accompanied by four Yumi Masters, Elisabeth's dream comes true, and she ends up in a civilisation that is about to be destroyed by a natural catastrophe.

Over the next two weeks, they have to train an army, defeat the high priest at his own game and save a young boy's life. But it's not all bad news, the people are wonderful, and the food is even better. Before the dreaded day dawns, they discover how the Lemurians intend to survive.

# THE GOLDEN PHOENIX
# BOOK FOUR

Accompanied by a few feisty friends, Addric embarks on a mission to rescue his brother's girlfriend from the clutches of a necromancer with delusions of grandeur.

To save Elisabeth, they will have to battle it out in the Roman arena, cross the Arctic Ocean on a crystal powered boat, venture deep into the bowels of the Earth, and then brave the fires of hell on a volcanic planet on the verge of a major transformation.

It will take something more than sharp claws and attitude to defeat a necromancer at his own game, but these boys are Yumi Masters, and they have a few tricks up their sleeve.

# INSTANT KARMA
# BOOK FIVE

The people of Earth have become obsessed with electronic devices, but if they want to survive, they have to make the biggest sacrifice of all. The big guys upstairs are willing to give them one more chance, but only if they change their ways.

Yumi Master, Addric Sharano, has been assigned the task of dragging them back from the brink. Unfortunately, there is a time limit on this deal. Addric spearheads a team of people who use every trick in the book.

Earthlings are about to find out that not all aliens have a bulbous head and big green eyes. Sit back and enjoy the ride as Addric reveals a few of his hidden talents.

# QUIETLY THEY CAME
## BOOK SIX

Yumi Master extraordinaire, Addric Sharano is back, and he is in fine form in this light-hearted adventure. Addric's new mission is to rescue forty-two orphans from Pompeii, before they are incinerated by the volcano.

Accompanied by his best friends and glamorous offsiders, Lady Felicity, and her sister, Countess Demetra, two exponents of the fine old art of subterfuge, and the modern version of sorcery, Addric comes up with a clever if not complicated plan.

However, there is one little catch. These kids have a greater purpose in life. They were born with a coded message in their DNA, and it is just waiting for an opportunity to be expressed.

Addric is not known as the master of spin for nothing, so, he takes the kids by the hands, and they dive into the deep end. And when they come up for air, they hit the big time.

Addric is the man with golden touch when it comes to doing the impossible, and he doesn't fail to deliver the goods in this rollicking romp of a story. Sit back and enjoy a ride that starts in Pompeii and ends on some of the great stages of the modern world.

## TEACH ME HOW TO FLY
## BOOK SEVEN

The future of an inconspicuous village is threatened by an ungodly invader, but a prophecy states that a messiah will come to their rescue.

The first person on the scene is a Yumi Master with a history of battling the bad guys. And not long after, the real messiah appears in a blaze of glory.

Disposing of the invaders is a serious business, but they have quite a few tricks up their sleeve, and the most potent weapon in their armoury is the power of sound. And when they are not doing that, they entertain the musically inclined villagers with a selection of inspirational songs from the 20$^{th}$ century.

## A PRAYER FOR BROTHER WILLIAM

After he loses his parents, William Cahill, retreats into a world of his own and his life would have spiralled out of control if it had not been for Aunt Augusta. She drags him back from the brink and transforms his life and that of his siblings, but Augusta Cahill is no ordinary woman.

She might be dreadfully wealthy and a pathetic old socialite, but she can be a force to be reckoned with. A story about life, death and suffering on the home front, a place that can be as perilous as a battlefield.

This novel, which is both historical fiction and a romance is also a tender portrayal of love in some of its myriad forms. It was inspired by an old family legend and is a story that breathes life into a bygone era with vivid authenticity.

# THE GODDESS OF GOOD FORTUNE

The Sequel to The Snake Charmer's Wife

When she is offered the opportunity to dispose of a recalcitrant necromancer, the illustrious Lady Felicity Originalis jumps at the chance. Lady Felicity is not your everyday detective. In fact, she is not a detective at all. She is an exponent of the fine old art of subterfuge, and the modern version of sorcery.

Felicity uses every trick in the book to protect a $9^{th}$ century Arabian knight from the clutches of an evil Vizier. Memphalut el Shakar is the quintessence of a self-obsessed despot with the sharp but beady eyes of a pack hound.

Old-fashioned methods of torture are never on the agenda for Lady Felicity. She prefers to use other much more subtle forms of persuasion.

## A TALE OF AN ARABIAN KNIGHT

In the fabled city of Aggrabad, nestled in the Rub al-Khali Desert, a tale of epic proportions unfolds. This lost city of the Bedouins, likened to the Atlantis of the Desert, is a masterpiece of glistening white limestone, a freshwater oasis, shrouded in mystery and romance.

At the heart of this story stands Hakim, the noble Captain of the Guards, who finds himself caught in a web of intrigue and sorcery woven by a tyrannical Sultan and the wicked Vizier, Memphalut al Shikari.

The Vizier, a practitioner of the dark arts rules through fear and cruelty, disposing of his enemies in the most horrific ways. Hakim and his fearless girlfriend, Zenobia must do everything in their power to make sure that the plans of this evil Vizier never come to pass.

## I WILL BE PRAYING FOR YOUR SOUL

This story follows the journey of a cruel, violent and troubled soul, Justin Valéry, a twelve-year-old boy who torments everyone including his sister Majella and his family. After a terrifying experience in a church in Madrid, Justin mysteriously disappears, and finds himself in an alternate reality. He meets a mysterious man who informs him that he must embark on a journey of atonement and redemption. Justin undergoes a series of strange and challenging experiences in equally challenging environments and is forced to confront the consequences of his actions.

## THE PASSIONFRUIT HOTEL

In a world where the culinary elite reign supreme, a tantalizing tale of revenge, betrayal, and supernatural intervention unfolds. At the heart of this delectable drama is Susannah Velasnikov, a Contessa whose life takes an unexpected turn when her good-for-nothing brothers meet an untimely demise. She reinvents herself with a new life as the proprietress of The Passionfruit Hotel, but things take a turn for the worst when she becomes embroiled in a web of shady dealings and ill-fated entanglements with the notorious Lord Alfred Chili Pepper.

## ABOUT THE AUTHOR

Vincent Gilvarry is a writer from tropical North Queensland in Australia, a multifaceted author with a rich and vivid imagination.

With a foundation in the visual arts, his transition into the realm of literature was sparked by a life-changing situation that inspired him to embark on a literary career and an odyssey that has lasted for over 25 years.

He boasts an eclectic repertoire that highlights his versatility across various genres and his fantasy fiction books in particular are a testament to his unparalleled imagination and to his narrative prowess.

All rights reserved.
Copyright
2024
©

Milton Keynes UK
Ingram Content Group UK Ltd.
UKHW021941281024
450365UK00018B/1212